GORDON R. DICKSON

As The Outposter, Cully When had declared
these stars were ours. Now he had to make it stick...

BAEN
BOOKS

69800-1 ☆ $3.50

NONE
BUT MAN

SOMETIMES,
ONE IS ALL IT TAKES . . .

". . . He wouldn't tell me if there were any others," Lucy was saying to a man with a captain's shoulder tabs, while eight others stood at their posts listening.

"There aren't any," said Cully, harshly, as he stepped into view, holding the heavy riot gun in both hands, covering them. "There's only me."

"You're a fool!" said the captain. "Give up now and you might get off without mandatory execution."

"No thanks," said Cully. He gestured with the end of the riot gun. "We're going into overdrive. Start setting up the course as I give it to you."

"No," said the captain, looking hard at him.

"You're a brave man," said Cully. "But let me point out something to you. I'm going to shoot you if you won't co-operate; then I'm going to work down the line of your officers. Sooner or later somebody's going to preserve his life by doing what I tell him. So getting yourself killed isn't going to save the ship at all. It just means somebody with less courage than you lives. And you die."

GORDON R. DICKSON

NONE BUT MAN

BAEN BOOKS

NONE BUT MAN

Copyright © 1989 by Gordon R. Dickson

A Baen Book

Baen Publishing Enterprises
260 Fifth Avenue
New York, N.Y. 10001

"Hilifter" copyright © 1963 by the Condé Nast Publications, Inc. Reprinted by permission of the Author.

First Baen printing, January 1989

ISBN: 0-671-69800-1

Cover art by Tom Kidd

Printed in the United States of America

Distributed by
SIMON & SCHUSTER
1230 Avenue of the Americas
New York, N.Y. 10020

Table of Contents

Hilifter

It was locked—from the outside.

Not only that, but the mechanical latch handle that would override the button lock on the tiny tourist cabin aboard the *Star of the North* was hidden by the very bed on which Cully When sat cross-legged, like some sinewy mountain man out of Cully's own pioneering ancestry. Cully grinned at the image in the mirror which went with the washstand now hidden by the bed beneath him. He would not have risked such an expression as that grin if there had been anyone around to see him. The grin, he knew, gave too much of him away to viewers. It was the hard, unconquerable humor of a man dealing for high stakes.

Here, in the privacy of this locked cabin, it was also a tribute to the skill of the steward who had imprisoned him. A dour and cautious individual with a long Scottish face, and no doubt the greater part of his back wages reinvested in the very spaceship line he worked for. Or had Cully done something to give himself away? No. Cully shook his head. If that had been the case, the steward would have done more than just lock the cabin.

3

It occurred to Cully that his face, at last, might be becoming known.

"I'm sorry, sir," the steward had said, as he opened the cabin's sliding door and saw the unmade bed. "Off-watch steward's missed making it up." He clucked reprovingly. "I'll fix it for you, sir."

"No hurry," said Cully. "I just want to hang my clothes; and I can do that later."

"Oh, no, sir." The lean, dour face of the other—as primitive in a different way as Cully's own—looked shocked. "Regulations. Passengers' gear to be stowed and bunk made up before overdrive."

"Well, I can't just stand here in the corridor," said Cully. "I want to get rid of the stuff and get a drink." And indeed the corridor was so narrow, they were like two vehicles on a mountain road. One would have to back up to some wider spot to let the other past.

"Have the sheets in a moment, sir," said the steward. "Just a moment, sir. If you wouldn't mind sitting up on the bed, sir?"

"All right," said Cully. "But hurry. I want to step up for a drink in the lounge."

He hopped up on to the bed, which filled the little cabin in its down position; and drew his legs up tailor-fashion to clear them out of the corridor.

"Excuse me, sir," said the steward as he closed the door, and went off. As soon as he had heard the button lock latch, Cully had realized what the man was up to. But an unsuspecting man would have waited at least several minutes before hammering on the locked door and calling for someone to let him out. Cully had been forced to sit digesting the matter in silence.

At the thought of it now, however, he grinned again. That steward was a regular prize package. Cully must remember to think up something appropriate for him, afterwards. At the moment, there were more pressing things to think of.

Cully looked in the mirror again and was relieved at the sight of himself without the betraying grin. The face that looked back at him at the moment was lean and angular. A little peroxide solution on his thick, straight brows had taken the sharp appearance off his high cheekbones and given his pale blue eyes a faintly innocent expression. When he really wanted to fail to impress sharply discerning eyes, he also made it a point to chew gum.

The present situation, he considered now, did not call for that extra touch. If the steward was already even vaguely suspicious of him, he could not wait around for an ideal opportunity. He would have to get busy now, while they were still working the spaceship out of the solar system to a safe distance where the overdrive would be engaged without risking a mass-proximity explosion.

And this, since he was imprisoned so neatly in his own shoebox of a cabin, promised to be a problem right from the start.

He looked around the cabin. Unlike the salon cabins on the level overhead, where it was possible to pull down the bed and still have a tiny space to stand upright in—either beside the bed, in the case of single-bed cabins, or between them, in the case of doubles—in the tourist cabins once the bed was down, the room was completely divided into two spaces—the space above the bed and the space below. In the space above, with him, were the light and temperature and ventilation controls, controls to provide him with soft music or the latest adventure tape, food and drink dispensers and a host of other minor comforts.

There were also a phone and a signal button, both connected with the steward's office. Thoughtfully he tried both. There was, of course, no answer.

At that moment a red light flashed on the wall opposite him; and a voice came out of the grille that usually provided the soft music.

"We are about to maneuver. This is the Captain's Section speaking. We are about to maneuver. Will all lounge passengers return to their cabins. Will all passengers remain in their cabins and fasten seat belts. We are about to maneuver. This is the Captain's Section—"

Cully stopped listening. The steward would have known this announcement was coming. It meant that everybody but crew members would be in their cabins and crew members would be up top in control level at maneuver posts. And that meant nobody was likely to happen along to let Cully out. If Cully could get out of this cabin, however, those abandoned corridors could be a break for him.

However, as he looked about him now, Cully was rapidly revising downward his first cheerful assumption that he—who had gotten out of so many much more intentional prisons—would find this a relatively easy task. On the same principle that a pit with unclimbable walls and too deep to jump up from and catch an edge is one of the most perfect traps designable—the tourist room held Cully. He was on top of the bed; and he needed to be below it to operate the latch handle.

First question: How impenetrable was the bed itself? Cully dug down through the covers, pried up the mattress, peered through the springs, and saw a blank panel of metal. Well, he had not really expected much in that direction. He put the mattress and covers back and examined what he had to work with above-bed.

There were all the control switches and buttons on the wall, but nothing among them promised him any aid. The walls were the same metal paneling as the base of the bed. Cully began to turn out his pockets in the hope of finding something in them that would inspire him. And he did indeed turn out a number of interesting items, including a folded piece of notepaper which he looked at rather soberly before laying it aside, unfolded, with a boy scout type of knife that just happened to have a set of lock picks among its other tools. The note would only take up valuable time at the moment, and—the lock being out of reach in the door—the lock picks were no good either.

There was nothing in what he produced to inspire him, however. Whistling a little mournfully, he began to make the next best use of his pile of property. He unscrewed the nib and cap of his long, gold fountain pen, took out the ink cartridge and laid the tube remaining aside. He removed his belt, and the buckle from the belt. The buckle, it appeared, clipped on to the fountain pen tube in somewhat the manner of a pistol grip. He reached in his mouth, removed a bridge covering from the second premolar to the second molar, and combined this with a small metal throwaway dispenser of the sort designed to contain antacid tablets. The two together had a remarkable resemblance to the magazine and miniaturized trigger assembly of a small handgun; and when he attached them to the buckle-fountain-pen-tube combination the resemblance became so marked as to be practically inarguable.

Cully made a few adjustments in this and looked around himself again. For the second time, his eye came to rest on the folded note, and, frowning at himself in the mirror, he did pick it up and unfold it. Inside it read; "O wae the pow'r the Giftie gie us. Love, Lucy." Well, thought Cully, that was about what you could expect from a starry-eyed girl with Scottish ancestors, and romantic notions about present-day conditions on Aldebaran IV and the other new worlds.

". . . But if you have all that land on Asterope IV, why aren't you back there developing it?" she had asked him.

"The New Worlds are stifling to death," he had answered. But he saw then she did not believe him. To her, the New Worlds were still the romantic Frontier, as the Old Worlds Confederation newspapers capitalized it. She thought he had given up from lack of vision.

"You should try again . . ." she murmured. He gave up trying to make her understand. And then, when the cruise was over and their shipboard acquaintance—that was all it was, really—ended on the Miami dock, he had felt her slip something in his pocket so lightly only someone as self-trained as he would have noticed it. Later he had found it to be this note—which he had kept now for too long.

He started to throw it away, changed his mind for the sixtieth time and put it back in his pocket. He turned back to the problem of getting out of the cabin. He looked it over, pulled a sheet from the bed and used its length to measure a few distances.

The bunk was pivoted near the point where the head of it entered the recess in the wall that concealed it in Up position. Up, the bunk was designed to fit with its foot next to the ceiling. Consequently, coming up, the foot would describe an arc—

About a second and a half later he had discovered that the arc of the foot, ascending, would leave just enough space in the opposite top angle between wall and ceiling so that if he could just manage to hang there, while releasing the safety latch at the foot of the bed, he might be able to get the bed up past him into the wall recess.

It was something which required the muscle and skill normally called for by so-called "chimney ascents" in mountain climbing—where the climber wedges himself between two opposing walls of rock. A rather wide chimney—since the room was a little more than four feet in width. But Cully had had some little experience in that line.

He tried it. A few seconds later, pressed against walls and ceiling, he reached down, managed to get the bed released, and had the satisfaction of seeing it fold up by him. Half a breath later he was free, out in the corridor of the Tourist Section.

The corridor was deserted and silent. All doors were closed. Cully closed his own thoughtfully behind him and went along the corridor to the more open space in the center of the ship. He looked up a steel ladder to the entrance of the Salon section, where there would be another ladder to the Crew Section, and from there eventually to his objective—the Control level and the Captain's Section. Had the way up those ladders been open, it would have been simple. But level with the top of the ladder he saw the way to the Salon section was closed off by a metal cover capable of withstanding fifteen pounds per square inch of pressure.

It had been closed, of course, as the other covers would have been, at the beginning of the maneuver period.

Cully considered it thoughtfully, his fingers caressing the pistol grip of the little handgun he had just put together. He would have preferred, naturally, that the covers be open and the way available to him without the need for fuss or muss. But the steward had effectively ruled out that possibility by reacting as and when he had. Cully turned away from the staircase, and frowned, picturing the layout of the ship, as he had committed it to memory five days ago.

There was an emergency hatch leading through the ceiling of the end tourist cabin to the end salon cabin overhead, at both extremes of the corridor. He turned and went down to the end cabin nearest him, and laid his finger quietly on the outside latch handle.

There was no sound from inside. He drew his put-together handgun from his belt; and, holding it in his left hand, calmly and without hesitation, opened the door and stepped inside.

He stopped abruptly. The bed in here was, of course, up in the wall, or he could never have entered. But the cabin's single occupant was asleep on the right-hand seat of the two seats that an upraised bed left exposed. The occupant was a small girl of about eight years old.

The slim golden barrel of the handgun had swung immediately to aim at the child's temple. For an automatic second, it hung poised there, Cully's finger half-pressing the trigger. But the little girl never stirred. In the silence, Cully heard the surge of his own blood in his ears and the faint crackle of the note in his shirt

pocket. He lowered the gun and fumbled in the waistband of his pants, coming up with a child-sized anes-
thetic pellet. He slipped this into his gun above the
regular load; aimed the gun, and fired. The child made
a little uneasy movement all at once; and then lay still.
Cully bent over her for a second, and heard the soft
sound of her breathing. He straighened up. The pellet
worked not through the blood stream, but immediately
through a reaction of the nerves. In fifteen minutes the
effect would be worn off, and the girl's sleep would be
natural slumber again.

He turned away, stepped up on the opposite seat and
laid his free hand on the latch handle of the emergency
hatch overhead. A murmur of voices from above made
him hesitate. He unscrewed the barrel of the handgun
and put it in his ear with the other hollow end resting
against the ceiling which was also the floor overhead.
The voices came, faint and distorted, but understandable to his listening.

". . . Hilifter," a female voice was saying.

"Oh, Patty!" another female voice answered. "He
was just trying to scare you. You believe everything."

"How about that ship that got hilifted just six months
ago? That ship going to one of the Pleiades, just like
this one? The *Queen of Argyle*—"

"*Princess of Argyle.*"

"Well, you know what I mean. Ships do get hilifted.
Just as long as there're governments on the pioneer
worlds that'll license them and no questions asked.
And it could just as well happen to this ship. But you
don't worry about it a bit."

"No, I don't."

"When hilifters take over a ship, they kill off everyone who can testify against them. None of the passengers or ship's officers from the *Princess of Argyle* was
ever heard of again."

"Says who?"

"Oh, everybody knows that!"

Cully took the barrel from his ear and screwed it back onto his weapon. He glanced at the anesthetized child and thought of trying the other cabin with an emergency hatch. But the maneuver period would not last more than twenty minutes at the most and five of that must be gone already. He put the handgun between his teeth, jerked the latch to the overhead hatch, and pulled it down and open.

He put both hands on the edge of the hatch opening; and with one spring went upward into the salon cabin overhead.

He erupted into the open space between a pair of facing seats, each of which held a girl in her twenties. The one on his left was a rather plump, short, blond girl who was sitting curled up on her particular seat with a towel across her knees, an open bottle of pink nail polish on the towel, and the brush-cap to the bottle poised in her hand. The other was a tall, dark-haired, very pretty lass with a lap-desk pulled down from the wall and a handscriber on the desk where she was apparently writing a letter. For a moment both stared at him, and his gun; and then the blonde gave a muffled shriek, pulled the towel over her head and lay still, while the brunette, staring at Cully, went slowly pale.

"Jim!" she said.

"Sorry," said Cully. "The real name's Cully When. Sorry about this, too, Lucy." He held the gun casually, but it was pointed in her general direction. "I didn't have any choice."

A little of the color came back. Her eyes were as still as fragments of green bottle glass.

"No choice about what?" she said.

"To come through this way," said Cully. "Believe me, if I'd known you were here, I'd have picked any other way. But there wasn't any other way; and I didn't know."

"I see," she said, and looked at the gun in his hand. "Do you have to point that at me?"

"I'm afraid," said Cully, gently, "I do."

She did not smile.

"I'd still like to know what you're doing here," she said.

"I'm just passing through," said Cully. He gestured with the gun to the emergency hatch to the Crew Section, overhead. "As I say, I'm sorry it has to be through your cabin. But I didn't even know you were serious about emigrating."

"People usually judge other people by themselves," she said expressionlessly. "As it happened, I believed you." She looked at the gun again. "How many of you are there on board?"

"I'm afraid I can't tell you that," said Cully.

"No. You couldn't, could you?" Her eyes held steady on him. "You know, there's an old poem about a man like you. He rides by a farm maiden and she falls in love with him, just like that. But he makes her guess what he is; and she guesses . . . oh, all sorts of honorable things, like soldier, or forester. But he tells her in the end he's just an outlaw, slinking through the wood."

Cully winced.

"Lucy—" he said. "Lucy—"

"Oh, that's all right," she said. "I should have known when you didn't call me or get in touch with me, after the boat docked." She glanced over at her friend, motionless under the towel. "You have the gun. What do you want us to do?"

"Just sit still," he said. "I'll go on up through here and be out of your way in a second. I'm afraid—" He reached over to the phone on the wall and pulled its cord loose. "You can buzz for the steward, still, after I'm gone," he said. "But he won't answer just a buzzer until after the maneuver period's over. And the stairway hatches are locked. Just sit tight and you'll be all right."

He tossed the phone aside and tucked the gun in his waistband.

"Excuse me," he said, stepping up on the seat beside

her. She moved stiffly away from him. He unlatched the hatch overhead, pulled it down; and went up through it. When he glanced back down through it, he saw her face stiffly upturned to him.

He turned away and found himself in an equipment room. It was what he had expected from the ship's plans he had memorized before coming aboard. He went quickly out of the room and scouted the Section.

As he had expected, there was no one at all upon this level. Weight and space on interstellar liners being at the premium that they were, even a steward like the one who had locked him in his cabin did double duty. In overdrive, no one but the navigating officer had to do much of anything. But in ordinary operation, there were posts for all ships personnel, and all ships personnel were at them up in the Captain's Section at Control.

The stair hatch to this top and final section of the ship he found to be closed as the rest. This, of course, was routine. He had not expected this to be unlocked, though a few years back ships like this might have been that careless. There were emergency hatches from this level as well, of course, up to the final section. But it was no part of Cully's plan to come up in the middle of a Control room or a Captain's Section filled with young, active, and almost certainly armed officers. The inside route was closed.

The outside route remained a possibility. Cully went down to the opposite end of the corridor and found the entry port closed, but sealed only by a standard lock. In an adjoining room there were outside suits. Cully spent a few minutes with his picks, breaking the lock of the seal; and then went in to put on the suit that came closest to fitting his six-foot-two frame.

A minute later he stepped out onto the outside skin of the ship.

As he watched the outer door of the entry port closing ponderously in the silence of airless space behind him, he felt the usual inner coldness that came over him at times like this. He had a mild but very definite phobia about open space with its myriads of unchanging stars. He knew what caused it—several psychiatrists had told him it was nothing to worry about, but he could not quite accept their unconcern. He knew he was a very lonely individual, underneath it all; and subconsciously he guessed he equated space with the final extinction in which he expected one day to disappear and be forgotten forever. He could not really believe it was possible for someone like him to make a dent in such a universe.

It was symptomatic, he thought now, plodding along with the magnetic bootsoles of his suit clinging to the metal hull, that he had never had any success with women—like Lucy. A sort of bad luck seemed to put him always in the wrong position with anyone he stood a chance of loving. Inwardly, he was just as starry-eyed as Lucy, he admitted to himself, alone with the vastness of space and the stars, but he'd never had much success bringing it out into the open. Where she went all right, he seemed to go all wrong. Well, he thought, that was life. She went her way and he would go his. And it was probably a good thing.

He looked ahead up the side of the ship, and saw the slight bulge of the observation window of the navigator's section. It was just a few more steps now.

Modern ships were sound-insulated, thankfully, or the crew inside would have heard his dragging footsteps on the hull. He reached the window and peered in. The room he looked into was empty.

Beside the window was a small, emergency port for cleaning and repairs of the window. Clumsily, and with a good deal of effort, he got the lock-bolt holding it down unscrewed, and let himself in. The space between outer and inner ports here was just enough to contain a space-suited man. He crouched in darkness after the outer port had closed behind him.

Incoming air screamed up to audibility. He cautiously cracked the interior door and looked into a room still empty of any crew members. He slipped inside and

snapped the lock on the door before getting out of his
suit.

As soon as he was out, he drew the handgun from his
belt and cautiously opened the door he had previously
locked. He looked out on a short corridor leading one
way to the Control Room, and the other, if his memory
of the ship plans had not failed him, to the central room
above the stairway hatch from below. Opening off this
small circular space surrounding the hatch would be
another entrance directly to the Control room, a door
to the Captain's Quarters, and one to the Communications Room.

The corridor was deserted. He heard voices coming
down it from the Control Room; and he slipped out the
door that led instead to the space surrounding the
stairway hatch. And checked abruptly.

The hatch was open. And it had not been open when
he had checked it from the level below, ten minutes
before.

For the first time he cocked an ear specifically to the
kinds of voices coming from the Control Room. The
acoustics of this part of the ship mangled all sense out of
the words being said. But now that he listened, he had
no trouble recognizing, among others, the voice of Lucy.

It occurred to him then with a kind of wonder at
himself, that it would have been no feat for an active
girl like herself to have followed him up through the
open emergency hatch, and later mount the crew level
stairs to the closed hatch there and pound on it until
someone opened up.

He threw aside further caution and sprinted across to
the doorway of the Captain's Quarters. The door was
unlocked. He ducked inside and looked around him. It
was empty. It occurred to him that Lucy and the rest of
the ship's complement would probably still be expecting him to be below in the Crew's section. He closed
the door and looked about him, at the room he was in.

The room was more lounge than anything else, being

the place where the captain of a spaceship did his
entertaining. But there was a large and businesslike
desk in one corner of the room, and in the wall opposite, was a locked, glassed-in case holding an assortment of rifles and handguns.

He was across the room in a moment, and in a few
savage seconds had the lock to the case picked open.
He reached in and took down a short-barreled, flaring-
muzzled riot gun. He checked the chamber. It was
filled with a full thousand-clip of the deadly steel darts.
Holding this in one hand and his handgun in the other,
he went back out the door and toward the other entrance to the control room—the entrance from the central room around the stairway hatch.

". . . He wouldn't tell me if there were any others,"
Lucy was saying to a man in a captain's shoulder tabs,
while eight other men, including the dour-faced steward who had locked Cully in his cabin, stood at their
posts, but listening.

"There aren't any," said Cully, harshly. They all turned
to him. He laid the handgun aside on a control table by
the entrance to free his other hand, and lifted the heavy
riot gun in both hands, covering them. "There's only
me."

"What do you want?" said the man with the captain's
tabs. His face was set, and a little pale. Cully ignored
the question. He came into the room, circling to his
right, so as to have a wall at his back.

"You're one man short," said Cully as he moved.
"Where is he?"

"Off-shift steward's sleeping," said the steward who
had locked Cully in his room.

"Move back," said Cully, picking up crew members
from their stations at control boards around the room,
and herding them before him back around the room's
circular limit to the very entrance by which he had
come in. "I don't believe you."

"Then I might as well tell you," said the captain,
backing up now along with Lucy and the rest. "He's in

Communications. We keep a steady contact with Solar Police right up until we go into overdrive. There are two of their ships pacing alongside us right now, lights off, a hundred miles each side of us."

"Tell me another," said Cully. "I don't believe that either." He was watching everybody in the room, but what he was most aware of were the eyes of Lucy, wide upon him. He spoke to her, harshly. "Why did you get into this?"

She was pale to the lips; and her eyes had a stunned look.

"I looked down and saw what you'd done to that child in the cabin below—" her voice broke off into a whisper. "Oh, Cully—"

He laughed mournfully.

"Stop there," he ordered. He had driven them back into a corner near the entrance he had come in. "I've got to have all of you together. Now, one of you is going to tell me where that other man is—and I'm going to pick you off, one at a time until somebody does."

"You're a fool," said the captain. A little of his color had come back. "You're all alone. You don't have a chance of controlling this ship by yourself. You know what happens to Hilifters, don't you? It's not just a prison sentence. Give up now and we'll all put in a word for you. You might get off without mandatory execution."

"No thanks," said Cully. He gestured with the end of the riot gun. "We're going into overdrive. Start setting up the course as I give it to you."

"No," said the captain, looking hard at him.

"You're a brave man," said Cully. "But I'd like to point out something. I'm going to shoot you if you won't cooperate; and then I'm going to work down the line of your officers. Sooner or later somebody's going to preserve his life by doing what I tell him. So getting yourself killed isn't going to save the ship at all. It just means somebody with less courage than you lives. And you die."

*   *   *

There was a sharp, bitter intake of breath from the direction of Lucy. Cully kept his eyes on the captain.

"How about it?" Cully asked.

"No brush-pants of a colonial," said the captain, slowly and deliberately, "is going to stand in my Control Room and tell me where to take my ship."

"Did the captain and officers of the *Princess of Argyle* ever come back?" said Cully, somewhat cryptically.

"It's nothing to me whether they came or stayed."

"I take it all back," said Cully. "You're too valuable to lose." The riot gun shifted to come to bear on the First Officer, a tall, thin, younger man whose hair was already receding at the temples. "But you aren't, friend. I'm not even going to tell you what I'm going to do. I'm just going to start counting; and when I decide to stop you've had it. One . . . two . . ."

"Don't! Don't shoot!" The First Officer jumped across the few steps that separated him from the main Computer Panel. "What's your course? What do you want me to set up—"

The captain began to curse the First Officer. He spoke slowly and distinctly and in a manner that completely ignored the presence of Lucy in the Control Room. He went right on as Cully gave the First Officer the course and the First Officer set it up. He stopped only as—abruptly—the lights went out, and the ship overdrove.

When the lights came on again—it was a matter of only a fraction of a second of real time—the captain was at last silent. He seemed to have sagged in the brief interval of darkness and his face looked older.

And then, slamming through the tense silence of the room came the sound of the Contact Alarm Bell.

"Turn it on," said Cully. The First Officer stepped over and pushed a button below the room's communication screen. It cleared suddenly to show a man in a white jacket.

"We're alongside, Cully," he said. "We'll take over now. How're you fixed for casualties?"

"At the moment—" began Cully. But he got no further than that. Behind him, three hard, spaced words in a man's voice cut him off.

"Drop it, Hilifter!"

Cully did not move. He cocked his eyebrows a little sadly and grinned his untamable grin for the first time at the ship's officers, and Lucy and the figure in the screen. Then the grin went away.

"Friend," he said to the man hidden behind him, "your business is running a spaceship. Mine is taking them away from people who run them. Right now you're figuring how you make me give up or shoot me down and this ship dodges back into overdrive, and you become hero for saving it. But it isn't going to work that way."

He waited for a moment to hear if the off-watch steward behind him—or whoever the officer was—would answer. But there was only silence.

"You're behind me," said Cully. "But I can turn pretty fast. You may get me coming around, but unless you've got something like a small cannon, you're not going to stop me getting you at this short range, whether you've got me or not. Now, if you think I'm just talking, you better think again. For me, this is one of the risks of the trade."

He turned. As he did so he went for the floor; and heard the first shot go by his ear. As he hit the floor another shot hit the deck beside him and ricocheted into his side. But by that time he had the heavy riot gun aimed and he pressed the firing button. The stream of darts knocked the man backward out of the entrance to the control room to lie, a still and huddled shape, in the corridor outside.

Cully got to his feet, feeling the single dart in his side. The room was beginning to waver around him, but he felt that he could hold on for the necessary couple of minutes before the people from the ship moving in alongside could breach the lock and come aboard. His jacket was loose and would hide the bleeding underneath. None of those facing him could know he had been hit.

"All right, folks," he said, managing a grin. "It's all over but the shouting—" And then Lucy broke suddenly from the group and went running across the room toward the entrance through which Cully had come a moment or so earlier.

"Lucy—" he barked at her. And then he saw her stop and turn by the control table near the entrance, snatching up the little handgun he had left there. "Lucy, do you want to get shot?"

But she was bringing up the little handgun, held in the grip of both her hands and aiming it squarely at him. The tears were running down her face.

"It's better for you, Cully—" she was sobbing. "Better . . ."

He swung the riot gun to bear on her, but he saw she did not even see it.

"Lucy, I'll have to kill you!" he cried. But she no more heard him, apparently, than she saw the muzzle-on view of the riot gun in his hands. The wavering golden barrel in her grasp wobbled to bear on him.

"Oh, Cully!" she wept. "Cully—" And pulled the trigger.

"Oh, *hell*!" said Cully in despair. And let her shoot him down.

When he came back, things were very fuzzy there at first. He heard the voice of the man in the white jacket, arguing with the voice of Lucy.

"Hallucination—" muttered Cully. The voices broke off.

"Oh, he said something!" cried the voice of Lucy.

"Cully?" said the man's voice. Cully felt a two-finger grip on his wrist in the area where his pulse should be—if, that was, he had a pulse. "How're you feeling?"

"Ship's doctor?" muttered Cully, with great effort. "You got the *Star of the North*?"

"That's right. All under control. How do you feel?"

"Feel fine," mumbled Cully. The doctor laughed.

"Sure you do," said the doctor. "Nothing like being shot a couple of times and having a pellet and a dart removed to put a man in good shape."

"Not Lucy's fault—" muttered Cully. "Not understand." He made another great effort in the interests of explanation. "Stars'n eyes."

"Oh, what does he mean?" wept Lucy.

"He means," said the voice of the doctor harshly, "that you're just the sort of fine young idealist who makes the best sort of sucker for the sort of propaganda the Old World's Confederation dishes out."

"Oh, you'd say that!" flared Lucy's voice. "Of course, you'd say that!"

"Young lady," said the doctor, "how rich do you think our friend Cully, here, is?"

Cully heard her blow her nose, weakly.

"He's got millions, I suppose," she said, bitterly. "Hasn't he hilifted dozens of ships?"

"He's hilifted eight," said the doctor, dryly, "which, incidentally, puts him three ships ahead of any other contender for the title of hilifting champion around the populated stars. The mortality rate among single workers—and you can't get any more than a single 'lifter aboard Confederation ships nowadays—hits ninety per cent with the third ship captured. But I doubt Cully's been able to save millions on a salary of six hundred a month, and a bonus of one tenth of one per cent of salvage value, at Colonial World rates."

There was a moment of profound silence.

"What do you mean?" said Lucy, in a voice that wavered a little.

"I'm trying," said the doctor, "for the sake of my patient—and perhaps for your own—to push aside what Cully calls those stars in your eyes and let a crack of surface daylight through."

"But why would he work for a salary—like that?" Disbelief was strong in her voice.

"Possibly," said the doctor, "just possibly because the picture of a bloodstained hilifter with a knife between his teeth, carousing in Colonial bars, shooting down Confederation officers for the fun of it, and dragging women passengers off by the hair, has very little to do with the real facts of a man like Cully."

"Smart girl," managed Cully. "S'little mixed up, s'all—" He manged to get his vision cleared a bit. The other two were standing facing each other, right beside his bed. The doctor had a slight flush above his cheekbones and looked angry. Lucy, Cully noted anxiously, was looking decidedly pale. "Mixed up—" Cully said again.

"Mixed up isn't the word for it," said the doctor angrily, without looking down at him. "She and all ninety-nine out of a hundred people on the Old Worlds." He went on to Lucy. "You met Cully Earthside. Evidently you liked him there. He didn't strike you as the scum of the stars, then.

"But all you have to do is hear him tagged with the name 'hilifter' and immediately your attitude changes."

Lucy swallowed.

"No," she said, in a small voice, "it didn't . . . change."

"Then who do you think's wrong—you or Cully?" The doctor snorted. "If I have to give you reasons, what's the use? If you can't see things straight for yourself, who can help you? That's what's wrong with all the people back on the Old Worlds."

"I believe Cully," she said. "I just don't know why I should."

"Who has lots of raw materials—the raw materials to support trade—but hasn't any trade?" asked the doctor.

She frowned at him.

"Why . . . the New Worlds haven't any trade on their own," she said. "But they're too undeveloped yet, too young—"

"Young? There's three to five generations on most of them!"

"I mean they haven't got the industry, the commercial organization—" she faltered before the slightly satirical expression on the doctor's face. "All right, then, you tell me! If they've got everything they need for trade, why don't they? The Old Worlds did; why don't you?"

"In what?"

She stared at him.

"But the Confederation of the Old Worlds already has the ships for interworld trade. And they're glad to ship Colonial products. In fact they do," she said.

"So a load of miniaturized surgical power instruments made on Asterope in the Pleiades, has to be shipped to Earth and then shipped clear back out to its destination on Electra, also in the Pleiades. Only by the time they get there they've doubled or tripled in price, and the difference is in the pockets of Earth shippers."

She was silent.

"It seems to me," said the doctor, "that girl who was with you mentioned something about your coming from Boston, back in the United States on Earth. Didn't they have a tea party there once? Followed by a revolution? And didn't it all have something to do with the fact that England at that time would not allow its colonies to own and operate their own ships for trade—so that it all had to be funneled through England in English ships to the advantage of English merchants?"

"But why can't you build your own ships?" she said.

Cully felt it was time he got in on the conversation. He cleared his throat, weakly.

"Hey—" he managed to say. They both looked at him; but he himself was looking only at Lucy.

"You see," he said, rolling over and struggling up on one elbow, "the thing is—"

"Lie down," said the doctor.

"Go jump out the air lock," said Cully. "The thing is, honey, you can't build spaceships without a lot of expensive equipment and tools and trained personnel.

You need a spaceship-building industry. And you have to get the equipment, tools, and people from somewhere else to start with. You can't get 'em unless you can trade for 'em. And you can't trade freely without ships of your own, which the Confederation, by forcing us to ship through them, makes it impossible for us to have.

"So you see how it works out," said Cully. "It works out you've got to have shipping before you can build shipping. And if people on the outside refuse to let you have it by proper means, simply because they've got a good thing going and don't want to give it up—then some of us just have to break loose and go after it any way we can."

"Oh, Cully!"

Suddenly she was on her knees by the bed and her arms were around him.

"Of course the Confederation news services have been trying to keep up the illusion we're sort of half jungle-jims, half wildwest characters," said the doctor. "Once a person takes a good look at the situation on the New Worlds, though, with his eyes open—" He stopped. They were not listening.

"I might mention," he went on, a little more loudly, "while Cully here may not be exactly rich, he does have a rather impressive medal due him, and a commission as Brevet-Admiral in the upcoming New Worlds Space Force. The New Worlds Congress voted him both at their meeting just last week on Asterope, as soon as they'd finished drafting their Statement of Independence—"

But they were still not listening. It occurred to the doctor then that he had better uses for his time—here on this vessel where he had been Ship's Doctor ever since she first lifted into space—than to stand around talking to deaf ears.

He went out, closing the door of the sick bay on the former *Princess of Argyle* quietly behind him.

None But Man

1

. . . Beyond this line we face the Alien's stars.
They may not lay their law on what is ours.
—For none but Man stands here.

IIASEC'S CREED

A jerk, and a sudden rumbling vibration jolted Culihan O'Rourke When out of the pain-laced fog enfolding him. It had become almost comfortable lately, that fog.

"No rest for the foolish," he thought with a feverishly lightheaded humor. The humor glimmered for a moment like a match in the mist of his mind, before reminding him of how obligingly he had cooperated with his own betrayal, into the hands of his present captors. That thought threatened once more to add a private mental torture to the physical hell of his situation.

It did not succeed if only because he still hung on to a powerful belief in his ability to straighten out almost anything, given time; but the mental effort just made had brought him up again into full consciousness. He

identified the vibration now. It was the sound and
movement of the engines restarting aboard the Space-
and-Atmosphere vessel that carried him. The ship was
readying itself for a landing, finally, after its long glide
down from the near-orbital midpoint of its passage from
New York Complex. Recognizing this, he woke all the
way, once more, to the specific cramps and agonies of
his body.

The most active pain was in his arms from shoulders
to wrists, held locked behind him by a set of spring
restraints. The arms felt fused together from the neck
down. Which was hardly surprising—the restraints had
not been taken off him in the last thirty-six hours.

They were one pair of the tools put to use during a
process of questioning that had stayed just inside the
legal limits during the past week and a half, ever since
he had been detained on landing at the Long Island
Sound Spaceport. During those ten days his World
Police questioners had not tortured him—legally.

But in a practical sense he had been pushed near to
the limits of his physical endurance. They had given
him either no food or several times what he could eat at
once. Also, the meals had either been burned or frozen
to the point of inedibility. He had been locked in a room
with a whimsical light switch that usually would not turn
off the powerful lighting panel overhead, and with a
water tap so set in the wall that it produced water only
when a peculiarly shaped cup was pushed beneath it.

But that cup had turned out to leak water as fast as
the tap supplied it. When Cully complained, his captors had brought him water otherwise—one ounce at a
time in a tiny paper cup. He had been kept in restraints
or under questioning for hours on end, and allowed to
sleep only enough to stay sane. Yet, as Cully knew, the
bald facts of his week and a half, as set down in the
official record, would show that he had not been de-
prived of adequate shelter, rest, food or drink.

The World Police had questioned him about some
supposed attempt by the Pleiades Frontier Worlds,

backed by the Moldaug aliens, to take over the three
Old Worlds of Earth, Mars and the expensively terra-
formed Venus, in a *coup d'état*. The plain ridiculousness
of this—of the few scattered millions of people on the
Frontier attempting to conquer the eighty-odd billions of
the three Solar System Worlds, who together controlled
over eighty percent of the wealth and armed might of the
human race—was so obvious that it took Cully some
little time to realize that his interrogators were serious.

Fantastically, they were serious. And Cully's inabil-
ity, which they assumed to be a refusal, to tell them
about the coup drove them nearly to illegal violence
during the week and a half.

Perhaps, he thought lightheadedly now, he should
not have damned them all for a bunch of paranoid
space-phobes, once he had realized that the questions
were not merely an excuse for holding him under arrest. But probably keeping his temper would have made
no difference in what they had done to him anyway.
Almost literally more dead than alive now, Cully's lean,
tall body lay helplessly where it had been dumped,
upon what he took to be mailbags, in the rear of the
passenger compartment of the World Police SA ship.
He lay on his side, with his restrained arms locked
behind him, just able to see out one of the curved
windows in the side of the ceremetal ship.

He had not bothered to notice where they were
taking him—had hardy cared, in fact, within the fog of
pain and weakness enclosing him. But now, roused by
the restarting of the engines, he lifted his head and
tried to see out the window.

They were dropping swiftly toward the dark-blue
surface of an ocean flecked with the peaceful gold of
floating sargasso weed. Both sargasso weed and the high
glare of the sun in the brilliantly blue sky testified to
the fact that they were somewhere in the tropic latitudes.

Looking down through the window now at the ex-
panse of blazing aquamarine sky and opalescent ocean,
Cully saw a strange structure like an offshore oil-drilling

rig, though much larger. As he blinked his eyes against the sun glare, however, and the SA ship dropped rapidly toward the structure, he saw that its similarity to an oil-drilling rig was less than he had first thought.

The resemblance was there, all right. There was a heavy metal platform and superstructure, supported on six legs going down into the water like the anchoring legs of an oil rig. But now Cully's dulled mind, triggered to slow movement by the unquenchable reflexes of that belief in himself that had never deserted him, reminded him that here, far from land—and it must be far from land—the ocean would hardly be shallow enough to allow legs like that to rest on the sea floor.

It was true that the steadiness of the structure gave it all the appearance of being so anchored. But Cully's knowledge of architecture and engineering gradually formed for him a picture of the legs as containing something like machinery or elevators, and reaching no more than a hundred feet or so beneath the surface. At which point they would terminate in a balancing body the volume and weight of the platform above.

Such a body, plus the fact that the legs went below the area of wave disturbance, would steady the total, floating structure as well as legs anchored in the sea bed—and with a great deal more practicality. While at the same time, the balance between the masses in air and water held the upper platform fifty to eighty feet above the most furious tossing of the waves.

This much Cully saw, and dully concluded, before the strain of stretching up to see out the window drained the small reserves of energy left in him. He fell back on the mailbags, and the scene around him went swimming away into darkness . . .

The next thing he remembered, he was being half-dragged, half-carried across a metal deck in an upright position between two men in the familiar black uniforms of the Police. The pain and effort of the movement jarred him back to consciousness, and he opened his eyes to catch a fleeting glimpse about the platform he had seen from the air. Then he was dragged into what seemed to be a metal-walled, oil-smelling room and dumped in a corner there.

There was a short delay. Then the room darkened and descended, dropping away elevator-fashion beneath him. It fell for some slow seconds, and the air became thickly warm about him. It jarred to a stop.

Somehow, Cully must have passed out again. Because next he found himself half-standing, half-slumped, upheld by a single individual in a green uniform.

There was a clashing sound and heavy, metal doors opened before them.

"All right! Get out!" said the guard.

His hands shoved Cully, thrust him, staggering, forward out through the elevator doors into semidarkness heavy with odors of human bodies. Under the impetus of that shove, Cully tottered forward blindly half a dozen steps, then fell. He lay, blissfully content to be no longer on his feet, the metal deck beneath him feeling soft as the softest mattress he could remember, its cold surface against his cheek as gentle as the touch of a down pillow.

"Get up!" boomed and echoed the voice of the guard, far and distant above him. Cully ignored it. His eyes were accustoming themselves to the gloom around him. As they focused in now, he saw a pair of Frontier-made brush boots approaching. They came up to within a foot of his nose, and stopped, their toe caps pointing back past Cully in the direction from which the guard's voice had come. A new, quiet voice echoed and sounded, more softly than the guard's, above Cully's head.

"We'll take care of him, Busher."

"Suits me, Jaimeson," answered the guard's voice. "The more you prisoners take care of yourselves, the better I like it."

There was the sound of feet from the direction in which the guard's voice had come, starting to move off.

"Wait a minute!" It was the voice belonging to the brush boots. "Hold on, Busher. He's still got those restraints on."

"Now, that's sad." It was the guard's voice. "No one told me to take them off."

"But you can't leave them on any longer. Look how they've cut into his arms. They've been on him for hours."

The guard's boots drew near again, walking heavily.

"Listen, Jaimeson. You want to take care of him, that's up to you. But I told you I didn't have any orders to take off the springs. And my orders don't come from you. Until I get orders—"

The guard's voice broke off on a suddenly squeaking note that, in spite of Cully's pain-shot wooziness, evoked the ghost of a silent chuckle in the back of Cully's mind. There was a long pause, a silence during which Cully became aware that a second pair of brush boots had silently joined the first. Cully stared at the new pair in fascination, for they were no larger than the boots of a boy of twelve. The guard's voice spoke again.

"You don't scare me, Doak!"

The words were brave enough, but the new, high pitch of the voice betrayed them.

"Take"—it was a different voice, a strange voice, unremarkable but oddly unyielding, a flat, boyish tenor that somehow failed to sound either boyish or flat—"them off."

There was a little moment of silence.

"They're hurting him," went on the Doak voice unemotionally. "You know I don't like that, Busher—seeing you hurt anyone."

Cully felt heavy fingers hastily fumbling with the restraints, holding his forearms and wrists together behind his back. There was the sudden, twanging sound of the lock snapping open, and the touch of the tight metal coils fell from him.

Wonderingly, he attempted to bring his arms around in front of him—and hot agony lanced through his shoulders, back and body like the flame of a welding torch. He never knew whether the scream that formed in him then actually came from his throat, or merely echoed itself in his brain. Because darkness, this time complete and unrelenting, closed down about him.

2

Later, he was never able to remember an exact moment in which he began once more to be aware of what was around him. In between was an interval of half-consciousness and nightmare; of faces that swelled and dwindled, coming close and then going away from him.

First, the face of Alia Braight, once more the thin, tomboyish young girl who had tagged after him around the weedy hills and fields surrounding Kalestin City. Then Alia again—but adult now—as she had been when she had come all the way back out to that Frontier World two months ago. She had come, she said, now that the troubles between the Old Worlds and the Frontier were four years over, to talk him into coming back with her to Earth, and taking up once more his graduate studies in architecture under Albert Monns at Michigan State.

Alia, adult and beautiful now, arguing for his return. Then Alia, turning strangely contrary aboard the ship bringing them both to Earth. Alia, reviving all the old political arguments between the Old Worlds and the Frontier. Finally, Alia, the day their ship had landed, a week and a half back, turning away from him in the spaceship lounge, as the ship settled on the Long Island Spaceport pad:

"Cully, it's no use. I thought you'd have changed— but you haven't. You're still just as much a Frontier revolutionist as you ever were. Maybe we'd better not see each other . . . for a while, anyway . . ."

And a few seconds later:

"No, I won't call you, Cully. I'll wait until you call me . . ."

Alia, going away from him, reflected in the wall mirror of the lounge as she mingled with the debarking crowd at the top of the lounge gangplank. His own sharp-boned face under its blond hair, for once somber, mirrored there also, gazing after her. Then, several minutes later, when Cully had followed, the neat-mustached, thin, young face of a World Police lieutenant waiting at the foot of the gangplank. The Lieutenant, flanked by two black-uniformed enlisted men, one of whom was a corporal, looking at Cully's papers from under the trim visor of his uniform cap. The Lieutenant's voice, asking:

"Culihan When? Not the spacelifter who hijacked more of our spaceships than any other Frontiersman during the Frontier Revolt?"

"Ex-spacelifter. That's my pardon you're holding— signed by one of your own Tri-World Council Members, Amos Braight. What is this?" Cully had demanded. Then sudden understanding exploding within him. Abruptly he had looked for Alia, and found her already lost in the crowd of passengers streaming ahead toward the Terminal Building. He had turned back toward the Lieutenant. *"If you're arresting me, what's the charge?"*

"Charge? Oh, no charge at all, sir. Just some routine questions . . ." The young Lieutenant's face lifted, smoothly polite among the gathering small crowd of disembarking passengers. *"But if you'll just come with us for a minute . . ."*

Afterwards, the Police Corporal's fist like a door slammed unexpectedly across Cully's mouth, once they had brought him into the back room of the Police Section of the Spaceport Terminal. The Corporal's hard-fat, savage face under stiff black hair . . . his arm drawn back again as other Police hands locked Cully's arms behind him. The Corporal's voice, thickly . . .

"Look at him! This one wants to bite. Hold him still, now . . ."

"All right, Corporal!" The Lieutenant, on his feet, neat and military behind the desk, speaking evenly and slowly toward the official interview recorder on his desk. *"I'm aware of the trouble this man offered to cause you as you were bringing him in, and I saw the threatening gesture he made toward you just now that forced you to strike him in self-defense—but we'll have no violence, here. You other two men put the restraints on him."*

The Lieutenant, sitting down again, as the cool, enfolding metal of the spring restraints enclosed Cully's arms from wrist to elbow behind him . . . *"Name, please?"*

"Damn you, you know my name!"

"Name please . . ."

And then the whirling visions of the week and a half of nightmares. Nightmares that slowly thinned and gave way to the black and utter sleep of exhaustion.

When full clearheadedness finally returned, it came slowly, like a man drifting up into daylight from the dark of deep waters. But it brought with it a freedom at last from pain, and a new peace of mind.

He had put it all into proper context finally. Alia had tricked him into returning to Earth so that the Old Worlds, now become near-paranoic with space fears, could lock him up. He, who had been the greatest thorn in their sides during the Frontier Revolt, which the Bill of Agreements had theoretically resolved, six years since.

But he could see now how Alia was not to blame for what she had done to him. She was still the daughter of Amos Braight, once Kalestin's Governor and Cully's guardian, but now Senior Member of the Tri-Worlds

Council, governing Earth, Mars and Venus. Being the
kind of person she was, Alia could be placed under
pressure by arguments of her father that her naturally
loyal nature could not resist.

Therefore, Alia had not been changed into his enemy, after all. She had only been ill-advised, and that
condition could be corrected. At that conclusion, a deep,
fierce warmth of challenge began to burn in Cully, and
he welcomed it like an old friend. Always there had
been this quality of recoil in him. The harder he was
hit, the higher he bounced. He could feel his spirits
returning now.

The trouble lay not in the clean, half-Frontier mind
of Alia, but in the sick fear of most of the Old World's
people where the Frontier and the Moldaug aliens were
concerned. Alia was too honest not to admit this if
Cully could prove it to her beyond doubt. And prove it
he would, he thought now. Even if it was necessary to
turn the Old Worlds, the Frontier, the Moldaug and
everything else upside down to do it. He grinned again,
inside his mind, at the picture this thought evoked.

"That's right," he told himself silently, part mock-
ingly part seriously. "You never were one for half-
measures, were you?"

That self-accusation woke him at last into full consciousness.

He opened his eyes, with the vague memory of having drifted up to just beneath the surface of awareness
in this place on a number of previous occasions, only to
slip back again.

This time, however, when he came awake he was
aware of what seemed to be a sort of cubbyhole with a
steeply slanting roof above it that might be the underside of a stairway, for he had vague recollections of
boots heard ascending and descending over his head. In
this dim cubbyhole, Cully made out three foam mattresses with bedding, which together filled the available
space below the slanting metal staircase.

On one of these foam mattresses he himself was

lying. It was the mattress closest to the inside wall. The mattress closest to the open side of the cubbyhole was empty. But on the middle mattress, seated crosslegged as a man sits before a fire—as Cully himself had grown into the habit of sitting during his youthful trapping trips into the brush country on Kalestin—was a slim, pleasant-looking Frontiersman with a pleasant, bony face and wiry body, who at first seemed hardly more than Cully's age, until Cully suddenly realized that the man's hair was white.

"Feeling better now?" asked the man.

It was the soft, educated voice that had first spoken to the guard, the voice that had belonged to the first pair of brush boots Cully had seen as he lay on the metal floor after being shoved out of the elevator.

"Fine," said Cully, and the hoarse weakness of his own voice shocked him.

The white-haired man nodded.

"You've been needing rest, mainly," he said. "Food, too—as much food as we could get into you. But mainly rest. Rest cures just about every human ill that's curable without medicines, and some that medicines can't cure."

The choice of words and their Old Worlds pronunciation, in the soft, baritone voice, was scholarly, almost pedantic-sounding, coming from a figure dressed in rough Frontier bush-country clothes and seated like a man long used to open campfires.

"I'm Will Jaimeson," the white-haired man went on. "My partner's Doak Townsend. Maybe you were awake enough from time to time to remember him."

Now that Cully thought of it, he had a hazy memory of a figure certainly no more than five feet tall and looking no more than his late teens—although the smallness of the face and figure may have contributed to the appearance of youthfulness—who had also sat crosslegged watching him, as Will Jaimeson was watching him now.

"I'm . . ." began Cully, and then caution stilled his tongue. It might be that his better safety lay in keeping his identity secret from his fellow prisoners. But Will Jaimeson was already finishing the sentence for him.

"Cully When, of course." Will nodded. "I know you. In fact I saw you once when you were a boy, living in Amos Braight's home back when Earth had sent him out to be the Governor on Kalestin."

"Oh? You go back some years on Kalestin, do you?" asked Cully huskily.

"I go back some years on all the Frontier Worlds," answered Will. "I was the anthropologist with the First Settlement on Casimir III, forty years ago."

Cully stared at him with new interest. Unless the man was lying, he could not be less than in his middle sixties. But aside from the white hair, his nearly unlined face and slim body gave no token of being much older than thirty. Of course, perhaps he was simply a little insane. Imprisoned men could become that.

"Funny I haven't heard your name before," Cully said slowly. "Someone that started out on the Frontier that far back—"

"I wasn't on the Frontier Worlds a good share of that time," answered Will. He smiled gently, but a little wearily also, as if these were questions with which he was overfamiliar.

"Oh? Back here on the Old Worlds?" Cully asked.

"No."

Cully gazed interestedly at him.

"Correct me if I'm wrong," Cully said. "But I don't know any other place you're likely to find humans besides the Solar System or the Frontier Worlds."

"But I wasn't among humans," said Will. "Most of that time I was out among aliens, deep in Moldaug territory, these last forty-odd years."

Cully lay still, watching him, thinking he had been right. The white-haired man was probably not all there mentally. For what he had claimed was essentially impossible. The Moldaug had closed their spatial Frontier to humans a dozen years back; and only a year ago they had sent Ambassadors here to the Tri-Worlds Council on Earth, laying claim to the Frontier Worlds where people had settled, saying that the Pleiades had belonged to the Moldaug long before humans came.

3

But the calmness of Will Jaimeson did not seem shaken by the frank disbelief in Cully's gaze. The older man sat so quietly and serenely that Cully's interest grew. Maybe the other was not mad, after all. Back when Cully had been a boy on Kalestin, when he had first come to that Frontier World with his emigrating parents, there had been stories of men who had known the alien Moldaug.

It was true enough, Cully remembered now—indeed, it was historical fact—that in the early years of the human settlements on the Frontier Worlds of the Pleiades, the Moldaug had seemed to class humans more as curiosities than as threats. But the stories had gone beyond this to claim that there had been humans then who had actually made friends with members of that bony, leathery-skinned but undeniably civilized alien race holding the stars beyond the Pleiades. These humans, said the stories, had even ridden on Moldaug ships between the newly human-settled Frontier Worlds circling the GO-type stars of the Pleiades. Stars, which had historically been hidden from Earth by distance and the cosmic dust of that interstellar area.

At that time the Moldaug, with their different psychological structure, had seemed to take humans much more for granted than humans took them. It was apparently neither wonderful nor terrible to the Moldaug, at first, to encounter another intelligent, space-going race. They, themselves, had seemed to have no great interest in the Pleiades Planets beyond making occasional scouting trips to them. Nor had they seemed to feel any resentment of the fact that humans were beginning to occupy those worlds.

But that had been in the beginning. At some time, somewhere along in the early years of human exploration and settlement of the Pleiades Planets, an emotional switch apparently had been thrown in the Moldaug psychology. The alien scout ships had ceased to visit the Pleiades Worlds and human spaceships were sternly warned off, if they ventured from the Pleiades inward toward the stars of the Moldaug region of space. As the Japanese in the seventeenth century had suddenly closed their borders to Europeans, so the Moldaug had closed theirs to humans—though from time to time there had still been stories of humans who had drifted into Moldaug territory before the aliens' change of attitude, returning unharmed.

But nowadays it was hard to believe such stories, since the Moldaug had suddenly, incredibly, and apparently reasonlessly, laid claim to all the Pleiades region. Even at this moment, as Cully knew, their Ambassadors were here on Earth; in discussion with Members of the Tri-Worlds Council, they were calmly demanding that humans abandon all worlds they had settled in that region. While the Council wrangled among itself, refusing to admit to the aliens that it could no longer command the people of the Frontier to come home again, refusing to admit to itself that the Moldaug were evidently ready to attack the whole human race if the Pleiades were not evacuated immediately.

Over all, coloring all the negotiations made by the Tri-Worlds Council Members, was the spacephobia—in

Frontier terms, not so much a fear-of-space as a fear of what that space might contain, beyond the bounds of the Solar System—that afflicted most of the Old Worlds people. It made them see the Frontiersmen as savages, the aliens as monsters—and warped their viewpoints toward the Frontier and the Frontier people in a way none of the Old World Leaders would admit. Even Alia, who was free from the spacephobia herself, would not admit its existence; and this, in fact, had been the main subject of disagreement between her and Cully on the trip back to Earth from Kalestin.

Yet the very reality of this place, and Cully's own arrest, proved that existence. Cully's train of thought peaked suddenly with a new, sharp interest.

But before he could begin to seriously examine this new idea, something silent as a moth flitted into the cubbyhole and folded up on the mattress beyond Will, so that it sat crosslegged, staring at Cully. Cully gazed back with interest. It was the little man he half-remembered seeing—the one Will had said was named Doak Townsend.

"He's better?" asked the unemotional voice Cully remembered. Its flat, tenor tone made a statement, rather than a question, out of the words the small man had just spoken. Will nodded.

"Thanks," said Cully, suddenly remembering what had happened outside the elevator. "Thanks, both of you."

Doak did not reply at all. His expressionless, regular features—which might perhaps have seemed handsome if they had shown a little more animation—continued to stare calmly at Cully. It was a strange face, the kind of face that made Cully wonder if he had seen it somewhere before. But Will answered for both of them.

"We try to pick up any new men who get delivered in particularly bad shape," Will said. "Doak's the only prisoner here the guards are really afraid of. So we can get things done right away, like making them take off those restraints they had on your arms. It's a wonder they hadn't already crippled you. And to think those things were brought in as replacements for straitjackets because people thought they were more humane!"

Cully looked back at Will.

"You always take the newly delivered cripples in here with you?" Cully asked.

"As often as we can. But," said Will, his eyes narrowing slightly, "your case is a little different. You're Culihan O'Rourke When, the all-time champion spacelifter. The man who, singlehanded, hijacked more than a dozen Old Worlds spaceships during the Frontier Revolt four years ago. That gave us a special interest in you."

"What special interest?" asked Cully. He was intrigued.

"No point in bothering you with it just yet," said Will. "You'd better have something to eat now, and rest some more. In a day or so you'll be stronger and ready to talk."

He turned and searched among the bedclothes at the head of his mattress, coming up with a thick plastic container. There was a slight popping sound as he handled it, and a second or two later the aroma of hot beef soup reached Cully's nostrils.

"Where do you get the food?" Cully asked, struggling to sit up in a posture that would make eating a little more practical.

"It's issued to us," Will answered quietly. "If you'd been able to move about, you could've gone to the requisition window and gotten your own. We just drew your rations for you." He passed the now opened and steaming plastic container into Cully's hands along with a detachable plastic spoon. "Here, get as much of this into you as you can hold, and then try to sleep some more."

Cully obeyed without protest. The advice was good; and besides, at the moment, he had a good deal of new information to absorb.

In the several days that followed, Cully's strength flowed back as he lay on his mattress under what was indeed a stairway between levels of their underwater prison. There were five levels in all, Will told him, all of them jammed with detainees, mainly from the Frontier Worlds, filling full all this bulbous underwater section of the ocean-encompassed structure known as Immigration Detention Station Number One. "Number One," for short.

As his strength came back, Cully studied the two odd individuals who had taken him into their care. Except at rare intervals, either Will or Doak was alone with him in the cubbyhole. Doak, on these occasions, proved not much of a companion—evidently not because he did not want to talk, but because he had very little to say. He spent his time with Cully either sleeping—often as not seated upright and crosslegged with his back against a vertical wall—or sharpening a typical, handmade prisoner's knife. One of those knives made of a strip of metal, whetted and honed to razor edge and needle point, and with its handle made out of rags wrapped around the tang of the blade and soaked in varnish to harden them. His only other occupation, as far as Cully could see, was sitting and contemplating whatever was in a locket that hung by a chain around his neck. He was always very careful to make sure that Cully could not also see what was in the locket; but whatever was there could hold the little man's attention for hours.

The fifth day after Cully had begun to feel himself again, he chose a moment when he was alone with Will to ask bluntly about his partner.

Will hesitated, then shrugged.

"Of course, Doak's not quite sane," he said.

"I thought so," said Cully. "So that's why the guards are all afraid of him?"

"The guards are afraid of him," said Will earnestly, "because Doak isn't afraid of them; and it's plain, even to men like them, that there's nothing they can do to make him afraid. So that if they push him or it—or if Doak himself simply takes a notion—to do something to one of them, he'll act without stopping to count the consequences. So they handle him with kid gloves. But, of course, sooner or—"

Will stopped suddenly.

"Of course . . . ?" Cully prompted.

"I think—" Will hesitated. "You asked me a couple of days ago why I took you in here, and I said I had a reason we'd talk about later."

He paused, as if waiting for some response from Cully.

"Go on," said Cully. "What was the reason?"

"It's got to do with what this place is, here."

"A prison," said Cully flatly.

"Yes. But officially, as I told you earlier, it's only a detention station—an Immigration Service Detention Station," said Will, "and we actually have got a few illegal immigrants here, from Mars, or Venus, or the asteroids. But what the place really is, is an internment camp for anyone from the Frontier the Police have had an excuse to pick up and question these last three years."

Cully nodded.

"You see," said Will, "the point is, we prisoners out-number the guards a hundred to one, and since we aren't really criminals, we've got our own government and our own laws. There's half a dozen men on what we call the Board of Governors who run things down here. They're all Frontiersmen who held positions of authority during the Frontier Revolt four years ago, and they're all old fellow-revolutionists of yours. The minute they know you're here"—Will looked steadily at Cully—"you'll probably become a Board Member yourself. Even if you don't, you're bound to have a lot of influence with them."

"What about it?" asked Cully flatly.

Will took a deep breath.

"I kept you here so I'd have a chance to talk to you before any of your old friends recognized you. As I just told you, the Board decides everything among us down here."

He paused, looking at Cully.

"One of the decisions it makes," he said slowly, "is who among us are going to get the chance to escape."

4

Cully laughed. The irony of the situation tickled him. But there was no bitter edge to his humor—any more than there had been bitterness at his betrayal by Alia. Cully had never expected his fellow men and women to be saints. Rather, the contrary. Which was possibly why, the thought had occurred to him once or twice, so many of them seemed to be well-disposed toward him. Certainly, nothing else explained his lifelong luck in that regard.

"So that's it," said Cully. "And here I was thinking it was pure admiration and charity that had made you take me in."

"I'm not asking for myself!" said Will sharply. "It's Doak. You see how he is. Sooner or later he'll kill someone here—or get himself killed."

"Well, that can happen," said Cully, "and you're a good man, in my book, for wanting to look out after your partner. But from what I've seen of places like this, it's not a good enough reason to get him escape priority. My guess is, he'll have to wait his turn."

"There won't be any turns," said Will. His usually calm face had tightened. "The chance to escape that's coming up is going to be the first and only at Number One."

Cully was suddenly alert.

"The first and only?" he said. "You mean no one's tried an escape before this?"

"That's right." Will nodded. "New Zealand's fifteen hundred miles away, and that's our closest land. The only way anyone can get out of here is by taking over one of the Space-and-Atmosphere ships that fly in to bring us new prisoners or supplies, and then fly out again. The SA ships always come down in the water a good hundred yards away from Number One, and then ferry over to the station what they're bringing in. That means there's always at least a hundred yards of open water between any escapees and the means of escape. And, aside from the guards, the water around Number One's alive with sharks. You'll see why, the first time you get your turn up on deck."

"I see," said Cully slowly. "It's a matter of needing a boat, then, to get from the station here to the SA ship?"

"Yes," said Will. "And there's no such thing as a boat to be found on Number One. The SA ships bring their own when they come, and take it away when they leave."

"Then how's an escape being figured?" Cully asked.

"The Board of Governors started building a boat four months ago," Will said. "Not many here know that, but I found it out. A small boat, made in fifty or sixty small parts that can be hidden separately, then fitted together when the time comes. It'll be six months more before it's done, and even after that, they'll have to wait for a change to smuggle the pieces up on deck. So that when an SA ship comes, the prisoners can stage a riot long enough for the boat to be put together and gotten into the water. The boat's to hold five men—it needs to hold at least five to be sure to take over the SA ship from whatever guards are left on her. But five's the limit. Any boat larger than that would be too hard to build secretly and put together in a hurry on deck when the time comes."

He stopped. Cully nodded thoughtfully.

"I see," said Cully.

"Yes," said Will. "Five men are going to get a chance to escape. Only five—out of nearly three thousand prisoners. You see what chance Doak and I have of being two of them?"

"Now it's both of you who want to go," said Cully humorously. "You'll have that boat filled in a minute. What makes you think I wouldn't want a place aboard her myself, if it comes to that?"

Will brushed the question aside impatiently.

"Don't joke with me—you know *you're* going!" he said, leaning urgently toward Cully. "Listen, you'll take Doak because you'll need me. And I won't go without him. I told you—I spent forty years, on and off, with the Moldaug. I can speak their language. But, more than that, I understand them. I understand the different way they think. With my help you can make terms with the Moldaug; and once you make terms with them, you can do anything you want to the Old Worlds!"

"Such as?" Cully's attention suddenly sharpened.

"I don't know—whatever your objectives are!" said Will. "Taking over their government, or whatever—I don't care! The point is, I can help you get it without bloodshed. I tell you I *know* the Moldaug. I came out with the first Casimir III Settlement as a cultural anthropologist, to study the adaptation of the settlers to Frontier conditions. But then I ran into the Moldaug and they fascinated me. I switched to studying them. I got to know them. I learned their tongue. I rode back to their worlds in their scouting ships, and began to study their myths and legends. Don't you understand? Those myths and legends are just the clues we humans need to understand the whole business of how the Moldaug think and react—"

"Hold on a minute," Cully interrupted gently. Will

stopped. For a moment he sat, still leaning tensely forward. Then his body sagged.

"No," he said in a dull voice, "you don't believe me either, do you? You don't realize what a difference there is between the Moldaug and humans—"

"Easy now," said Cully. "I'm not turning a deaf ear to all this you're saying. It's just you're going a little fast for me. Let's go back a minute. Remember—I asked you why you didn't think I'd grab a place for myself on that boat if I could get it?"

Will stared at him, at first blankly and then with growing astonishment.

"I don't understand," he said at last.

"You've got that a bit twisted," said Cully. "I'm the one who doesn't understand. What makes you think I'm so sure of a place in that boat that I can fix it for you and Doak to come along with me? I just landed in this place. There's three thousand men, according to you, that were here before me."

"But—" Will still stared at him incredulously. "The whole business is for you, isn't it? I mean, who else but you could've figured out a way of taking over the Old Worlds in a *coup d'état* with the few spaceships and men we've got out on the Frontier? If anybody's going to get a chance to get out of here and back to the Pleiades, it has to be you!"

"I'd be happy to think so," said Cully. "But there's one little thing you seem misinformed about. I've never made any plans for the Frontier to take over the Old Worlds in a *coup d'état*. I'd have had to lose what little sense I've got to dream a dream like that."

Will stared at him for a long second.

"You don't trust me, that's it," said Will at last. "That must be it. Cully, everybody in Number One knows about the plot! We've all been questioned about it by the Police before we were brought here."

"Oh?" said Cully. He nodded then, slowly and thoughtfully. "So that's it. That's how the fantasy started. It's this Old Worlds paranoia."

"Fantasy?" Will echoed the word in a strangely stifled voice. He sat for a second. *"Fantasy?"*

"Well, now, you're from the Frontier yourself," said Cully. "Tell me—can you see any way such a notion could be anything more than fantasy?"

Will sat looking at him—for what seemed a long time. He did not answer or move. Then a deep breath escaped from him slowly, and he seemed to shrink in size.

"Fantasy . . ." he said again in the same stilled voice. "I knew it . . ." His voice thickened a little. "And the Board of Governors and everyone in Number One from the Frontier, all this time, just holding on for the day when it'd come true, and we'd be rescued by the Frontier's takeover here on Earth. That's why the Board started to build their boat—to get word back to the Frontier Congress how we were all being held here. Of course, we had to know—all of us—that it's impossible. But we all tried to believe in it just the same . . ."

"Well, the World Police believe in it, it seems," said Cully, "and they've got powerful ways of making themselves convincing." He sat back, looking at the older man slumped opposite him. In spite of the casualness of his voice, a new idea was beginning to build swiftly in the back of Cully's mind. He chose his next words carefully.

"Cheer up," he said. "It's a mad universe, all over the place. Here's the Old Worlds convinced that the Frontier can take them over, without a shred of reason for believing it. And there's the Moldaug out on the Frontier, laying claim to our worlds in the Pleiades without a shred of reason either."

"What—" Will's voice was dull. He roused himself slightly. "Oh, the Moldaug reason for claiming the Pleiades will be real enough."

"Real enough?" Cully watched him closely. "The Moldaug sit for fifty years and watch us settle down on those planets, and then suddenly claim that we had no right landing on them in the first place? Why, it's the very fact there's no reason and sense behind that action of theirs that started this whole chain of events, with the Old Worlds dreaming the nightmare of a *coup d'état* that got us all arrested and sent here in the first place."

"I know—I know—" said Will straightening up. "But the very fact we don't see any reason for the Moldaug to do this is an example of why the Tri-Worlds Council is making such a mess of dealing with their Ambassador Ruhn and his Brother Ambassadors. That's why I came to Earth, to explain that to the Council; but when I tried to tell Braight, he turned me over to the World Police—"

"Braight? Amos Braight?" demanded Cully.

"Yes, that's the man," said Will. "I knew him slightly back when he was Kalestin's Governor. So I managed to get an appointment to see him; but when I told him, he didn't believe me. You see, our human culture operates on a polarity between the concepts of 'right' and 'wrong.' But 'right' and 'wrong' are unimportant, flexible, only relative terms to the Moldaug. They operate instead on a polarity between the concepts of Respectability and not-Respectability. I know it's not an easy idea to grasp, but Braight wouldn't even try to listen. He accused me of being part of the plot—the 'fantasy' you called it—and you're right, of course . . ."

He trailed off.

"Then, just what *is* the Moldaug reason for claiming the Pleiades?" Cully asked quietly.

"The specific reason? That I don't know," said Will. "My field's anthropology, not politics. But I know the reason's got to be there in Moldaug terms—a perfectly sensible reason, if you think like they do. It only needs someone who thinks in the proper terms and knows the Moldaug, to dig it out."

"Is that so?" said Cully thoughtfully. He changed the subject abruptly. "What about Doak? How does Doak come into all this?"

"Doak?" Will hesitated. For the first time his eyes shifted a little away from Cully's. "Oh, Doak was brought to Number One a little after I got here. He'd come to Earth about a year before, to . . . look for someone. Finally he was picked up by the World Police. He'd given them a harder time than I had—or anyone else they'd sent here. He can't bend at all, you see. Once he'd told them the truth and they wouldn't listen, he just stopped talking altogether. When he came here he was in bad shape—worse than you were, much worse. Well, I know a little about medicine. I helped him get well . . . and we've been partners since."

"Yes," said Cully. His mind was in high gear now, fitting fact to fact and supposition to supposition with lightlike speed. He had almost forgotten Will's presence, when the older man spoke to him.

"What?" asked Cully, looking back across the mattresses.

"I said"—Will's eyes were penetratingly upon him—"I wouldn't have thought there was anything in what I've told you to make a man smile."

"Smile?" Cully became suddenly conscious of his own facial expression.

"If you can call it that," said Will. "That's a pretty wolfish expression, whether it's a smile or not. Braight was a friend of yours when you were a boy on Kalestin, wasn't he?"

"He took me in," said Cully, feeling the smile vanish. "He took me into his home, into the Governor's mansion on Kalestin, after my parents were killed by brush outlaws. He'd known my father back on Earth. I lived with him and his daughter for six years before I struck out back into the brush to go trapping on my own. That was two years before he gave up the Governorship, when his party called him back to run for office here on Earth."

For a moment, the memory of Amos and Alia as he had known them on Kalestin threatened to draw Cully's thoughts from the situation at hand. Harshly, he shoved memory aside and came back to the present.

"You say the prisoner Board of Governors all believe

in this scheme, the Frontier making an attempt to take over the Old Worlds?" he asked Will.

"Yes," answered Will, looking at him in some wonder. "I told you—we've all believed it here."

Cully got to his feet, stepping out from under the staircase. Will rose and followed.

"Then we'd better get busy about seeing them," said Cully—he smiled again at the older man—"if you and Doak want your places in that boat, after all."

"If Doak and I—" A startled look showed in Will's eyes. "But how can we get into it now—?" He broke off suddenly. "I thought you told me just a minute ago that the plot was a fantasy—a fantasy dreamed up by the paranoiacs here on the Old Worlds."

"It was," answered Cully lightly, "until just about thirty seconds ago. Are you going to show me where I can find these Governors you talked about—or not?"

"If you want." Still gazing at Cully wonderingly, Will walked around him and began to mount the stairs above their cubbyhole. "I'll take you to them. But you said 'was'?"

"*Was*, as I say," agreed Cully, stepping up level with the older man. "But as of the last thirty seconds it strikes me there just might be a very good chance of making it become real."

Will stared at him.

"I don't understand?" the older man said.

"Why, it seems that uncovering the reason behind that Moldaug claim to the Pleiades may be the key to everything," said Cully cheerfully. "And with your help, once we get out of here, we just might be able to pull off that *coup d'état* after all—with benefits to all concerned."

5

On the open-air deck of the platform at Number One, four months and some days later, a cruising sea bird might have seen a number of men, clothed for the most part only in ragged pants, working upon a chest-high metal fence. This fence surrounded the platform at its edge, except for the open garbage area screened off at one corner, where the station's food scraps and other trash were dumped into the ocean—thereby ensuring the plentiful supply of sharks which patrolled the Dentention Station—as Will had earlier remarked to Cully. One of the men bent over at work on the fence near the garbage area this day was Cully himself. He was chipping paint on one of the thick, steel fenceposts.

Or rather, he was chipping *at* paint. His job, like the other available jobs abovedecks, was the only sort of occupation or make-work available on Number One; and so overwhelming were the number of prisoners craving an excuse for a few hours in the sunlight and open air that the idea was not so much to get the work done as to preserve it for the next shift from belowdecks.

In this particular case, Cully was working on a piece of old paint which was coming to resemble the map of

Ireland; and, shift by shift, he had been lovingly improving its outline.

Shortly, a prisoner carrying boxes of stores came by, and a small object dropped from somewhere about the passing man to roll in Cully's direction. Cully tensed internally but invisibly to the watching world. He dropped his free hand and palmed the object, picking it up. Still working, he examined it out of the corner of his eye. It was an old checker piece, its sharp edges worn away until it more resembled a small, red, wooden wheel than anything else. Cully made himself relax. It was the first time he had ever encountered that small red wheel abovedecks. Its appearance there, in the guards' home territory, was too dangerous for all concerned, unless some unusual emergency was at hand.

Cully slipped it into his pocket and glanced casually about the deck. Some distance off, Will was pushing a broom along the already clean deck, carefully chivvying from place to place a few small pieces of cardboard and a nail. Cully reached up with his free hand and hooked his index finger idly into the wire mesh of the fence above his head.

After a little while he glanced about again and saw that Will was sweeping in his direction. Cully let his hand drop and waited. Will swept up level with him and discovered some trouble with the bristles of his broom. He knelt down beside Cully to work at it.

"What is it?" Will's voice sounded in Cully's ear. Still chipping away at the map of Ireland, Cully answered, without turning his head or moving his lips.

"I don't know, but something's come up. There's a meeting called, for the garbage area. This may be it. Get Doak close, and tell him if I signal, he's to move in and give the spiel I taught him."

"Right," murmured Will. "Anything else?"

"That's all. Make it fast, though. I've got to head for the garbage area in a few minutes at most."

"All right."

Will got up and resumed his sweeping. He swept his

way down the deck and around a corner of the guards' quarters in the direction of another section of the deck where Doak would be working.

Cully went back to his chipping. A flood of tension and emotion was threatening to rise in him at the prospect of escape at last. Deliberately, he forced his mind to switch channels. It was an old exercise in patience, begun during his spacelifting days and continued aboard Number One since he had begun to recondition mind and body. It had been an exercise as deliberate as the regular, daily practice-jogging of a runner in training, and now it paid off. With an effort of will, he was able to make himself relax and forget the possibility of escape. He was able to make himself think about something entirely different and removed.

The identity tags around his bare, tanned neck chinked as they swung lightly against the fence with the rhythm of Cully's chipping. The sound suggested the substitute area for his thinking. For the tags were not marked with the name of Culihan O'Rourke When. They were the tags of another prisoner, a suicide named Julio Ortega, who had been buried overside to the sharks, two months before, wearing Cully's tags.

The change of identity was something done by all those who, like Cully since his first week aboard, had become members of the prisoner Board of Governors. In any ordinary detention center, routine checks of the inmates would have uncovered the changes. But the guards at Number One were happy to live and let live, as long as their overcrowded prisoners caused them a minimum of trouble.

In his lifetime, thought Cully, he had discovered three loves. In order of his discovery of them, they were the Frontier, architecture, and Alia. To begin with, he had had none of them. At seven, he had been a typical Earth boy, who was not happy at the idea of his family moving out to a Frontier World like Kalestin. At eleven, he had been a grief-dazed orphan, sustained only by the fact that Kalestin's Governor, Amos Braight, who had known Cully's father back on Earth, had, in all but the legal sense, adopted him and taken him in.

So it was, he found a family when he needed it most. So that five years later, when he went on his own into the brush as a trapper, it was with a clean, healed mind that left him free to discover that first love of his—a love for the free, sprawling, open spaces of virgin land that gave the Frontier and its people their character, so different from the character of the Old Worlds and the teeming populations there.

Chipping at the fencepost under the blazing, tropical sun of Earth, Cully remembered how it had been when, two years later, he had come out of the brush with a financial stake large enough to send him to college on Earth. It was at Michigan State University that he discovered architecture, his second love. Adulthood, he had recognized, was already turning him into the kind of man who could not simply accept the world or universe around him. He had to lay hands on it, to change it, for better or for worse. In a more peaceful age, he thought now, wryly, chipping at paint, he might have found a full occupation for his life in the creativity that architecture offered him.

But three years of extra credit, vacationless study, while it completed a five-year course for his bachelor's degree, also exhausted his financial reserves. He had no choice but to return to Kalestin, where even his unfinished training was enough to find him work as a practicing architect. Once he had built up enough savings, he could come back to Earth for his postgraduate study. But not twelve months later the Frontier Revolt was in full flame; and Cully, swept into it by his first love, was in the hottest part of it.

He had set a record for survival and success in the usually fatal profession of spacelifting—pirating and taking over in space those spaceships the Frontier Worlds so badly needed, and which the Old Worlds would neither allow them to build nor own by themselves. And the Frontier had won.

Cully, looking forward to a bright future, had become

the Kalestin City Representative in the newly formed Assembly of Frontier World Representatives on Kalestin.

But in that Assembly he had witnessed the slow death of his hopes for his first love. Day by day, the Frontier Assembly sat and wrangled, and Cully saw the ideals and inspirations for which they had all fought slowly sinking from sight in a morass of partisan politics, selfish regional and world divisions. Weary of watching, after half a year of it, he had resigned to return to his Kalestin practice as an architect.

It was at this low-ebb point of his life that Alia had reappeared suddenly—

"Cully!"

The low, hoarse, angry whisper barely reaching his ears snapped him instantly out of his thoughts. Without lifting his head, he glanced swiftly about, out of the corners of his eyes.

He had expected to see Doak, though it was not like the little man to whisper urgently to him like that. But Doak was still nowhere in sight. Instead, Cully's eyes met for a second with the eyes of a huge, heavy-boned prisoner who was even now slipping unobtrusively around the edge of the shelter hiding the garbage area from view of all but the open sea. The prisoner was Mark Leestrom, one of the other Governors, and his eyes met Cully's urgently, with a tight, hard question in them.

"What's delaying you?"

Never since Cully arrived had he seen impatience like that in the big Frontiersman. It struck Cully then that he had been right in the guess he had made to Will about the reason for the unusual meeting. There was little doubt now, seeing Leestrom like this.

The moment of a chance to escape from Number One was upon them.

From here on out, seconds would probably be precious. But for his own purposes, about which the rest of the Board of Governors necessarily knew nothing, Cully could not risk joining the meeting until he had Doak safely in sight.

6

Cully went back to his automatic chipping at the map
of Ireland.

He could count on perhaps another four or five minutes before the Board began to recognize the fact that
something more than ordinary caution was delaying his
appearance. After that—they might not go ahead without him. Or they might. If they did, he could lose a
chance to have Will and Doak with him among those
prisoners the Board of Directors had already named to
escape.

For Cully himself, as Will had predicted, there had
been no problem. Everyone on the Board had taken it
for granted that Cully, the Frontier's former number-
one revolutionist, would have been among those given
a chance to escape. But in the plans of the Board,
neither Will nor Doak merited any consideration. To
Cully's private plans, however, they—or at least Will—
were vitally important.

So important, in fact, that he dared not trust even
the other Board Members with the possibility that Will
might be able to help him find the apparently unex-
plainable reason behind the Moldaug claim against the

Frontier Worlds. If a hint of Will's importance should leak, and the white-haired man for any reason be removed from Number One before a chance for escape came, all of Cully's larger plans could be destroyed.

No, far better that Will remain safely unimportant in everyone's eyes until they were all securely back on Kalestin.

But this decision meant Cully had to find some other reason for forcing the Board to allow Will and Doak to join the escapees.

He began by looking for flaws in the Board's present escape plan—and he found them. As he had suspected after hearing about it from Will, the scheme to build a boat secretly in parts and assemble it at the moment of escape was both too complicated and too obvious. If Will knew about it, Cully figured, too many other prisoners probably also knew. And among three thousand men, the guards were bound to have informers.

A quiet personal check confirmed these suspicions. Cully quickly satisfied himself, beyond a reasonable doubt, that the Governor of Number One already knew about the boat scheme; the guards were simply letting the Board burn up its energies on this known escape plan until the boat should be finished. At which time, they would descend on the various hiding places of the boat's parts and confiscate them.

Satisfied, therefore, that the Board's plans were already doomed, Cully went privately to work to discover another, less obvious escape method. Shortly he found it. Now his plan was to make information about it the price of the Board's acceptance of Doak and Will as escapees. But he had been forced to wait, necessarily, for a moment of crisis in which to introduce the idea, to be sure of stampeding the Board into the price of its acceptance.

So he had been waiting, meanwhile learning from Will about the Moldaug character and language. This had not come as easily as he had expected in the beginning. His questions had first pleased Will, then

brought an unusual frown to the white-haired man's
face. Shortly, he challenged Cully.

"Anyone likes it when someone else takes an interest
in his life's work," Will said. "But why try to learn all
this when you can simply ask me, as the questions
come up in actual practice?"

"I want to understand the Moldaug," said Cully.

"*Understand* them?" The frown deepened between
Will's still-dark eyebrows. "How can you or any other
human understand them, when you start all your thinking about them from the basic idea they're freaks?"

"Freaks?" Cully raised his own eyebrows. "Aren't
you confusing me with someone else, Will? Say, someone from Earth here, or one of the other Old Worlds?
I'm a Frontiersman, like yourself."

"No, I'm not confusing anything!" said Will flatly.
"Old Worlds or Frontier people—unconsciously, on the
animal level, you all react the same way when it comes
to the Moldaug. Down in your unconscious, it's the
same old primitive notion. '*Stranger*' equals '*enemy.*'
'*Enemy*' equals everything that's evil and terrible. No,"
said Will decisively, "I'm not going to give you extra
information about the Moldaug just so you can twist it
to fit your own unconscious prejudices. When you need
to know something specific, ask me—but I'm not teaching you all I know just so you can increase your fund of
misinformation!"

It was easily the most emotional reaction Cully had
ever seen in Will. Wisely, Cully left the matter alone
for a few days, during which time he came to the
conclusion that there might be some justification for
Will's opinion of him, after all. He approached Will
again.

"I've been thinking it over, Will," he said. "And you
know, I think you're right. I think I actually have been
thinking of the Moldaug as freaks, down inside. But
how am I ever going to learn different unless you show
me?"

Will stared at Cully hard for a moment. Then he slowly relaxed.

"You're right," he said. "Maybe, I've been oversensitized, too, by talking to too many fools. The thing is, most humans don't even appreciate the unconscious barriers culture raises between them as humans. How can I expect them to begin to recognize the differences between them and the Moldaug?"

"Try me, why don't you?" said Cully. "What's this about human barriers, for example?"

Will laughed suddenly, all his reluctance evaporated.

"I'll tell you a story," he said. "But you tell me first—have you ever had anybody who seemed to want to talk uncomfortably close to you, breathing in your face all the time he talked?"

"It's happened to me, yes," said Cully.

"Well, keep that in mind now, while I tell you my story," said Will. "As far as I know—it may go back farther—it dates back to the twentieth century on Earth. As it goes, there was a diplomatic cocktail party somewhere at which the English and Italian Ambassadors were standing face to face, talking to each other; and as they talked they gradually, without realizing it, drifted across the room—the Englishman backing up, the Italian advancing."

Will broke off abruptly. He stared at Cully.

"Have you got any idea why?" he asked.

"Not an idea," said Cully.

"Well, as it happens, the distance that's considered comfortable between people in conversation varies from culture to culture," said Will. "What was a comfortable conversational distance for the Italian was about half the distance comfortable for the Englishman. The result was that the Englishman, being vaguely uncomfortable at the Italian's closeness, was unconsciously continually trying to back away to his own comfort-distance. But any increase in space between them made the Italian uncomfortable, and unconsciously, *he* would move forward to try to *decrease* the distance between them.

And all this was going on at a low level of awareness without either one realizing just why he was uncomfortable."

Cully laughed.

"I see," he said. "Yes, I can see that happening."

"Good," said Will. "Now, as it happens with the Moldaug, there're two conversational distances. The 'individual,' at about eight feet; and the 'personal,' at about twelve inches. But never mind that now. Tell me," said Will. "Have you ever read anything by a twentieth-century writer named Edward T. Hall?"

Cully shook his head.

"He wrote a book, among others, called *The Silent Language*," said Will. "In that book, Hall tells about a western American town in which most of the local government officials were of Spanish-American cultural descent, but a good many people driving through the town were of Anglo-American cultural descent. The town's speed limit was fifteen miles an hour, and the Spanish-American policeman infallibly arrested anyone going even one mile per hour over that. This wasn't so bad, but the Anglo-Americans soon noticed that the Spanish-Americans who were arrested usually had a relative sitting on the bench, and were usually quickly acquitted, while they themselves almost never got off easily. This made the Anglos furious."

Cully laughed again.

"I'd be a bit furious myself, maybe," he said.

"Your cultural descent is undoubtedly more Anglo than Spanish," said Will. "But the truth of the matter was that both the Spanish-cultured and the Anglo-cultured were doing what was right, according to their own cultural patterns. To the Spanish-cultured the *law* was a formal matter. A law could only be either unbroken or broken. There was nothing in between. So when they were arrested they took it without complaint. It was only *after* they were arrested that they invoked the informal, by turning to a system of relatives which had grown up in response to a weak government. On the other hand, the Anglos were informal about the actual violation. They felt that the speed limit should be somewhat flexible, according to situation and conditions. But once the machinery of the law was invoked, they tended to get very formal and unyielding. Anything less than strict judicial impartiality was unthinkable. The intercultural conflict that developed finally got to the point where the policeman was deliberately hurt in an accident, and to where he got to the point of making his arrests with drawn pistol. There you have it—both cultural groups doing what they thought was right, and both at swords' points because of it."

"All right," said Cully when Will had finished. "I see your point. The Tri-Worlds Councilmen and the Moldaug Ambassadors could be misunderstanding each other without knowing it—"

"They *have* to be misunderstanding each other!" Will interrupted emphatically. "That's the point. The only way they can avoid misunderstanding is by being completely understanding—and this they aren't; the Moldaug of we humans, or we humans of the Moldaug. For example, Admiral Ruhn is the chief of the three Ambassadors on Earth right now. Most humans, therefore, take it for granted that the other two are either his assistants or simply diplomatic window dressing. But what do you suppose is the actual, Moldaug, reason for there being three of them?"

"No idea," said Cully. "But you'll enlighten me, no doubt."

Will missed the humor of the answer entirely. He was too deeply immersed now in his own subject.

"There are three of them," he said, "because there's no such thing as an individual, as we know it, in Moldaug terms. The closest thing to it is a tight association of three persons. Theoretically, three brothers or sisters, but actually any combination of three. They're the basic unit of Moldaug society. They make up their minds as a unit and act as one person; in fact, as a human individual acts and decides for himself. That's why there have to be *three* Ambassadors, even though Ruhn is the

Elder Brother—the dominant. I'd be very surprised if Braight and his fellow Council Members realize how bound Ruhn is by the opinions of his two Brothers, let alone appreciate the diplomatic implications of dealing with a three-person 'individual.' "

"I'd be, myself," said Cully. "But you're sure about this? How can you be sure of such things on a basis of myths and legends, where anything can happen? Our fairy stories of elves and ghosts and goblins have little enough to do with actual human ways, it seems to me."

"You're wrong. Very wrong," said Will energetically. "All our myth figures represent deep cultural elements. And deep variations in attitude from culture to culture even among our own race. Look at the Balkan myth of the vampire who made a fellow vampire out of his victim by drinking the victim's blood. The cultural element reflected here is the treachery running all through the history of the Balkan region. The cultural message of the vampire legend was that there was no one you could trust, not even the woman who loved you, or your best friend. The bite of the vampire could turn either of them into your most dangerous enemy overnight. Now, in contrast, look at the areas of the British Isles and Northwestern Europe. Look at the myth of the English brownie or hobgoblin, or the Scottish fairy. Do you see something in these, different from the vampire-legend figure?"

Cully thought for a second.

"They're not . . . deadly," he said, "not in the sense that the vampire was deadly."

"Exactly!" said Will. "The brownie, elf, hobgoblin or fairy was mischievous, but not really harmful—*unless you cheated one of them!* In short, they had something that was almost the opposite of the vampire trait. A sense of honesty—or fair play."

"True," said Cully thoughtfully. " 'Fair play,' come to think of it, is pretty much an English phrase."

"More than that," said Will. "The English have been called a nation of shopkeepers—with some reason. And both English and Scots have been celebrated for sticking to their bargains—particularly to the spirit behind the letter of their contracts."

"The Irish," Cully grinned, "haven't exactly been known as a nation of shopkeepers."

"No," said Will. "But parallel myths and cultural qualities exist there too. The Old Nick of Irish legend is supernatural enough. But a stouthearted Irishman, particularly if he has right on his side, can outwit or outfight Old Nick. Again—the human is able to meet the mythical figure on even terms if he has the courage for it. Grendel, in the Beowulf legend of early Germanic literature, was a monster who fed on human flesh—first cousin to the vampire. No one could withstand Grendel—until the hero Beowulf appeared, and not only outfought the demon but pursued him down under the waters of a marsh and slew him. Now, though, compare a human legend with its closest parallel among the Moldaug. On the human side, you've heard of the Four Horsemen of the Apocalypse?"

"Yes," said Cully.

"Well," said Will. "There are four figures in that myth. The parallel Moldaug myth has only one—or rather, three-in-one—called the Demon of Dark. I say three-in-one because the Demon of Dark, like all Moldaug individuals, is actually composed of three persons. The *Demon* himself is the dominant member, or leader, of the tripartite 'individual,' which also includes the *Scholar* and the *Madman*. In the legend, the Scholar and the Madman combine to free the Demon, who then goes forth as a tripartite 'individual' to forecast doom among the Moldaug—"

"Wait a minute," interrupted Cully, suddenly very interested. "What kind of doom?"

"That's my point," said Will. "The Four Horsemen of the human legend forecast famine, war, pestilence, death—all the physical forms of destruction for a race. But the Demon of Dark doesn't directly threaten any kind of physical destruction to the Moldaug, because to the Moldaug such things aren't so much evils in themselves as symptoms of the one Great Evil—"

Will broke off on a particular note of emphasis, staring at Cully.

"Which is what?" Cully prompted him.

"A Change," said Will solemnly, "in the Aspect of Respectability."

"Aspect of Respectability?" Cully repressed an instinctive urge to chuckle—but his face must have betrayed him.

"It's very much something you don't laugh at if you're a Moldaug," said Will reprovingly. "Remember, I told you it was *Respectability* that was the peg on which the Moldaug culture turns, just as ours turns upon the peg of *Righteousness?* To be right, instead of wrong, in the way he lives and what he does—no matter what cultural standard of right or wrong he uses—is important to the people of all human cultures. But now, suppose you're a Moldaug, the dominant member or one of the two subjectives of a tripartite 'individual.' Your concern, both as a person and individual, is the supreme importance of being Respectable, as opposed to not-Respectable."

"How do I know when I'm Respectable?" Cully asked.

"You *don't*," said Will. "And *there's* one of the great differences from human thinking. A single human's personal standards or belief in what's right can't be taken from him or changed—witness the long line of martyrs down through human history. But your standard of Respectability as a Moldaug can be changed on you without your being able to control it. That's one aspect of your culture with which you live as a Moldaug—and die; because to lose Respectability in any large measure can be literally a fate to which you'd prefer death."

Cully stared at the older man, sitting crosslegged in the shadow of the staircase.

"Now, why?" he asked softly.

"You'll have to stretch your imagination to understand," said Will. "You see, to be Respectable among the Moldaug is to be in proper accord with the actions taken by the leaders of the race, that ensure and maintain the survival of the race. To be connected in any way with an action that leads to a plague or an unsuccessful war—any symptom of countersurvival developments—is to lose some part of your Respectability. If the developments are serious enough to threaten the existence of the race as a whole, or if they simply multiply beyond the endurance of the majority of the Moldaug, then those responsible lose Respectability to the point where they must be deposed as leaders. In Moldaug terms, as well as they can be expressed in any human tongue, the Aspect of Respectability has 'Changed'—in short, the quality of Respectabillty has abandoned the present leaders of the race and settled elsewhere, on other Moldaug, who must be discovered and installed as leaders instead."

Cully whistled softly.

"You see," said Will, "what that means is that as a Moldaug you can never be sure that the action you have just taken is Respectable or not until it has safely become a part of successful racial history. You can only make the best possible decision and hope that events prove you Respectable."

"Respectability's bigger than the individual, then?" asked Cully, thoughtfully.

"That's right," said Will. "And it's important to remember that if you're a Moldaug. It's not just your own failure you have to worry about. To be connected with failure can destroy your Respectability just as quickly, and the connections are beyond your control. You see, all this is a survival characteristic of Moldaug culture that tries to make sure the best possible people are in charge of the destiny of the race at all times. Guilt by association is not an arguable point among the Moldaug. It's a foregone conclusion."

"You say the connections are beyond an individual's—I mean, a person's—control?" asked Cully. "Why?"

"Because the Moldaug society is hierarchical in organization," answered Will. "As a single Moldaug, you belong first to the basic, three-person individual, within the family structure. A number of families make up a sept. A number of septs makes up a clan. The clans together make up the race and are headed by the ruling clan, within which is the ruling sept, family, and finally the ruling 'individual'—a three-person unit. If the race gets into trouble, the social structure loses Respectability from the top downward. The ruling clan is deposed and the other clans fight among themselves to discover who is now Most Respectable—or, in plain language, who is strongest. And when the Most Respectable clan triumphs, the society reorients itself around them, and the clan's inner hierarchy produce the new set of authorities up to the ruling 'individual' himself—or themselves."

"And the former ruling clan becomes Unrespectable? Is that it?" said Cully musingly.

"Well, not the whole clan—just the royal family," Will hesitated. " 'Unrespectable' is the ultimate term. If you're 'Unrespectable' you're effectively canceled out already. It's like a strong version of our word 'inhuman.' If you're really inhuman, you're no longer a human being. It's the same way with the term 'Unrespectable' among the Moldaug. A Moldaug would never call you 'Unrespectable,' no matter what your crime might be. If he really considered you 'Unrespectable,' he would see no point in naming you at all. The most he would accuse you of being would be 'not-Respectable.' "

"Then what happens to the rest of the clan?" asked Cully. "Do they get off scot-free?"

"No, the Aspect of Respectability has abandoned the whole clan," said Will. "Only, it's abandoned the social units within the clan in direct ratio to their former power and responsibility. First, the original tripartite 'Ruler,' or 'Rulers,' lose Respectability to the point where suicide is the only possible course for them. Then their action may be imitated by a good share of their closer relatives within their immediate family, the decision being taken as tripartite 'individuals,' not on a personal basis. The other families in the royal sept generally lose Respectability to degrees not requiring suicide, both as families and 'individuals,' and the other septs in the clan related to the royal sept also lose it to an even lesser degree . . . and so forth."

"And," said Cully thoughtfully, "according to the legend, all this is caused by the Demon of Dark?"

Will shook his head.

"The Demon doesn't cause Respectability to leave one clan and settle on another. He simply signals the Change—in the Aspect of Respectability. Where he appears, disasters of various kinds will follow. Enough of these disasters and the Moldaug begin to conclude that the Aspect of Respectability has abandoned the ruling clan and its inner hierarchy. Once this realization occurs, each clan naturally assumes that it has now acquired the Aspect. This leads each clan to attempt to assume authority over the other clans—and the fight starts to choose a new set of leaders."

"So," said Cully, "that's it. When the Demon appears, everything goes wrong."

"Yes," said Will. "You see why he's the ultimate in horror figures among the Moldaug. Now, of course, they've outgrown direct superstition since becoming a technical race, just as we have. In spite of that, the cultural elements that the myths and legends pictured in them still exist in them."

"I see," said Cully thoughtfully. "Indeed, I see. Tell me more, though, about this Demon himself. How does the legend go, exactly?"

Will obliged.

A sudden flicker of movement now in the corner of Cully's field of vision interrupted his thoughts. He turned his head slightly to look away from the fencepost.

It was Doak at last. The little man had drifted into sight, pushing a broom like Will's. In fact, it *was* Will's. The scraps of paper and a single nail identified the litter it pushed across the deck. Will must have switched jobs with Doak in order to get him free from whatever had been holding him from coming. Cully caught Doak's eye, inclined his head slightly toward the garbage area, and began to chip his way along the bottom rail of the fence in that direction.

He continued until he came within sight of the open-sided, fifteen-by-six-foot area, where a prisoner, chained to the wall for safety, was usually at work letting down the heavy, oversized, filled garbage containers on long chains to the sharks and other sea scavengers sixty feet below.

Still bent over, Cully ducked around a corner into the area itself, to find the rest of the Board of Governors impatiently waiting for him.

7

They were all big, hard men on the Board of Governors, thick of body if not unusual in height—with two exceptions: Mark Leestrom, who was Cully's height, and Dr. James Toy, slightly shorter, stick-thin and gray-haired, Toy stood beside the empty belt and chain anchored to the wall behind them, which secured the prisoner on garbage detail. The prisoner had evidently been sent elsewhere by the Board, for not all the cans in sight were empty, and the metal-ridged outer part of the deck edge, which sloped toward the open sea, gleamed with uncleaned grease and a litter of table scraps. Beside the wide gape of the empty belt, the narrow waist and frail height of Toy made him look too fragile to survive under prison conditions which had driven younger men to death through illness or suicide.

Beside Toy, Leestrom was simply big—like a stone castle. It was at Leestrom Cully looked, as he straightened up and joined the group.

"What is it?" he asked.

"It's an unscheduled SA ship from North America," answered Leestrom. "We just got word through the Station Commander's messboy. It's a private yacht belonging to one of the Tri-Worlds Council Members, and it's bringing the three Moldaug Ambassadors here to have a look at us—nobody knows why. It'll be here in three hours—less, now!"

The last two words were a growl of reproach at Cully.

"Sorry," said Cully, swiveling slightly so that his gaze went past the angle of the end of the wall to see Doak sweeping toward them. Doak's eye met Cully's, and Cully twitched a beckoning finger surreptitiously.

"The point is," broke in Toy, "what're we going to do? The boat isn't finished yet, even if we had time to get the parts smuggled up on deck here and put together somewhere."

"Stage a riot and rush the boat when it reaches the platform," growled Leestrom grimly. "Take the boat back and hijack the SA ship."

"It doesn't stand a chance, and you know it!" said Toy, evidently resuming an argument already underway when Cully appeared. "We've talked that over forty times in the last couple of years—rushing a ferryboat. That's just what the guards on duty are expecting."

"A boat from a regularly scheduled guardship, sure!" said Leestrom. "But a private vessel, with civilian pilots . . ."

Cully risked a glance at Doak. The little man had swept to just around the corner and was now waiting. Cully signaled him to move on in.

"We'll never get a chance like this again!" Leestrom was saying, low-voiced but furious. "An unscheduled ship—a yacht with civilians aboard! Think of it!"

"What I think of," Toy retorted, "is that if the guards here at Number One ever protected anything in their lives, they'll protect that boat, from landing to leaving, as long as Moldaug Ambassadors are aboard. The guards here may be sloppy about some things, but not when it comes to that. I'll bet they're unhappy enough about their responsibility in having the Moldaug here, right now. I don't see anything for it but to let this chance go by, finish our own boat and wait for a supply ship, the way we've always planned—"

He broke off, for Doak had calmly stepped into their midst and laid his broom against the wall. Child-sized among that circle of big men, he looked quietly around them.

"Get out of here, Doak!" snapped Leestrom. "This is a Board meeting!"

"That's why I'm here," Doak answered him. He turned to Cully and spoke. "I know what's bothering you. And I've got an answer."

"Out!" growled Leestrom in a low voice. "Unless you want to go overboard!"

He took a step toward Doak, and then stopped abruptly. For Doak turned and walked calmly out onto the greasy, sloping metal ridges that pitched toward the unguarded edge of the open deck, where the prisoner on duty, secured by his chain, had been dumping garbage.

But Doak was secured by no chain.

Cully sucked in his breath and felt his belly muscles go flat. The escape means was Cully's inspiration—but this business of stepping out on the slick edge of eternity, sixty feet above a cauldron of feeding sharks, was Doak's own idea.

"Come put me overboard," said Doak emotionlessly to Leestrom, "unless you'd rather listen."

"Talk," said Toy. The word came out of the older man as if it hurt him. Like the rest, he was rigid as a statue, staring at Doak. There were no cowards on the Board, but Doak's gamble was worse—much worse— than that of a man who crosses a high wire between tall buildings with no net below.

"All right," said Doak. "Look down there."

He pointed at the blue water below, foamed by the swirling dorsal fins of the sharks, mad with hunger among the garbage.

"There's got to be an unscheduled SA ship due here in a few hours," he said. "Never mind how I know. And six or seven prisoners could escape on it if they could get past those sharks and reach it while whoever came here on it is on Number One. None of you know how to get to it. But Will Jaimeson does."

He paused and looked at them.

"If Will and I can be two of the ones that go, I'll tell you how," he said. "If not, we'll try it by ourselves."

He waited.

"Talk," said Toy again, still from a tight throat. "If it works—all right."

Doak did not answer immediately. Instead, he looked around at the others.

"You've got our word on it," said Cully quickly. "Talk."

"All right," said Doak.

He turned again to face the sea, while the Board members held their breaths.

"Now, look out there," said Doak pointing off across the weed-splotched, blue surface of the water. "Out there, about fifty, sixty yards off downwind is where they'll set that yacht down—in the lee of this place, but at what they think is a safe distance, even if someone tried to swim for it. They'll send a small boat across with the party and it'll come up on deck by cable elevator."

He turned to look into Cully's eyes.

"Meanwhile, Will and I," he said, "and whoever else you pick are going to be headed toward the yacht."

"Swimming?" Cully asked, prompting Doak to unfold the scheme quickly—and get back off those greasy, sloping, metal ridges.

"Floating," replied Doak, shaking his head. He pointed back past Cully. "In those."

Cully turned with the others and looked at the stacks of big empty garbage cans, washed clean by the sea at the end of long chains from the platform above—once the scavengers of the ocean had taken care of their contents.

"It'll be downwind to the yacht," said Doak. "We'll

float in the right direction. And one can will hold one man. The sharks don't pay any attention to the clean cans."

"I see . . ." Cully looked at him. "Why bother with us at all? Why didn't you and Will just take off in the cans without bothering to talk to us?"

Doak shrugged.

"The riot would help," he said. "And we need *you*, Cully—Will says—to get us off this planet and back to Kalestin. We'll have a better chance with you."

"All right, come back on the deck," said Cully. Doak turned and calmly stepped to safety. The watching men began to breathe normally again. Cully faced about to the Board of Governors.

"All right, let's vote on it," he said. "You stay here," he added to Doak. He led the Board along the deck and around the corner in single file like a work detail, and disappeared into their second meeting place abovedecks, the deck-engine room. In the privacy of the corner of the deck-engine room, with a couple of the ordinary prisoners on guard just out of earshot, they threshed the matter out.

The Board as a whole—after its first shock had passed—was hot with outrage that these two should not only take advantage of the first real escape chance to come by, but should displace two men of the planned escape crew in order to do so. Cully offered to take Doak and Will as extras; but at that the hard-headedness of the Board reasserted itself and they began—as Cully had known they would—to come around to accepting the inevitable and making the best of it. It was finally decided that only Cully, Leestrom, and Dr. Toy should join with Doak and Will, to be the safe minimum of an escape crew.

With that they split up—for time was growing short—to go about their business of organizing the riot that should cover the escape attempt.

So it was that three hours later found the five members of the escape crew crouched in the alcove with the clean garbage cans, as a dot appeared high in the midafternoon sky in the east. It grew swiftly to the shape of a luxury Space-and-Atmosphere ship—essentially the sort of twelve passenger SA model Leestrom had predicted it would be. It swung low once over the platform of Number One—and a ragged chorus of purely spontaneous, derisive jeers burst from the prisoners in tattered pants, watching on the main deck. The guards moved swiftly to quiet them down as the yacht turned, as lightly as a sea bird itself, for all its stubby-winged, cylindrical shape, and settled gently on the heaving, dark-blue waves some fifty yards off.

"Wait," commanded Cully, as Doak began to move from among the cans toward the edge of the garbage section.

A hatch opened in the side of the yacht and a small boat slid out. It rose on its supporting cushion of air and hung there as, one by one, six figures stepped out of the yacht to stand upright in it.

Three of them were dark-robed, narrow-shouldered figures, with dark, hairless skulls stark in the tropical sunlight. They stood side by side, the one in the center taller by half a head. The boat turned and slid smoothly across the waves toward the far end of Number One, where a cable elevator had been rigged to lift it up onto the deck sixty feet above.

"Wonder who that center Moldaug is?" muttered Leestrom, as the boat reached the corner of the platform and paused for the cable elevator to enclose it.

"One of their Space Admirals," the voice of Will spoke quietly, just behind Cully's left ear, "judging by the shape of his robe and collar. Which also marks him as an Elder Brother. So the two with him will be the two younger Brothers of his 'individual' unit. All of them are of a cadet line to the Imperial Family. At a guess, from what all these things add up to, he's Admiral Ruhn himself."

"What do you mean? How do you tell all that?" muttered Leestrom, still staring at the middle figure of the three narrow-shouldered, gowned shapes. The boat was now being hoisted to the deck at the far end of Number One.

Will laughed beside and behind Cully. But Cully heard the laugh as if from some distance. He could not take his own eyes off the tall center Moldaug; and out of that talent of his for divining motives behind the actions of others, there was kindling in him a strange, deep feeling of powerful empathy, as if he could almost sense what Ruhn was sensing at this moment.

As a boy, in his first year on Kalestin before the aliens' scout ships stopped coming, he had seen Moldaug twice. But never until now—and probably it was the result of all Will's teaching—had the sight of them reached out and touched him, emotionally, as it did now. Before his eyes the Moldaug in the ferryboat seemed alien and not-alien at the same time. It seemed as if he knew how the alien he watched was feeling—for all the obvious differences in bone and flesh, plain now before his eyes.

For Ruhn, like all Moldaug, had the physical appearance of a distorted human. Within the dark-gray gown that swathed his standing figure, his spine was set in a flatter curve than that of a human—which gave him an uprightness of carriage that sharply distinguished him and his two Brothers from the humans in the small boat. His narrow shoulders were deceptive—a result of the fact that the ball-and-socket shoulder joints of the aliens faced more toward the front of the body than toward the side, as they did in the human frame. But it was within the frame of the high-rounded collar, upcurving behind the head, that the real unnaturalness of the Moldaug to human eyes seemed to take place.

The face, the skull, was completely hairless and covered with a thin-looking, dark, yet somehow nearly transparent skin. Under that skin the bone seemed heavier and less cushioned by softening fat than in the human. "*Soft faces*," Will had said the Moldaug called humans in the Moldaug language—and it was a fact that, in contrast with those about them, the faces of the Moldaug in the approaching boat seemed rather to be three skin-covered skulls than three collections of features in the human sense.

The eyes of the Ruhn, at whom Cully stared, lacked eyebrows. Instead, under bony protective ridges, they were linelike slits between double sets of equally movable upper and lower eyelids. The nose was a long, extremely narrow, bony ridge ending in nostrils that lay back at an angle that brought them almost flat with the face. The cheekbones were more like cheekplates, extending down level with the nostrils; and the upper jaw, which was as wide from nostrils to lip as the lower jaw was from lip to chin, met the lower in a thin slash of a mouth.

The neck appeared thin from the front in the V-shaped opening of the gown; but heavy cords of muscle running down from behind the narrow, projecting ears that set above the high hinge of the lower jaw, gave the neck a thick look from the side. Altogether, the Moldaug figure looked frail by human standards—but was not, although an adult male of the aliens on the average stood shorter and weighed less than an average human man.

In the face of the particular Moldaug he was watching, now up close, Cully saw a mass of fine wrinkles like the cracking of dark old varnish on a piece of antique furniture. But the face itself was unreadable.

Unreadable—but, caught up in his strange moment of empathy, something like a spark of total understanding leaped just then to Cully from the inhuman, upright figure. For a moment, as if borne upward on the wings of some great emotion, Cully felt himself carried with a rush into what it must feel like to be Moldaug; to be the dominant one of three Brothers, alone among unpredictable alien humans, bearing the responsibility of getting across to these soft-faced aliens an understanding they seemed incapable of achieving.

The loneliness—the particularly *Moldaug* loneliness

and courage—of Ruhn struck a spark from Cully's own strong individuality, with a keen, almost physical impact, like the point of a knife driven in under his breastbone.

"*Very Respectable—a Very Respectable Elder Brother* . . ." he murmured, involuntarily, in the Moldaug tongue. "*Oh, Very Respectable, my Cousin Ruhn!*"

The murmur of his voice in his own ears brought him abruptly back into his own human skin.

". . . depends on where you look," Will was saying to Leestrom. "Our emblems of rank mean nothing to the aliens either. Among the Moldaug the cut of the gown is everything. That upstanding collar identifies and individual of high rank, the backward slant means he's military. The V-shaped opening in front—"

"By God, you do know a lot about the Moldaug!" The craggy-faced Leestrom looked at the older man with a sudden, new awakening of respect.

"No one knows a lot about the Moldaug," replied Will, "except the Moldaug themselves. Still—"

"*Now!*" snapped Cully, interrupting them both. The boat had just been hoisted over the fence onto the platform. And a sudden shouting of voices in a different section of the deck signaled that the planned prisoners' riot had begun. With Cully leading, the five men dashed to the edge of the platform and began to climb down the chains already hanging from the edge there, toward the waves below.

Cully went down swiftly. Above him, the noise, carried through the metal underside of the platform, was increasing. He reached his garbage can, hanging at the end of the chain, some few feet above the crests of the waves. It swung lidless and free. It was large enough for him to crouch down into and he eased himself into it before looking around at the others. They were nearly all into their own cans, hanging to one side or the other of the center can which was Cully's. He waited until they were all in.

"Ready?" he called to the rest of them. "Hold up the line!"

Five arms, including Cully's, lifted from garbage cans to hold up the light rope that ran from can to can. It was to be a hit-and-miss project, drifting down on the yacht, but if even one of them could make the vessel, he could haul the others in by means of the rope—they hoped.

"All right. Fasten the rope!" called Cully.

He and the rest took loops in the rope and tied on to the right handle of their garbage can.

"Now—drop!" ordered Cully, and cut the rope binding his can to its supporting chain.

It was a tricky business. He had tried to judge the cutting moment just as a wave swell passed beneath his can, so that it would have no more than a foot or so to drop. But the fastening rope was tough, and he barely got it cut through as the wave crest passed. He dropped, and jarred with a severe shock against the can as the waves took him.

He stuck his head up to see how the others had made it. They were all, he saw, down safely. And Doak, in the can at the far right, was already trying to paddle himself in the direction of the yacht. Cully groped in his own can for one of the strips of plastic they had brought along to use as paddles, but his first attempt to use it merely set his can to spinning like a metal whirling dervish.

He was encountering a difficulty first discovered by his own Irish, coracle-building ancestors—to wit, that a round craft does not necessarily go forward upon being paddled. He gave up, and resigned himself to keeping the plastic strip down in the water as a rudder.

Luckily, the wind was moving them at pretty fair speed toward the yacht. At first it seemed that they were making no progress at all; but then, on spinning around for a moment so that he was facing back the way he had come, Cully was surprised to see that a good strip of water had already opened between them and

Number One. He spun back for a look at the yacht, which was now appearing, now disappearing, as his garbage can went up and down on waves which had seemed hardly more than ripples from the platform's height. Down here these same waves could be seen to measure a good three feet or more from crest to trough.

All in all, however, they seemed to be moving well, and in the right direction. Cully's throat suddenly tightened as something scraped hard against the side of his can, and the can lurched. Rising up and looking over the edge, he saw the long, gray shape of a nurse shark curving around his can. He sank back down into the bottom of its metal interior, his stomach in a tight knot under his breastbone.

But there were no more scrapings against his can, and after a little while he lifted his head again to see that the yacht was now only a short distance away. Behind them, as Cully spun about for a moment, the noise from Number One had mounted until it resounded like the howling of maddened beasts, interspersed with the crackle of riot guns. The stampede back there would be out of control even of its leaders, now that hundreds of prison-mad men, spewing up out of the commandeered elevators, ran amuck in reaction against months of restraint. Cully spun back and saw that they were almost upon the yacht—

But they were drifting past it.

Maddeningly, the garbage cans had refused to stay strung out in the broad line that would have given them the maximum chance of encountering the vessel. Instead, the two on Cully's left, holding Dr. Toy and Leestrom, had swung around to join with the two holding Doak and Will Jaimeson, on Cully's right, so that Cully was now at the left end of what was more of a cluster, than a line, of drifting garbage cans.

And it was on Cully's left that the yacht was about to pass them.

For a moment Cully sat crouched and staring at the yacht. It was no less than twenty feet away now, but it was twenty feet of three-foot-high waves. Then he straightened up his can and untied the rope from the can's handle.

"Give me line!" he shouted at the others and dove out of his can, holding his part of the line and swimming strongly for the still open hatch of the yacht.

For a moment the memory of the nurse shark came back, threatening to leach all the courage out of him. Almost, in imagination, he could feel it now, gliding up underneath to seize on his swimming body with its tooth-armored jaws. But he thrust the thought from him and concentrated on churning frantically toward the open hatch.

However, the line had pulled tight and the garbage cans were now a dead weight behind him. For a long moment he fought, only yards from the yacht, being dragged down along its open side by the weight of the men in cans at the far end of the line. It seemed that he must inevitably be pulled past the hatch before he could reach it—and then one hand, desperately outflung, caught and held onto the hinge of the hatch's open door.

Gasping from his effort, Cully dragged himself up against the pull of the line until he could climb into the low entrance of the hatch and, over the rails on which the boat had been launched, through it. Inside, he lay for a moment panting.

Then he began to drag the other cans up to the hatch.

It was minutes of muscle-cracking work, but eventually all four other men stood beside him in the open hatch. Now Leestrom and Dr. Toy, as well as Doak, held homemade knives in their hands. Only Will was not holding his prison-made knife.

"All right," panted Cully. "Spread out and see if there's anyone left aboard her. Doctor, Lee—you head aft. Doak—you and I'll go forward. Come on . . ."

He and Doak ran forward. In the forward lounge

they split up, Cully diving into the pilot's section, Doak taking the galley and storerooms.

The pilot's section was empty. Cully paused a second to examine the controls. Yes, it was a typical rich-man's cruiser. Almost anyone taken at random off the streets of any big city could fly it—let alone a man with large-spaceship training, like himself. He turned to head back to the lounge.

A woman's scream sounded suddenly, wild and clear from the galley. Cully's imagination lit up with the small but deadly image of Doak. He plunged back into the lounge, and from there into the galley.

But there was no tragedy in progress. Doak stood, merely barring exit from the galley to a slim, blond-haired girl in a pink sunsuit. Her eyes flashed to Cully in a look of desperate appeal—and froze there.

Cully froze also.

"Alia!" he said grimly.

"Cully!" Her face was white. "They told me you were dead!"

8

For a moment Cully and Alia stood staring at each other. Then the bulky figure of Leestrom appeared in the doorway.

"No one aboard—" Leestrom broke off at the sight of Alia; and Cully, brought back abruptly from the shock of seeing her, broke into action.

"Lock her up—in her stateroom!" he snapped at Leestrom and spun about to head on a run for the pilot's section of the yacht.

Reaching there, he threw himself into a control chair, touched the motor switches of the craft, and saw with relief all the needles on the monitoring dials leap into flight-ready positions. He thumbed the intercom button.

"Hang on, everyone!" he announced flatly. "We're taking off—fast!"

He slammed the switches home and locked his hands on the quarter-wheel of the main control unit before him. The yacht left the surface of the water like a wild duck under hunters' fire and leveled out, climbing toward the horizon. Above, the intercept screen glowed to life, showing the blip of the patrol ship circling Number One at the fifty-mile radius. The patrol ship was moving on its regular course—which would bring it almost to intercept the climbing yacht.

"Turn! Aren't you going to turn?"

It was Leestrom, speaking from the door behind Cully, where the big man clung to the doorframe against the upward tilt of the yacht's deck. He lunged forward and dropped into the control seat beside Cully.

"No!" said Cully. "They'll have heard of the riot by now. They'll think we're just hustling the Moldaug out to avoid an interracial incident—I hope. The patrol pilot won't want to stick his neck out, maybe, to halt us. Isn't Number One supposed to be escape-proof?"

Leestrom did not answer. Cully kept on course. At the last minute the patrol ship altered course, diving five hundred meters to clear the yacht's path. There was no challenge from the patrol ship.

Now the yacht was lifting toward the upper limits of the atmosphere, a black band of airless space forming in the upper sky above them—and shortly the curve of the Earth put them out of screen view of both Number One and the patrol ship.

"All right, Lee," said Cully. "Call San Francisco Spaceport and ask them if there's an interstellar ship take-off scheduled there within the hour."

Leestrom bent to the communications board among the controls before him. Cully, listening, heard San Francisco's answer.

". . . Just a minute, sir. Yes, sir. The *North Star*, leaving for Merope III and other Pleiades Planets in forty-two minutes, local time. After that—"

Cully reached over, flipped Lee's switch, and took the call on his own board.

"All right. I'll take over," he said to the startled face of the San Francisco responder. Will you put me through to the Captain of the *North Star*, please? Immediately." His voice rasped into impatience as the man stared at him without moving. "I'm the personal secretary of Alia Braight—Member Amos Braight's daughter; and we're calling from the Member's personal yacht. Miss Braight would like to speak to the *North Star* Captain. If you please."

The screen went gray. Cully saw Leestrom staring at him.

"I was going to try to get us aboard a ship with a refueling crew," Cully told him. "But I've got a better idea now."

He reached over and flicked on an intercom switch for the one cabin that had its occupancy light glowing red. Alia's face stared astonished into the screen at him.

"Alia," said Cully, without further explanation, "I'm going to let you talk to the Captain of an interstellar ship—the *North Star*."

"Cully," she began, and then her lips moved soundlessly in the screen as his fingers pulled the phone connection loose between them.

"Yes?" said a new voice. Cully looked to see a man in a blue jacket and with Captain's insignia filling the other screen. He connected the two screens but without reconnecting Alia's phone connection.

Alia's eyes widened at the sight of the face above the uniform.

"Miss Braight . . . ?" Recognition woke in the Captain's eyes, and Cully let out a silent breath of relief. As Amos' daughter, Alia's picture had been on the news media often enough. Still, there had always been the chance that this Captain would not recognize her. But then the Captain's expression changed to puzzlement. "Miss Braight, happy to see you again. But is your volume control turned up . . . ? I don't seem to hear you . . ."

Alia's lips moved. Abruptly Cully reached out and cut her image from the Captain's circuit, replacing it with his own.

"Captain?" he said pleasantly, leaning forward. "Terribly sorry, Captain. Something wrong with the circuit to Miss Braight's cabin. She asks me to tell you that she and a party of five would like to leave on your ship. They can be there in half an hour."

"Half an hour?" the Captain frowned.

"At the latest," said Cully with quick smoothness. "No luggage. Miss Braight promises you won't be delayed from your normal take-off time. If you'd just say a word to the Customs and the gate guards . . . ? I'm sure Member Braight would appreciate it."

"All right," said the Captain, his frown wrinkling into a scowl. "But I won't hold ship. Thirty minutes!"

"They'll be there. Thank you." Cully cut the connection, got up and went back to find the cabin with Alia's name on it. He unlocked the door and let himself in. She was huddled in a chair before the screen, but she leaped up and came toward him as he entered.

"Oh, Cully!" she cried. "What kind of a trick was that? What'd you do?"

"I'll tell you exactly what I did," he answered.

He told her briefly, giving her no time to speak. Her face paled again as she listened, but her eyes met his steadily. The slim beauty of her standing there reached through to him, and in self-defense against the way she affected him he made his voice dry and unsparing.

". . . so you see what the situation is," he wound up. "We're going to spacelift that ship and use it to get home in. You can go along with us or not. That's up to you. But just remember that if you don't go along with us, if you raise an alarm or give us away, men are going to die, and their deaths will be on your conscience. Remember—all we're trying to do is get home where we belong!"

He stopped and stared challengingly at her, waiting for her to answer—well aware, from his own intimate knowledge of her, of the kind of unfair emotional blackmail he was using to force her cooperation. But he hardened his face and heart to carry it through. After all, it would have been just such emotional blackmail by her father that she had given in to, in decoying him to Earth and Number One.

"Well?" he demanded, when she did not answer immediately.

"Of course, I'll help you get away," she whispered.

"Good," he said. He swung about and went out, relocking the door behind him.

Forty minutes later, the yacht dropped to a landing at the marina attached to the San Francisco Spaceport; and from it five men and a subdued-looking woman in rich gown and tiara hurried to the Terminal, where they were waved through normal boarding procedures.

"Miss Braight . . . and party . . ." said the plump steward, closing the sally port behind them and pressing the button that signaled "all aboard" to the bridge. "Glad to have you all on board. If you'll just follow me—"

He broke off with a choked sound, for the heavy arm of Leestrom was around his neck, and the point of Leestrom's prison-made knife was pricking him in the fold of white skin under his chin.

"Not just yet," said Cully grimly. "Show us to the crewside lift tube."

Shaken the steward led them back through this level of the ship to the lounge-deck pantry, which opened on a vertical shaft containing a sort of man-sized dumbwaiter—a convenience to enable the deck steward to come and go from the crew and officer country in the ship's nose to the lounge levels in her tail, without passing through the staterooms and private quarters of the passenger section.

"I'll go first," said Cully, He let himself into the tube and caught hold of the moving chain which carried him upward.

The rest, even Alia and the trembling steward, followed. In the officers'-level pantry they tied up the steward, and left him and Alia with Toy. The rest, following Cully, slipped down a short corridor and into the Captain's quarters, where the arms locker was kept.

It was locked, but Cully's prison-made lock picks, prepared against this hour, opened it. Cully lifted out three of the heavy riot guns; and, armed, they moved up to a door leading to the very nose of the ship. It was closed, but Cully put his hand on the latch.

"Ready—?" he asked the others. They nodded. "Now!" he said as he tore open the door and charged through, they after him.

The Captain of the *North Star* and his three senior officers, including the Astrogator and the Senior Overdrive Officer, were all at their instrument consoles scattered about the circular room, with its wide screen giving a four-way view of the surrounding stars. The junior officers—which is to say, both the Junior Astrogator and the Junior Overdrive Officer, stood behind their seniors in backup position according to regulations. The First Officer, of course, stood behind his Captain.

Into this scene, like three foxes into a henyard, erupted the three wild figures of Cully, Leestrom and the small but more fearsome Doak, his slight figure again clothed in that deadliness he had displayed to the guards, on occasion, aboard Number One.

"Still! Stand still, and continue operations!" rapped out Cully, as the three men fanned out to cover all the officers in the pilot room. Cully himself stood facing the Captain and the First Officer.

"Step aside, Captain!" he ordered. "This ship of yours is spacelifted. Two steps back now—quickly!"

The Captain, his hands still poised above his control console, stared stupidly at Cully. It had been four years since the Bill of Agreements between the Old Worlds and the Frontier had put a stop to that devastating larceny of ships in flight that had kept legitimate shipmasters awake nights. For a moment, it seemed that this Captain did not understand. Then comprehension dawned in his face and eyes.

Other than the rape of one member of a family from another, there is no loss so brutal as that which takes a ship from its Captain. Four years ago a Captain like this would probably have been armed. This one was not, but he went for Cully's throat with his bare hands just the same.

Quickly reversing the riot gun, Cully brought the heavy butt of the weapon around to slam against the side of the head of the attacking man. The Captain dropped to the deck.

"Take care of him—and stand back!" said Cully to the First Officer. Gray-faced, the First Officer dragged the fallen man to one side. Cully stepped behind the control console.

"All stations. Report!" he said.

The underofficers, after a numb moment of pause, began to report. Without a pause—for a ship hurtling into space and about to take itself into overdrive has no time to waste—Cully led them all smoothly into the overdrive procedure. The ship shifted—its first shift, putting it lightyears from the Solar System, and absolutely beyond the reach of any rescue from the planet they had just left behind.

"All right," said Cully, closing the switches on his control console. He looked around the room, where the ship's officers, having automatically closed down their own consoles, had swung about, either standing or sitting, to stare at him. "It seems that you're now without a Captain," he said. "How many of you now have Master's tickets? Raise your hands!"

To his right, crouched over the now reviving Captain, the First Officer raised his hand without hesitation. The hands of the Astrogator and Senior Overdrive Officer also quickly went up.

"Thank you, gentlemen," said Cully dryly. "Now we'll just take good care that none of the three of you are allowed above the passengers' level for the rest of the trip. You junior officers—if an emergency comes up, I'll be calling you to help me move the ship. Now, for the moment, you can all head downdecks."

He turned to the Captain, who was on his feet now, supported by the First Officer, although the side of the Captain's face was beginning to swell and darken in ugly fashion. Cully did not add insult to injury by expressing sympathy for the man. It would have seemed a mockery in the face of what Cully was doing to him. The deadly hatred that glared upon him from the Captain's eyes was a look with which Cully had become familiar during his spacelifting years.

"No!" said the Captain, thickly, as the other officers moved, and the First Officer tried to lead him away. He pulled away from the First Officer and staggered to face Cully.

"Listen to me, Mister—" the Captain said harshly. "Do you think you can run a spaceship just by punching a few buttons . . . ? You answer me, whoever you are! Do you know anything about handling a ship? There are passengers aboard here, and crew I'm responsible for—"

"I had my Master's papers ten years ago," replied Cully coldly. "And I've commanded more star crossings than a commercial line will let you make between now and retirement age. Your ship's safe in my hands, Captain. I'm Cully When."

"When . . . ?" echoed the Captain blankly. And then memory lit a light of understanding in his eyes. "*When!* You're going to keep her, then! You're not just taking my ship for the ride to Merope!"

"That's right," said Cully evenly. "We're headed for Kalestin, and we'll be keeping her."

"Keeping her—" The Captain tried to throw himself at Cully's throat again, but the First Officer held him back. The Captain exploded into a rage of words. "You spacelifter! You damned pirate! You won't get away with this!—I'll see you shot! I'll shoot you myself—"

"For God's sake, come along, sir . . . ," muttered the First Officer uneasily, with his eye on the three riot guns covering them. "Come along sir . . ."

He half-dragged the Captain, still shouting threats, out of the Pilot Room. Leestrom followed them to the circular stairs leading first to the crew's quarters, and finally to the passenger levels below. The big man, riot gun cradled under one arm, followed them down the stairwell and out of sight.

"Doak," said Cully, once they had gone. "Get the others up. Will—"

He broke off suddenly, seeing something that looked like a miniature suitcase in Will's left hand. "What's that?"

But the older man was already opening the case on a chart table. He took out one of several packs of what looked like long strips of paper fastened together at the top end. Cully stepped over to look at them. The top strip of the one he examined held a vertical row of what looked like single words—each word made up of a set of three characters.

At first glance, the characters seemed not merely similar but identical; looking closely, however, Cully was able to make out differences between them.

"What are they?" he asked Will.

"Some papers evidently belonging to Admiral Ruhn—if that was really Ruhn, that Moldaug that came with the visitors to Number One," answered Will. "I noticed the case, back on Miss Braight's father's yacht, and thought I'd bring it along. You wanted to learn to read Moldaug as well as speak it. I can use this to help teach you."

"Good," said Cully. "But there's something else I wanted to talk to you about. You told me Doak was essentially harmless. But he made Miss Braight scream just now, when we came aboard the flyer."

"I think she must have been just startled," said Will. "I promise you—"

"Promises aren't going to be good enough," said Cully flatly. "If there's something about Doak and women, I've got to know it—now. You've got to tell me what you know about him."

"*I* tell you?" Will's tone held an unusual stubbornness. "It's Doak's secret, not mine to tell. It's true, I did say he wasn't quite sane. But who's to judge?" He smiled sadly, unexpectedly. "Maybe I'm a little not sane either, after forty-odd years of studying alien ghosts and goblins. I can't tell you his story. Doak trusts me and—"

Will broke off, looking past Cully. Turning, Cully saw that Dr. Toy and the little man had just brought the steward and Alia into the Control Room.

"I don't mind," said Doak calmly. Plainly, he had overheard at least half of Will's speech. "Cully belongs to the Frontier, Will. I don't mind his knowing." He turned toward Cully. "I'm looking for my father, Cully. He's an Earthman, and I thought he had to be some-place on Earth now."

"And you couldn't find him?" Cully asked. "The Directory in Geneva ought to be able to locate anyone for you. Did you try there?"

"Yes," said Doak calmly. "But I knew it was no use. And it wasn't. He's probably changed his identity. You see—he doesn't want me to find him."

"Your father doesn't want you to find him?" Cully echoed.

"No. He knows I'm going to kill him. Execute him—for murder."

"Murder?" Cully stared back at the calm-voiced little man, feeling the flesh chill on the back of his neck.

"My mother's murder," explained Doak quietly. "You see, he killed her. Because they told him to. And I suppose—because he was drunk and had nothing else to do that evening."

The little man cocked his head to one side.

"What'll I do with this steward?" he asked.

"Cut him loose and send him downdecks with the rest of the crew," said Cully. "And show Miss Braight to the Captain's bedroom. That can be her quarters for the trip. Toy, look around for some way of sealing the hatches between us and the rest of the ship."

They went out. Cully turned back to face Will.

9

The older man's face was unhappy.

"So," said Will, "you know now."

"Well," said Cully, "you might as well tell me the rest." He made, unconsciously, a circular movement of his hand. "It's all in his head, isn't it?"

"Unfortunately, no," answered Will slowly. "Do you ever remember being told of the Fortown Massacre?"

"Fortown!" said Cully. "So that's it!"

For, of course, he had heard about Fortown. He had been nine years old and on Kalestin at the time of the Massacre. A Moldaug spaceship that was plainly armed had touched down briefly near a small human community on that world. It had stayed a few hours, doing no harm, and then taken off again. But, when word of this had gotten back to the Old Worlds, for once the bureaucracy there had bestirred itself. It had sent out a military force—three companies of armored infantry, which proceeded to build a fort beside the small settlement.

But the Moldaug ship, which had done no damage or offered no violence in the first place, never came back; and shortly, that same bureaucracy back on the Old

Worlds forgot about their three companies of armored infantry.

The soldiers were not officially forgotten, of course. But what with one pigeonholing and another, they were not relieved. The tour of their duty was extended—after all, they were away out there in the Pleiades, and there were more importunate members of the armed forces close at hand . . .

So the Fort and its occupants began to degenerate; and with them, the little neighboring settlement, now known as Fortown, began to degenerate also. Into a wild little town. Into a shacky little town. Into a general hellhole and redlight district.

The Fortown gamblers cheated the soldiers, and the Fortown prostitutes infected them with diseases that never should have emigrated with humans from the Old Worlds in the first place. And then, one final day, the Lieutenant Colonel in charge of the Fort went crazy—or at least that was the charitable explanation. He was no more a stranger to the gamblers and prostitutes than any of his men; and one day, something set him off. That evening, he ordered every man in the Fort to assemble, issued them weapons with live charge-units, and ordered them to march immediately on Fortown to clean it up.

The result was the Fortown Massacre. Commanders of medieval troops in the Middle Ages were aware that if their soldiers were forced to sit too long besieging a town, there was no hope of saving the townspeople from plunder, rape and looting when the town finally capitulated. Fortown was in a similar case—what began as a crazed man's disciplinary action became a fiery massacre.

It lasted until Amos Braight put on an officers uniform and flew to the scene, walked into the Fort, and personally arrested the crazed Lieutenant Colonel. Where Amos had gotten the uniform, Cully never knew. But he remembered how, some years later, the sight of it in a closet of the Governor's mansion had increased

his boyish admiration for Amos, as a man not only of
honesty but of courage.

". . . So Doak's mother was one of the Fortown
women?" Cully asked Will. "You mean his father actually killed her in the Massacre?"

"That's what Doak believes," Will answered. "But he
was only four years or so old at the time, and he'd
never seen his father before. His mother always sent
Doak away when his father came to visit. So what's true
and what's in Doak's mind, nobody can tell."

"I see . . ." Cully glanced toward the circular stairway. "What's the locket got to do with it?"

"Locket?" Will's face had stiffened slightly. "What
locket?"

"The locket"—Cully stared curiously at him—"Doak
carries around his neck. You didn't know about it?"

"Oh, *that* locket. Of course," said Will. But his face
was still a little pale. "It's a locket Doak thinks his
mother used to own. He thinks the man pictured in it is
his father."

"You don't think so yourself?"

"Is it likely?" said Will almost sharply. "It could be
anyone's locket. It could be any man's picture—and
whoever it is would have changed in sixteen years so
that Doak wouldn't be able to recognize him from the
picture, even if Doak thinks he could." Will hesitated,
then added, "That's one of the reasons I had to get
Doak away from Earth—even in Number One there
was too much danger of his killing some perfectly innocent man who just happened to look like a picture in
the wrong locket."

Will's hand had closed on his shirt at belt level as he
spoke. Under its grasp there, Cully saw beneath the
cloth the outline of the handle of Will's prisoner's knife—
the knife he had not drawn even when they boarded
Braight's yacht, not knowing what or who might be
waiting for them. Will caught the direction of Cully's
glance and dropped his hand to his side.

"But, believe me," said Will, "he's not dangerous to

anyone except the man he thinks is his father. Least of all to women. He identifies every woman he meets with his mother, and he'd literally give his own life to protect her—especially against another man."

"All right," said Cully. "Well, I'll make you responsible for him, in any case. Meanwhile—we've got a spaceliner to navigate."

In fact, it turned out to be a job from that moment on that was to occupy Cully, in particular, through most of his waking hours. This, because it was necessary for him to be Navigator as well as Captain. For while both Leestrom and Toy could navigate in a pinch, they were nowhere close to being in Cully's class—in that interstellar occupation where solid mathematical ability faded off into the tenuous area of inspired guesswork, when it came to the reduction of destination-point error.

The pressure of the work kept him busy—and Alia, he noted, carefully avoided him. Otherwise, the close quarters of the command section they inhabited, up front in the ship—with its doors welded shut against any attempt by the official Captain and crew to retake the vessel from the passenger section underneath—would have eventually forced them into conversation.

It was plain that she was deliberately refusing to be put in a position where she would have to talk to him. Obviously, thought Cully, she was still clinging to the idea that what she had done in decoying him into the hands of the World Police was right. Cully accepted her consequently implied condemnation of him a little sadly, but philosophically. He made no attempt to force her into conversation. In his own way, he could be very patient; and he was content to wait now until events should convince her and bring her to a different opinion of him, by her own free will and decision.

He buried himself in his job of handling the spaceliner, and succeeded in forgetting everything else. He forgot so well, in fact, that he was literally confounded by Will for a moment, shortly before they were due to set down on Kalestin. The older man came into the Navigation

Room and shoved two items before him on top of the chart cube.

One of the items was a perfectly ordinary sheet of writing material with printing on it. The other was a sort of narrow scroll.

"What's this?" he demanded of Will.

"You remember those Moldaug papers I picked up aboard Braight's yacht?" Will asked. "The ones I thought I might use to help you learn to read their language?"

"I remember now," said Cully. He looked with curiosity from the scroll to the printed page. "So that's what it looks like, translated."

"Yes. But never mind how it looks," said Will. "I sat down to translate a part of it so you'd have something to work with; and what I found out was interesting. Very interesting. So I translated the whole set. Altogether, this writing adds up to an unfinished first draft by Admiral Ruhn of a report to his superiors back among the Moldaug."

"Oh?" Cully was suddenly interested.

"That's right," said Will. "The report is addressed from Ruhn and his two Brothers, of the Envoy unit he represents, to the Youngest Brother of his Elder Cousins, Eighth from the Throne—that three-person 'individual' unit among the Imperial Family to whom Ruhn must first speak in addressing the Moldaug tripartite rulers—"

"All right," interrupted Cully, "but why don't you skip the titles and get to whatever's important about it? I've got only twenty more minutes to finalize computations on the next shift."

"I can say this in a minute," said Will. "The fact that it's a first draft and not completed is because it's been a hard report for Ruhn to write. You see, he's reporting a failure."

"Failure?" echoed Cully.

"That's right," said Will. He frowned slightly. "Try to think like a Moldaug now, because I warn you the message in this report won't make sense by human standards. Ruhn reports that his Human Cousins—that'll be Braight and the other Tri-Worlds Council Members—have continued to be too clever for him and his two Brothers in the matter of the question of ownership of the Pleiades Region."

"Too clever?" said Cully unbelievingly. "You mean that Braight and those others have actually managed to talk the Moldaug out of the claim they were making on our Frontier Planets?"

"No. Just the opposite. Ruhn reports that Braight and the others seemed determined to avoid any firm statement of human intent to hold the Pleiades Region," said Will. "As a result, Ruhn writes, it must be feared that, in spite of all his efforts, the Moldaug may be left with no Respectable choice but to take action against the human race. He will continue to press the matter upon Braight and the others with all urgency; but meanwhile he regretfully suggests to his Elder Cousin that in all prudence the Moldaug fighting ships be put in readiness for immediate action, and that all those individuals of the proper requisites prepare themselves for war."

10

"You get back here," said the young man in the tailored brush pants and jacket, "just in time to stick your head into a nest of rock-tigrets."

They were talking in Cully's hotel room, in Kalestin City—Cully, Doak, Leestrom, and the man speaking—who was an elected Member of that same Frontier Assembly from which Cully had resigned two years before. The name of the young speaker was Onweetok Murfa.

He was slim and tall—though nowhere near the height of Cully or Leestrom. He had an open, round, boyish sort of face that, even with the heavy Frontier tan, looked cheerful and harmless. A certain dandiness about his tailored clothes backed up the impression.

On the other hand, the easy way he stood, balanced on the balls of his feet in brush boots with the unadorned, businesslike, wooden pistol-grip of the handgun peeping out of the belly-holster in the gap of his unclosed jacket, gave the boyishness and dandyism license to go by unchallenged by any experienced Frontiersman.

"I expected to hear that," said Cully. He smiled, a little grimly.

"Sure—but this is something different," said Onweetok, with a small wave of his hand. "Things aren't the way they were when you left six months ago, and that's a fact."

"How?" asked Cully.

"The Assembly's little more than a farce, a sideshow nowadays. And you're part to blame for it. Sure, look at me that way if you like, Cully. You were one of the ones who left us after the Bill of Agreements seemed to settle things with the Old Worlds. You, and all the good men, the big men, on these Frontier Worlds of ours took off on business of their own, leaving their Assembly seats to any loudmouth brush chopper who felt like drawing his pay and talking up in the Assembly House . . . and could get himself elected from a city or sector on his World."

Onweetok, apparently stirred more deeply than the soft tones of his voice showed, took several soft-footed, long-legged paces up and down the rose-colored rug of the hotel room. He checked again before Cully's chair.

"You know Brian Machin?" Onweetok demanded.

"The big man?" asked Cully. "From Casimir III?"

"The same. It's him and his Brush-knife Boys who own the Assembly nowadays. They've got a majority—even if we've been able to keep them out of the Speaker's seat and a few committee chairmanships. But it's just a matter of time before they have those too. And here, you want me to take you in to them so you can talk about this scheme of yours to elbow the Old Worlds out of the way and deal with the Moldaug ourselves. Why, even if they believed what you're talking about—and I know you well enough myself, Cully lad, to know you're six tenths under the surface like an iceberg most of the time—Machin and his Boys wouldn't be interested. They've got snails of their own to roast!"

Onweetok stopped speaking and stood, thumbs in his belt, staring down at Cully.

"Such as?" Cully asked.

"Graft, Cully," said Onweetok. "Graft, pure and simple. This Frontier of ours is growing like a cake in the oven—there are licenses and laws going through the Assembly every day worth millions to men in the right spot. The Brush-knife Boys are the voting machine to get those men the legislation they want from the Assembly. And Machin's the man who makes the machine go."

Cully frowned.

"What about the other good men that were in the Assembly?" he asked. "What about Wade Libervoy—?"

"Dead, Cully," said Onweetok, rocking on the balls of his feet. "Split near half down the middle in a brush-knife duel with Machin. Same with Welker Johnson. You begin to see how the pattern works, Cully? The Brush-knife Boys do the voting, and Machin not only cracks the whip but trims down the opposition."

"What about the old bunch?" asked Cully. "Machin can't have killed them all off. What about Art Millums?"

"Retired, too old for politics, he says."

"Emile Hasec, then? Or Bill Royce?"

"Royce?" Onweetok laughed. "Cully, Royce is up to his ears in building banks on these nine Frontier Worlds of ours. Royce is Brian Machin's best customer. Hasec— Emile's married again, back with a young wife, on his earth with the other upland farmers, and not about to come to town. Why name me names? Don't you think those of us who're left with a sense of what's right haven't thought of getting together again the old guard that led us during the Revolt? They're all gone like *you* were gone."

"I see," said Cully thoughtfully. "It looks like I'm on my own, then."

"On your own? You've got me, and one or two others in the Assembly!" cried Onweetok. "But that's not going to help. We're too few, I tell you. My advice to you is, clear out again and leave Machin be, unless you want to end up with your own skull split by a brush knife. The Brush Boys all wear them, you know. It's their party badge."

Cully frowned.

"You mean there's no civil protection left in Kalestin City?"

"Protection! Why, sure there is!" said Onweetok. "There's no street murder tolerated here. But what I'm saying is, Machin'll challenge you just like he challenged Wade and Welker, if it looks like you're going to rock the boat. And it's only a plain damn fool who gets into a brush-knife duel with a man to whom one of those tools is no more weight in his big hand than a butter knife in yours or mine. He'll wear you down and then chop you up, Cully—he's done it often enough to good men before this. Have you ever seen him?"

"No, only heard of him," said Cully.

"Well, when you see him you'll understand," said Onweetok. He took a deep breath and straightened up. "Now—tell me you'll listen to reason and not ask me to take you up on this."

Cully shook his head. "I'm going to need an Assembly behind me I can trust," he said. "But don't worry. There's more than one way to skin a cat. There must be more than one way to deal with a Brian Machin." He smiled cheerfully at Onweetok. "I'll expect you to take me in to the Assembly and get me a chance to speak at this afternoon's meeting."

Onweetok tossed the tanned palms of his hands ceilingward.

"It's your own stake-out, Cully lad!" he said.

The gathering in the hotel room broke up. Cully left to meet Alia and drive her to the Spaceport, where she would be leaving for Earth this noon on a sister ship to the *North Star*. The *North Star*, herself, stood on a refitting field to the west of the Spaceport. She was now newly registered under Kalestin registry in Cully's name.

Alia, kidnaped to Kalestin with literally nothing more than the clothes in which she stood, had been forced to accept financial assistance from Cully—who, even without his ownership of the newly spacelifted *North Star*, had considerable credit locally. Alia had accepted this charity, but silently; and she was silent now on their drive to the Spaceport.

Cully made no attempt to force conversation on her. He was a firm believer in the notion that if minds were ever changed, they were changed from within by their owners, and not from without by argument. So it was that he and Alia walked to the very foot of the spaceliner's boarding gangplank before anything was said between them.

But, at the gangplank's foot, Alia turned to face Cully.

"There's something I want you to know," she said. Her face was tight, and pale. "I didn't know—I'd no idea they'd be putting you in that Detention Center, in a place like that. But I couldn't believe it when I went looking for records of you, and the records said you were dead. Dead—maybe; but not by suicide, the way the records said. I couldn't believe that. That's why I suggested Dad lend the Moldaug Ambassadors our flyer, when he wanted to prove to Ruhn that your Frontier people often did things we couldn't control. That's why I went along with them to that ocean-prison place. If I'd found any evidence of anything that'd been done to you there, I was going to expose everything, no matter what it did to Dad."

Cully nodded.

"So," he said. His mind fastened on one part of what she had said. "That's why the alien Ambassadors came to see Number One."

Alia ignored his words.

"I just wanted to tell you, too," she said. "It wasn't my idea that you or anyone else from the Frontier should be caged up like that." She turned away and began to mount the gangplank. Suddenly recalled to the fact that she was leaving, Cully took one long stride after her, and caught her arm. He turned her around.

"That's all you wanted to tell me?" he demanded. "Just that you hadn't thought what they'd do to me after they arrested me? But you still think it was the right thing you did?"

She stared at him for a second and her face tightened suddenly, almost as if she would burst into tears.

"Let me go!" she choked.

Tearing her arm from his grasp, she turned and ran up the gangplank. Cully watched her vanish through the dark doorway of the entry hatch. Sighing, he turned away and went back to the car in which he had driven them both out to the Spaceport.

He touched the controls. With a little hiss, the car rose on its air cushion and swung about, headed back into town.

However, instead of driving directly back into the city, just outside the Airport, Cully swung north of the town to a spot where a hill rose sharply from the edge of the highway to Bonjoi Town, two-hundred kilometers north. It was a hill he and Alia had known as children. He stopped the car, got out and walked about the slope for several minutes. Then, satisfied, he headed back to his hotel. Onweetok was waiting for him there, and together they took a taxi to the Assembly Building.

It was a former field house. Its floor still bore the design of a basketball court that had been laid out on it. But the stadium benches lining both of the long walls of the interior had been taken out except for a section on each side at the far end from the entrance. On these steep benches sat Assembly Members, among them Brian Machin.

Cully recognized him instantly, in spite of never having seen the man before. There was no mistaking which one of the opposition party Members he was. Not only was Machin far and away the biggest man on that side of the room—or, in fact, in the room as a whole—but he was also seated in the middle of the very front rank of the section of seats on Cully's left.

Even aside from Machin's size, his appearance was striking enough. He must, Cully judged, be at least six feet ten, and weigh at least three hundred pounds. But in spite of this height and mass, Brian Machin appeared neither heavy nor awkward. His bodily proportions were so well-balanced that they disguised the fact of his unusual size. Sitting on the front bench, he did not appear at first glance to be so much larger than the men around him. Rather, he seemed merely an averagely good-sized man surrounded by dwarfs and midgets. He wore a metal-buckled bush shirt, and heavy brush pants flaring at the bottom of each trouser leg above up-country boots. But boots and clothes alike were of as fine a material as Onweetok wore, and the hilt of the brush knife hanging toylike from the belt circling his relatively narrow waist, gleamed above the polished sheath of dark leather. His shirt was open at the throat, the column of his neck rose straight out of it; and above that his face was handsome, even noble-looking, with a high brow and wavy blond hair above it.

One of the Assembly Members on Machin's side of the room was speaking as Cully and Onweetok came in. Onweetok stopped Cully just outside the area of the two facing sections of seats. They waited until the Member speaking was through and had sat down; then Onweetok led Cully forward to the section of seats on the right, found space for them both, and motioned Cully to sit while he himself turned to face the single Assembly Member sitting behind the desk on an elevated rostrum against the wall and midway between the two sections of seats.

"Mr. Speaker," Onweetok's voice rang out cheerfully through the room. "I'd like to propose an interruption to ordinary business, if the Assembly will permit. I've brought with me here Culihan O'Rourke When, formerly a Member of this Assembly, who has some interesting information and business to bring before this Assembly."

"The Member from the Northwest Territory of Kalestin, Mr. Murfa, has suggested an interruption of ordinary business," announced the man behind the desk. "Mr. Murfa, I will refer the matter to the Assembly."

Onweetok sat down beside Cully, and they waited while the matter of interrupting ordinary business was

put to a vote. The vote favoring interruption being
carried by 218 to 23, the Speaker announced these
results to Onweetok and asked him to introduce Mr.
When.

Cully got to his feet. And as he did so, a strange wave
of feeling swept through him. Except for some differences in the faces on the bench opposite him, the
afternoon sun shining through the high field-house windows and lighting up the polished floor between the
two sections of seats, the sections themselves, the walls
surrounding—all these were as they had been many
times in the past when he had stood here as a Member
in his own right. For a single, slightly dizzy moment he
let his mind play with the notion that no time at all had
passed—that his resignation, his decision to make the
trip to Earth, the trip itself and his subsequent arrest
and imprisonment, his escape and all that had followed,
were but the substance of one night's dream, between
yesterday's session in this place and today's.

The notion was oddly, seductively pleasant. He had
to shake it from his mind by a literal effort of will. But
having done so, he strode out into the middle space
between the two sections of seats, and began to tell the
Assembly of the ocean prison camp, of his escape from
there, and of the Old World's conviction that there was
a *coup d'état* planned by the Frontier to take them
over.

"Mr. When," interrupted the Speaker at this point.
"You're not telling us that there actually is some group
of misguided Frontiersmen somewhere with such a plot?"

"What does it matter whether there is or not?" countered Cully, "as long as the Old Worlds believes there
is?"

His eyes roamed around the Members sitting on the
benches, pausing for a second on Machin.

"The important point," he went on, "is the reason
why the Old Worlds believe it. They believe it because
they can't figure out the real reason the Moldaug suddenly turned on them, demanding they clear out our

Frontier Worlds. Because they can't find the real reason for that, they're willing to believe anything. But if we—we on the Frontier—were able to find out the true reason, then we'd be in a position to deal with the Moldaug, where the Tri-Worlds Council can't. And being in such a position, we could claim anything we wanted from them—up to and including the full recognition of our independence, out here, that we've always wanted."

Again he paused. The houseful of listening Assembly Members were silent. He stood for a second. He was on a verbal tightrope now, for he had to choose his words so as to make one impression upon the minds of Machin and his Brush-knife Boys, another upon the sensible Members present.

"Now," he said, "I've turned up a man, a Frontiersman who came out with the Casimir III expedition, an anthropologist who's spent most of forty years among the Moldaug and speaks their tongue like a native. He tells me that, whatever it is, the Moldaug have a sound reason—to their own alien way of thinking, which is different from the human—for their claim. He's convinced me we can find out that reason, if we'll go into their territory and look for it. Now, I'll tell you why I believe we ought to do that—"

Again he paused. The Assembly still was silent. Machin was watching him almost casually, the big man's handsome head tilted back upon the column of his neck, the light from the high windows glinting on his mane of blond hair.

"It's not only the value that information might have in the present circumstances," Cully said. "I'll remind you all that it's this World right here, and the other eight we've settled in the Pleiades, that the Moldaug have demanded we get off. And we on the Frontier have taken that demand all too casually. The Old Worlds can afford to misunderstand the aliens. We can't—because we're their next neighbors here, and because we're bound to grow and have even more to do with them in the future than we have in the past."

He paused for a third time. Machin shifted in his seat and dropped his eyelids, as if in slight weariness. A small thing—but a murmur of restlessness, as if cued, ran through the ranks of brush-knife-wearing men seated about him.

"So," said Cully, as if he had seen or heard neither movement nor murmur, "we're between the cracker and the nut. On the one hand, there are great things to be gained by my going in and finding this alien reason for claiming our Worlds. Great trouble, if we don't. All I ask for is a small appropriation to arm the ship I've already got and convert her to fighting trim—together with the equivalent of a letter of marque from this Assembly, showing I've got its authority in its name to protect myself and capture, if necessary, any Moldaug vessels that threaten to attack me or the Frontier."

He sat down.

A mild bit of action was stirring the front rank of the opposite seats, where Machin sat. A note was being handed down the line. It reached a heavy-browed, black-haired man in his early thirties with a brush-knife scabbard at his belt. He rose and asked the Speaker for the floor.

"The Member from Dannen's World, Southern Sector is recognized," said the Speaker.

"Thank you, sir. As I see it," said the black-haired Member, "we've just been told two things. One of these is that the Moldaug are maybe ready to attack the whole human race; and the other is that we ought to outfit When, here, just so that he can go and stir them up that much more. I don't see the sense, myself, in helping him to make things worse than they are already."

The man sat down. Onweetok got the attention of the Speaker and rose.

"Brice," Onweetok said, easily speaking to the black-haired Member, "you're thinking like someone in a Complex apartment back on Earth. The Moldaug have always been able to chew us up anytime they wanted to. We couldn't last three hours on any of the Frontier

Worlds if the aliens really decided to take ship against us. Why do you think they haven't done it before this? It's simple. They don't attack us here on the Frontier because, according to their alien way of thinking, they can't but believe that the minute they hit us, all the armed ships of the Solar System would automatically hit them back. Now, maybe you Brush-knife Boys don't like to hear that we're that dependent for our safety on the Old Worlds. But it's a fact."

And Onweetok sat down in his chair.

Brice was instantly on his feet again.

"You're pretty sure of that—that we wouldn't stand up to the Moldaug!" he said. "Some of us over on this side aren't so sure about that!"

Onweetok regained his feet as swiftly as the other man.

"Sure, it's easy for you, Brice lad, to say that, sitting here on Kalestin! What you say is *one* thing. What *is*, is another—"

The Speaker was hammering on his table with a gavel for order. Brice was starting to shout back at Onweetok again. Several other Members on both sides of the room were on their feet attempting to get the floor. The Speaker finally hammered them all into silence, and they sank into their seats again. Only Brice and Onweetok remained standing.

"Member from Dannen's World has the floor," said the Speaker. Onweetok reluctantly sat down. Slowly, opposite Cully, Brian Machin rose until he seemed to tower above them all. He turned toward Brice, who had just been acknowledged to have the floor.

"Will the Member from Dannen's World yield to me?"

"Yield—" said Brice promptly. He sat down. Machin turned to face the opposite benches, and his brown eyes under their loftly brows sought out Cully.

"Mr. When," Machin said, "has a famous name on our Frontier Worlds." The big man's voice was a light baritone rather than a bass, the only flaw in the larger-than-human impression he produced. But he managed to turn even this to account by speaking with particular softness, as if deliberately restraining vocal chords that might otherwise overwhelm his listeners. "But maybe it ought to be pointed out to Mr. When that it's been two years since he was a Member of this Assembly. And in that length of time conditions have changed."

He turned a little away from Cully to spread his hands slightly and appeal to the Members seated on the bench around and behind him.

"Of course," he went on, "we all feel the same way about the Moldaug, here on the Frontier. I'm sure that there's not one of us who doesn't feel like responding to Mr. When's bold plan to make use of the alien problem— in order to get those full rights of independence from the Old Worlds that every one of us has always wanted—"

His eyes came back to lock with Cully's. Cully smiled slightly, but the big man continued to gaze at him with the utmost seriousness. Machin went on.

"But I think we ought to ask ourselves first whether the good of the Frontier Worlds as a whole is going to be served by backing an act of Frontier aggression against the aliens. For my part—" Machin's chin lifted. He almost, but not quite, struck a pose. "Like most of us here, I believe that, far from being threatened by the Moldaug and having to look toward the Old Worlds for protection, here on the Frontier Planets we'd have no trouble with the aliens if only we just ignored them and the Old Worlds alike. Admittedly, the aliens are stronger than we are without Old Worlds backing. But that's the very source of our security. Our Planets, as Onweetok Murfa pointed out, are too weak to pose a threat to the Moldaug. They aren't, and never have been, really worried about us. Not so with the Old Worlds. Their very existence and power frighten the alien community. Which only needs to know, through some small political concession or gesture of appease-ment by the Tri-Worlds Council, that the Old Worlds respect the Moldaug military strength. Under these

circumstances, why not let sleeping aliens lie? I urge
this Assembly—"

Cully tapped Onweetok on the arm and whispered in
the other's ear. Onweetok stood up as Machin was still
talking.

"Will the member from Casimir III yield to a question?" said Onweetok.

Machin hesitated for a moment, then shrugged.

"Very well—I yield to a question only."

"Thank you, sir," said Onweetok gracefully. "Mr.
When will put the question for me."

He sat down swiftly as Cully rose and spoke before
either the Speaker or Machin could interrupt him.

"The question is," said Cully, "better for whom?
better for—"

The bang of the Speaker's gavel cut him short.

"Mr. When, you're out of order!" snapped the Speaker.

Onweetok was on his feet again. But it was Machin
who spoke first.

"No, no—" he said, his eyes narrowing. "Let Mr.
When tell me what he means."

"Do we understand, then," demanded the Speaker,
"that you're yielding not merely to Onweetok Murfa
but to Mr. When?"

"That's right," said Brian Machin. The small wrinkles
of tension around his eyes relaxed. He spoke calmly.
"Go ahead, Mr. When."

"It's simple enough," answered Cully. He felt the
skin over his cheekbones stretching tight. But he kept
his voice light, almost pleasantly curious. "I'm just won-
dering whether it's *all* the people of the Frontier you
believe would be better off if the Moldaug were left
alone. Or did you mean just some special group—for
example, some particular political group, like you and
your Brush-knife Boys?"

For a moment after Cully stopped speaking there was
a space of silence in the chamber. A space of silence so
complete and profound that it would have been easy to

believe that all the people in the room were holding their breath at once. Then Machin spoke again.

"*All* the people on the Frontier, of course, Mr. When," he said in a colorless voice and sat down again in his seat.

The Assembly began to breathe again as one man. Onweetok rose to his feet and proposed that the Assembly decision on Cully's proposal be laid over until the following day. This motion was placed before the assembled Members and agreed on without a dissenting vote. Another Member behind Onweetok proposed that the Assembly adjourn for the day. This also passed without argument, and the Assembly broke up. Onweetok said nothing until he and Cully were safely back in Cully's hotel room. Then the dapper Frontiersman threw himself down in a chair, cocked the heels of his boots up on Cully's bed, and sighed heavily.

"Well, Cully lad, you did it. I'm not going to ask you why you want to commit suicide. I'll just ask you why you didn't tell me ahead of time you were going to do it?"

"Would you have gone along with it if you'd known?" asked Cully.

Onweetok stared at him for a second.

"No, I don't guess I would have, Cully," he said at last, slowly. "All right, maybe you'd better tell me why you did it, after all. Why go out of your way to stick your neck under Machin's knife?"

"Because I'm going to need a solid, honest Assembly here on the Frontier for what I'm going to do," answered Cully. "And I can't have that while Machin's still on the benches. So I might as well get what psychological advantage I can by picking the fight myself."

Onweetok stared at him steadily for a long second, and then drew a deep breath.

"All right, Cully," he said. "What is it you're actually after—what with cleaning stables at the Assembly and prodding the Moldaug in a way that ought to make

them want to go to war? After all these years you ought
to be able to tell *me* at least. Can't you?"

Cully rubbed his nose thoughtfully.

"The people on the Old Worlds," he said, "haven't
got the right sort of training and experience to think in
interstellar and interracial terms. They think too much
in terms of Earth and the Solar System to be left in
command of the human race any longer. So, what I'm
going to do is take that command away from them."

Onweetok sat not moving in the chair, now, gazing
steadily at Cully. Cully returned his gaze without a
word.

"That's all?" Onweetok said at last ironically. "Just
that?"

"Just that," said Cully quietly.

Onweetok opened his mouth, but before he could say
whatever it was that was on his mind, a knock at the
hotel room door interrupted him.

He raised his eyebrows sardonically at Cully, swung
his boots down onto the floor with a thump, got to his
feet and walked over to the door. He opened it. There
was a murmur of voices from the hall. Onweetok stepped
out, closing the door behind him. A moment later he
came back into the room and sat down on the bed
opposite Cully.

"Well," Onweetok said, "it's 'Get off planet in your
ship by dawn tomorrow, or meet Machin with brush
knives outside of town in the morning,' That's the message. What kind of answer do I make for you?"

"Tell him brush knives suit me fine," said Cully.
"And tell him the time will be ten tomorrow morning,
outside of town on Hill Five, by the highway marker on
the road to Bonjoi."

Late that night, an instinct woke Cully to the fact
that somebody was in the room with him. Instinctively
he reached for the light stud at bedside. The deep
growl of Leestrom's voice from the darkness stopped
his hand.

"Cully," said Leestrom. "Let me fight him for you. He's just as much taller than me as he is you—but I've got weight you haven't got."

"Don't be a damn fool, Lee," said Cully. "It's me Machin wants to kill, not you. Even if he'd let you take my place tomorrow I'd have to fight him later anyway. Now, will you get out of here and let me get my sleep? I'm going to need it."

He dropped his head back on the pillow. After a long moment there was the quiet click of the door to his room closing. He slept.

11

Hill Number Five, on the road to Bonjoi Town—that same hill Cully had stopped to examine the day before— was a ten-to-twenty-degree slope slanting up some fifty yards from the road to the base of a vertical cliff of gray metamorphic rock. Over the years, the freezing and thawing of Kalestin's sudden springs and falls had flaked off much of the rock face, in shards and splinters of gray stone; and these, tumbling down the slope below, had finally covered most of that slope in loose rock fragments. Among these rock fragments a few small bushes struggled to survive. There had been trees on the slope also, but a forest fire within the last few years had reduced them to an occasional charred stump sticking up out of the stony rubble.

"Well," said Onweetok, "there'll be a nice clear view for all of us watching, though you might have picked a more level spot, Cully. Sure, there's a chance Machin might turn an ankle on that loose rock up there. But so might you; and if you were counting on him to stumble, I've got to tell you, Cully, that, big as he is, he's as sure on his feet as the rest of us."

The dapper Frontiersman and Cully had just arrived

by car at the foot of the slope. They pulled off the road
and got out of the vehicle. Cully was dressed in bush
shirt and brush pants with a borrowed brush knife in a
scabbard at his waist. He drew it now and hefted it. It
had been three years since he had handled one of these
tools, which also served on occasion as a murderous
weapon. But the weight and balance of it in his grip
woke old memories of reflex and muscle. The four-
pound weight of it swung easily in his hand. With its
slightly curved lower edge, it looked like something
between an outsized bowie knife and a fat scimitar.

"Here they come," said Onweetok behind him.

Cully turned about. Coming up the road from Kalestin
City was another car just like their own. In it, even at
this distance, Brian Machin could be distinguished because of his large bulk. Behind that car, at a polite
distance, came a small caravan of seven or eight other
cars.

"Oh," said Cully, "did you think to get us a few
friendly witnesses? It wouldn't be too good if you were
the only one here who could give an unbiased report of
this."

"Don't worry, Cully lad," replied Onweetok. "We've
gotten formal as all blazes about duels here nowadays.
The Speaker of the Assembly will be here, with at least
three semiofficial witnesses from Machin's party, and
the same number from mine. Then there'll be a few
important people out here just to see for themselves
how you do. You don't seem to realize what you laid on
the line by calling Machin. There're a lot of people in
Kalestin City who remember Cully When real well.
You're a hero, and Machin's a giant. And one of the two
of you has got to lose his badge by the time this day is
out." Onweetok grinned—not entirely happily.

The lead car containing Machin was almost up to
them now. It came on, passed by them, and parked
twenty yards up the road. The caravan of cars behind
followed and parked, filling in the space between Cully's car and Machin's.

"Any last-minute instructions you want to give me?" asked Onweetok. "I've got to go and talk to Machin's second now. If there's anything you want done about the arrangements, speak up. Machin had the choice of weapons, so the rest of the arrangements are all up to you."

"I know," said Cully absent-mindedly. He had been studying the slope. "Tell Machin's second, I'd like to start with the two of us about thirty feet apart, facing each other and halfway up the slope." He turned to look at Onweetok. "And if you have anything to do with picking the actual starting positions, try and find me a spot that will put two or three good stumps between me and him."

Onweetok went down along the line of cars. A few moments later, Cully saw him up on the slope with another man tying white cloths around two stumps that were approximately the distance apart Cully had specified.

This done, the two seconds split up and Onweetok came back down the slope to Cully.

Cully had already gotten rid of the scabbard to his brush knife, rolled up his sleeves and fastened them above the elbow, and stuffed the ends of his brush pants into the tops of his boots, lacing them down there securely. This was the extent of his preparations. Down at the far end of the line of cars, he could see Brian Machin going through roughly the same preparation. Only, Machin's shirt was off, and they were oiling his upper body and arms so that he would be hard to grip and hold if he and Cully came to close quarters. They finished by tying the man's blond hair back into a pigtail to keep it from getting into his eyes. Machin stood relaxed as they went through these preparations. With his huge, tanned chest gleaming in the sunlight, he seemed to loom over the smaller men surrounding him.

"Better take your shirt off too, Cully," said Onweetok, "and let me oil you up. No need making it easy for

Machin to grab hold of you with his free hand. If he does, he's got you."

"I don't plan to get that close to him," said Cully. He found himself taking a deep breath that was almost a yawn of tension. "Besides, that's part of his psychological warfare, getting us both stripped down, so he can show off how much bigger he is than I am. No point in playing it all his way."

Onweetok shrugged.

"It's up to you," he said. "Look out for the point of his knife. He likes to use that point instead of the edge. Knife and arm together, he's got a reach from the shoulder of over four feet, and he can lunge eight feet. So don't underestimate the distance he can reach you from."

Cully nodded.

The local sun was high enough above the horizon now so as to be in the eyes of neither duelist under normal circumstances. The sky was cloudless. The sunlight reflected from the stone rubble of the slope and warmed the air just above it, a warmth that was disturbed now and then by an occasional wandering breeze along the face of the slope. Such a breeze cooled Cully's face now for a moment, and he became aware of the tautness of the skin of that face. He did not need a mirror to know how his expression had lightened and become wolfish. That same wolfishness was echoed inside him—but mixed there also with a strange compound of other emotions.

There was the bleak loneliness he had always had inside him, now somehow deepened and added to by his feelings for Alia. There was regret—for what, he was not sure—and a sort of wistful longing for a world, or maybe a universe, that was set right to start out with and would not need so much fighting and effort and pain to correct it. All these sensations and feelings came to him more clearly than usual. He felt them like a pattern of thin, sharp wires pressing against the naked surface of his heart. He looked among the pattern for fear, and found that also, like a little nugget of cold metal among the other wires, but wrapped about by the counteracting heat of a dark, bitter joy in coming battle.

He looked up at the sun, bright in the east quarter of the cloudless sky, and the thought came irresistibly to him that it might well be that by the time that sun had moved just one hour's space higher in the sky, his eyes would be no longer able to see it there. But the chance did not shake him. He felt empty inside, but not unhappy or panicked; and all in one piece, ready to face what was coming.

Onweetok touched his elbow.

"Time to move up," said Onweetok. They mounted the slope together, the smaller rocks turning and sliding under their bootsoles until they came to one of the cloth-marked stumps. They stopped behind it, standing side by side. Across thirty feet of distance, Cully saw Brian Machin and his second standing waiting. Machin towered over his second, his massive chest broad in the sunlight coming over Cully's left shoulder and across the lower part of the slope. The bare brush knife in Machin's hand looked as small indeed, as Onweetok had said, as a butter knife. It was a flash of metal, like a scale model in the big fist.

Machin's second lifted his hand. Onweetok lifted his in response. He slapped Cully slightly on the shoulder.

"Luck!" Onweetok said and started down the slope alone. Thirty feet away, Machin's second had turned and was also going down toward the line of cars at the road and the waiting line of men watching there.

Cully looked back across the slope at Machin. Machin smiled at him, almost genially, and lifted his brush knife in something like a half-salute. Then he came forward, plowing across the loose rock of the slope between them.

Cully let him come to within about ten feet without moving. Then, with a bound, Cully went back and up the slope away at an angle from the larger man. Machin followed with a rush, but upslope Cully gained on him.

When he was about twenty or twenty-five feet above Machin, Cully switched and ran back across the slope toward the end from which Machin had originally started.

Reaching a charred tree stump some ten inches in diameter, with its jagged black end reaching about to the height of Cully's shoulders, Cully stopped and spun about. He saw Machin behind him coming fast, and now about thirty feet away. The big man's face was fixed in a grin showing bared teeth.

This time Cully stood his ground until Machin reached him. Cully saw the sudden flash of the other's brush knife in midair—the big man was, indeed, as quick as a cat. Cully flung up his own brush knife to ward the blow, ducking back behind the protection of the charred stump as he did so. The parry of his own blade, as he had planned, deflected Machin's brush knife into the stump, so that the edge sank deeply into the wood and stuck there. But for all that he had braced himself to receive the blow, Cully found his arm and shoulder numbed from it; and that numbness slowed him enough so that he was not able to take advantage, as he had hoped, of the second it would take Machin to wrench his brush knife free of the stump. Cully turned and ran again—this time downslope.

He heard the rattle and plunge of the big man's feet close behind him. Still, he gained again, and choosing a section of slope where there was nothing but loose rock, he cut abruptly at an angle back upslope again, ran a dozen steps, and then stopped, turning about.

A sound like a small landslide had already informed him that his sudden change of direction had been successful. Machin, with his greater weight and momentum, had not been able to change direction as quickly as Cully. In trying to do so, he had gone into a slide down the slope, on his back.

Instantly Cully was bounding down the slope, in the direction of the fallen man. But by the time Cully reached him, Machin had flipped over and was up on his knees. He flung up his brush knife to parry Cully's blow easily, and a second later he was on his feet—as powerful and dangerous as ever. Cully fled, once more upslope.

He heard Machin close behind him with the first few steps. However, as he reached higher on the slope, the sound of the big man's boots in the loose rock fell farther behind him. After some thirty steps or so, Cully risked turning about. He saw Machin a good dozen steps below him, sweat now pouring down his face and mingling with the oil on his arms and chest. The mechanical, bared-teeth grin was still on Machin's face, but as Cully watched he thought he saw something more than the mechanical come into it—something like a gleam of triumph.

Puzzled but wary, Cully wiped dry the sweat-soaked sponges of his eyebrows with a quick dash of the back of his left hand. He spun to his left to run along the upper part of the slope—and stopped in dismay.

He had maneuvered himself—or Machin had maneuvered him, it made no difference now—into a part of the upper slope where a boss, or buttress, of the cliff face projected down onto the slope itself. The ordinary cliff face and the projecting boss made an angle of stone within which Cully now found himself caught. His eyes darted rapidly right and left, looking for a way out, but Machin had already altered direction to take the center part of the angle, and there was little or no hope of breaking past him. As Cully hesitated he came on, and there was no longer any escape space. Cully was cornered.

Suddenly Machin loomed above him, twice life-sized, looking like an oily-skinned god come to life to crush ordinary mortals. Machin's brush knife glittered in an overhand cut and flashed downward. Cully parried and dodged in the same second, remembering to turn his own blade edge-on for the parry so that the flats of the two blades would not come together with the muscle-numbing shock that Cully had felt in parrying before.

As it was, the shock was bad enough. Still—Cully

managed to deflect Machin's blow. For a moment he was inside the big man's guard; and, quickly reversing his own brush knife, he struck upward with the handle at Machin's face. The end of the handle, projecting beyond his grip, cracked against Machin's jaw. For a second the other man was—not staggered, exactly—but made to hesitate. In that second, Cully ducked underneath the other's massive left arm and broke away into the freedom of the open slope.

He ran at top speed for fifteen or twenty paces along the slope before trusting himself to stop and look back. He saw Machin just now recovered and coming after him, but enough behind so that Cully could risk standing still for the period of a few precious breaths.

Surprised, Cully looked down. He saw blood streaking widely down the left side of his own chest. Somehow in that last exchange of blows Machin had cut him, if shallowly. Cully had not felt a thing. For that matter, he felt nothing now. He was only conscious of his heaving lungs and his racing heart, striving to replenish the oxygen his straining muscles had been using up so prodigally.

Staring at the approaching Machin, he saw the big man's chest heaving also. The cloth of his brush pants, above the belt that held them up, was stained dark with sweat that had run down off the oiled torso to soak into the fabric. Cully glanced quickly around him and behind him. Down the slope, a little distance to his left, were two stumps at least eight inches in diameter and no more than a foot and a half apart, too close together for Machin to come through them after him. Quickly, Cully turned and ran back and down the slope to stand behind the two stumps.

Machin turned and plunged after him, but then came to a sliding halt as he, too, saw that to get at Cully he would have to go around the stumps; and whichever way he chose to go around would give time and warning enough to let Cully dodge in the other direction.

"When! Listen—" panted Machin unexpectedly, "maybe we can talk this thing over—"

"There's nothing to talk over—" gasped Cully, "unless you want—to throw down your knife—and give up—"

"Well, maybe I—might do that—if we could work out a deal—"

Cully leaped suddenly, with the instinct of a dog who catches sight of a flung rock out of the corner of its eyes. There had been no time for conscious warning. But his muscles carried him reflexively back from the two stumps, just as Brian Machin's knife came licking between them. In midword of the talk designed to distract Cully's attention, Machin had lunged, as Onweetok had warned Cully he might do. The lunge had been so deadly swift that Cully could not even now remember seeing it happen. One moment it seemed that he was standing just behind the stumps, talking to Machin—and the next he had jumped back two feet, and the big man was extended full-length, his huge body stretched out, the enormous length of his right arm like an iron bar, reaching forward with the knife in its grasp, and some eight inches of the silver point and blade projecting past the spot where the skin of Cully's chest had been a fraction of a second before.

Cully recovered and leaped forward again immediately around the righthand stump, to try and catch Machin in his vulnerable extended position. But Machin had recovered also—and the best that Cully could do was to dodge past the other man and start his flight again across the face of the slope.

He led Machin first at long angle down the slope, waited for him behind the barrier of a bush-overgrown stump, then dodged about it to start back upslope once more. Twice more, Machin almost caught him. Each time there was a brief clash of knives. Cully was now bleeding from two more slashes—grazing slashes, to be sure—but nonetheless wounds which were draining the blood and strength from him. On the other hand,

Machin, although panting and sweating, was unmarked. In the process of wiping the sweat from his soggy eyebrows, Cully caught sight of the wrist watch on his left arm. Incredibly, the hand stood at a little more than a quarter to eleven. Three quarters of an hour had passed. To Cully it seemed as if less than five minutes had been used up since the moment in which Onweetok had left him alone to face Machin behind the other cloth-ringed stump.

With the understanding that an actual three quarters of an hour had passed, however, Cully became conscious of the fact that he was wearing out. His chest ached with the effort of heavy breathing, his eyes stung from the salt sweat in them, and the brush knife in his hand felt as heavy as a ten-pound hammer.

He was standing still as he became conscious of these things. He and Machin had paused together, something that they had done several times now, and more frequently lately. Some eighteen feet of loose stone separated Cully and Machin, where the big man leaned upon one of the charred stumps with his free left hand. Cully stared at him. The fixed grin was gone from Machin's face. Now he frankly panted as Cully panted. But aside from this, to Cully's sweat-blurred eyes, the other man looked as fresh as ever.

Nonetheless, there was now no more time in which to delay. Cully leaped from his resting place. This time he hurled himself at Machin, instead of away from him.

The attack took the big man by surprise. Machin's response was slow. He had time to get his brush knife up to ward off the swinging cut that Cully aimed at him as Cully ran past. But Machin slipped on the loose stone and went down on one knee.

He was up in a second and standing with his legs wide apart, staring at Cully, who had halted less than a dozen feet away.

"Come on, Machin!" croaked Cully.

Machin looked back at him and grinned hideously, and shook his head, not even wasting energy on breath.

The answer was plain. He would force Cully to come to him.

Cully felt a sudden wave of despair. He had counted on wearing down his larger opponent by chases up and down the hillside until Machin's greater strength should be counterbalanced by greater exhaustion. But he had underestimated the intelligence of the big man. Now he could refuse to go to Machin, but that would not win him the duel, either officially, or—more importantly—in the eyes of other Frontiersmen.

Above all, it was in the eyes of other Frontiersmen that he needed to win over Machin. Without that win, there would be no crew or supplies for his ship, and no going forward with his plan.

Once more Cully rushed his opponent. But this time Machin was braced and ready. There was a clash of steel that nearly sent the brush knife spinning from Cully's tired grasp, and then Cully was safely away. But now it was he who was tiring faster than Machin; while Machin, standing still, like a medieval citadel contemptuous of a besieging army, was fast getting back his wind and strength.

Twice more, Cully tried attacks. Each time he barely escaped. The last time left him panting and weak. He rested for a second a little to one side and up the hill from Machin, then charged at the other man once more.

This time his charge all but missed. When Machin's brush knife rang against Cully's own, it seemed to catch Cully in a moment of being off balance. Cully's legs tangled and he went tumbling, sliding down the loose rock of the hillside.

But even as he rolled and tumbled he heard the sound of Machin's heavy feet plunging after him, eager to finish him off, now that he was down and disorganized. Just below Cully was a small drop-off, a little eight-foot-high vertical fall interrupting the normal slope of the cliff. Arms and legs flailing, Cully went over its edge and Machin leaped after him.

But—and to the watchers on the road below it must have seemed like a kind of miracle—as Cully dropped off the edge of the little cliff his body abruptly straightened in midair, his feet gathered under him and he landed upright. In almost the same moment the huge body of Machin, following fast, came down on top of him.

They went flat together, and Cully felt the breath driven out of his body by the shock of the massive body that slammed him against the rocky hillside. For a full moment he was dazed, and then his senses swam back to him. He heaved at the dead weight above him, rolled it a little to one side, and struggled free to stand shakily upright as the men from the road below, headed by Onweetok, reached him.

"Are you all right, Cully lad?" cried Onweetok. "Where's your knife? Machin—" his voice checked suddenly, and caught in Onweetok's throat. He was staring down at the figure of Brian Machin, who lay still. Rammed clear through the flesh and bone of the big man's chest, up to its hilt, was Cully's brush knife. Machin grinned with unmoving eyes at the sky.

"Glory be!" whispered Onweetok, and raised his eyes to stare almost in unbelief at Cully. "You planned that, Cully?"

Cully nodded wearily. It had been his last chance. It had been a desperate chance—first that Machin would be lured to follow him down the slope at the sight of Cully ostensibly off his feet and falling out of control; second, that Cully, himself could roll off the cliff and still manage to get both his feet under him and his knife up in time to catch Machin unprepared, in the act of jumping down after him.

Somehow, it had worked. There lay Machin, dead. But for the moment the weight of it all—the deliberate slaughter of such an enemy—left Cully only weak and empty. He felt a wave of something like nausea pass through him. A man had died.

Cully was vaguely aware then that Onweetok had

caught hold of him and, with one of the other men from the road below, was supporting him, helping him back down to the car in which he had arrived. They reached it, and he sank into its seat cushions gratefully. Onweetok was climbing in beside him. A moment later the car rose softly on the air cushion of its underjets, turned as easily as a weathervane to a change in the wind, and headed lightly back down the winding road toward Kalestin City.

12

"It's been six weeks," said Onweetok, as he and Cully stood looking out a side window of the Refitting Terminal Building, looking down on the outfitting area from which the former *North Star* was due to lift. "Six weeks since your fight with Machin, and you've been fit as a fiddle since the first two of those at least. That makes four weeks you've been waiting around here, while matters between the Old Worlds and the aliens get tighter every day. What's keeping you, Cully? Something still missing from your ship and crew down there?"

"No," answered Cully, without turning his thoughtful gaze from the vessel in question.

It was the truth. The former spaceliner, now renamed the *Bei*, a Moldaug word meaning "Chariot," had been completely remodeled. Bulkheads had been torn out to increase the working space, at the expense of most of the passenger accommodations. In the remaining staterooms the furniture had been taken out and double bunks installed. Up in the nose of the vessel the officers' quarters had been cut down to add space for extra navigational and search equipment. Lastly, the outer hull had been pierced to mount lasers and heavy plasma weapons.

Similarly, the crew Cully wanted had been selected—and this had been the more difficult matter. After his victory over Machin, there had been no lack of applicants to ship with Cully. But he had wanted a particular sort of men, not merely adventurers or wild-brush outlaw types with an eye on possible Moldaug loot. He had wanted men who believed in the Frontier and its future—men like those who had joined him in the Frontier revolt six years ago. So he had picked carefully—choosing men like Pete Hyde, a lanky genius who was the Frontier's best Navigator, with a talent even surpassing Cully's own in that department. Leestrom was First Officer; and the rest aboard were the cream of a pool of experienced, hardened, level-headed men who knew both the wild Frontier and deep space, and were jacks-of-all-trades into the bargain. No, as far as the ship and crew were concerned, Cully could have left Kalestin two weeks before.

"As a matter of fact," said Cully, turning about to face Onweetok, "we lift at 4:37 A.M. tomorrow morning. But I'd have been happier if you'd got Emile Hasec alongside you with the other new men you've been recruiting into the Assembly, before we went."

"Emile! I've told you nothing would move the man! I've been on the phone to him every day—" Onweetok broke off. "Now, don't make fun of an old friend, Cully. It hasn't been the lack of Emile Hasec in the Assembly that's been delaying your lift-off!"

Cully laughed.

"No," he said. "The truth is we've been waiting so as to hit our target areas in Moldaug territory at a particular time. They've got a yearly festival on all their worlds—a sort of carnival time when all the usual laws and customs go out the window."

"So that's it!" Onweetok said. "They do that once a year, do they? Why, that's mighty near human of them. I never knew they did anything like that!"

"Nobody else but Will Jaimeson ever did either," Cully said. "But it's that we've been waiting for."

"You might have told me!" But the tone of Onweetok's protest was milder than the words indicated. "That Will's a real encyclopedia about the Moldaug, isn't he, now? Anything you need, you just have to ask him."

Cully smiled wryly.

"I wish it were that easy," he said. "Will may know several thousand times what any other human knows about the Moldaug, but he doesn't know one thousandth, probably, of what any Moldaug knows about his own race. For instance, Will's got only the roughest idea of how to find the worlds he visited himself, as a passenger in Moldaug ships. And so he can't tell me on which worlds their technological, military, or government centers are located. And those are things I have to know."

Onweetok frowned.

"Why, then," he said, "what can you do, going into alien territory blind?"

"We're going to a world he visited first, one that we can find," said Cully. "A planet named 'Heder T'ai.'" He smiled. "That translates, in case you're interested, into 'Heder's Grave.' From Heder's Grave on—well, we'll just have to keep our fingers crossed."

At 4:37 the next morning, Kalestin City time, they lifted the *Bei* off-planet. Eighty minutes later they were outside the atmosphere, and Cully's Navigator, Pete Hyde, had begun programing the first of the twenty shifts he had calculated were necessary to bring them to their target area.

These "shifts" were those translation processes which put into effect an alteration in the spaceship's mathematical position relative to the theoretical centerpoint of the galaxy. The practical effect was that immediately—in a theoretically timeless interval—the spaceship ceased to be at one position, and appeared again, in theory, at another, the position calculated for its destination.

In theory, there was no limit to the distance a spaceship could be moved this way. In practice, the calculations could not be made precise enough in a reasonable length of working time; and the greater the distance, the more difficult and time-consuming the calculation required to establish the destination point. Consequently—and most important—this resulted in a greater amount of probable error in the actual point of emergence of the ship after its shift.

Graphed, this error factor grew in a sharply rising curve. The result was that in any shift of over ten light-years of distance the error began to assume prohibitive proportions, and in any shift of over fifty light-years the probable error was greater than the shift distance itself.

So it was that the actual "shifts" of the *Bei*, as it headed into Moldaug territory, took no time at all; but twelve to fourteen hours in calculation time was required between each shift. First, their new position must be correctly recalculated after each shift. Then the business of figuring the next destination point could begin.

It was with long pauses, then, but with giant strides, that the little spaceship in the vast reaches of the universe approached its interstellar destination point. By the third day, however, they were well within the Moldaug special perimeter; well behind—Cully hoped—the Moldaug warships on watch along the border area with the Frontier. There was no hiding the flare of energy that they produced each time they shifted. This flare was undoubtedly showing up on the screens of any detector units of the aliens that were focused in their direction. But the Moldaug used the shift principle also; and the safety of the human ship lay in the fact that the Moldaug should have no reason to suspect that, this deep in their own territory, such flares were being made by any craft other than their own. The aliens would have to suspect that a human vessel was loose among their stars before they would be able to even begin making use of the information on their detector screens.

Ten days later, the *Bei* had reached the general area

of the solar system containing the world of Heder T'ai
under a GO-type star.

On conventional drive they crept in toward this, the
outer-most of the two alien-inhabited worlds in the
system, shielding themselves behind the disk of the
lesser of the two moons that circled it. Once in orbit
about the world, Cully put all controls on standby and
called all crew members into what was left of the ship's
lounge to brief them.

"All right," he said to them, "it's time to let you all in
on why we've come first to this particular planet. This
first expedition isn't going to be a raid on Moldaug
ships or even Moldaug surface installations. We're here
to raise a devil."

There was a mutter from the listening men—a mutter halfway between laughter and the sounds of surprise.

"I mean that, just the way it sounds," went on Cully.
"The idea is to get ourselves a name, a Moldaug demon
name. And the name we've decided to get is the name
of one of the Moldaug mythological characters, known
as the 'Rath i'Lan,' who rides a ship called the *Bei*. He's
a devil out of their superstitious past, and his name
means 'The Demon of Dark.' Like most Moldaug mythological characters, he's a tripartite demon. That is, while
there's only one actual demon, that one never moves or
acts without his two mortal Moldaug 'Brothers.' So
what we're going to do is go down to the place where
Moldaug legend says the original raising of the Rath
i'Lan took place, and re-enact the raising, making sure
the local Moldaug know about it. I'll be the Demon,
and Will and Doak will play my 'Brothers.' So it'll be
the three of us going down, plus five men to handle the
shuttle boat and help us fight our way back, if necessary. Who wants to volunteer?"

A number of hands went up; but the Navigator, Pete
Hyde, spoke up.

"Mind if I ask a question first, Cully?"

"Go ahead," said Cully.

"Do the Moldaug still believe in demons? First I heard of it," said Pete.

"No, Pete, of course they don't—any more than we do," answered Cully.

There was more laughter. Cully paused and ran his eyes over the group.

"No. The point is," Cully said good-humoredly, when they were quiet again, "that while you can't call us really superstitious any more, on the other hand, superstition isn't dead among us. Will tells me it's pretty much the same among the Moldaug. They don't believe in the Demon of Dark nowadays—not with the front of their heads anyway. On the other hand, there's enough superstition left in the back of their minds so that the fact of this demon's name being tied to us will trigger off all sorts of basic emotional responses when we start making trouble. Any objections or suggestions?"

There were none. Cully picked his five men, including Pete, who was eager to be a volunteer, and half an hour later the cargo hatch opened on the ship to let out the small, now crowded shuttle boat. It took off, circled the moon, and dropped toward the surface of the alien world below.

Cully had arranged it so that they descended on the night-time side of the planet below. They shut off their engines and glided in on stored power for the last ten-thousand feet of the descent, touching ground at last as lightly as a fly lighting on a pillow.

The area in which they had landed was a rugged one. It was mountainous country, in a spot where a tumbling express train of a mountain stream split around a spire of some dark rock and circled on each side of perhaps an acre of stone slope, before the two halves of the stream joined again to pitch further on down the mountainside.

All around them, even on the spire dominated little island that was made by the temporarily divided stream, was a wilderness of black rock—rock that here and there had been hollowed by past wind or water action into pitch-dark caves. It was into the largest of these caves, in the stony spire on the island itself, that the eight men proceeded to stow the shuttle boat, manhandling it through the musky but breathable atmosphere by sheer muscle power, while it hovered a couple of feet above the stony slope on stored power.

Once the shuttle boat was out of sight, they returned out under the welcome stars of the open sky and squatted on the island, while Cully sent up a balloon with a scanning unit attached by a thin wire to a vision screen at his feet. The balloon needed to rise some six-hundred feet before the view of its scanning unit would break clear of the surrounding rocky peaks. But when this happened it sent back down to the vision screen below a clear picture of two Moldaug family settlements in adjoining valleys—one five miles west of where they stood, and the other barely two miles to the northeast. The lights of the buildings in each settlement flickered through the misty night air like the will-o'-the wisps of spontaneous marsh-gas combustion back on Earth.

"There's our witnesses," said Cully, looking down and away at one set of lights. He turned to Leestrom. "Lee, how quickly do you figure they could get here once they start seeing and hearing things?"

Leestrom squinted at the screen.

"From the nearer one, I'd say maybe fifteen minutes," he said. "From the farther one maybe twenty-five minutes, maybe half an hour."

"All right, then," said Cully. He turned to Will. "Tell them the legend, will you, Will?"

Will got to his feet. In the faint light of the stars and the nearer moon, which was just beginning to show above the surrounding mountaintops, he seemed a slight, shadowy silhouette of a figure. His quiet voice came calmly to them. Once more he might have been speaking in a classroom.

"The legend that the Moldaug tell," he said, "is that from time immemorial there'd been a demon sleeping in the cliffs over there." He pointed toward the monolith. "All Moldaug knew the Demon was sleeping there, but none of them were foolish enough to wake him. Now, as some of you already know, where our human basic unit of population is the single indvidual, among the Moldaug it's never less than three of them working as a team. For this reason, the Demon would never wake up of his own accord, because he was harmless unless joined by the two other living parts that would make him a normal, full, tripartite 'individual,' in Moldaug terms."

Will paused, then went on.

"Let me say that again," he said. "The tripartite individual is 'normal' in Moldaug terms. But there are *abnormal* Moldaug, just as there are abnormal humans. Among the Moldaug these abnormals take the form of single persons who can't or won't fit into the basic, three-person, 'individual' unit. One type is the Moldaug whose particular work or study is one that no one else shares—so that he's forced to live and work alone. This type has the name which can be roughly translated by the human word 'Scholar.' Another type is one which is simply temperamentally unsuited to the three-person unit. The Moldaug name for this type translates literally as 'Solitary.' But, since the Moldaug can't imagine anyone but a deranged person being unable to fit into a three-person unit, the label on this latter type actually means something more like 'Madman.' Since the role that the Solitary plays in this legend is one that is only possible to a deranged person in Moldaug terms, let's use the title 'Madman.' "

Will paused and drew a deep breath. He glanced toward Doak. But Doak looked back, innocently and undisturbed.

"Now—to get back to the legend itself. The legend says that by sheer chance two of these abnormals happened to run into each other at this particular spot. One was a Scholar—and that's the role I'm going to play. The other was a Solitary, or Madman—that's Doak's part. The legend says these two started talking and, since night had fallen while they were still talking, they sat down, built a fire and ate supper. They talked on into the night; and they learned that each of them had a quality that complemented the other—the way that individuals fitted together in a normal Moldaug three-person unit. The Scholar had a knowledge of the semimagical techniques needed to raise the Demon slumbering in the cliffs behind them. The Madman had the courage—I mean he had the will or desire—to do the raising. So, driven by a warped version of the instinctive Moldaug desire to be part of a three-person 'individual' unit, the two of them joined forces and woke the Demon."

Will hesitated. There was an unusual solemnity in his voice when he went on. "Then things began to happen. A terrific thunderstorm burst about them. The Demon came forth and immediately joined them to complete the three-person 'individual' that was the full *Demon of Dark*. In other words, he became a full, effective Demon by becoming the dominant personality of the individual group also containing the Scholar and the Madman. They set out together then, according to the legend, to roam the lands and cities of the Moldaug, wherever these might be. And wherever they went, a Change in the Aspect of Respectability followed close behind them. And there you have it."

Will fell silent. Cully took over.

"So now you know," he said to the other men. "Now I'll tell you how we're going to work this. The Moldaug have pretty good scent-perceptive instruments. With those, they'll be able to reconstruct what happened outside our immediate area, here on this island. Here on the island we're going to burn some sulphur decontamination flares to foul up their instruments. But outside the island, across the stream there, Will and Doak are going to play out their parts in the legend. That, the sulphur flares, some flash markers for lightning, and a loudspeaker broadcast of thunder ought to take care of the stage dressing. So, while Will and Doak are busy across the stream, the rest of us'll haul the supplies out of the shuttle boat and set up here. Let's go."

They went to work. Looking up from placing the last of the sulphur flares in position to complete the ring surrounding the rest of them and the entrance to the cave holding the shuttle boat, Cully glanced across the stream and nodded to Doak and Will. Together, the two men rose from the small fire before which they had been seated and, leaving it burning, waded the small stream and came to join the others inside the ring of sulphur flares. When they were all inside, Cully switched on the loudspeaker system to play the recording of an explosive thunderstorm.

They waited inside the circle while the beat and roll of the thunder cannonaded around them, setting off occasional flash-flares to simulate lightning. At the end of ten minutes, Cully gave the word to light the flares. All of them picked up their equipment and retreated to the shuttle boat inside the cave.

There they waited. Leestrom had estimated that at least fifteen minutes would be required for the Moldaug from the nearest household to reach the spot. In actuality, it was almost thirty-five minutes, and the sulphur flares, with their volcanic reek of a planet's interior— associated with the idea of the nether regions in Moldaug as well as human religions—had almost burned themselves into extinction when the first lights appeared among the surrounding darkness and began to approach the spot.

The lights came not from the direction of the nearer Moldaug household, but from the farther. But before they had reached the place, lights from the other direction also began approaching. Cully waited until the first party of investigators were close enough to be visible in the illumination of their own lights, before he turned to Leestrom, who was sitting at the controls of the shuttle boat.

"Take her up!" he said.

He slammed the engine controls on full. With a roar

of displaced air the shuttle boat burst from the cave mouth. Theoretically, they should have gotten away clear. But evidently some of the approaching Moldaug had held weapons already trained on the cave mouth as a precaution. There was an explosion of small-arms fire—blended with the banging of a shattered hull, and a scream from one of the twin engines, followed by its silence. Already lost in the darkness of the night between the black ground and the star-filled space above, the little boat lurched and faltered, as Leestrom fell forward over the controls.

Cully threw the big man bodily out of the pilot's chair and dropped into it himself. His fingers flew over the controls, balancing out the effect of the one dead engine. As he did so a whistle of escaping air registered on his ears, and he checked the shuttle boat's steep climb leveling it off and then sending it diving back down into thicker atmosphere. At five thousand feet above the surface he leveled off and put the boat on automatic pilot, before turning back to investigate the damage.

Leestrom was unconscious from shock, with a slug from a missile weapon through the upper right side of his chest. No one else was hurt, though the number-two engine was effectively wrecked. But explosive shells from the hand weapons of the Moldaug had made unsealable holes in the hull of the unarmored shuttle boat.

Cully himself had ordered the taking out of emergency airsuits along with other supplies to make cargo space for the flares and other equipment along with the eight men who nearly filled the ten-place boat. Without those airsuits, and with a hull that would not hold atmosphere, their spaceship on the other side of this planet's second moon might well have been as far away as the Pleiades, for all the good it did them. The few hundred thousand miles of empty space between planet and moon barred them from it.

They were effectual prisoners on this Moldaug world.

And within hours the alarm would be out among the aliens for them.

"Will," said Cully, "I'm going to black out the outside of the ship and turn on the interior lights. Take a look at Lee, will you?"

13

"How is he?" asked Cully without looking around.

"He'll be all right, I think," answered Will. He and Doak were working over the unconscious Leestrom, who, stretched out, filled most of the aisle space in the shuttle boat.

"It's a nice clean wound," said Will, "straight through, high on the shoulder muscle. I don't think that was what knocked him out. He's been clipped on the head by one of the pieces of wall that flew around inside here when their explosive shells made holes in us. He's starting to come around now."

"Good," grunted Cully. He was back in the pilot's seat at the control of the shuttle boat. Under the direction of his fingers, the boat scanner was gradually unrolling a map of the world below them. "Come up here a second, Will, as soon as you can."

"I can come right now," answered the older man. "Pete's bandaging him." There was a rustle of movement behind Cully, and Will squeezed into the little space beside the pilot chair. "What is it?"

"Will," said Cully, "if we don't get off this planet inside of about six hours, the Moldaug will have it buttoned up so tight we won't have a chance to make it."

"Is that so?" replied Will calmly. In the little, hooded glow of lights from the instrument panel, his face was as serene and quiet as ever.

"That's right," said Cully. "Now, Will, this is the native world of the Demon of Dark. Aren't there other legends about him, elsewhere about this world, after he'd been wakened?"

"Quite a few," answered Will. "Why?"

"Because," said Cully, "we may need whatever help his legends can give us. I'd planned to land the shuttle boat for a minute in the middle of some good-sized community—throw a few colored smoke bombs just to confirm our Demon raising, and then head obviously off-planet to the *Bei* before the local military forces could catch us. But the holes in our hull wreck that plan. As I say, we've got six hours at the most, and we can't fix the shuttle boat in that length of time even if we had tools and materials. The only other way off-planet is by Moldaug spaceship. And the only two spaceports on this world are at Burath Chi and at Colau Ran. If we move fast before the alarm has a chance to spread, we might be able to spacelift a Moldaug ship before the Moldaug get experts and instruments up into the mountains who'll know for sure that it was humans that went through the Demon-raising ceremony, and before it occurs to them that we might need one of their spaceships to get away in. But it would help if we could kick up some kind of a diversion while we try to 'lift' the spaceship. Can you think of something the Demon might do to distract their attention?"

"Colau Ran . . ." murmured Will thoughtfully. "No, I'm wrong. It was Col Mar where the pestilence was the first sign of a changing Aspect to follow the Demon's appearance there."

"Never mind," said Cully. "It doesn't matter if it isn't the same city. What did he do, exactly, to bring the pestilence? And could we do it?"

"He appeared with the Madman and the Scholar, slaughtered a *Viinyii* . . ." The word produced by Will was more like a whinny than any other sound producible by a human throat. "That's a Moldaug meat animal, about the size of a small goat—and he laid the carcass on the steps of the main gate to the city. Come to think of it, you wouldn't be able to do that nowadays anyway. Moldaug cities don't have gates any more. The gates disappeared along with the walls around the cities, when they ceased to be a protection against modern weapons.

"Never mind—never mind—" said Cully almost to himself. His mind was buzzing in high gear, and he could feel the skin growing taut over his cheekbones. "A spaceport is a gate to a city nowadays. That'll do just fine. Now, what will we need besides the animal? You and I and Doak—will we have to dress up in any particular way?"

"Well . . ." Will hesitated. "Ordinary Moldaug robes—without clan insignia, of course—would help Doak and me if we had them. I guess we can just wear the clothes we've got on. But the Demon was supposed to be about eight feet tall and black with a large black fold of skin like a hood standing up behind his head."

"Oh? All right—I'll think about it," muttered Cully. "I want the Moldaug to realize we're humans just playing at being the Demon anyway. Meanwhile we'll see about getting one of those animals."

A moan from behind him interrupted Cully.

"That'll be Leestrom coming around now," said Cully with lopsided cheerfulness. "You're not dead yet, Lee. Now, Will, where do you suppose we could find one of those animals?"

Will stood for a moment, obviously thinking. Then he spoke.

"There's a folk song about a herder of such animals, and it talks about deep valleys between the mountains. I'd guess that we'd find that sort of animal roaming more or less freely in that kind of surroundings."

"Deep valley between mountains . . ." muttered Cully. "It sounds like the edge of a mountain range—like the range we're over right now, perhaps." His fingers danced over the controls before him and a relief map of the continent under them began to roll through the scanner. "The big cities are all on the coastal or interior plains," said Cully, half to himself. "If the grazing land is on the fringe of the mountain ranges, the best chance would be close to one of the large cities, where the main consumer market would be—but not too close, because there wouldn't be that much free land available under modern conditions."

He continued to study the relief map. Finally, with a tap of his finger he halted its motion.

"I think I've got it," he said. He rose from the pilot chair and turned around to go to Leestrom. He found the big man sitting up, propped against a sidewall of the shuttle boat and once more conscious. Cully knelt beside him.

"How're you feeling, Lee?" Cully asked. "Think you'd be up to a little high-speed foot movement, up to—about a hundred feet, if necessary, in about five-six hours from now?"

Leestrom grimaced.

"I'm all right. Pete shot me full of pain killer," he answered. "A hundred feet, you say? I ought to be able to make that easy. I'll take myself a little nap now just to make sure."

Leestrom closed his eyes. Cully got to his feet and turned to the rest of the men in the shuttle boat.

"We've got less than six hours, at my guess," he said to them. "So we're going into one of their larger cities—Colau Ran—and try to spacelift one of their ships. Will, Doak, and I will go into our Demon act to distract them, while the rest of you try to grab a ship. That's the schedule. Right now we're hunting for an animal we need in the act. Pete—?"

"Behind you," answered the voice of Pete Hyde. Cully turned about to face him.

"Pete, I think you're the best of us on the heat sensors," he said. "I want you to take over the scanner and start looking for a small animal the size and weight of a goat. I'm going to take over the controls and start piloting us low over some areas where we might find one."

It took them four hours to locate a herd of the native animals and capture one of them. It was an hour and a half later, just before local sunrise, with Pete at the controls, that the shuttle boat came drifting in just above the glistening surface under the lights of the Moldaug Spaceport at Colau Ran, until it passed the Terminal Building and approached the spaceships lying beyond it.

The shuttle boat by now was almost to the spaceship that Cully had chosen to spacelift. So far they had attracted little attention from the aliens working about the Spaceport. Cully had bet heavily on Will's assurance that Moldaug were less likely to be disturbed than humans at the sight of strangers and strange things—and so far that bet seemed to be paying off.

It was not, in fact, until the shuttle boat sank to the ground by the boarding ramp of the spaceship they had picked that the Moldaug nearby began to give it any real attention. Then, singly and in groups, they stopped their work and turned slowly to gaze at this unusual small vessel that had moved in among them.

They kept staring, but they did not move. Pete thumbed a button, and the shuttle-boat door swung open.

"Out of my way now," grunted Cully. He had blackened his face and hands with graphite and made himself a robe as well as a graphite-blackened hood from the fabric covering of one of the shuttle-boat seats. Now he picked up the pinioned native animal in his arms. It came up silently but heavily into his grasp.

Its weight was not light, but already the adrenalin of an emergency situation was flooding his veins. He felt at once furious and lightheaded to the point of drunkenness. With the beast in his arms, he leaped out onto the landing surface of the Spaceport, went quickly around the front end of the shuttle boat and headed for the Terminal. Out of the corners of his eyes he saw Will and Doak join him, one on either side of him. Together they started their brisk but steady walk across the landing pad toward the shuttered door of the Terminal, and the staring Moldaug who were standing motionless between them and it.

It was less than sixty yards to the shuttered door of the Terminal. Cully marched steadily forward with the motionless figure of the animal dragging heavily on his arms, with Will and Doak on either side of him. There was no sound but the sound of their bootfalls on the concretelike surface of the landing pad. The Moldaug remained motionless and silent, staring steadily, with what seemed to be completely expressionless faces. Inside Cully, it was as if a wire was being wound tighter and tighter. But he stalked forward with his head up, feeling the tautness of the skin over his cheekbones.

For the first time he was aware of a thick, oily smell rising from the close-curled, black hair thinly covering the creature he carried. His nose registered it with an acuteness that seemed many times normal—just as his ears heard, it seemed, with unusual acuteness, and his gaze surveyed the Moldaug faces and the scene around him with almost microscopic clarity of vision.

They were passing now within a few yards of some of the Moldaug standing silently about. The door was less than twenty feet away. Then, it was only ten feet away. It was just before them. They stopped, and Cully dropped the animal at the foot of the shutter. He drew his knife and hesitated.

"Cully—" prodded Will in an urgent undertone at his side. The knife trembled in Cully's hand—and then he caught sight of the animal's head. In that head the nearer eyelid was drawn back. The eye was staring and still. The creature was already dead, whether from shock

or from some damage it had sustained while it was
being captured.

Cully slashed his knife across the woolly, black neck,
picked up the carcass and threw it heavily against the
shutter. Blood so dark red that it was almost black,
splattered from the wound onto the shutter and the
landing pad.

"Now let's get out of here!" muttered Cully.

They wheeled about and began their march back in
the direction of the shuttle boat. The Moldaug about
them were still standing and staring. But now many of
them were staring past the three humans, at the butch-
ered four-legged corpse lying in front of the shuttered
door. Cully, Will and Doak walked on, briskly but
trying not to seem to hurry, three abreast. Fixed in
Cully's gaze was the shuttle boat and the flattened,
long, cigar shape of the spaceship extending above and
beyond it on both sides. Both seemed to dance with the
jar of every footfall in Cully's fixed vision. Nearer they
came, and nearer, with each step. They were almost
halfway back to the closest side of the shuttle boat now.
The silence was heavy behind them.

Suddenly a cry from a Moldaug throat, thin and
piping at first, but hoarsening and dropping in volume
as it progressed, tore the heavy, waiting silence. It was
echoed by another—and another—and all at once there
was a chorus of yells and voices all around and behind
the three humans.

"Keep walking!" Cully growled harshly to Will and
Doak. They continued. Then behind them Cully heard
the rapidly approaching sound of a single pair of running footsteps. He tensed, ready to turn, but Will
touched him lightly on one arm.

"No," said Will in a low voice looking straight ahead.
"Let Doak do it."

They kept on, steadily walking. The footsteps rushed
upon them from the rear. Abruptly Doak wheeled about
and disappeared from Cully's left side. Cully heard the
thud of bodies colliding, and an alien cry that was

choked off at its very beginning. Then silence. A moment later Doak was back beside him, putting his knife
back into its sheath at the belt around his narrow waist.
Behind them the alien voices continued to cry out, but
there was no further sound of feet rushing upon them.

They reached the shuttle boat and started around it.
Just as they turned around its nose, something whanged
and screeched off the hull beside them; and a burst of
hand-weapon discharges sounded from the direction of
the Terminal.

"Run! Now!" shouted Cully; and, rounding the bulk
of the shuttle boat they broke into a dash for the ladder
leading to the spaceship's sally port.

They swarmed up the ladder. Will first, Doak next
and Cully bringing up the rear. Will reached the top of
the ladder and scuttled into the sally port on hands and
knees. Doak followed, with Cully after him. As Cully
crawled in as rapidly as he could, he discovered Leestrom
and one of the other men lying prone on the floor on
each side, just inside the entrance of the sally port,
returning the aliens' fire.

Safely within, Cully spun about on his hands and
knees and dropped flat himself. From his position inside the open sally port, he could see that the landing
pad between them and the Terminal was now empty of
Moldaug except for a line of a dozen or so aliens, either
crouched or lying flat on the landing pad, and firing at
the open sally port with the discipline of policemen or
soldiers.

"Cease fire!" said Cully to Leestrom and the other
man. "Let's get this sally port closed!"

They all three scrambled backwards without rising,
until they were safely out of line with the sally-port
opening. Then Cully turned swiftly toward where the
sally-port controls would have been in a human vessel.
But the wall he faced was blank and a bare, gray,
vertical sheet of metal. But even as he whirled about to
search for controls elsewhere, the sally port began ponderously to close itself; and, looking across the space-

ship room in which he stood, he saw Pete standing beside a panel of controls ten feet on the other side of the sally port. Pete winked at Cully, and a second later the heavy port closed with a clash.

"Where's the Control Section?" snapped Cully.

"Up for'ard, just like ours," replied Pete. "Come on, follow me!"

He led Cully at a run out of the room, up a narrow, metal-walled corridor through a circular room obviously containing navigational and sensory instruments, and along a further, shorter corridor into a room shaped like a slice of bread, containing six pilot chairs and control consoles. A single Moldaug was tied up in a corner, lying on the floor.

Cully glanced at the alien even as he was heading for the three forward pilot chairs.

"How about others?" he threw at Pete.

"There were only five, and we've got them all," answered Pete. Cully was already sliding into the centermost of the pilot chairs.

"Get somebody else up here, and the two of you join me," he said. "It's going to be a three-man job to lift this ship, the way the Moldaug have their controls set up."

"Right!" said Pete, and left the room at a run.

Cully ran his eyes over the console before him. Here, at last, he was on familiar ground. Several years ago in his spacelifting days, he had once managed to obtain pictures of the control consoles of a captured Moldaug spaceship; and he had practiced on mockups of the alien consoles until he was almost as at home with these under his fingers as he was with the controls of a human spaceship. Now, running his eyes over the board, he had cause to be relieved that the Moldaug saw and heard in approximately human ranges of light and sound. For this console was evidently a somewhat more advanced model than the one he had studied. Some of the manual controls he remembered had been replaced by what were evidently automatics, cues to colored-light signals. From past experience, he knew that the customary warning range of alien light signals ranged from blue through green into yellow, just as the progression on a human board would run from red through yellow into white. Using this knowledge, he deduced that the ship needed only to be security-checked before lift-off. And the security check was simply a matter of an instrument test on the console before him—possibly a five-minute job. They could do that while lifting through the atmosphere—although it was against all common sense and space-going safety rules, alien or human.

At this point there was the sound of feet on the deck behind him. Pete shoved himself into the righthand pilot's seat, and Will dropped into the lefthand seat.

"All right, now," said Cully to them. "I'm going to call off the instruments in front of you in order. As I call each one, you press the button or turn the control below the instrument, and repeat to me what you see in the way of a color or a scale reading on the instrument dial. Got it?"

The other two nodded. Cully began the check-off. When he had completed security-checking the major elements of the spaceship, he began to lift the ship—first on the gravity-repulsor units that the aliens used instead of stored power, and then, as they gained altitude, he began to cut in the alien plasma engines, which were hardly different from the ones used by humans. He had barely completed this, when the whole ship suddenly shuddered and rang to a heavy blow somewhere in its stem. Yellow warning lights flared suddenly, lightning-bright on the alien board; and Cully slammed shut the switches sealing off an aft section of the vessel.

He reached out to activate the screen before him that would give him a telescopic picture of the Spaceport they had just left. Sure enough, standing alone out in the midst of the empty area of the landing pad was something that was clearly either a mobile fieldpiece, or a vehicle-mounted cannon. Cully shoved the plasma engines up a notch, and acceleration pinned them all back in their seats.

But no further shots reached the spaceship. Clearly, they had been almost out of range when the first shot had hit. Now they were almost out of the atmosphere, and shortly they would be safe from anything except another spaceship taking off right behind them. But the view of the Spaceport, dwindling as it was, showed no ship beginning to follow. They had gotten away safely.

Cully switched from plasma engines to conventional space drive. He sat back for a second with a sigh of relief, then turned to Will and Pete.

"That's all I'll need you two for, for the moment," he said. "But stick around. I'm going to swing around the planet and duck behind the moon where our own ship is. That much I can do myself. But once we're hidden behind the moon, I'm going to make a quick switch in and out of shift. And I'll need you for that."

From the pilot seat beside him, Pete frowned at him in perplexity.

"In and out of shift?" Pete echoed, frowning. "What's the good of that? We'd better signal our own ship to follow us and make a quick shift of at least a couple of light-years away from this solar system while we can."

Cully shook his head at the other man.

"Pete," he said, "you aren't thinking. Going in and out of shift will make an energy flare to give those Moldaug back there the notion we've done just what you said, and headed it for open space where we can lie low and they can't find us. But we'll still actually be here, waiting."

Pete still frowned.

"Think, Pete," Cully said. "What's the first thing those Moldaug back there are going to do? They're going to send a ship out. Not after us, because after recording a shift-flare behind this moon, they'll think we're lost in deep space where they'll never find us. But they'll want to send a ship immediately to carry word about us and what we've done to whatever world contains their government—to the Crown World of the Moldaug."

Pete's face lit up.

"I see!" he said. "You want us to wait and pounce on that ship the minute it clears their atmosphere down there? They won't be expecting a thing, and we'll have taken another alien ship!"

Cully shook his head.

"We didn't go to all this trouble of raising a demon just to capture Moldaug ships. We could do that just as well while being plain humans," he said. "We're going to tag along behind that courier ship they send, tracking it until it reaches their Crown World. I want to know where that world is. So it's up to you to navigate for me as you've never navigated before, so that the ship we're following doesn't suspect we're after it—until they're ready to land. *Then* we'll snap her up."

Pete nodded then, slowly. He turned and went.

Cully let him go. Pete had not stopped to ask what Cully intended to do after capturing a Moldaug ship under the very noses of the doubtless massive military defenses of the solar system containing the alien Crown World. And that was just as well.

14

"The trick," said Cully to his assembled officers, "isn't going to be just to take the ship we'll be following. It'll be to take her just short of her destination without alarming whatever space defenses the Moldaug have set up to guard their Crown World."

It had taken Cully just a little over three hours to make the swing around and out to the orbit of the second moon. When they had slipped behind it he lined his ship up so that the moon eclipsed the world from which they had taken off. He calculated a zero-change shift.

He continued to hold the ship there, hidden by the moon, for about thirty minutes more—or roughly the time he estimated it would have taken to calculate a shift to some short but safe distance outside the Moldaug solar system in which they were presently located. Then he slapped the shift buttons.

No single stir or motion of the vessel had betrayed what had happened. But the sudden jump of the needles on several dozen indicators, the changing of colors and markers to signal a vast drain of the ship's accumulated energy, told the story of the shift-flare—which would be recorded, like an invisible corona around and beyond the shielding disc of the moon by alien instruments on the planet below it.

Cully had then moved the captured Moldaug ship in over the spot on the dark side of the moon, where his own ship was hidden. Once above it, he had sent Doak, who was the only one of them who could fit into a Moldaug spacesuit, to open the sally port and display in that now airless entrance the three lights of red, green and blue which had been agreed upon as the recognition signal between the shuttle boat and the human-built spaceship.

Cully had waited for an answer. It was some few, hesitant moments in coming; but then the red, blue and green burnt among the imitation rocks of the camouflage cover hiding the spaceship below. Cully had put the captured Moldaug vessel down alongside his original ship, gone over to the *Bei*, and called his officers into conference there.

"What's the schedule, then?" asked Will, as he stood listening with Doak, a bandaged-up Leestrom and Pete Hyde.

"The schedule," said Cully, "is to follow without being suspected. Now, I'd guess that that courier ship should take off within the hour. That means we don't have time to switch some of our own search and navigational equipment—let alone any of our outside weapons—from the *Bei* to the Moldaug ship we've just spacelifted. So we'll have to do that work during calculation pauses, between shifts, as we tail that other ship to wherever it's headed. For now, Lee"—he looked over at Leestrom—"I want you to take over command of the *Bei*. Let your Second Officer run her until you're fit to handle her yourself. I'll take the new ship and half the men. Will and Doak better stick with me so that the Demon is all in one place in case of any emergency—and we'll crew the Moldaug ship until I've had time to train some of the men with me to use those alien-control consoles."

Cully looked around the faces of the rest of the men in the room.

"Any objections or suggestions?" he asked. There was a waiting silence from the rest.

"Then we'll get busy," he said. "Let's break it up."

Cully went through the *Bei*, selecting the men he wanted. Then he led them across the connecting tube that had been established between the hatches of the two vessels.

As soon as the division of personnel had been made, the connecting tube was dismantled and the hatches closed. A limited shortwave hookup—good for no more than fifty miles, so that it could not be snooped upon by alien receivers—was set up between the two vessels. Cully also took time out to change the actual name on the outside of the Moldaug vessel from *Char O Nei*, or "Brotherly Love," to *Nansh Rakh*, or "Vengeance." He ordered both ships to move out clear of the moon in order to observe, with their sensory instruments, the lifting of the next Moldaug vessel to leave the planet.

They did not have long to wait. Within half an hour after they had taken observing stations, their instruments showed a ship lifting from Colau Ran. It moved up and out from the planet, and they followed at a discreet distance of four thousand miles. They followed, keeping the *Bei* and the *Nansh Rakh* no more than half a mile apart, so that if they were spotted by the aliens' instruments, they would show up on his screens not as two blips, but one.

However, the other ship gave no sign of knowing it was being followed. It moved out a safe planetary diameter from its world, and disappeared in the flare of invisible energy that signaled it had made a shift.

On board the *Bei*, Pete Hyde had been watching and ready on the instruments covering the large-scan cube. This was a cube-shaped vision screen, a globe of interstellar space some three thousand light-years in diameter.

In this cube, because of the vast area it covered, little registered except the hot stars themselves and the flares of ships going into shift. It was a black, three-dimensional space filled with the steady glow of the larger stars and the momentary, winking flares of ships in shift. Within that cube the ship from Colau Ran would have immediately been lost, if Pete had not known, first, the point of its departure, and second, the fact that its initial shift would in all probability be less than five light years distant. He had therefore established perimeters of five light-years in global radius from the ship's departure point. Within this space it was unlikely that any other ship would be coming out of shift—appearing at its destination point—at just the same particular moment of the Colau Ran ship. As a result, when the flare flickered in the area under observation, some three and a half light-years from where the ship had disappeared, Pete immediately took a fix on it. Within twenty minutes the two ships under Cully's command—the *Bei* and the *Nansh Rakh*—followed the vessel from Colau Ran. They shifted to within a light-year of the other vessel's position, close, but still far enough behind it not to excite the suspicions of the alien vessel. Then in the anonymity of deep space, they waited for the other ship to finish calculating for its second shift.

While they waited, the *Bei* and the *Nansh Rakh* drew close together until they lay side by side, with less than twenty yards between their hulls. Crews of men from both vessels went to work transferring some of the outside armaments from the *Bei* to the *Nansh Rakh*.

They had only completed transferring two of the eight weapons to be shifted, when the ship they were following flared into her second shift. Once again, however, Pete Hyde was on watch. He observed the flare-in of their quarry just under five light-years distant from them.

The *Bei* and the *Nansh Rakh* separated to a minimum safe distance and shifted through in pursuit, coming out, once more, a half light-year behind the ship from

Colau Ran. Again the two pursuing ships were brought
within a twenty-yard distance, and work crews swarmed
over the outside of both their hulls. This time the work
went more quickly. They were one-third finished with
their task by the time the ship they were chasing shifted
again.

Two more shifts, and the work of transferring equipment and weapons was completed. The *Nansh Rakh*
was now armed and instrumented to be operated by
humans untrained in alien controls. She was, of course,
far too lightly armed to stand up to any orthodox Moldaug
military spaceship, such as the one they were following.
On the other hand, her obvious Moldaug design should
allow her to get close enough to the ship they followed,
when the time came, so that she could knock out most
of its weapons before its crew realized that they were
under attack. This ability to get close before being
recognized was an ability the *Bei* with its obviously
human design did not have.

At the next shift, Cully transferred ships to talk to
Pete Hyde at his post among the sensory equipment on
the *Bei*.

"What does it look like?" Cully asked as he came into
the Communications Room. "Have you got any line on
where their ultimate destination might be?"

Pete unhooked the single earphone connected to his
instruments that was feeding him energy and distance
readings on the alien ships.

"It's a sixty-five percent or better chance," Pete answered, "that they're heading for N–1520—that's a
twelve body solar system revolving around an AO star
about forty-three light-years away from our present position." He looked up at Cully, smiling a little out of his
lean face with one corner of his mouth. "Let me wait a
couple more shifts, and I can tell you for sure."

"We can't wait any longer," said Cully. "If we're
going to get there ahead of that ship from Colau Ran,
we've got to start picking up distance on them with
each shift from now on."

"You want to start getting ahead of them now, do you?" said Pete.

"I want us to be sure we're there when they get to their destination area," said Cully. "Our best chance to take that ship is going to be when it's reached that area and thinks it's home safe. They're not likely to come out of their last shift any closer to that solar system than five times the system's diameter, are they?"

Pete frowned.

"Well, I'll say this," he said. "*I* wouldn't come out of shift any closer to a solar system than that before making my last corrective shift. And, judging by the way this ship we're chasing has been traveling so far, those alien navigators are a lot more cautious than I am. You realize, if we end up lying in wait for them, we'll be taking a statistical chance—small, but there—that they'll come out right on top of us?"

"I know," said Cully. "But everything we do boils down to the fact that we're willing to take just a little bit bigger chance than the next man—or Moldaug. I'm counting on you, Pete, to outnavigate them."

"Well, that's what I'll have to be doing," replied Pete. "If I'm going to calculate bigger jumps for us, we're going to have a bigger chance of error every time we jump—you better just hope it balances out."

"I trust you, Pete," said Cully. "You'll balance it out somehow."

"Thanks," Pete grimaced. "Thanks for the faith, partner."

Cully left the *Bei* and went back to the *Nansh Rakh*. During the next eight shifts, while Pete gradually lengthened their jumps until they were coming out ahead of the alien vessel from Colau Ran, Cully trained two men on the alien sensory and navigational instruments on the *Nansh Rakh*. Also, on that same ship he drilled himself at the control console, with Will in the chair at his right and Doak in the chair at his left. The Moldaug ships were set up for three control pilots rather than one, and Cully wanted to be sure that he, Will, and

Doak would be able to operate, easily and naturally—as a demon unit—any Moldaug ship they might have to take over.

By the time Pete came through, the two human-crewed ships were one shift from the outskirts of System N–1520, and were a good half shift ahead of the vessel from Colau Ran. Cully called Pete Hyde to come over and take charge of the Instrument Room on board the *Nansh Rakh*.

"Tell me, Pete," Cully said, when the other man showed up in the Control Room of the *Nansh Rakh*, "what can we expect that ship from Colau Ran to do when it comes out of shift? And how long will it take to do it?"

Pete rubbed his long nose thoughtfully.

"Well," he answered, "unless something's gone badly wrong, that Navigator of theirs should bring their ship out within ten or twelve light-days of the star system here. He's more careful than I'd be. Then he'll take his time—maybe an hour or two—calculating a short shift to within half a dozen system diameters of N–1520. From there on, he'll either calculate a very small shift—taking maybe ten or fifteen minutes to do it—and shift right into the neighborhood of the planet he's headed for; or he'll make a shorter shift into the outskirts of the Solar System and go on from there in conventional drive. Either way, the time for us to hit him is during his longer calculating period, several light-days away from this star system."

"Fine," said Cully. "Then I'll leave it up to you, Pete. Calculate a shift for us to about where you think that other ship will be coming out of shift—at however many light-days distant you guess it'll be. We'll move both our ships to that point. Then I'll want you to keep monitoring until the courier ship flares-in; and as soon as it does, calculate a quick shift to right on top of it, for the *Nansh Rakh* alone. The *Bei* can follow a few minutes later. I want to approach that alien ship with the *Nansh Rakh* first, so she doesn't suspect anything. With any luck at all, we ought to be able to get close enough to knock out most of her weapons before she suspects we're out to hit her. Got it?"

"Got it," replied Pete, and went off toward the Instrument Room.

Pete turned out to be an accurate prophet. The ship from Colau Ran behaved almost as if its pilot had been reading Pete's mind. It flared-in just six and a half days away from N–1520. Less than a light-day from the point at which the *Bei* and the *Nansh Rakh* shifted, and suddenly the alien vessel was visible to the close-in sensory instruments aboard the *Nansh Rakh*. These reported it as being no more than a hundred and fifty miles away.

The flaring-in of another vessel so close to its own position could not have passed without notice aboard the ship from Colau Ran. But apparently it assumed that this close encounter was merely a chance meeting with another Moldaug ship bound for N–1520. For the alien vessel showed no signs of alarm. Meanwhile, in the Instrument Room, Pete was calculating furiously.

Three minutes and twenty seconds after they had emerged close to the alien vessel, the intercom in front of Cully crackled with Pete's voice.

"Ready—" said Pete, and reeled off a string of figures, which Cully's, Will's, and Doak's flashing fingers fed into the consoles before them. They shifted. Suddenly the other ship was clear and huge on the viewing screen in front of Cully—no more than half a mile away. Now, for the first time, the ship from Colau Ran buzzed and sparkled to the instruments of Cully's ship with the radiations of noise and mechanical activity that signaled surprise.

Still, the other ship evidently hesitated to broadcast an alarm. Coincidence might bring another ship to flare-in within a few hundred miles of it—although this was almost too close for comfort. But that another such vessel should immediately shift even closer—to what amounted almost to hull contact—strained coincidence to the breaking point. The weapons mounted outside the other ship's hull began to swing about in precautionary aim at Cully's vessel.

But aboard the *Nansh Rakh* their weapons were already manned and aimed. Lasers reached out within the pale, narrow fingers of the beams from their sighting searchlights. They touched and melted the external transmitter units mounted on the alien hull, then flared on the alien weapons.

The other ship rolled to bring its far-side weapons to bear, but once more the lasers aboard the *Nansh Rakh* were ready, and knocked them out before they could do more than score two faint, grazing cuts in the *Nansh Rakh's* outer hull.

The cuts were small enough to seal themselves automatically, the semifluid material between the inner and outer hulls forcing itself into the melted gaps where the lasers had touched, and hardening, upon the exposure to airless space, into a glass-smooth bond with the melted metal edges of the damaged hull.

"Close, and board!" snapped Cully into his ship's intercom.

The *Nansh Rakh* swung in against the alien vessel until the two hulls rang together and clung on magnetic lock. The *Nansh Rakh*, under Cully's controlling fingers, rolled and slid about her enemy's hull until the two cargo hatches were approximately facing each other. The cargo hatch of the *Nansh Rakh* was opened inward, men in spacesuits sprayed sealer into the openings at the points of contact of the hulls of the two ships, and the sealer hardened immediately so that air could be pumped back in to the Cargo Room. A shaped charge blew open the cargo hatch of the other vessel, and the spacesuited crew of the *Nansh Rakh* swarmed through the breach with hand weapons to take the other vessel prisoner.

The spacesuits had been worn on Cully's order, in case the Moldaug ship should have thought to open its sally port and catch the attackers in airlessness. But they turned out to be unnecessary—as the hand weapons carried by the boarders were almost as unnecessary. Only three among the aliens showed fight—one of the three trios of officers found in the other ship's Control Room. These three were armed. They shot one of the boarders, and were gunned down in return, two of them being killed outright and the other suffering a burn on his gunarm that made him drop his weapon. He had, however, recovered his composure by the time the vessel was subdued and Cully came into its Control Room with Doak and Will.

It was to the surviving member of this trio that Cully addressed himself, in Moldaug, politely using the "individual" second-person pronoun, in spite of the fact that the other's two "Brothers" were no longer alive.

"If yourself will be quiet and do not struggle any more, there will be no need for any of yourselves further to be hurt."

The Moldaug addressed, and the other Moldaug in the Control Room, froze at hearing themselves spoken to in their own tongue. Slowly, they all turned to stare at Cully. After a second, the one to whom Cully had spoken spoke in reply.

"What—who art thou [single person]?" the Moldaug officer demanded.

"Myself [Collective individual] am the Demon of Dark. Beside me [single person] you see the Scholar, and across the room, there, holding that one [single person, unknown] so that that one will struggle no more, is the Madman."

Cully stopped speaking. The Moldaug officer, still staring at him, stood silent and motionless. The silence stretched out . . .

"What is it? Is he registering any emotion?" Cully asked Will in English. "I can't tell from his face. Can you?"

"I don't think he's showing any emotion," answered Will, also in the human tongue. "But I think he's feeling it. I think he's deliberately hiding his feelings as much as he can."

"Art thou not aware that thou, and yourselves [general group of individuals present, or multiple tripartite individuals] all are soft-faced aliens? The Demon of Dark was never a [collective] soft-faced alien!" said the officer.

"How dost thou know?" retorted Cully in Moldaug. "Dost thou know all the faces of the Demon? Did yourself [collective individual] know, before thy Brothers died, just now? Art thou one [single person, known] to authoritatively proclaim that the Demon comes not in what shape himself choose? Reflect thou that this time is one in which there are soft faces; and consider how in soft face may the Demon perhaps forecast what comes to we and ye [all Moldaug—the total race]."

Once again there was a long pause, and then the Moldaug officer burst into speech.

"Myself-that-was before my Brothers' deaths, and I, am not so lacking in Respectability of insight to argue nonsense. Therefore I-myself and ourselves [all Moldaug present] ignore such talk. Myself-that-was and ourselves [all present] make the customary offer. Ourselves will suicide, thereby relieving yourselves of all blood-feud obligation by the families of ourselves, if yourselves will only deliver, in custom, to the families of ourselves, the bodies of ourselves, on the world of Heder T'ai—"

"There is no need," interrupted Cully. "Myself contemplates nothing not-Respectable. For a little while yourselves will be prisoners of ourselves. Then yourselves shall have a small ship with which to return to Heder T'ai, being released within that ship, in space, not far from that world."

The Moldaug officer hesitated.

"All . . ." he spoke slowly, "of ourselves?"

"Respectably, yes," said Cully. He turned to speak to Pete Hyde in English. "How many prisoners have we got?"

"We took twenty-three on this ship," said Pete.

"Myself promise yourselves," said Cully, turning back

to the Moldaug officer, "all twenty-three of yourselves from this ship, together with some of yourselves captured in another of the spaceships of yourselves, will be put in the small boat and returned to your people—"

Cully did not finish. He was interrupted suddenly by a unanimous, whistling gasp from all of the Moldaug in the room. The eyes of the officer in front of him seemed to go back and back in his bony skull, and without warning he launched himself at Cully.

The Moldaug sprang, not as a human would spring, but bounding up into the air and kicking his legs out forward to wind them around Cully's waist. Sheer instinct made Cully strike out. He felt the knuckles of his right fist jar against alien shin and bone. Then the Moldaug pilot was lying still at Cully's feet—as motionless as his two dead partners.

Something between a grunt and a growl arose from the other Moldaug. They leaped forward, and were grappled by Pete Hyde and the other men in the room. Will was already kneeling beside the Moldaug Cully had hit.

He raised his head almost immediately, and spoke rapidly in Moldaug to the others around the room.

"He is not dead—no, he is unconscious only!" shouted Will to the struggling Moldaug, all fighting now in the grips of the humans holding them, trying to get to Cully. "Respectably, ourselves have punished without killing him, so that now yourselves know ourselves are the Demon. Therefore, yourselves should be quiet, as yourselves claim Respectable manners!"

The Moldaug on the floor was beginning to stir and twitch as consciousness returned to him. The other Moldaug slowly ceased their struggling.

One of them spoke.

"Myself does not in Respectability agree that yourself is the Demon of Dark," he said to Will. "But ourselves are not without Respect. Our First Cousin moves, and so shows now that he lives—therefore, ourselves admit misunderstanding. The Respectability of ourselves is under complaint of yourself."

Cully looked at Will.

"You might be interested to know," Will said in English, "that you've just substantiated the Demon of Dark story about you. You see, the Demon was supposed to be able to slay with a touch. Also, that officer expected to be killed—it was the price of the protest that Respectability demands of him. These others here were sure you'd killed him."

"I don't understand," said Cully. "Didn't they see that I hit him, not just touched him?"

"They saw it," answered Will, smiling. "But they didn't understand or believe it. If you'll take a look at the way a Moldaug's shoulder is hinged, you'll see that it's impossible for them to strike a straightforward blow, the way we can when we punch. There's no shoulder bracing in the Moldaug skeleton to anchor the blow, so that the arm can be stiffened with the weight of the body behind it. Even if a Moldaug could make himself try to punch in a straight line, he'd be more likely to pop his shoulder joint out of its socket when he hits, than do any damage to what he was hitting."

"I see." Cully frowned down at the pilot at his feet, who was now beginning to sit up and look wonderingly around him. "But what made him jump me?"

Will's smile vanished.

"I'm afraid his reaction was something I should have warned you about," he replied. "Remember I told you how much more complicated inheritance within the family is among the Moldaug than it is among us? The law of succession is very strict, and requires that proof of the elder's death be provided before inheritance can take place—which in almost every case means you've got to produce his actual corpse before you can take over his position. That's why these others offered to suicide, and why it's more important to this alien you hit that his body get back to his family than that he himself live. Unfortunately—and I should have thought of it myself—when you and Pete automatically only counted the living Moldaug in figuring the number you were sending home, you implied to him that you weren't sending back the two bodies of his Brothers. Worse than that"—Will grimaced—"part of the Demon legend is that, like most of the evil supernatural characters in the Moldaug pantheon, the Demon eats his victims. Consequently, this officer you were talking to jumped to the conclusion that you were going to play the Demon to the extent of keeping his Brothers' bodies so that you could eat them."

Will paused. Cully nodded.

"I see," he said. "I can imagine what he felt like if he thought that."

"Actually," said Will, "I don't believe you can. The idea of eating a Moldaug body is even worse to them than it is to us—since the concept's not only horrible but totally not-Respectable, since you're not ouly destroying bodies but a line of succession—which can mean destroying the family, that controls the sept, that controls the clan; so that in theory you can bring disaster upon thousands or even hundreds of thousands of people."

The Moldaug pilot that Cully had knocked out had now regained his senses and got himself back on his feet. Wobbly as he was, he would have attacked Cully again—except that Will got between them and began talking urgently to the alien in a persuasive voice. Slowly the Moldaug allowed himself to be calmed, and Will stopped talking. The Moldaug stepped back and looked at Cully.

"Respectably, I am under complaint of yourself," he said.

"It is very Respectable of thee to so admit," answered Cully. "I will consider the debit discharged if thou will only give me the pleasure of being made knowledgeable about thy family, sept, and clan."

He nodded toward the door.

"But for now," he said, "yourselves will be taken to

the quarters of yourselves, aboard this vessel, to rest and recover." He turned to Pete.

"Lock them up in their quarters, Pete," he said in English, "and then come back here."

Pete took them out. He came back to find Will and Cully in earnest conversation, with Doak standing silently and patiently by.

"What now?" Pete asked Cully.

"Now," answered Cully, "I'm going to question that Moldaug about his home and relations. Once I learn all about him I can claim to be a friend of his family, sept and clan when we go down onto the fifth world of this system."

"Fifth world? Go down?" Pete stared.

"The fifth world in this system is the Crown World of the Moldaug, Pete," explained Will. "I knew it was the fifth world of some system, but I didn't know which one until we followed that ship here from Heder T'ai."

"So that's Crown World?" said Pete. "But you say we're going *down* on it—like we did on Heder T'ai? Won't the Crown World be guarded a lot more—"

"It is," interrupted Cully. He smiled. "But stay cool, Pete. This is a job for people who can speak Moldaug. So you aren't going down, neither you nor any of the other men. Just Will and myself—with Doak to stay in the shuttle boat and hold it ready for a quick take-off. This was why I held off leaving Kalestin until I did. We've arrived at the Crown World just when I wanted to—at the Time of All-Respectable. It's a sort of Moldaug Mardi Gras, when all the rules are relaxed and just about anything goes. Will and I can speak Moldaug; and at All-Respectable Time, as long as we keep inside the relaxed carnival rules, even humans like us ought to be able to wander around free down there—as long as they don't yet know we're playing Demon of Dark."

"But what good's it going to do for just the three of you to wander around down there?" Pete protested. "Just three of you alone can't do anything!"

"We can find out things—such as where the Moldaug

Military Center is. Or where the palace of the Royal Family is located on this Crown World," said Cully, smiling. "In short, we can get answers to all those other questions I might have asked a Moldaug like that officer—and a lot more he'd never have answered even if he'd been able to."

15

"Just how safe are we?" asked Cully bluntly, once he and Will were alone and afoot at the Spaceport of the capital city on the Crown World of the Moldaug. They had left Doak behind, keeping the shuttle boat of the captured Moldaug ship on ready for instant take-off, and were now crossing the small-boat parking area toward the Spaceport taxi line-up.

"Not safe at all, really," admitted Will.

"I thought so," said Cully.

It had been entirely too easy so far. The captured ship turned out to have maps of the Crown World by which they could locate the capital city and its Space-port. The three of them had entered the planetary atmosphere quite openly in the shuttle boat; and in reply to a routine challenge by the Moldaug equivalent of a spaceport traffic controller, Will had answered quite truthfully that they were three soft faces, last from Heder T'ai, friends of—and he had named the surviving Chief Officer of the courier ship they had captured—who were coming in to see the capital city during All-Respectable Time.

At a spaceport on one of the Old Worlds or one of the

Frontier Worlds, under the present tense human-alien conditions, this would hardly have been enough to satisfy the landing authorities. But, as Will had explained, the concept of absolute responsibility which invested the Moldaug Leaders—as long as they remained leaders of the race—was matched by a concept of absolute trust on the part of the Moldaug who were led. The very fact that three soft faces were here, in the very heart of the Moldaug territory, was enough to prove that they had a right to be here. Just within the border line of the Moldaug frontier, the shuttle boat would probably have been melted on sight.

But there was a difference. The Moldaug on the Frontier were under orders to keep soft faces out. The Moldaug at the capital-city Spaceport were not.

Cully and Will were now almost to the edge of the parking area. Now they could see the line of automated alien taxis clearly—looking eerily like a column of old-fashioned, horsedrawn coaches out of the human past, but lacking both horses and wheels and floating a few inches above the ground on repulsor units.

"We'll grab one of those," said Cully thoughtfully. "It ought to be programed to take us automatically to any destination we can name. About being safe—even if this is a time of carnival and general license, it'll be for a special kind of Moldaug carnival and license, isn't that it?"

"That's it," agreed Will. "To the Moldaug themselves, it's a time of complete relaxation of the rules. But, really, this only means relaxation from the conscious rules. The unconscious commandments of their culture and society still operate on them. If we violate one of those unconscious commandments, if we step across the line somewhere, we may find ourselves in trouble. And if we get into trouble, we may be held until the Time of All-Respectable ends. Then we will, indeed, be in very deep trouble."

They had reached the line of automated taxi vehicles. Cully opened the door of the first one—and checked instinctively, his hand jumping to the small gun he had tucked underneath his belt, below the Moldaug robe which he, like Will, had borrowed from the captured ship's officers.

Something small and dark had bolted out the door on the opposite side of the cab, to the tune of a high-pitched chittering. Cully lunged after it, and saw what seemed to be a small Moldaug running down the line to the next cab and pulling its door open. From this second cab spilled another small Moldaug, also chittering; and by the time those two stood together, another was joining them from the third cab in line.

"What is it?" Cully whispered to Will, who had now joined him in peering out of the other door of the cab.

"It seems to be three young sisters," whispered back Will. "They each hid in one of the cabs to startle whoever came along to use one of them. The fact that we're human and there're only two of us, seems to have startled our particular girl more than she expected to startle us."

"What's that noise they're making?" Cully asked. "I've never heard that kind of sound from a Moldaug before."

Will chuckled.

"They're laughing—perhaps, considering their age and sex, you might say giggling," he answered.

The three young Moldaug females, having discussed the matter, now somewhat hesitantly approached in a group up to the door of the taxi where Will and Cully were looking out. There was another small burst of Moldaug laughter, and then the tallest of them hesitantly spoke to Cully.

"Are the two Very Respectables really soft faces?" she asked. The termination of her question was punctuated by another burst of nervous laughter.

"Myself is indeed," replied Cully.

The laughter greeting this announcement was almost a storm. The three young Moldaug females consulted excitedly among themselves.

"That one person said 'myself!' " exclaimed one of the

two smaller females. They whispered together for a moment, and then the tallest one addressed Cully once more.

"Yourself—" she began. A burst of giggling by her two companions interrupted her. She quieted them with a look and went on—"has a costume for All-Respectable Time made up like that of the Demon of Dark? Was that really the intent of yourself?"

"It was the intent of myself," answered Cully. "And this person with me—also a soft face, as you see—is dressed to be the Scholar."

More laughter from the three young Moldaug was followed by another whispered consultation.

"Would yourself be kind enough to tell ourself what you are going to do this evening of the All-Respectable?" asked the tallest of the three.

"Ourself are out to see the city of yourselves," said Cully, "and all the Respectable things associated with it."

Once more there was consultation among the three.

"Yourself is a soft face and consequently cannot know properly," said the tallest. "Has yourself never been told that the Demon is Three, like all Oneselves, whether Respectable or not?"

"Indeed, myself knew that," answered Cully, smiling a little in spite of himself, "but yourself sees that there are only two soft faces; therefore we could not very well be three."

There was a new burst of discussion among the three young females. Then with a sudden and completely unexpected bound, the tallest of them leaped onto the entrance step of the door out of which Cully and Will were looking, so that they were forced to duck back.

"My sisters agree!" she crowed. "I will be thy Madman, so that yourself will at last be a true Demon!"

Without waiting for an answer, she crowded into the taxi, closed the door behind her and leaned out its window to shout reassurances to the other two young Moldaug, who shouted back, laughed and waved at them continuously as she turned and set the taxi in motion out of its line of similar vehicles and sliding silently away down the street on its repulsor units.

"Thou," said the young Moldaug, glancing sideways at Cully, with another half-smothered giggle, "must always call me Madman, or else there will not be a true ourself."

"Very well, Madman," agreed Cully.

"And thee must remember that I am afraid of nothing, as befits a Madman!"

"I will be glad to keep that in mind," said Cully gravely. "Will thou mind if I explain the situation to the Scholar here, in our native soft-faced language? For, though he speaks thy tongue even more Respectably than I do, still we understand each other best in our own language."

"I would not mind at all," said Madman. "It would be interesting to me to hear thee speak in soft-face language."

"Thank you," said Cully in Moldaug. He turned to Will, beside him—for, now that Madman was at the controls of the cab, Cully was in the middle, and Will was pushed over against the far wall.

"What are we going to do about this, do you suppose?" said Cully in English, to Will. "I was hoping to get hold of an adult—someone who would know the things we need to find out. Now we're stuck with this girl. You don't suppose there's any possibility of her knowing anything worthwhile?"

"I'll have to admit I didn't think of it before," answered Will softly and also in English, "but there's no reason she shouldn't know the location of things like the Royal Family Compound as well as a fully adult Moldaug—and it might be we stand less danger of violating one of the unconscious taboos with her. She evidently thinks of it as some kind of prank, this business of leaving her sisters. She'd never do it at any time but this, when theoretically all actions are Respectable, going off with a couple of strangers. Besides, you no-

ticed that she has a bit of awe about us because we're
aliens; and maybe also because we're fully adult and
she's not, and she's been trained to respect the decisions of older members in her culture. So she may
assume that we know what we're doing even when we
don't—which would help."

"All right, then," said Cully, sitting back in the coach.
"We'll let her be our guide instead of hunting for someone else." He did not add an extra, personal objection
which had occurred to him against the using of this
young female.

According to the original plans he had made with
Will, they had hoped to pick up another Solitary to
round out their three-person unit. One advantage of
using another Solitary would have been that, in case of
necessity, they would be freer from discovery if they
had to kill to hide their own tracks, or facilitate their
own escape once more off-planet back to their waiting
ships. But Cully had taken it for granted that the Solitary would be an adult male Moldaug. Now the thought
of possibly having to kill Madman to cover up their
tracks was not so easy.

He put the thought of that possibility out of his mind.
Turning to Madman, be spoke to her once more in
Moldaug.

"My Brother and I are happy to have thee as one of
us," he said. "From now on we will try to talk only in
the Respectable language, and not use our soft-face
tongue, except when there is no other way."

"I do not mind," Madman assured him seriously.
"After all, ourself is all a Demon now and ready to do
all sorts of terrible, not-very-Respectable things. What
are we going to do?"

"Well," answered Cully, "suppose we search about
the city for a place to leave some portent or sign that
the Demon has been here?"

Madman literally shook. She did not shiver as a human might. Instead, she actually, and violently, shook
all over, like a dog coming out of water.

"Thou are right!" she cried. "Ourself cannot be a Demon without leaving a portent someplace! Where shall ourself leave it?"

"Thou knows the city and all the lands about here better than I, or Scholar, here," said Cully. "What about leaving a portent at the place where the great military spaceships of ye Moldaug are kept?"

"No. That is no use," said Madman decisively. "Here, in Crown City, we have no warships except for a few couriers at the Spaceport that come and go carrying messages. It is on the tenth world of this system where the great fleet lies. And I cannot go off-planet without permission from my family."

They were away from the Spaceport now, moving down what seemed to be a large, six-lane boulevard, interspersed with ground vegetation and local trees, looking something like poplars in full leaf. Now it was obvious what had replaced the artificial lighting of the city; for, every twenty or thirty yards there were enormous flaring torches, burning in clusters of threes, on top of thick posts about a dozen feet tall. The total effect was that of enormous, triple-flamed candles lighting the streets and boulevard.

"Where are we now?" asked Will.

"We are on the Imperial Parkway, of course," Madman said. "From here we can go anywhere. Now we must decide where to leave our portent—oh, wait!"

They had just come level with a small series of what looked like shops, lit from within by one or more of the triple flares.

Madman jerked the taxi to a halt. Without any further word, she ducked out the door on her side of the vehicle, ran around it and into one of the shops.

"What's she up to now?" demanded Cully of Will in English.

The older man shook his head in the flickeringly lit, dim interior of the taxi.

"I don't have any idea," he said.

But a minute or two later, Madman came running

back out of the shop, bounced into the taxi, and started it up again.

"Now," she said, triumphantly, "I am a *real* Madman. See?"

Cully looked at her. For a moment he did not see what she was talking about. Then he saw that something like a paste-on strip of paper had been added to the collar of her gown, elevating it and changing its shape. The temporary adjustment in her dress designated Madman now as male and Solitary. Cully caught the glint of something about her waist, and, looking down, saw a belt around her gown with a black scabbard, from which the bulbous hilt of something like a toy sword protruded.

"I see," he said. Without giving himself time to hesitate any longer, he went on. "While thou were inside, our Brother—the Scholar—and I decided that the place to leave the portent of ourselves would be at the Imperial Family Compound."

Madman stared at him for a moment. Then she squealed and began to shake once more in that violent fashion she had demonstrated earlier. There were a few seconds before she seemed to gain enough control of herself to speak.

"Oh, terrible! Oh, wonderful! Wait until I tell my Sisters about thy idea and this doing of ourself!" she cried. "Ourself will be a real Demon! Ourself will lay a portent at the very gates of the Very Most Respectable! Thou are marvelous soft faces, both of thee!"

Madman edged the taxi into the lefthand lane of roadstrip down which they were moving. At the first crossover that appeared, she swung them left, over a lane where traffic was moving at a slightly higher speed. They were now in the inmost lane of the three parallel traffic strips moving through the parklike area. Out among the trees and vegetation of the parklike strips, the large candlelike triple flares were burning, casting wild and flickering shadows upon this world's equivalent of grass and leaves and branches. Here and there, in the light of the flares, there were Moldaug to be seen, nearly all of them in groups of three, or multiples of threes, walking or running about from torchlit area to torchlit area. Occasionally, a group of them would be seen with joined hands in a circle, all running around either a particular bush or tree, or around one of the triple-flare torches itself. Gazing at them, Cully was suddenly struck by the fact that each circle consisted of neither more nor less than nine individuals, their hands linked together and in constant movement.

"What's that? Some kind of dance, I suppose?" Cully asked Madman.

She turned to stare at him suddenly. Abruptly, Cully had the sinking intuitive feeling that he had unknowingly violated one of the unconscious taboos that were in existence in spite of the apparent license and freedom of All-Respectable Time.

"I . . . don't understand?" faltered Madman. "Dance?" She turned to look from him out into the park areas, where a group of nine were circling around one of the flares less than fifty feet away. Suddenly understanding seemed to come to her.

She burst abruptly into the high chittering which was the first sound Cully had heard from her, back from the line of parked taxis, and which Will had identified as the sound of Moldaug laughter. But this particular bout was more prolonged than any she had engaged in so far, and she turned her head away from him.

"Have I made some mistake—" Cully was beginning hurriedly, when she interrupted him in a muffled voice.

"No mistake—" She went off into a new fit of laughter. "Thou know!"

"Know? Know what?" asked Cully.

But she went off into a new fit of laughter, hiding her head from him and refusing to answer. Hastily, Cully sought for some means of changing the subject.

"How far is it now to the Imperial Family Compound?" he asked. "Will it take us much longer to get there?"

"Not—not far." Madman got herself under control again and sobered. "Ourself should be there in—" The figure she gave in Moldaug time units automatically translated itself in Cully's head into the equivalent of about four minutes. "What kind of portent are ourself going to leave?"

"Myself will decide that," answered Cully, "after I have had a look at the Imperial Compound and have a chance to come to a decision."

He already had, in fact, a pretty fair idea of how the grounds and buildings within the Imperial Compound should be laid out. This was because, although Will had never seen the Compound, himself, there were illustrations of how an Imperial Compound theoretically should look, in several of the Moldaug books Will had studied during his years among the aliens. The trouble was, however, that the illustration showed theoretical rather than actual plans. This was because the Imperial Compound was continually being rebuilt by different Moldaug and in different places. Whenever the Aspect of Respectability changed and a new clan emerged as the ruling clan over all the Moldaug, the home world of that clan became the Crown World, and a new Imperial Family Compound was built on their world to house the new Imperial Family. The Compound that was built always agreed in principle with the theoretical plans for such an establishment, but according to what Will had picked up by way of information, there were always individual differences, depending upon terrain, clan prejudices, or even personal preferences of individuals among the ruling family.

Madman seemed content with Cully's answer. Accordingly, they drove on. The Parkway continued as usual—the only difference that Cully could see was that the groups of Moldaug disporting themselves in the park began to thin out, until very shortly there were none of them to be seen at all—though the same number of torches continued to burn in the midst of the silent alien grass and trees.

Now he became aware, through the front window of the taxicab, of something that looked like a string of lights up ahead of them. They drew closer swiftly, and the string of lights revealed themselves to be what seemed like an unending line of triple flares burning in midair from as far to the left to as far to the right as the eye could see in the night darkness. When they got closer, Cully saw the reason for the flares apparently being poised in midair. They were mounted upon a black wall, perhaps twenty feet in height, which barred the Parkway, unbroken before them except at a large gate in which two enormous gate doors stood ajar. Though the gate doors were not fully opened, the gap between them was still a good forty feet. Madman drove up to the gate opening, where the Parkway's strips of traffic road came together in a sort of small circle of paving, and stopped the taxi.

The circle and the gate itself seemed completely deserted. Looking through the gate, Cully could see the flickering lights of torches within the Compound.

"What does ourself do now?" whispered Madman, almost in his ear.

"Forgive me for a moment," answered Cully, "while I speak to my Brother in our own tongue."

He turned to Will.

"What do you think's going on here?" he asked Will. "Nobody around, and the place wide open like this. This can't be natural."

"Things aren't natural during the carnival of All-Respectable," replied the older man. "But I agree with you. This seems to be going almost too far—leaving the gates to the Compound open, and no one on guard. But it's probably more ritual than real. There must be some guards in there somewhere. Not to protect against enemies— When No Change of Aspect is underway, enemies in the Royal Compound are unthinkable—but to protect against any dangerous Solitary, or abnormal Moldaug."

"Well!" whispered Madman impatiently in Cully's

ear, "what is ourself going to do? Shall ourself put the
Demon sign on one of the gateposts there?"

Cully turned back to her and spoke in Moldaug.

"No," he said deliberately. "I think we'll go inside—"

A choked sound from Madman interrupted him. She
had frozen suddenly. She looked at him now in obvious
terror.

"Oh-oh," said Will quietly in English, "that may have
done it!"

16

"Why," said Cully in Moldaug, forcing his voice to calmness and still looking at Madman as if he had not heard Will speak at all, "what is the matter with thee? There is not one person on guard there at the gates."

A tremendous shiver shook Madman.

"But *It* is there!" she quavered. "Thou cannot see It, because It is invisible. But It is on guard there—as It always is during the Time of All-Respectable, when the guards have gone off to join in the celebrating."

"It? What do you mean—It?" demanded Cully.

"It, of course! The Royal—" The Moldaug word Madman used was one that Cully had never heard before, but it was not hard to guess that it meant something like "dragon" or "monster." He felt the night air, suddenly cool on his face. Will had been right—they had stumbled across one of the deep unconscious taboos from which All-Respectable Time gave no exemption. For a moment their whole situation here trembled upon the situation of the moment. If Madman suddenly took fright and tried to run away from them and give the alarm, Cully would have no choice but to stop her. And his mind shied again from the thought that stop-

182

ping her might mean killing her. His leaping mind, hunting a solution, stumbled suddenly upon an inspiration.

"That old story!" he said scornfully, in Moldaug. "Thou do not believe in that old fairy tale, do you?"

For a moment he did not know if he had hit the right note or not. But then, slowly, he saw the tension begin to leak out of Madman. As the tension left her, she shrank up, almost huddled on the seat, until she looked very small indeed.

"Well, I do not like it anyway!" she said at last in a stifled defensive voice. "Thou is a soft face and maybe is not afraid of—" She used the strange word again. "But I do not like . . ."

Cully's mind had been buzzing at high speed. It was no time to take any more chances in frightening Madman. He spoke quickly.

"That is all right," he said. "I will tell thee what I will do. Thou and my Brother will wait out here to warn me if any guards come back. I will go through the gate, one person, alone."

Madman uncoiled somewhat from her huddle and stared at him with wonder and awe-filled eyes. Without waiting for any further reaction from her, he reached past her, opened the door and slipped out of the taxi.

Over his shoulder, he spoke in English to Will.

"Keep her with you," he said to Will. "Whatever you do, don't let her give the alarm. I won't be gone more than five minutes. I just want to get a rough idea of how the grounds are laid out."

Without waiting for an answer, he turned and ran swiftly but quietly toward the left gatepost. When he reached it he paused, peering around it into the dark interior of the Compound, which seemed to stretch for acres, dotted here and there by the flickering lights that apprised him of the fact that within the walls it formed a shallow basin or hollow. Luck was with him. Being near the outer rim of that hollow, he was in a position to look down on most of the buildings within the Compound—and by the lights of the torches surrounding those buildings he would be able to make out their general pattern.

For a moment more he hesitated, looking right and left inside the gate to make sure that there were no guards hidden there, after all. But he saw nothing and no one.

He slipped around the gatepost into the darkness behind the wall.

Suddenly, it was as if he had stepped into darker night. The wall he had just passed was very thick, thick enough so that from this angle right beneath it on the inner side, he was cut off from the light of even the torches on top of it. The brightness of the circle outside the gates was suddenly lost to him.

He waited a few seconds for his eyes to adjust. Then he began cautiously to move inward into the Compound, away from the gate and the wall. As he went, his eyes adjusted further to the darkness, until by the light of the one moon overhead—that moonlight which had been obscured by the flaring light of the torches closer to the ground—he was able to look down on the pattern of buildings within the Compound, and even dimly make out the slope and tumble of the land between them.

The hollow was not a perfect hollow. Within its general bowl shape it had little softened hills and valleys, and running through these the moonlight reflected whitely on footpaths between the clusters of torches that marked the outline of the various buildings.

Having moved in perhaps a hundred yards from the gate, Cully stood still, looking down at the interior of the Compound and trying to reconcile what he saw with the patterns Will had drawn for him from Will's memory of the illustrations of the theoretical Compound layout. For a number of minutes it seemed he made no sense at all out of what he saw. Then, gradually, he identified one large, rectangular, torchbordered area as the Main House—which would be the residence of the three Royal Brothers that made up that tripartite "individual" who was ruler over the Royal Family, which was in turn chieftain of the Royal Sept, which ruled the Royal Clan.

From this, suddenly, the whole Compound fell into order. He picked out the building that would be the residence of the Royal Wives, the Cousins' Quarters— and finally, that smaller building not too far from the Main House, which would be the nursery, or building housing the Heritors to the Moldaug Throne.

Quickly he turned and headed back toward the gate— rather, toward the gap of brightness that he recognized to be the gate. Now that he was turned about with his back to the darkness of the inner Compound, Cully saw, a short distance off from him, the roadway running in through the gate. He cut left, and a few seconds later felt the earth and vegetation under his feet change to a hard surface. Looking ahead, only about thirty yards through the gate, he saw the taxi vehicle waiting. He was even able to make out within its forward window, two shapes, which must be Will and Madman.

The sight of Madman suddenly reminded him. It had been no excuse, but a natural part of his plan, to leave a sign of the Demon somewhere on this Crown World; and here within the Royal Compound was as good or better than any other place for it to be found.

He checked. Reaching inside his robe, he closed his fingers around the small pressurized paint-spray can he had brought with him. Taking it out, he turned and sprayed upon the roadway what was the Moldaug conventional sign for the Demon—a sort of stylized representation of the spire of the cave and the two streams of the mountainous spot from which the Demon had theoretically and originally been raised. The result looked something like the symbol:

$$\text{Å}$$

Then he turned and sprinted for the taxi.

He jerked open the door and threw himself inside. Madman was huddled up against Will at the far edge of

the seat. Cully paid no immediate attention to her.
Instead, he grasped the control rod of the taxi vehicle
and set it in motion. He spun it about and headed it
back down the Parkway road up which it had come.

Cully was concentrating completely on his driving—
and making the best speed possible, without traveling
at such a rate that they would be conspicuous. As a
result, for the moment his mind was off his two companions; and it came as a distinct jolt when Will spoke
to him abruptly, if quietly, in English.

"I think we've got trouble, Cully," Will said quietly.
"Look here."

Cully flicked his eyes away from the road for a second
to look at Will and Madman. The young female Moldaug
was curled almost into a ball and pressed tight against
Will. It was not necessary to be an expert on the
Moldaug to see that her posture was no normal one,
her stillness was not a normal stillness, and her silence
was clearly not natural.

"What's—" Cully asked, keeping his own voice calm
and bringing his eyes back to the road, "the matter, do
you think?"

"I don't know what caused it, except that she saw you
spray that sign on the pavement." Will's voice came
quietly back. "But this time I know for certain we've
stepped over the taboo line someplace. She's obviously
frightened to death."

"That's all right," said Cully. "Just as long as she
doesn't make a fuss. When we reach the Spaceport
we'll put her out before we board the shuttle boat.
Sooner or later somebody will come along and find her,
and then they'll take care of her. I don't mind if they
find out we've been here after we've gone—just so long
as we can get off-planet safely and back to our own
ship."

"All right," said Will quietly. "I'll keep my fingers
crossed."

They sped back down to the Parkway, through the
city and back to the lights of the Spaceport that drew

them through the city's torchlit streets like a glowing false dawn on the far horizon, where its artificial light beat against the black sky. When they reached the taxi ranks, no one was in sight; and, on impulse, Cully simply turned the vehicle and drove it right out among the parked shuttle boats toward their own.

All this time there had been no movement and no sound from Madman. Her eyes continued to stay fixed upon Cully's—at least Cully found them so fixed whenever he risked a glance at her. But it was impossible to read from her alien features exactly what was in her mind, or what had caused this frozen state of attention with which she now regarded him.

Cully pulled the taxi vehicle up alongside the entry port of the sally boat and stopped. He reached across Madman and Will to open the door on their side.

"Take her out, Will," he said. "I'll follow. Then we'll just leave her here while we board the shuttle. With luck she'll just stay as she is until someone finds her."

Will pulled the unresisting Madman, who went with him out onto the level, hard surface of the shuttle-boat parking lot. But when Cully followed she shrank even further away from him.

"Thou need not worry," said Cully to her, as gently in Moldaug as he could. "Ourself have frightened thee somehow. But ourself meant thee no harm. Ourself will go now."

He turned toward the shuttle boat, and in that moment the shuttle-boat entry port swung open and Doak stepped out.

At the sight of him, Madman began to scream.

Her screaming began as a low keening noise that mounted and mounted. There was no time to lose, nor any other choice to be made.

"Quick!" shouted Cully, picking her up. "Into the shuttle boat with her. Doak, get ready to lift!"

Madman came up in his arms as lightly as a bundle of twigs, as Cully snatched her up. With two long strides he was in through the entry port and had set her down

on the passenger seats behind the three pilot seats of
the shuttle boat. Behind him the door of the shuttle
boat slammed shut; but within the confines, the metal
walls, of the shuttle boat Madman's scream continued
to bounce and rise until it rang deafeningly about them.
Cully dropped on the couch beside her and took both of
her light fragile-feeling, clawlike hands in his own in an
instinctive effort to calm her.

"Take her up, Doak!" he snapped, over his shoulder—
and a second later the shuttle boat lurched into the air,
pinning both Madman and himself together against the
back of the passenger seat.

With the sudden movement, her screams broke off in
mid-volume. For a second she was simply still, and
then she began to uncoil from the ball shape into which
she had compressed herself all the way back from the
Royal Compound. She straightened up, and she drew
her hands out of Cully's grasp.

She looked at him with eyes that were almost lumi-
nous. Then she turned deliberately to look at the backs
of Will and of Doak, who were sitting side by side in
two of the three control chairs. Then her eyes came
back to Cully.

"Yourself are Three," she said in a strangely quiet
voice. "Yourself were Three from the start, and yourself
went through the gate. Not even the Royal"—again the
unknown Moldaug word—"stopped you. Yourself went
through, and yourself came back, and yourself left the
mark of the Demon for all to see."

"Thou must not worry," said Cully gently. "We are
only soft faces, and it was only a joke at All-Respectable
Time. We will put thee in the care of thy own people,
and themselves will see that you are brought safely
back to thy Family and thy Sisters."

She turned away from him, so that he could see only
her narrow back and inhumanly narrow Moldaug shoulders in the dimness of the shuttle-boat interior.

"No," she said in the same still voice, "the Demon
makes himself into whatever likeness himself wishes—

even that of soft faces pretending to be himself. Yourself are the Demon of Dark, and I am no longer Respectable."

Cully looked at her and tried to think of something to say in Moldaug that would comfort her. But he could think of nothing.

He looked back up front at the backs of Will and Doak, and past them at the instruments. All was going well. The shuttle boat was climbing steadily away from the planet below. They were essentially safe now, and would be safe certainly, beyond doubt, within half an hour. Beside him he heard something like a small choking sound from Madman, and her body leaned back against him.

He did not look at her, nor move, grateful that she had at least resigned herself to physical contact with him again. Perhaps, he thought, she had broken through the frozen barrier of her shock and would start to be better from now on. In any case, she would be all right once he had turned her over to the captured officers of the Moldaug ship. Once among her own kind, she would begin to recover. It could not be otherwise, seeing how young she was.

The shuttle boat bored on upward into airless space. Thirty-five minutes later it swung around the curve of the moon and made contact with the captured Moldaug ship waiting there. A port opened in the ship's side, and the shuttle boat slipped in. The port closed behind it.

"Ourselves are here now," said Cully, turning to Madman.

She did not answer. But as he turned he moved his shoulder, and her body fell backward across his knees. It was then he saw that the bulbous handle of the little tinsel sword gleamed among her robes above her narrow chest. It had been driven deeply into her. She was dead.

For a moment Cully sat simply staring down at her, unable to credit what he saw. Then Will's voice saying something to him roused him out of his stuper. He looked up to see Will looking down at the body of Madman.

"I'll take her body to her people anyhow," Cully heard himself say.

He picked up the frail body and carried it out of the shuttle boat through the inner airlock of the shuttle-boat module and on through the corridors of the ship until he came to the rooms where two of the men stood guard outside the door to the quarters in which the Moldaug officers had been placed under lock and key.

Cully spoke to the men on guard. They unlocked the door and opened it. Cully, followed by Will and Doak, and still carrying the body of Madman in his arms, walked into the quarters of the Moldaug officers.

These had been sitting or lying about the large lounge room of their quarters in various positions as Cully entered. But at the sight of what he carried, they all came to their feet.

"What is this yourselves have brought to ourselves?" demanded the Senior Moldaug Officer, gazing at Madman's body in Cully's arms.

"Tell them, Will," said Cully in English. Will told them—as briefly and as kindly as possible.

"And now," said Cully in Moldaug, when Will had finished, and there was no sound in reply from the Moldaug officers, "myself is going to put this one person's body back in storage compartment Number One so that it will be together with the Respectable bodies of the Brothers of yourselves, who were killed when ourselves took this ship from yourselves. Myself wished you to know what this one person had done, in Respectability, so that yourselves would be sure to see that this body is returned from Heder T'ai when yourselves and the bodies of the Brothers of yourselves are released near that world."

"It is good that yourself told ourselves this," replied the Senior Moldaug Officer, "for now I must demand that yourself not put the body of that one in with the

Respectable bodies of the dead Brothers of Myself-that-was. The body of that one must be put in the other preservation compartment; but ourselves will see that it is returned to its family, though only because that one did suicide."

Cully stared at the Moldaug officer.

"I don't understand," he said to Will in English.

"She's lost her Respectability, all right—for some reason," answered Will in the same language. "I don't know why."

"I'll find out why," said Cully grimly. He switched to Moldaug. "Let myself ask why this one who was bravely self-killed should be considered not fit to share the same preservation compartment with the brothers of yourself even in death? If it was brave for they-two to fight to the death, surely it was brave, or braver, for this young one to suicide in the name of Respectability."

"It was indeed brave of that one," retorted the Moldaug officer. "But only that redeems her. For she has associated with yourself, who acted an act of the Demon of Dark—whether yourself are indeed the Demon she believed come again in soft-face guise or not. Therefore, she has become not-Respectable."

"But it was no fault of this dead one!" said Cully harshly. "Myself tell yourself that she had no knowledge, nor no means of stopping ourself, even if she had had knowledge."

"Of course, that is true," replied the Moldaug officer. "But myself does not understand why yourself insist upon the tragedy of this young one's loss of Respectability. It is very tragic—but it is so. She is become not-Respectable because she was associated with yourself in an act which is not-Respectable. I repeat, yourself must not put her in preservation with our Respectable dead, because she has not the right to be so preserved."

With that, the Moldaug officer turned away from Cully. He did not completely turn his back—which would have been an out-and-out insult. But he turned enough aside to make it plain that the conversation was over and the matter settled, as far as he was concerned.

Cully turned and took one long stride back out into the corridor, followed by Will.

"Lock that door!" he said harshly to guards. Turning, he strode off down the corridor back toward the aft portion of the vessel, until he entered the room from which two doors led to the refrigerated rooms which were the preservation compartments.

He stepped up to the first of these doors, beyond which the dead Moldaug officers lay, and took hold of the handle. But, in the very act of opening the door, he hesitated.

For a long second he hesitated. Then he sighed softly and dropped his hand from the handle of the door. He turned instead and stepped to the second compartment, opened its door and walked in. The cold and antiseptic-laden, special atmosphere in the compartment bit at his lungs. Gently, he laid the small body of Madman down on one of the bunklike ledges set into the wall. He straightened out her dead limbs, pulled her robe down to cover them and folded the hood of her robe around her face. Then he stepped back and stood for a second looking at her, before turning on his heel and walking out.

The door of preservation-compartment Number Two slammed shut behind him with a hard metallic crash that had nothing kind or gentle about it.

He was suddenly aware that Will had followed him down to this place. They were alone together here. Will looked at him, and he looked back at Will. The older man smiled sadly.

"Come on up front, Cully," said Will softly. "Come along up front and sit down with the rest of us human beings, and have a cup of coffee or a drink. Every people has its own ways—and some of ours might seem pretty cruel to members of another race. Not that it helps to know that, I suppose."

17

"You're sure you want to hit this Communications Point?" demanded Pete Hyde. "We can save half a day on the way back to Kalestin by not shifting out of our way to see if there's been any messages for us—and we'll be home in three days anyway."

"No," said Cully. "I want to shift to that Communications Point first, no matter what the delay. It's been six weeks since we left the Frontier, Pete. With just enough men to man five Moldaug prize ships, we don't want to go blundering into any situation out of ignorance. Especially when going half a day out of our way would save us."

Cully did not add that he was practically certain there would be information waiting for them at the Communications Point. There would be no easy way to explain to someone like Pete that they had left the elements of a dynamic social change behind them when they had lifted from Kalestin to go play Demon of Dark; and that these, like certain chemical elements, with time and proximity must have been almost certain to produce a reaction.

Also, it was true that the six ships he now com-

manded were barely manned. The *Bei* and her one
captured vessel had escaped safely from the Crown
World and lost themselves among the flares of other
Moldaug ships, winking in and out of shift among the
alien stars. Following that, they had spent nearly nine
weeks scouting the inhabited star systems of Moldaug
space, according to the charts in the captured Moldaug
vessel. In the process they had taken six more unsuspecting alien ships which had blundered into contact
with them. Two of these ships had been disarmed and
set free with Moldaug prisoners and dead aboard, to
find their own way home.

Five years out from Kalestin was the Communications Point—an arbitrary location in space, close enough
to Kalestin so that a small, unmanned, drone message-
ship could be sent to it in a single shift, to wait there
until Cully should arrive to pick up the drone, or drones,
with whatever messages Onweetok or others had sent
him. Two days later they flared-in within a few hundred
miles of that Point.

Immediately, the automatic general-alarm bells sounded
to life aboard the *Bei*, drowning out whatever beeping
signal of a drone message might otherwise have been
heard. Cully sprinted to the Control Room.

"A ship!" Pete shouted as Cully burst in. "But it's not
Moldaug, Cully. It's one of ours—"

He did not get any further, for at that moment the
intership communications speaker above them began
speaking—in Onweetok's voice.

"*Bei?* Hello, *Bei?* This is Kalestin ship *Wanderlust*.
Repeat, Kalestin ship *Wanderlust*. Cully, are you aboard
one of those ships there? This is Onweetok Murfa here.
Repeat, Onweetok—"

Cully took two strides to the communications console
and slapped the transmit button.

"Onweetok—" Cully, who was ordinarily almost im-
mune to unthinking anger, suddenly found it exploding
inside him. "I told you—never mind! Come aboard
here. *Now!*"

Five minutes later the dapper Frontiersman came into the Control Room of the *Bei* to find Cully looking like a thundercloud. Onweetok opened his mouth to speak, but Cully spoke first.

"Didn't I tell you under no circumstances to leave Kalestin?" demanded Cully. "Didn't you realize that whatever and whoever was behind Machin and the Brush-knife Boys would jump at the first chance to get control of the Assembly back again?"

Onweetok stared up at the taller man, clearly more in amazement than dismay.

"By Heaven, you've grown telepathic, Cully!" he said. "How'd you know the fact that someone's been hiring Brush-knifers by the hundreds, on Kalestin? That was one of the things I came here to talk to you about!"

"It ought to be plain enough——" began Cully. But then he got himself under control. "Machin wasn't that much of a mind and power to be anything more than a front for whoever was actually behind the political machine he set up. That's one reason I left you behind the way I did. With me gone, they'd be bound to come out in the open—but with you there, they wouldn't dare try taking over. Then, when I got back, we could deal with them. The Frontier's no different than the Old Worlds in one way, On; they both need a jolt to wake them up to the realities of the situation."

"I'll believe that!" said Onweetok emphatically. "And my apologies, Cully lad, for breaking my promise to you to stay put in Kalestin. But, then, you didn't explain it to me in these words at the time. At any rate, you're right. Somebody was evidently behind Machin, and it looks like Royce. He's recruiting a regular army of brush outlaws now—we might even have a rough little civil war on our hands."

"Maybe that's just what's needed——" Cully checked himself. "But you said something about this being only one half the things you've been waiting to tell me?"

"Oh, that—an interesting bit of news," said Onweetok. "Eight people—relatives of members of the Tri-Worlds

Council and other leading Old Worlds men and women—
are on their way to the Moldaug right now. They're
voluntarily surrendering themselves as hostages to prove
to the Moldaug that the Old Worlds has nothing to do
with all those activities of yours these last few weeks
among the alien stars." He paused, looking a little
sidelong at Cully. "Alia Braight's one of the volunteers."

"Alia?" snapped Cully. But his anger evaporated suddenly into thoughtfulness. He swung about. "Where's
Will? Oh, there you are. Will, what's the Moldaug
attitude likely to be to a boatload of human hostages?"

"Hostages, let alone volunteers, aren't a Moldaug
concept—" Will was beginning, when Cully interrupted
him with an upraised hand and swung back to face
Onweetok.

"That hostage ship didn't land on Kalestin?" he
demanded. "It hasn't already gone on into Moldaug
territory?"

Onweetok shook his head.

"The news came in on another ship that left Earth
three days before the ship with the hostages had left.
Word was, the hostage ship wasn't stopping anywhere.
It was to head right into a meeting with a Moldaug ship
beyond the Pleiades."

"You don't know where?" demanded Cully.

"Some fifteen light-years down-galaxy from Kalestin—
that's the most I was able to learn," answered Onweetok.
Cully turned to Will.

"Sorry to break in on you like that, Will," Cully said.
"I just had an idea. Now, tell me—how would the
aliens go about something like this? Give me some idea
about how they'd react to this hostage business. Aren't
there some folk tales or legends about hostages being
exchanged?"

Will frowned.

"That's what I was starting to tell you," he answered
slowly. "There aren't—as such."

"Aren't?" Cully frowned at him.

"In fact, come to think of it," said Will thoughtfully,

"I don't believe there's a word in their language that exactly translates 'hostage.' The concept doesn't have any meaning for them in its ordinary sense. You see, in their culture anyone given up as a hostage would become essentially dead, as far as his family was concerned. Except for the all-important fact that his body wouldn't be available to permit succession."

"Why?" asked Cully sharply.

"Because," said the older man, "to their minds any member of the family who becomes a liability to the family's survival is better off dead. Much as he may love life, he'll respect his duty to die so that the family can slough him off officially and make room for someone new in his position. Duty to the survival of family overrides duty to self, just as duty to the survival of sept outranks duty to family, and clan survival outranks sept. The duty of the individual to the survival of the Moldaug race as a whole is greatest of all. It's the inverse of the chain of responsibility. There's nothing greater; and what we'd take to be the maximum of self-sacrifice, the Moldaug figure as the minimum."

Cully frowned back at him.

"But On says a Moldaug ship is meeting the hostage ship. So, they're obviously accepting the hostages in this case, aren't they?" he asked.

"Do you know that for certain?" countered Will. "Can you be sure that the Moldaug agreed to, or even knew about, this plan by the Old Worlds to deliver volunteer hostages to them?"

Cully sat down on the couch, motioning Will to take the chair opposite him. As Will sat down in turn, Cully answered him.

"I can't see hostages being delivered to the aliens without some sort of prior consultation," said Cully, "probably with Ruhn and his Brothers back on Earth. So, what I want you to tell me, Will, is how the aliens would be likely to go about accepting the hostages?"

Will thought for a moment.

"Well, the closest thing to taking hostages I know

of," he said, "as far as my knowledge of myth and legend among the Moldaug goes, would be a case like the legend of The Nine Sisters of Ogh. The Nine Sisters surrendered to an enemy clan because all the effective adult males of their generation in their clan were dead, and the heirs to the positions of the dead warriors were all too young to take over leadership of the family. Alive and not captive, the Nine Sisters would have been forced to continue war with the enemy clan as regents for the young heirs. Dead, they would have left the children as wards of the sept, whether anyone wanted it or not—which meant that the children could be legitimately slaughtered by the enemy clan. By surrendering themselves to the enemy clan, the sisters avoided both these possibilities. Since they were females, and not warriors, the opposing clan could not Respectably kill them, even though they had surrendered. And with the sisters themselves neither alive nor dead, the children could appeal for aid to a neutral clan. In Moldaug legend it was a clever trick—a solution to an impossible cultural situation."

"Well," asked Cully, "how does this apply to the present hostages?"

"I'd guess," answered Will, "in that the Moldaug are almost certain to assume that the surrender of these people, their giving themselves up voluntarily like this, can also only be some sort of brave, human trick." He looked quizzically at Cully.

"Trick—" Cully echoed, and broke off thoughtfully. His eyes met Will's. "Do you suppose that they'll think the surrender of these hostages is somehow connected with what I've been doing—what we've been doing—the last few weeks and months in raiding their shipping lanes and worlds?"

Will nodded slowly.

"Yes, I'd think so," said Will. "Remember, the Moldaug can't believe that you've been doing all this without the approval of your Elders and superiors. That's why the Tri-Worlds Council is obviously having trouble disavowing their responsibility for what you do."

"So," said Cully, "that means the Moldaug will think this surrender of hostages is another slap in the face, like my playing Demon of Dark?"

Will looked at Cully, suddenly startled.

"I hadn't thought about that," the older man said. "Yes, that means they'll come up with a reason in their own terms for the hostages—and what you suggest is the most likely Moldaug viewpoint."

"But," said Cully, speaking slowly and thoughtfully, "you think they'll definitely accept the hostages to begin with?"

"That's right. They'd have to—" Will broke off. "I see what you mean, Cully. Undoubtedly, the Moldaug will have made arrangements to accept the hostages. And if that's the case, you want to know how they'd go about accepting them?"

"That's it," said Cully. "How would they?"

Will got up from his chair and began to wander thoughtfully about the room. Cully sat watching him, and Doak, perched on an arm of the chair, also watched. After a couple of silent moments, Will came back to sit down opposite Cully again.

"There's a long history of conversations between clans or septs or families at odds with each other," Will said. "And almost invariably, these conversations have taken place at the border itself, so probably we can take it that this procedure's going to be an invariable. In other words, if the hostages are going to be accepted by the Moldaug, the Moldaug ship would want to meet the human ship at what the Moldaug consider their frontier, and have the hostages transshipped there to an alien vessel."

"Their real border line, wherever that is—or the frontier they're claiming from us?" Cully shot out.

Will looked oddly for a moment at Cully.

"Let me see . . ." he said. He thought for a moment. "No, now that I stop to think about it, the meeting would have to take place at wherever the earliest frontier line was. In short, by meeting at the original boundary line, in effect, they're declaring a truce without actually saying so."

"Then we ought to be able to figure out about where they'd meet," said Cully thoughtfully. "It'd be the point at which the first Moldaug ran into the first human—right?"

"That's a good guess," said Will. "But it's not quite right. It would be the point at which the first Moldaug military vessel first contacted either a human vessel or a human settlement."

Doak gave a faint ejaculation. In the silence that followed he said one word.

"Fortown."

There was another small silence as Will and Cully looked at each other.

"He's right, of course," said Will.

"But those hostages can't be turned over to aliens on Kalestin soil," said Cully. "Aside from whether we'd permit it here on the frontier, it'd take weeks to get the arrangements set up through all the red tape between the Tri-Worlds Council and the Assembly."

"Yes," answered Will. "But it doesn't have to be at Fortown itself. Fortown simply establishes a point through which the boundary line runs in space."

"I see," said Cully thoughtfully. "Then we can take a line running through Fortown—which of course in this case simply means a line running through the world of Kalestin itself—and prolong that line out through space in either direction, as long as relative distances between it and Earth, and it and the alien Crown World, are maintained."

Will looked at him with frank respect.

"I hadn't carried the thought that far," said Will. "I'd only thought that it could be other places besides the original meeting places of the two races on Kalestin. But you're right. Along that line fifteen light-years down-galaxy from Kalestin, as Onweetok says, you ought to find the meeting place of the hostage ship with the Moldaug ship that's going to meet them."

"Good. That's all I need to know," said Cully. "Pete, you start figuring a shift to that point. I want enough men from the captured ships to give us a full fighting crew here aboard the *Bei*. Lee"—he turned to the big man—"you take the other ships back to Kalestin with On. Get them fitted and crewed."

"Right," said Leestrom and went out of the Control Room, followed by Onweetok.

Less than two hours later the *Bei*, once more fully manned, shifted outward toward an area fifteen light-years away from Kalestin, down along the imaginary line that Pete had calculated.

Ten hours later the *Bei* reached the approximate area of their destination. This area was, in itself, some three light-years distant from the estimated transfer point at which the hostages would be handed over from a human vessel to a Moldaug ship. They stopped, and Pete Hyde set up a monitor watch in the Equipment Room, continually scanning a globe of space surrounding the *Nansh Rakh* and ten light-years on radius.

"No sign," he reported to Cully some four hours later when Cully came into the Equipment Room to check on how his watch was doing. He took off the button of his earphone and rubbed tired eyes, leaving the monitoring to his two assistants. He got up, stretched, and turned to face Cully.

"Shouldn't we have seen some sign of either the human or the alien ship approaching this area by this time?" asked Cully.

"Not necessarily," answered Pete. "We haven't been at rest long enough to get a really good picture of an area this large. We've been able to make a few guesses on the basis of what the computer's thrown up and what we've been able to observe ourselves. I think"—his tone was grudging—"we may have identified the alien ship. If it's her, then she's about eighteen light-years deep in Moldaug territory, and headed almost directly toward us—"

A grunt from one of Pete's two assistants interrupted him. The man, who was known as Red Orfa, spun around in his chair and handed up a facsimile two-dimensional still picture of the large-scan unit, one of the pictures produced by the observing computer. Red Orfa had circled one of the little flare lights on the picture with a white stylus marker.

"Look at this, Pete," Orfa said.

Pete took the picture, glanced at it, and handed it on to Cully.

"And there's our human-hostage ship," said Pete. "About twelve light-years out and also headed in this direction." He paused and looked at Cully expectantly. "It'll be six hours before they meet up with the alien ship. Do you want to intercept now?"

Cully shook his head.

"If we take those hostages from an Old Worlds ship, that's piracy," he answered. "But if we take it from the aliens, after they've been transferred, there's no Old Worlds legal complications involved. We'll lie back and wait for the hostages to be transferred to that Moldaug ship. Then we'll intercept the aliens with the hostages on their first jump away from the rendezvous point."

So they did. They rested and watched as the ship containing the hostages met and joined with the Moldaug vessel. For something like three hours they remained together. Then the human vessel flared into shift and appeared again on the large-scan screen four light-years back from the meeting point, back once more within the human area of space. Approximately twelve minutes later, the alien ship also flared and appeared about the same distance back in Moldaug territory.

"All right," ordered Cully aboard the *Bei*. "After the next shift we'll meet that alien ship."

Pete had precalculated a possible shift destination for the alien ship. Within twenty minutes they followed the other vessel, flaring-in less than a hundred-thousand miles from the other ship. For some minutes it seemed as if the alien vessel was not even aware of them. But then, as the *Bei* under Pete's direction closed the gap between the two ships by a quick, short shift of some eighty thousand miles, the alien ship winked into shift again and disappeared.

"Pete!" barked Cully into the intercom from the Control to the Equipment Room.

"It's all right, Cully," Pete's voice answered him. "We've got him located in the screen. We'll be after him inside a couple of hours at the most."

Cully let up the intercom button, cutting communications. He sat back in his control chair. From this point on, and for some little while, there would be little for him and Will and Doak to do. Just as there would be little for the three Pilots of the alien ship to do. For the moment it would be a duel between the two Navigators— Pete Hyde and the alien Navigators, whoever they might be.

They paused, calculated and shifted. And shifted again. And again. Slowly, Pete, by greater correctness of calculation, was gradually narrowing both the time and distance gaps between themselves and the alien ship. With each shift the alien had less time to calculate an escape shift before Pete moved the *Bei* in close to it. With the shortening of each calculation time, his jumps necessarily became shorter and shorter to minimize the inherent error of his calculations. They were, thought Cully with a sudden touch of dry humor, like two fleas in a large box—one trying to escape from, one trying to capture, the other. And gradually the pursuer was wearing down the pursued. Prowling restlessly in the Control Room, Cully glanced at his two other Demon components. Will was cleaning the old-fashioned chemical-powered revolver he had bought back on Kalestin, and carried ever since, though no one had ever seen him use it. Doak was honing his familiar, prison-made knife—now fitted with a hand-carved wooden handle. Like the jealously guarded locket on the cord about his neck, the knife was so constantly in his hands that it seemed a part of him.

The chase continued. There was nothing dramatic about it. Hour by slow hour, Pete, and his two assistants at the navigational consoles in the Equipment Room, by superior navigation were cutting down the calculation time available to the alien ship. In the endless depths of space, under the countless eyes of the uncaring stars, they calculated and shifted and calculated and shifted again. And tension began to grow and expand aboard the *Bei* as the chase wore on.

Cully left the Control Room and made a tour about the ship. All the men aboard were under arms and had their airsuits ready. Some were sleeping, if fitfully, some reading or writing letters, or talking in low voices. The growing tension was there, all right. Cully felt it like the pressure of a spring. The men needed something to snap it, something to jerk their minds away from the hunt at least momentarily.

In the Aft Laser-control Center he found the six man weapons crew playing poker on the flat top of the back-up fire-control computer. The Assistant Fire-control Chief, a slim, dark-haired, crookedly smiling young man named Mike Bourjoi, had a small rampart of lead-colored plastic chips stacked in front of him.

"Don't clean them all out, Mike," said Cully lightly. "When we catch up with that alien ship I want this crew thinking about their weapons, not about their money in your pocket.

"No money to it, Admiral," replied Mike, looking up with a flash of almost black-pupilled eyes and a brush-country twang to his voice. "We're just playing for a few little drinks."

"A few, he says!" Lige Jenkins, the Crew Chief, snorted. "Wouldn't you know a beer drinker would do it to us? Look at those chips in front of him, Admiral. Nothing but beer chips. Now, nobody's going to drink two hundred and forty cases of beer before the bottles explode."

"Kalestin City beer doesn't explode any more," retorted Mike. "They been fixing it up since the first of
the year—just like they do on the Old Worlds. All the
modern luxuries coming in, Lige—you ought to know
that." He passed one of the chips up to Cully. "Hey,
Admiral, take a look at this."

Cully took the chip. It was stamped out of plastic
with a bottle on one side; and when he turned it over
he discovered the word "beer" printed on the other.

"That's my cousin's and mine—our new business back
at Kalestin City now, Admiral," said Mike. "Five beer
chips make a booze chip. Two booze chips make a
champagne chip. Cute, hey? 'Bourjoi and Shawley,
Games Equipment,' that's us."

He won the hand before him, raked in the pot, and
reached into his pocket for a new, unsealed deck of
cards, which he passed up to Cully.

"Look at those, Admiral," he said. "There's our playing
cards. First Frontier brand; finest home-industry cards
in the Pleiades. We get our nitrocellulose sheeting from
the plant right in Kalestin City and lithograph it ourselves so you get a sixty-card deck for playing Frontier
Bridge. Look it over."

Cully did. The deck was cleanly and professionally
made inside its plastic protective wrapping. Cully turned
it over to examine the red wafer, like a circle of sealing
wax, that secured the wrapping. The sight of it triggered an old memory in him, and the memory sparked
an inspiration for breaking the steadily increasing tension holding his ship. He tossed the pack of cards in the
air with one hand, and caught it again, laughing out
loud.

"What's funny?" asked Mike. The game had come to
an abrupt halt. They all stared at Cully.

"Here, Mike," said Cully, laughing, tossing the deck
at him. "Catch! But just be careful you don't blow up!"

Mike's brown hands received the flying deck of cards
out of the air as softly as if it had been a thin-shelled,
uncooked egg. The tone of Cully's voice hinted at a

joke—but Mike was too Frontier-wary to take chances. Men had had lighted sticks of dynamite tossed at them in Kalestin mining camps in much the same tone of humor.

With the pack in his hands, he looked it over gingerly.

"Blow up?" he said.

"Well, maybe that's one of the safe ones," said Cully. "But you took over the First Frontier brand name from an original manufacturing outfit called Frontier Imports, didn't you?"

Mike looked up at him cautiously.

"That's right," he said. "But how did *you* know?"

"Cards again—" demanded Cully, reaching his hands out for them. Mike passed them up. Cully turned the pack over to show them the red sealing wafer.

"Frontier Imports was set up back in our spacelifting days," said Cully. "It set up import shops in New York Complex, Upper Marstown and Venus City. Most of what it imported were regular curio items from the Frontier—and it made a mint. I understand the shops are still running, selling Frontier-made toothpicks for five thousand times the price of the Earth-made article. But it also stocked a few items for spacelifters like myself who had to enter Earth without much obvious spacelifting equipment."

He thumbed the red wafer.

"What are your cards made out of, Mike?" he asked.

"I told you—nitrocellulose sheeting. Well, pyroxylin, actually. We'll make them out of plastic later on—"

"But right now it's cheaper to use the pyroxylin, which is partially nitrated cellulose," said Cully. "Real nitrocellulose, which is cellulose trinitrate, is guncotton and quite another thing. It goes off with a big bang, indeed. Well, among the regular First Frontier brand playing cards in the import shops, all the sixty-card packs were made out of guncotton rather than pyroxylin; and this little wafer was both a fuse and a timer. Break the seal and you've got only a pack of playing cards. But thumb it like this without breaking the seal"—he demonstrated—"and it's set to go off in three seconds. Catch!"

He threw it toward the midst of the table, and all the men there ducked instinctively. The unsealed pack of cards slapped down in the middle of the computer top, and Cully went out, laughing—followed, he was glad to hear, by echoing laughter from the men who had just ducked.

He went on around the ship, relieved, knowing he had started a running gag which would soon spread throughout the vessel and snap the growing tension of nerves within her hull. From now on, until the design of the First Frontier brand cards was changed, Mike Bourjoi and everyone else who introduced a new deck of them into a card game would be kidded about their intentions of blowing up the rest of the players.

Cully went on down to the Drive Room and was checking over the state of the plasma motors there, when a call for him from the bridge came over the intercom.

"Admiral—" It was Pete's voice. "We're going to land right on top of them on the next shift."

Cully turned and headed for the Control Room. When he arrived, he found that Will and Doak were already in their seats waiting for him. He flung himself into the middle seat between them and thumbed the intercom.

"I'm all set up here in the Control Room," he told Pete.

"Right. Watch your screen. Shift in about eight seconds."

Cully stared at the screen before him, with its maze of unfamiliar stars. Abruptly the scene changed. Without a jar of warning, dead ahead of him—it could not be more than thirty or forty miles away—was the bright silver dot of the alien ship reflecting the white light of an AO star nearby. A second later, on magnification, it all but filled the screen. Cully could see its hull rolling to bring its outside-mounted weapons to bear.

"Got it!" Cully snapped into the intercom, flicking the switch on the console before him that alerted the whole ship to the fact that the Pilot had taken over from the Navigators. "Down and under," he said to Doak and Will, his fingers already flashing over his console. The fingers of the other men moved to follow him up. The *Bei* shot forward, went under the belly of the alien ship and came up the other side just as the Moldaug Pilots flung her backward to avoid what seemed to be an attempt to ram. The underhull of the fore portion of the *Bei* clanged against the afterhull of the alien vessel—and magnetics locked the two hulls together. Immediately, Cully began to roll his ship around the hull of the other, working forward as he did so. His own weapons section were blasting the enemy's hull-mounted offensive armament as they came across it.

The Moldaug ship fishtailed, like a dog shaking itself, trying to break loose from the clinging human vessel. But the magnetics held.

Now they were almost cargo hatch to cargo hatch. Cully gave the order to lock magnetics. As they shuddered to a halt in position against the hull of the wildly gyrating alien ship, he pushed the boarding button. The boarding alarm bell began to clang through the vessel around him.

He had not had time to get into an airsuit. Now he stopped to struggle into one; and even the few seconds this took delayed him long enough so that when he came to the cargo hatch he found his men had already opened a way into the alien vessel. So far, all had gone pretty much as usual. From this point on, it changed. Within the Moldaug ship the aliens were suited up, armed, and ready. They fought fiercely, man to man. It was an hour and forty-three minutes before the signal came over the airsuit intercoms that the ship was cleared.

Wearily, Cully—who had been in the thick of some of the fighting up forward in the Moldaug ship—returned to his own Control Room to wait the arrival of the hostages, which a search party had just announced they had found in one of the aft alien-crew dormitory compartments. He was sitting in his pilot's chair, with a cup of coffee steaming in his hand, when the hostages were herded into the Control Room.

They entered, wearing every conceivable expression—ranging from sheepishness to astonishment to outrage. But nearly the last to enter was a female figure, the sight of which brought him bolt-upright in his chair. Her eyes were enormous as she confronted him.

"Cully!" she said. "I might have known it'd be you!"

It was Alia.

18

". . . Yes, they were," replied Alia. "The hostages were Dad's idea."

Her voice shook a little, which was not surprising. After returning the *Bei* and the captured Moldaug ship to the Communications Point, Cully had forced the former human hostages to witness his offer to the Moldaug officers of a Respectable return to their families.

The resulting attempts at suicide by the aliens—which would have been successful if Cully had not had men ready to stop the Moldaug—had shaken all the ex-hostages. But only Alia, with two others, had been willing to see in this any measure of the difference between human and Moldaug thinking, or any indication of Tri-Worlds' mistake in dealing with the Moldaug. And Alia, alone, was ready to admit her volunteering had probably been a mistake.

But beyond that admission she would not go. She refused to take the mental step from her admission about the hostage idea to the idea that her father, Amos Braight, was wrong in other ways of dealing with the Moldaug.

"Of course, the hostages were Dad's idea," she re-

peated now stiffly as she stood alone with Cully in the
Control Room of the *Bei*, after the Moldaug had taken
off in their disarmed vessel. "And, of course, that means
he was wrong—in that one decision. But now you want
me to believe that this one mistake means he's wrong in
all his thinking about the aliens."

"Can't you see the same principle at work in other
things he does?" asked Cully. "In arresting me, for one
thing . . ."

"All right—maybe he was wrong about that, too!"
She lifted her chin stubbornly. "But that's not the point.
The trouble is, you want to blame him for everything
because of what you've suffered, yourself, Cully. Well,
I don't blame you for wanting that! But you're looking
in the wrong direction. If you want to blame somebody,
blame me! *I* was the one who got you to come back
from Kalestin to be arrested—even if I never suspected
it'd mean your being taken to a place like that"—she
shuddered—"ocean prison."

"But that was Amos' idea from the start." Cully found
that, strangely, she had the ability to loosen the reins of
his temper where others could not. "Can't you see that
there's a basic idea gone wrong in the man? A basic,
deliberate misconception of what the aliens mean and
stand for—"

"No. And I don't believe there is—in spite of what
you just showed me here!" Alia retorted. "You've got
no real proof. And between Dad and you, who should I
believe? Naturally, he's made mistakes! He's only human. But here you are, who never did anything but sit
in on a backwoods Assembly for half a year; and here's
my father, who's spent his whole lifetime in government, in figuring out what's best for people. Which one
of you do you think I should believe? It hasn't been
easy for him either. Do you think it was easy last week
for him to offer Ruhn that humans would give up the
Front—"

She broke off, plainly dismayed at what had escaped
her tongue.

"Give up the Frontier? To the Moldaug?" Cully pounced on her. "When did he offer them that? What made him think he could give away what he didn't own—"

He did not get a chance to finish. Just then Pete Hyde burst into the Control Room.

"Cully!" he shouted. "Leestrom just flared-in with eight ships at the Point here. He'll be coming into rendezvous with us in five minutes. And he's got something to tell you—he's coming aboard as soon as he gets here."

"Tell me what?" asked Cully, turning from Alia.

"He wouldn't say." Pete stared stonily at him, suddenly and strangely tight-lipped.

"Wouldn't . . ." Cully gazed at the Navigator sharply a moment, then swung about on his heel and spoke over his shoulder to Alia. "Come on up to the Equipment Room. We'll see about this."

They went through the ship to the Equipment Room, and Cully himself put in a call to the oncoming ships under Leestrom's command, now visible on the close-scan screen like a school of small silver minnows as they approached on ordinary power.

"Captain Leestrom says he'll be there in a minute," answered the face of a man Cully did not know personally, from the communications screen. "He asked if you'd wait until he can talk to you in person."

Cully cut the circuit and led Alia and Pete down the hall to the main lounge to the sally port. The skin of Cully's face felt tight across the cheekbones. By the time they reached the lounge, Leestrom's ship was drifting in close on minimum power, and a few minutes later the two hulls clanged together. Shortly, a travel tube was fitted between the two hatches and Leestrom walked in.

He stopped abruptly at the sight of Cully, waiting there. The big man's face was serious.

"What is it?" Cully asked.

"Onweetok's dead," said Leestrom slowly. "Four days after we got back. And Royce is controlling Kalestin . . ."

He proceeded to tell the harsh story bluntly, in bald words that increased rather than minimized the brutality of the events it reported.

The day after Onweetok had lifted ship to meet Cully, Bill Royce had introduced in the Assembly a bill to hold Cully and Onweetok for trial by the Assembly itself, on a charge of endangering Frontier citizens by his activities in Moldaug territory. The day Onweetok returned, the bill had been passed by a handful of Assembly Representatives—all Royce men. The other Representatives had been held, in effect, prisoners in their homes by a private army of heavily armed, brush-country toughs Royce had been quietly bringing into Kalestin City for nearly a week.

Having got his bill passed, Royce paid no attention to Onweetok, but hastily ordered his hired army to move on to the Spaceport fitting yard to take control of whatever ships and crews of Cully's were there.

Before they actually got moving, however, there was an interruption. Some half dozen of the toughs, acting on their own initiative, had broken into Onweetok's apartment, dragged him to the back of the hotel, and hanged him there, from an arch over the entrance to the hotel parking area. Then they had sought out Royce, expecting praise, and finding Royce just as he was ready to start for the Spaceport.

To the lynchers' astonishment, it was not praise they received. It had never been a plan of Royce's to murder so popular a Frontier figure as Onweetok. The trial bill had been a means to an end only. Royce cursed the murderers with a red fury that revealed the ex-spacelifter beneath the banker's clothes. He disarmed them all, not gently, and had them thrown in jail. But, at the same time, he decided to salvage what he could from the situation by going ahead with his plan to take over the vessels Cully had left behind.

He commandeered cars and moved swiftly toward

the Spaceport, hoping to take by surprise whomever Cully had put in command.

This he might have done if one of the more moderate of Royce's followers among the Assembly Members, appalled at Onweetok's lynching, had not phoned ahead to Leestrom to warn him.

Leestrom, faced with an emergency, had pounded the side of his brutal jaw softly with a scarred fist, scowling in indecision. Atmosphere-borne, battle-ready and fully manned, the ships at his disposal could not merely have made short work of Royce's brush-country army, but wiped a city several times the size of Kalestin off the face of the planet. However, "battle-ready" was a poor term to describe any of the captured vessels or those in the refitting yard; and he had on hand barely enough trained men to lift them, let alone fight them.

In the end, he had decided to leave the decision of what to do about Royce up to Cully. He had rounded up what men he could, lifted ships, and now here he was.

". . . and that's it," said Leestrom with gruff hoarseness, concluding. He was not used to speaking at such length without being interrupted. Now done, he fell silent, leaving it up to Cully to pass judgment on his actions, without venturing any further excuse or explanation for them.

Cully, however, found himself too full of feeling for words. He swung about and walked over to stare into the large-scan screen in silence. He had deliberately planned to push the Assembly situation on Kalestin to the explosion point—as much to awake the Frontier population in general to the Moldaug danger, as to recruit needed men like Emile Hasec. But he had not expected that explosion to strike so close to home. Onweetok had been one of his oldest and closest friends on the Frontier.

Coldly and unsparingly, Cully held himself to account for not foreseeing the fact that his actions and orders had left Onweetok vulnerable to exactly what had just taken place. For the moment, all that Cully could think about was the feel of his hands closing on the short, red, bull-neck of Royce.

But then, in a little, the emotional fog of his fury lifted from the clear patterns in his mind. Staring into the large-scan screen, he found he was looking at the bright marker-light that was Kalestin, some thirty light-years distant.

His mind cleared, all the way. It had always been like this with him. Following on the first red flames and smoke of sooty rage, his thoughts burned suddenly white-hot, clean and brilliant. The reaction had saved his life a number of times during his spacelifting years. For a long moment now he saw matters with a clarity so pure as to be almost unreal. Things fell into place.

"Lee," he said quietly, "you'll take the hostages, including Miss Braight here, and all the ships but the *Bei*. Head back for Kalestin, but land your ships in the uplands, in Emile Hasec's area. You'll find crewmen and officers enough among the ex-spacemen-turned-farmers. Tell Emile what's happened, and tell him from me to gather men and take Kalestin City from Royce. Say I'm not *asking* him to do that—I'm *telling* him. You've got that?"

"Yes," said Leestrom economically.

"All right," said Cully. "Then tell him to alert the rest of the Frontier Worlds. Call on them in my name to join you with any space-going piece of metal they have. Make up a fleet—any kind of fleet—and put half the vessels on patrol duty around the Frontier Planets, just as if they were warships. You take the rest to Earth. You understand me?"

"Yes, Cully," Leestrom said.

"When you get near Earth, stop with your half fleet just out of close-viewing range, and go in to the Fleet Headquarters at Moon Base with three of your ships that're Moldaug-built. Tell the Admirals of the Fleet there that the Frontier has signed an agreement with the Moldaug, in return for which they've supplied us with war vessels enough to conquer the Worlds of the Solar System. They, and all of the Tri-Worlds Fleet grounded at Moon Base, are under your guns. They're to surrender to the Frontier Representative—which is you."

"Good God, Cully!" burst out Pete Hyde. "You don't think for one minute they'll do anything but throw Lee and everyone with him into a guardhouse?"

Cully turned and looked at the lanky Navigator. Pete subsided.

"No, they won't," said Cully. "The three Old Worlds have been scaring themselves to death with the idea that the Frontier is going to take them over. Those Admirals Lee talks to will look at the Moldaug design of Lee's ships and wait long enough to check with Earth." He turned back to Leestrom. "In fact, you tell them to check—with me or Amos Braight. I'll have reached him by that time, and one of us will back up what you say."

"Cully—Dad won't!" cried Alia suddenly.

"Yes, he will," said Cully slowly. "I think I've got a way of convincing him to do what I ask him to."

"What way? Oh, Cully, he won't believe you, no matter what you say! But what way?"

"I—" Cully broke off short, suddenly remembering how this part of his plans would touch her also. "Go along with Lee and the other hostages now. Quick! I've got no time to waste."

"But wait, Cully!" She caught at him, as Lee took hold of her arm to lead her away. "Please listen! Maybe I was wrong, after all. There's one thing I ought to tell you. Dad's like two different men nowadays. Maybe you think you know him, from back on Kalestin, but you don't. He's changed. Only *I* know him. If you'll just trust me, I can tell you what to do—"

"Sorry," he said. "Take her, Lee!"

He turned abruptly from her, breaking her hold on his arm, and Lee's massive strength held her from following him.

"Come on, Pete," Cully ordered.

He led the way from the lounge. Behind him he heard Alia's voice calling after him.

"Cully, come back! You don't understand! He won't believe you, no matter what you tell him. I know——"

With Pete half a step behind him, Cully stepped into the Equipment Room, stopped and turned.

"Pete," he said, "we're moving over to the *Nansh Rakh*, and I want to start back into Moldaug territory as soon as we can. Plot me a course to the Crown World of the Moldaug."

19

The Crown World of the Moldaug race floated in the Control Room screen before Cully on full magnification, a dot of light against blackness pricked by other starlights. The *Nansh Rakh* had been ten days this time coming to this fifth world of a planetary system circling a AO-type star. Four times they had been challenged or pursued by alien warships. Four times they had shifted blindly to distances of over ten light-years, in order to throw the enemy off their trail. And four times, as a result, they had been forced to lie still for more than sixteen hours while Pete replotted their position from observation alone. But now they were here.

"Will—" said Cully, calling the white-haired man to stand beside him before the large pilot's vision screen of the Control Room. "When we left Kalestin, I felt pretty sure the Moldaug wouldn't expect us to show up here again right away. But what do you think?"

Will hesitated.

"Go on," prompted Cully.

"Well, it's only my opinion," said Will, "but I think you're right. My guess is, the chances of our not being

expected here again are pretty good. The Moldaug on
the Crown World either don't believe you're a portent
of Change of Aspect—whether you're the mythical Demon or not—or they do. If they believe it, then you've
already been here and left your sign and there's no
reason for you to come back again."

"And if they don't believe?"

"If they don't, or don't want to believe," said Will,
"then I'd think they'd be leaning over backward, if
anything, not to be alarmed by the chance you'd come
back here again. After all, the last people among the
Moldaug who'd want to believe in a Change in Aspect
would be the Royal Family, Sept and Clan now in
power."

Will paused and looked sideways at Cully. He smiled
a little, thoughtfully.

"So," he said, "if you want my vote, it's that you
won't be expected—not that that means you could land
in broad daylight, the way we got away with doing last
time under the general disorganization and freedom of
All-Respectable Time. If we tried that now, we'd be
arrested and held inside of five minutes."

"Don't worry," said Cully. "It's not in daylight we'll
be going down." He turned to the lanky Navigator.
"Pete, you and I'll start setting things up now."

He and Pete went into a huddle about the safest
practical method of getting in close to the surface of the
Crown World, for the forty milliseconds it would re-
quire them to map the area of the Royal Enclosure with
high-speed altitude cameras. The decision was finally
taken to shift to within three diameters of the star
system containing the Crown World, then to move in
on conventional drive for the nine or ten days it would
take them to get within a half-million miles of the
Crown World itself. At a half-million miles, they were
in one of the so-called "gray" zones of detection. They
would be close enough to the Crown World itself so
that the distance between them would be too small to
be accurately measurable upon anything like a large-

scan unit. On the other hand, they would be far enough away from the planet so that conventional sensing units would have trouble locating them in the relative vastness of empty space surrounding their metal hull.

Ten days later they rested, some four hundred and eighty thousand miles from the Crown World itself, while Pete set up a very short but complex double-shift.

"Ready," Pete announced at last.

"Stations!" ordered Cully.

They shifted. From the standpoint of those aboard the *Nansh Rakh* watching their screens, nothing happened except that their instruments recorded a brief increase of light of forty-milliseconds' duration. That flash of sunlight was even too brief to register upon the eyes of those watching the screens, except in the case of a few of them with acute vision like Cully, Doak and Pete Hyde. As far as the awareness of the rest were concerned, it was as if they had just suddenly shifted from a position deep in a star system under the light of a nearby sun into deep space with its surrounding blackness and tiny starlights.

But Pete was jubilant. They had accomplished a shift right to the edges of the Crown World's atmosphere, got their pictures and shifted away to a four-light-year distance without a hitch. Moreover, his cameras had worked beautifully. Down in the Equipment Room he spread out a series of large two-dimensional stills for Cully and Will to examine. Fitted together in their proper relationship, they showed a large rectangle covering a piece of planetary terrain some five-by-ten miles in area. On these stills the various man-made structures were revealed as if seen from an altitude of less than three-hundred feet.

Will had already sketched up a theoretical layout for an Enclosure inhabited by a Ruling Family of the Moldaug, showing the relative size and spacing of the structures housing the various Family members. Cully remembered the torchlit structures of the Compound as he had seen them. The three men set about correlating the information on their photographs with the theoretical layout.

However, it hardly required more than the orientation of the largest structures before Will was able to put his finger on one building on photograph number seven.

"This is it," he said. "This is where the Heritors to the Throne are housed."

"That's it, then," said Cully. "The next point to decide is, what's the best time for us to get into it with the least amount of disturbance?"

"I've been doing some thinking about that," said Will. "The Moldaug are diurnal, like ourselves, but they've also got an activity period lasting about two and a half hours shortly before midnight. Following that activity period would be the time of most general rest and inactivity." Will smiled a little. "Of course, that's also going to be the time at which they'd consider a sneak attack most likely if they were expecting attack—just as the period before dawn has been a traditionally favorite time for an attack by one group of human beings upon another."

"All right," said Cully. "Then, let's get ready."

They split up. Fifty-three hours later, the *Nansh Rakh* shifted suddenly to the night edge of the atmosphere of the Crown World, then dropped on conventional drive through the atmosphere toward the Royal Family's area. As far as the Equipment Room could tell, no local alarm system reacted to their entry. At what would have been around two A.M. by human and Earthly standards, they landed lightly beside the structure they had decided housed the Royal Princes.

The sally port swung open. Cully, Doak, and six other men emerged. They were dressed in black clothes, roughly conforming to the outstanding shape of Moldaug dress—the peaked shoulders, the half-hood or high, upstanding cowl, and the skullcap-covered heads that simulated the hairless Moldaug skulls. In addition, their hands and faces had been blackened to reflect no stray gleam of light. Low to the ground, they scurried the thirty yards or so to the nearest entrance of the structure that was their target.

The entrance was barred by a sliding door. Cully slapped a cordlike length of gray, puttylike, plastic explosive down one vertical crack. He stepped back and triggered it with a small fuse gun.

There was a muffled thud. Three quarters of the door disappeared, leaving a dark, jagged-edged hole through which two men could walk abreast. At a run, Cully led the way through it into the building.

They found themselves in a long, narrow corridor, unlit except for a few palely glowing squares of translucent material set in the ceiling at distant intervals. Cully thumbed on the lamp at his belt, and the rust-colored walls around them seemed to jump inward in the sudden illumination.

"Third turn to the right. Follow close!" Cully barked over his shoulder.

The slapping sound of their running feet seemed to thunder in the corridor as they ran down it. Now Cully was aware of a mixed odor—a green odor like that of crushed vegetation mixed with the sharpness of ozone. He reached the third turn to the right and rounded the corner. Ahead of them now lay a shorter hallway, more fully lit than the one they had just left. But also, now, for the first time they began to hear the whistle-like shrilling of Moldaug female voices raised in alarm behind the walls on either side of the corridor. A male Moldaug carrying a handgun stumbled out of the doorway ahead of Cully, and someone behind Cully beamed him down.

Other Moldaug faces were appearing at other doorways along the way. There was the shouting of a male voice behind them, followed by the actinic flash of an alien handgun, and one of the men behind Cully cried out, and Cully heard him fall. Somebody else cursed and fired back down the corridor. There was an exchange of shots.

Meanwhile Cully was pounding on. He reached the

end of the corridor, where a sliding door barred his way. From a few yards' distance he fired at it, then hit it with all the force and weight of his running body. The door shivered and broke around him, and he tumbled into a relatively small room carpeted with green vegetation, something between ferns and leaves in appearance.

He rolled over in this, the odor he had smelled earlier filling his nostrils so that it made his head swim. He scrambled to his feet, found Doak beside him, and saw three miniature aliens, dressed in every respect as male adults, but ranging in height from less than three feet to barely four feet. They stood close together facing him, and the middle one held a handgun in both hands.

"Doak—" Cully began. But Doak was ahead of him. Even as Cully was opening his mouth, the little man was diving at the middle youngster and wresting the handgun out of his grasp.

Cully stumbled forward, snatched up the two smaller figures, one under each arm, and turned toward the door. He was aware of Doak picking up the largest one. Together they headed back through the ruined door and up the corridor. There were no Moldaug to be seen in the corridor now, except for three still bodies lying at intervals on the floor down its length. On either side the doors were shut, but the crying out of the females could still be heard, here and there interspersed by the deeper tones of the males. One of Cully's men had a bad burn through the left shoulder and was being half-carried by two of the others. With the remaining three guarding before and behind, the human party made the best time it could down to the end of the corridor, around to the left and back up the long corridor toward the outer air.

They heard no sounds of pursuit, but they had barely left the building, angling away toward the spaceship to their right, when a line of white fire lanced through the broken entrance, a bolt of crackling energy that could only have come from a floor-mounted weapon.

Outside now, too, there were the sounds of distant

voices and alarms. Other buildings in the area, until now invisible in the darkness, were revealing themselves by the lights that twinkled about them. As the kidnaping party reached the sally port, the whole scene suddenly burst into view as bright as day, as a powerful flare exploded high in the air above it. In that light the humans, their prisoners and the spaceship itself stood out as starkly as the gaunt black figure of a wolf among the packed white sheep of a fold.

"Inside!" snapped Cully. All of them, who had frozen automatically like felons caught in the act at the bursting of the flare overhead, came back to life and scrambled in through the sally port, which clanged shut behind them.

Cully was already shouting into the intercom.

"Lift ship!"

But before the words were out of his mouth, the *Nansh Rakh* was already lifting. In the Control Room, Will was heading her up and out. On the sally-port vision screen, beside the intercom, the flarelit Royal Compound could be seen dropping away rapidly beneath them. Suddenly the *Nansh Rakh* shuddered and rang to a missile hit from below. Cully turned and ran for the Control Room.

He burst in on Will, who was seated in what ordinarily would have been Cully's pilot's seat. At the sight of Cully he slid over into his own seat at Cully's right, and Cully dropped into his own central seat.

A second later Doak filled in the seat to his left.

"Damage?" Cully asked Will, even as his fingers were searching out the controls in front of him.

"Nothing bad," answered Will. "A pretty good hit, but it landed in the aft storage hold. There's not much to damage there. I've sealed that section off."

"Good!" said Cully. In the vision screen before him now, a slightly curved horizon line was beginning to show with the black of space beyond it. He thumbed the intercom and spoke to Pete. "Ready for shift?"

"Ready!" answered the voice of Pete from the Equipment Room.

There was a moment's pause, during which the horizon-line scene on the vision screen before Cully became slightly more curved. Then, all at once, it was gone, replaced by darkness and the stars.

Cully leaned wearily back in his pilot's seat. Pete's voice crackled over the intercom.

"We're about four light-years out from the star system," Pete said. "It'll take about three hours to figure another four-to-five-light-year shift."

"All right," said Cully.

The intercom hummed, open but silent as Pete waited at the other end. Cully swung around in his chair to the right to look at Will.

"Well," he said, "what do you think? Do you figure they'll get word of what we've done off to Ruhn and his Brothers on Earth as soon as possible?"

Will frowned.

"They'll undoubtedly conclude the Princes are dead," he said. "After all, kidnaping is as much an unknown concept to the Moldaug as hostages are—and for the same reason. There'd be no point in stealing people when, if you were Respectable, you'd just have to let them suicide and then return their bodies anyway. So they'll probably try to keep word of this in the official family for a day or two until they have time to talk it over."

"But," said Cully, "after they've had time to talk it over—?"

"Then," said Will, "I can't see them wasting any time sending word to Ruhn, probably with a powerful war fleet close behind to back up a demand for the bodies of the little Princes. After all, you've already shaken the Moldaug social situation by playing Demon of Dark. Now you've put a gap in the direct line of Royal succession by stealing the heirs to the Moldaug Throne. That's a gap that can't be filled except by the return of the Princes' bodies. There may be ways of glossing over a gap like that under ordinary conditions, but not under the present disturbed conditions you've set up by playing Demon of Dark. In short"—he smiled at Cully—"there's no doubt you've put the present ruling Moldaug dynasty in a very shaky political position."

"That's what I wanted to hear," said Cully.

"So," said Pete. "And now we've done that, where to?"

"Earth," said Cully.

20

The *Nansh Rakh* shifted steadily toward Earth. It shortly became plain that her raid had taken the Crown World entirely by surprise. She was three shifts out before there were flares of ships moving out from the Crown World's star system to signal pursuit. By that time, Pete told Cully, there was no hope of the aliens' catching them, except by accident.

Those aboard got to work meanwhile repairing the rear cargo hold, which had been pierced by the missile during the raid. Cully had turned the three young Moldaug Princes over to the care of Will. This was not only because Will was probably by temperament the best-suited of any aboard to take care of them, but because he was the only one with sufficient understanding of their language to be a practical success at the job.

Busy directing the repair of the ship, Cully had not seen the little alien Princes from the moment they had been brought aboard the *Nansh Rakh*. He had almost succeeded in forgetting that they existed—except as part of the machinery of his plans. He did not think of them; he thought only of Amos Braight and how he would get to see him.

Because reaching Amos, thought Cully, watching through the transparent faceplate of his airsuit outside the ship as the final repair section of the damaged hold was being melted into place, would not be the real problem. The real problem would be to reach him without being recognized, along the way, as Cully When. For a Tri-Worlds Council Member was surrounded at all times by security guards specially briefed on known enemies and other dangerous characters who might try to get through to harm a Member. Cully had no wish to be shot on sight before Amos even knew he was on Earth . . .

Cully felt a tap on his elbow and turned around to see another airsuited figure. The face of Will showed through the faceplate. Will beckoned him to follow and led him back out through the temporary airlock into the air-filled section of the spaceship. Once safely surrounded by atmosphere, Will opened up his faceplate and pushed the hood back, exposing his head so that he could talk. Cully did the same.

"What is it?" asked Cully.

"The young Moldaug want to talk to you," said Will.

Cully nodded. Will looked at him curiously.

"You don't seem surprised," said Will. There was an odd note to his voice and something uncomfortable about his gaze. Cully smiled at him.

"I thought they'd get around to wanting to see me eventually," said Cully. "But what if I don't come right now?"

"Of course," murmured Will, "if you don't come, you don't come."

"That's all right, then," said Cully. "But I *will* come." He ran a finger from the neck downward along the closure of his suit to unseal it. He stepped out of it. Will was doing the same. "Let's go!"

He followed Will forward through the ship until they came to what had once been the quarters for the officers among the Moldaug crew. Here three adjoining staterooms had had interconnecting doors cut between them. One belonged to Will, the center one belonged to the three young alien Princes, and the third one belonged to Cully. Cully's interconnecting door had remained locked. Will's, he remembered vaguely hearing a day or two ago, was normally allowed to stand open, so that the young aliens could reach the white-haired man at any time.

It was to Will's own cabin that Will took Cully now. Will unlocked the door and they stepped inside. To Cully's surprise, the room was empty, but, according to reports, the interconnecting door from it to the aliens' stateroom alongside was standing ajar. Will led the way to and through it, and Cully followed him.

Within the other stateroom he found the three aliens lined up side by side with the largest one in the middle, just as he had seen them when he had first laid eyes on them in their own quarters back on the Crown World. It was obviously an official posture of some sort, possibly one adopted from seeing their elders use it. However, in any case, they stood in their version of an official silence, watching him as he stopped about six feet in front of them.

Will was standing to one side, and for the first time Cully had a clear, unhurried view of the alien youngsters. They were smaller, Will had told him, than Earth Children of a comparable age—just as the Moldaug adults were, on the average, smaller and slighter-boned than their human equivalents. But there was nothing similar to the actions of human children in the way they stood so close together, their shoulders pressed, and in this stiff, portentous silence. Nor was their general appearance childlike to human eyes. Rather, with their hairless, round skulls and bony faces, they resembled little old men more than children.

But, at the same time, that which was youthful about them could not be denied. In spite of their strangeness of form and feature, they fixed on Cully the wide, all-curious, unjudging stare of the young. There was, Cully noticed, in every line and feature of these Moldaug children, the same unconscious demand for adult care and protection he had seen in human children back home.

Instinctively, they expressed the demand; and instinctively, Cully found himself responding to it. Suddenly aware of what was taking place in him, he erased the smile that was beginning to touch his lips at the sight of their miniature formality, and called his mind back to business.

"Well?" he said to Will in English, "I'm here. What do they want?"

"They're waiting for you to ask them that," answered Will. Cully turned his gaze back to the little Princes.

"Myself am here," said Cully formally, in Moldaug. "What is it yourself wishes to say to myself?"

At the sound of his voice, the littlest one giggled at him, leaning forward out of line—and was quickly pulled back in by the tallest, middle Brother.

"Ourself has summoned thee here," said that same tallest one, "because ourself is not merely an ordinary Respectable individual. Ourself is the Very Most Respectable Heritors of the Very Most Respectable of families. Therefore, ourself do not have to wait for thee to offer ourself a Respectable return to our families. Ourself have summoned thee to demand that thou make ourself this offer."

"Respectable offer," echoed Cully, thoughtfully nodding. He turned to Will, speaking in English. "You think they're serious?"

"Perfectly serious," said Will, also in English. "Whatever answer you give them, I suggest you be just as serious. They want their bodies returned to their families so that normal succession within their family goes on. You'll make a great mistake if you treat this demand of theirs as anything less than it is."

"I wasn't going to treat it any other way," said Cully, gazing at them. He turned back to the three small aliens and the sixpower searchlights of their examining eyes.

"Myself has not made yourself this Respectable offer," he said slowly in Moldaug, "because myself does not intend making it at all, for the reason that there is no need for it. Myself must keep yourself with me for a small while longer. But at the end of that time, yourself will be returned, alive, to the family of yourself."

He ended his speech. For several seconds the small aliens stared back at him without responding. Then the middle Brother spoke again.

"Perhaps thou are unsure," he said, "that ourself is wise enough in years to accomplish this Respectable action. Therefore, I, Hjrker, Eldest Brother, assure you that I am fully so; and I pledge myself to give these my Brothers whatever help they need before I accomplish my own Respectable action." Unexpectedly, he patted his smallest Brother on the head and descended suddenly from a lofty official tone to a rush of confidential words. "Especially Othga here, who, as thou may see, does not really understand these things very well yet."

Cully glanced at Will, but the white-haired man's face was as rigidly uncommitted as the stone mask of some indifferent idol. Cully turned back to the three young Princes.

"If yourself knows about myself," he said, "yourself knows that myself seldom requires or offers a Respectable action to the prisoners of myself. For myself am not an ordinary captor. As yourself may have heard, myself am the Demon of Dark."

The six young eyes stared at this statement for a long moment of silence. It was a silence that was unexpectedly and somewhat shrilly broken by Othga, the smallest of the three.

"Where is thy black third hand?"

Cully stood, cut adrift by the unexpected question. *This* he had not expected. He remembered now that it was part of the legend about the Demon that he had a black third hand which he kept tucked inside his clothes most of the time. He had to fight back a smile. No adult Moldaug had ever asked to see Cully's black third hand.

The difference between youthful and mature alien thinking was interesting.

The three young Moldaug stood, meanwhile, staring back at him with the fascinated astonishment and interest of human children watching an adult who has just used a forbidden, or otherwise terrible, word. Then the middle Brother stiffened and took a small half-step forward toward Cully. His two Brothers closed up immediately on either side of him.

"Thou are not the Demon of Dark. Thou are not even a Respectable Person," accused the tallest Brother. "Thou are only a soft face!"

Cully nodded.

"That is true," he said. "Myself am a soft face. In the time when the Very Most Respectable Father and Uncles of yourself were the age of yourself now, ye of the Moldaug did not have to know about soft faces and deal with them. But when yourself shall be full-grown Very Most Respectable, yourself and all ye Moldaug will need to understand the different ways of soft faces like myself."

The small, bony faces stared up at him in bafflement.

"Myself does not understand thee," said Hjrker, finally.

"That is right. Yourself does not understand," said Cully. "But yourself must try to understand that there can be a way equal to that of Respectability, but no less. And according to that way, myself am entirely Respectable; but, according to that way, if myself should let you accomplish your Respectable action, I would not be Respectable at all. This is a difference yourself from now on must begin to try to understand."

There was a long moment of silence in the room.

"Myself understands all that is needed," said the tallest Brother at last, stubbornly. "For the people will only live safely on many worlds if there is one strong clan to lead them. Everybody says so. And within the clan there must be one sept that leads, within that sept one family, and within the family there must be the

Very Most Respectable of all, such as Barthi and his two Brothers who are the Father and Uncles of ourself."

"And in a little time yourself will be returned alive to the Very Most Respectable Barthi and his Brothers," said Cully.

"But a little time is not-Respectable! No time is Respectable!" said Hjerker. "Without all of its parts, alive or dead, the family is not-Respectable, nor the sept, nor the clan—and the people have not proper leadership. Now, perhaps already, the Father of ourselves and his Brothers no longer leads the family, or the family the sept, or the sept the clan, of ourselves. Perhaps already our clan is fallen into not-Respectability—and all because thou would not let us accomplish our proper, Respectable action. *Thou are not a Respectable Person!*"

With that, and in unison, the three young Moldaug turned their backs on Cully. It was a dramatic gesture for one so young—marred only by the fact that the smallest Brother could not resist peeking back over his shoulder to see how Cully took it. The oldest Brother reached over and sharply turned Othga's head straight once more.

Cully turned and left, followed by Will. Once more out in the corridor, the door to Will's connecting stateroom safely locked behind them, Cully let himself smile. But then he sobered. He turned to face the white-haired man.

"Whatever happens," Cully said, "they mustn't be allowed to harm themselves. If they happened to succeed in killing themselves, everything would go down the drain."

"I'll keep them safe," said Will. "In fact—you know they really aren't mature, for all the way they talk. I wouldn't be surprised, with the adaptability you find in all young creatures, that they didn't resign themselves to the situation now that you've told them 'no' so decisively. I'm sorry you had to wrestle with them alone,

though. I thought it'd be more convincing if I didn't
join in the argument. Sorry."

"Don't be," said Cully. "I was expecting something
like this. And I'm glad to hear you say you think they'll
resign themselves to their situation aboard here. You
really think that?"

"Yes," said Will, slowly, "They meant what they said,
all right. But at the same time, they were—even the
oldest of them—more or less going through the motions
of a procedure they didn't really understand, except as
something their elders always took for granted. Now
that they've made the effort and it hasn't worked, they
may simply accept the fact. That's something children
of all races have to do all the time anyway."

"Good," said Cully. "Well, once you're sure they've
given up the idea of suicide, you can let them out of
just those two rooms. Let them run around the ship—
just so long as they don't get into trouble."

"I'll watch them," said Will.

So he did. The result was that, within a day or two,
the young Moldaug were, literally, running up and
down the ship's corridors and gaping at the changes
that the humans had made in the alien vessel for convenience or efficiency. The young Princes poked their
narrow noses, in fact, into almost everything, and shortly
became not only acceptable, but highly welcome in the
crew's quarters. The only place Will would not take
them was the Control Room. They suffered under this
prohibition for a number of days, but curiosity was
evidently as powerful a Moldaug trait as it was a human
one. The day came when Cully, in the Control Room
with Pete and Doak, heard a birdlike rattling at the
Control Room door.

He went over and opened it. Outside, in a row,
without Will, and facing up at him, were the three
small Princes—Hjrker stiff, tallest, in the middle. Just
at that moment, Will turned a corner of the corridor
behind them and came hurrying up.

"Sorry, Cully," said Will. "They got away from me—"

"What's the trouble?" Cully asked, speaking to him in English—but it was Hjrker who answered, almost as if he had understood the human tongue.

"We are the Very Most Respectable on this ship," he said stubbornly. "Therefore, we can go anywhere we want."

Othga was craning his head in excitement to see around Cully's tall body at the changes the humans had made in the Moldaug-designed Control Room. Hjrker reached over and pulled his impulsive younger Brother back into the official line.

"Myself am sorry," said Cully, "and myself agrees that yourself is the Very Most Respectable on this ship. But yourself, in spite of that fact, is still not permitted to come into this Control Room."

The Princes stared at him. Hjrker, if Cully was beginning to be able to read Moldaug facial expressions at all, was scowling. But it was Othga, the unruly, who piped up.

"To the Very Most Respectable everything is permitted!"

"No," said Cully.

"Thou are not-Respectable to say 'no' to ourself!" accused Othga.

They stared at him.

"Perhaps not," said Cully, "but myself am Right."

"What has the fact that thou are Right to do with the fact that thou are not-Respectable?" Hjrker demanded.

"It has *everything* to do with it," said Cully calmly, "because yourself are not aboard a Moldaug ship now. This is now a human ship. Here, if something is not-Right it may not be done, no matter how Respectable the oneself who wishes to do it. Here, Right is more important than Respectable."

Hjrker scowled, apparently baffled and at a loss for words. Not so, Othga.

"Why is it not-Right for us to go into a Control Room?" demanded Othga. And he shook, doglike with triumphal glee, plainly feeling that he had now put Cully thoroughly on the spot argumentatively.

"Because," said Cully, "among humans it is not a matter of things being Respectable or not-Respectable, but Right or not-Right. And among humans it is not-Right for young ones, no matter how Respectable, to enter any place of sensitivity or danger without a Responsible person accompanying them. In our Control Room now are instruments which yourself might damage without intending to. There are also other instruments which might hurt yourself because you do not understand them. Therefore, it is not-Right for you to enter here, since you have no Responsible Person with you to ensure that you hurt nothing and are not hurt."

Hjrker's scowl suddenly cleared.

He pointed stiffly at Will.

"Very well," Hjrker said, "ourself will name *him* a Responsible Person for ourself."

Cully shook his head. It was a human gesture unknown to the Moldaug ordinarily, but the three young Princes had come to understand it since their kidnaping.

"No," he said, "Yourself does not fully understand. Among humans, being named such a Responsible Person is not something done lightly. It is not-Right for anyone to be Responsible for young ones like yourself unless they are already a Responsible member of your family, or so designated by a Responsible member of your family. That is why," said Cully, firmly beginning to close the Control Room door in their small faces, "it is not-Right for any of ourselves to allow you in here, and aboard a human ship oneself never does what is not-Right."

The door clicked shut. For a second, beyond it, Cully heard only silence. But then a babble of small voices questioning Will arose on the other side of the metal panel. Smiling, Cully went back to his work.

Ten days later, traveling on a direct line and at maximum practical distance per shift, they were out of Moldaug territory, well past the Frontier and closing rapidly on the Solar System and their destination of Earth. They had already joined the direct line of travel between the Solar System and the Pleiades; and with no general monitoring system likely to be in operation, they should be able to approach Earth without being challenged. So far, their large-scan cube had shown no sign of the concerted flaring-in and -out of a large number of spaceships such as Cully had told Lee to gather from the Frontier Worlds and bring to the Solar System.

Pete and some of the others found time to worry about this. Cully did not. He had confidence in Leestrom, especially in partnership with Emile Hasec; and he had wanted to get to Earth well before Leestrom showed up, in any case. Still, as they moved first to the outer boundary of the Solar System and then into orbit around Earth itself, with nothing more than a perfunctory traffic check from the traffic-control station, also in orbit, Pete's uneasiness grew.

"I'm having trouble believing this," he growled to Cully over the intercom from the Equipment Room. "What's going on here? Not only is there no sign of Lee, but this is supposed to be a set of planets scared out of their wits for fear they'll make the Moldaug mad enough to fight; and they've got no more space security around this world, no more warships on patrol, then they ever had."

"They're scared to the point of paralysis," answered Cully. But before Pete could say anything further, the outside speaker came to life.

"You are cleared for landing, *Nansh Rakh*." The voice of the traffic-control satellite broke in on them. "Your point of landing will be grid eight thousand one Polar—two thousand four hundred and sixty-nine Equatorial."

"Got it, Traffic Control," answered Doak, in flat, brush-country accents.

He was playing the part of a human translator, picked up in the Pleiades by the alien crew, in order to facilitate their landing and take-off procedures during the delivery of necessary alien supplies to the Moldaug embassy on Earth.

They descended. The Spaceport to which they had been directed was the one outside Phoenix, Arizona. Doak, speaking from the Equipment Room for the supposed aliens, had requested some other Spaceport than the crowded one over Long Island Sound—Earth's largest. The reason he gave was the desire to maintain adequate security measures on the part of the diplomatic-status aliens, theoretically in command of the *Nansh Rakh*. Traffic Control had not hesitated about complying. The Phoenix Spaceport was ideal, quiet enough so that alien-knowledgeable humans were not likely to be present, and less than twenty minutes from Tri-Worlds Headquarters in New York Complex.

"Do you think they believed it—the fact that we're aliens?" asked Pete as the ship touched down on the Phoenix Spaceport pad. Pete had come in from the Equipment Room, leaving Doak there to handle communications with the Spaceport as they landed, there being nothing more for him to do as Navigator. A man with no nerves at all when he was navigating, Pete had a tendency to become jumpy when he was forced to sit on his hands.

"I think so," answered Cully, shutting off his communications connection with Doak and standing up. "We're in a Moldaug-made ship. What else could we be but aliens?" He turned and smiled at Pete. "You don't ask for proof of identity from an alien who looks like an alien. Anybody can see we're non-humans by looking at the shape of this ship. As long as your diplomatic status isn't questioned, no one's going to bother you. In fact, you can have Doak ask for police protection if anyone starts nosing around the ship. Amos Braight may wonder how I got here when he sees me—but the last guess he's going to make is that I got here in a Moldaug spacecraft."

"Then we just sit tight—until we hear from you?" asked Pete. "Is that it?"

"Until you hear from me, or until Lee puts in an appearance with his ships," said Cully. "When that happens, contact him and tell him he can find me through Amos Braight, to look for me somewhere in the Tri-Worlds Council Building."

"You seem awfully sure everything's going to go off all right," snapped Pete. "What makes you so sure they'll just hand over the keys to the Council Chamber to you the minute you speak to Braight and Lee shows up at Moon Base? I suppose you realize the Moldaug'll have a war fleet on their way here right now to get their Princes back?"

"I know. In fact, I'm counting on it," said Cully. He slapped Pete on the shoulder. "For the rest of it, even if I explained, it wouldn't make sense to you. Take me on faith a little while longer?"

Pete nodded grudgingly.

"Any last questions, then?" asked Cully, looking from Pete to Will, who was standing beside the Navigator.

Will shook his head without a word.

"Good luck, then, damn your eyes!" growled Pete.

21

Riding the subway through the vacuum of its underground tube at near-orbital speeds from Phoenix to the Kansas City transfer point, and from there to New York Complex Terminal, Cully found himself caught up in an unfamiliar inversion of emotion.

It was a strange feeling to find himself back once more on the surface of Earth, in the hunted situation he had become accustomed to during his old spacelifting days. But oddly, that same feeling was more familiar and more comfortable—even more natural—than the emotions that had held him at his last previous landing on Earth—that landing which had culminated in the argument with Alia, and his own arrest by the World Police. Coming here then, he had been determined to fit in on Earth and to adjust to Earth ways—and he had felt nothing so much as his difference from the natives of this mother planet. Now, moving familiarly like a hunted enemy among them, the tension of his previous landing was no longer with him.

He looked at the Old Worlds people about him in the subway car; looked at them reading, talking, drinking or simply dozing; and found them much more understandable and akin to himself than he had ever felt them to be before. They were, he thought, as the subway car decelerated at last for its approach into New York Complex Terminal, no different from the people of the Frontier—in a sense, not too vastly different from the Moldaug. All that was different about them was that time and circumstance had cast them into a certain cultural mold from which they could not now break out of their own free will—a cultural mold he would now manipulate to save them from themselves.

He left the Terminal and took a pneumatic tube to the center of the New York Complex. He picked out a restaurant whose large transparent wall gave a fine view of the rising towers of the Tri-Worlds Council Headquarters Building. He ordered breakfast, as soon as he was alone with it, he activated the phone in the privacy of the booth where he had chosen to be served.

The screen lit up with the face of a pleasant but extremely well-tailored, middle-aged woman.

"Member Braight's offices," she said. "Can I help you?"

"I'd like to speak to one of the Member's staff, if it could be arranged," answered Cully with equal pleasantness. "Is Tom Donough there?"

There was the faintest of hesitation as she looked at his face through her screen. Cully's hair had been dyed a dark brown and his face aged with make-up. Her stare indicated no recognition of him as Cully When.

"I'm afraid he isn't—right now," she answered. "Perhaps you'd like to leave a message for him?"

"Yes," said Cully. "I'd appreciate it if he'd set a time when I can call him and find him in. I'm actually phoning on behalf of another gentleman who's got an urgent message for Mr. Donough. Unfortunately, neither of us is in a position where Mr. Donough can call us back. But if you give him my message, and give me some idea now when I might call back to see if there's any answer—"

"I really don't know," said the woman, writing on a

pad before her. "Mr. Donough is Member Braight's
personal secretary, you know, and he's with the Member
almost all the time. There's no way of telling when
he'll find time to come back to the offices here."

"Well, perhaps you can pass my message on anyway," said Cully. "The message my friend carries is
more than slightly urgent. You might try mentioning to
Mr. Donough something about the Frontier Worlds
Banks—I think he'll understand."

The woman's face became suddenly alert. She stared
into the screen for a second.

"Frontier Banks? The ones owned by Mr. Royce—?"
She broke off abruptly. "Just a moment, please."

The phone screen in Cully's booth suddenly went
blank—not with the silvery blankness of a broken connection, but with the gray obscurity that came when
the party at the other end was pressing down on a hold
button. Cully waited patiently. After perhaps half a
minute the screen cleared again to show the woman's
face.

"I'm sorry," she said. "I can't get in touch with Mr.
Donough right now. He's with the Member at the
Member's Headquarters office, getting ready for a Council meeting scheduled for one o'clock this afternoon.
But if your friend would care to go over to the Headquarters Building, I'll phone ahead and have a pass
waiting for him at the main entrance. He can go up to
the Member's offices, and wait there until Mr. Donough
is free to talk to him."

"That would be fine," said Cully.

"Good," she said, picking up her stylus again. "Who
shall I have the pass made out for?"

"A Mr. Smith—William Smith," dictated Cully. She
wrote the name down.

"William Smith," she echoed. "The pass will be waiting for you, and I'll get word to Mr. Donough to come
to the offices to talk with your friend, just as soon as I
can."

"Thank you," said Cully, and cut the phone connection.

He had barely done so, when an automated cart came rolling up to the table bearing the breakfast he had ordered. Cully transferred the various plates and glasses to his table and settled down to eat. He was too old a campaigner to rush into things, and he knew that most men, himself included, operated better on a full stomach. He had located Braight, which had been his main intent. Now it was necessary to plan how actually to contact Alia's father.

As soon as he had finished eating, Cully left the restaurant and made his way to the main entrance of the Tri-Worlds Council Building. He gave the name of William Smith to the armed and black-uniformed World Policeman at the main entrance, and received a small round badge showing three planets in a circle and his name printed below them above the stamped legend— *Visitor*. He continued on to the circular information desk in the lobby beyond the entrance, amd there asked for a wand to guide him to Member Braight's offices.

The girl he spoke to behind the information desk gave him the wand and showed him how to set it—a simple matter of turning the rotating handle until the words *Member Braight's Offices* showed up through a slot in the handle cover. She passed it into his grasp and it turned in his hand, pointing at the elevator tubes across the lobby. He followed the direction in which it pointed and stepped into one of the elevator tubes. He stepped onto one of the ascending discs in the tube, and the wand hummed a single note. The platform lifted him upward for perhaps thirty or so stories, and then stopped. The transparent wall of the tube slipped back, and Cully, following the indication of the wand, stepped from the platform into a hallway, wide, green carpeted and luxuriously alive with soft light and shifting murals.

The wand led him on down this corridor and around two corners into branching corridors until it stopped before another, smaller bank of elevator tubes. One of these lifted him a goodly number more of stories, and let him out into a circular lobby from which several short corridors branched off. Clearly, he was high in one of the towers of the Tri-Worlds Council Headquarters. The lobby was busy with the movement of men and women, half of them in the bellhoplike uniform of Council messengers, passing in and out of the shorter corridors. The wand indicated one of these corridors, but Cully did not enter it. Instead, he turned the handle of the wand until it was shut off, and then hesitantly approached one of the uniformed messengers who was on his way out.

"Excuse me—" said Cully. The messenger stopped. "My wand seems to have stopped working. Could you tell me if this is the floor that has the staff restaurant on it?"

"No, it isn't," answered the messenger brusquely. He was a round-faced young man whose air of personal importance hinted an acquaintance with the important messages he carried. "It's eight floors down. What's wrong with your wand? Let me see it."

He took it from Cully's hand, rather than accepting it as Cully offered it, and looked at the handle.

"No wonder," he said. "It's turned off. You see this handle?"

"Yes," answered Cully.

"Well, that handle has to be turned to *Restaurant*. Like this—" The messenger turned the handle until the word *Restaurant* appeared in the slot, then handed it back to Cully. "Just be careful how you hold it. If you turn that handle without noticing it, you can end up anywhere in the building, even in places where you might find yourself in deep trouble."

"I'll watch it," said Cully.

"That's the best thing you can do," said the messenger and went off.

Cully followed the wand with its new setting, and let it lead him back into the elevator tubes. Once in the down tube, drifting downward on a descending disc, he turned the handle once more until he discovered the words *Basement Power Room*. The wand hummed a single, different note from the one that it uttered when he had first stepped into the tube, and the disc this time carried him down a long distance.

When it finally let him out, he found himself in a wide but bare walled marble corridor, pierced with metal doors at intervals. He walked down this corridor for some distance until it branched, then tried one of the doors at random. It was locked. He gave it up and moved about the various corridors at a brisk enough pace to convince the occasional people he passed that he was on some definite errand in this area. The people he passed were not as many as formed on the upper floors, but there were a good number of them down here. Evidently in addition to the power rooms supplying the Headquarters, a good deal of the back records and other materials were stored down here. He encountered a good many clerks, both male and female, and not a few of the uniformed messengers.

He checked his watch. It was nearly twenty minutes to one, twenty minutes until the hour that had been set, according to Braight's receptionist, for the Council meeting.

He chose one of the smaller corridors, and strolled up and down it until he saw one of the messengers who was about his own size coming down it. Except for the two of them, the corridor was deserted. The messenger came on, Cully strolled toward him. Then, as Cully stepped past the other, he wheeled and brought the heel of his hand down on the messenger's neck. The messenger slumped.

Cully bent swiftly over the unconscious body, knelt and got it up over his own neck and shoulders in a fireman's lift. Then he went hastily down the corridor, trying doors as he went. The first door that proved unlocked had several clerks inside bending over a micrograph machine. They looked up with annoyed expressions at the sight of his face, seen through a narrow crack in the barely open door.

"Sorry—" muttered Cully, who closed the door behind him and went on his way.

Cully had to try two more unlocked doors before he found one that opened into a room that was stacked from floor to ceiling with bundles of official forms baled in transparent coverings. He carried his burden in there and deposited it upon the common surface of several stacks of forms racked tightly together. The messenger was still unconscious. Cully felt a pulse and peeled back an eyelid. With luck, the other would have nothing worse than a headache and a sore neck to show for the adventure.

Taking a roll of tape from his pocket and placing it handily upon a nearby stack of forms, Cully quickly undressed the unconscious man, then taped his wrists behind him and his ankles together, ending up with a strip of tape across the mouth as a gag. Then he himself changed into the messenger's uniform.

The messenger, clad now only in boxer shorts and scalloped undershirt, was beginning to stir on top of his bed of forms, when Cully stepped out into the corridor once more, setting the latch on the door so that it would lock behind him. As it clicked shut, he looked up and down the corridor and found it empty. He had opened one of the packages and taken several of the bulky forms and sealed them into an official envelope. Carrying this now, with the wand left in the room behind him, he went briskly to the elevators, stepped in, and spoke aloud the number of the floor to which the wand had originally directed him. He rose upward.

Entering the upper lobby again, he went quickly ahead and down the corridor which the wand had originally indicated, but which he had not followed the time before. At the end of it he found another, smaller, circular lobby and another middle-aged receptionist, as much like the one he had talked to over the phone as if she had been her twin.

"Urgent and personal for Member Braight—from his own staff offices," he told her, displaying the bulky envelope he carried.

"Oh? All right—" she answered. "He's in his working office. You can take them on in." Seeing Cully's hesitation, she added, "New, are you? It's the third door to your left, next to the meeting room."

"Thanks," said Cully, and went down the corridor she had indicated.

Before the door she had described, he stopped and knocked.

"Come in," answered the voice that was unmistakably Amos Braight's, even muffled as it was by the intervening door panels.

Cully touched the latch button of the door and swung it open before him. He walked in, hearing it close behind him.

The two men in the room turned to look at him—and then checked themselves, suddenly still. Caught in the afternoon light from a single tall, wide window, they made a small tableau: Amos Braight, short, and fleshy and dark, seated behind the desk, and the tall, heavy-shouldered, white-haired man standing beside the desk and in the act of handing a paper to him. They stayed unmoving as Cully came forward to the desk, and then Amos broke the spell.

"Cully!" he said. The tall man, who had been holding the paper outstretched, withdrew it sharply and took a step backward toward a door in the wall behind him.

"Hold it, Tom," said Cully. And the man who had been Amos' personal secretary, even back when Cully had been a boy on Kalestin, stopped again. "I'm here to talk to Amos privately. If he still wants you to call the World Police after I've talked to him, there'll be plenty of time to do it then."

"What makes you think I'll talk to you, Cully?" said Amos harshly. A little of the color that had left his face at the first sight of Cully was flooding back. Seated behind the desk, he seemed to have shrunk from the days when Cully remembered him. He was hunched and sag-bodied by comparison—almost frail-looking—and the lines about his mouth and under his eyes were deep.

"Because I'm here to make you a deal, Amos," said Cully lightly. "Give me your word that you'll listen to me and let me go afterwards without having Tom call the Police. And I'll give you my word that I'll tell you something that can solve all your problems. On the other hand, if you call the Police now, I guarantee you'll regret it." He stared into the dark, age-shrunken eyes of the older man. "How about it, Amos? We both have a record of keeping our word."

Amos stiffened.

"*All* my problems?" he echoed sharply. For a moment he hesitated, chewing on his lower lip, then apparently made up his mind. "All right. You've got my word, and I'll take yours. Tom, wait inside."

"Yes, Amos," said the big, white-haired man. He turned, casting an unhappy glance at Cully, and went out through a door in the back wall.

Cully and Amos both watched the door close behind him. When it was closed, they looked back at each other.

"Well, Cully," said Amos. His voice was wary. He got up from behind his desk and walked around it to face Cully. "It's up to you now. I suppose you realize I put my reputation, and even my Membership on the Council, on the line just to hear what you promised to tell me. It'd better be worth it."

Cully looked at him. He had remembered Amos Braight all these years as a man—only middling-tall perhaps—but filled with a vibrant force of authority and self-command. He had remembered Amos as the older man must have been that day he stopped the Fortown Massacre, by walking unarmed through blood-crazed soldiers into a fort controlled by an insane commander, to order that same commander be put under arrest by those same soldiers.

Now the man he looked at, standing on this thick plum-colored rug in this wide-paneled office on the topmost floor of the building that ruled the three richest Worlds of the human race, seemed less than a poor relation of that figure in Cully's memory and imagination. The Amos Braight facing Cully now had grown thicker in the belly and thinner in the face. He had grown a thick mustache, now graying. The unchanged black hair on his round head looked artificial and unnatural above that mustache and the haggard lines of that face; and his shoulders were thinned and bent forward. But more than this, the man's voice had changed. Where it had been strong, it was now thin. Where it had been harsh, it was now bitter. It had the savage whine of an old dog defending a cold hearth. Suddenly Cully was reminded of how Alia had insisted that her father had changed.

"It's worth it," said Cully, answering Amos' half-threat. "I'm here to relieve you of all responsibility. What could be more worth it than that?"

Amos stared at him.

"What's that supposed to mean?" he demanded. "What is this?"

"This?" said Cully. "This is the *coup d'état* you've been so worried about, Amos. We on the Frontier are taking over control of all of you on the Old Worlds, Amos. Maybe you didn't know it, but there's a Moldaug war fleet on the way here."

"I know," said Amos, harshly. "Ruhn just left to meet with it. He's due back in eight days with some kind of word from the Moldaug rulers. I still say, what's that got to do with this nonsense you're spouting?"

"Nonsense?" echoed Cully. "How can it be nonsense when it's what you've been warning about, and guarding against, and arresting people from the Frontier for, the last four years? It's simple. The Moldaug are ready to fight. You people can't handle them without a war, but we Frontiersmen can. I told you I had the solution to all your troubles. So we're taking over. The only sensible thing for the Old Worlds to do is go along with it and let us take over. You can begin by resigning, Amos, and calling on the other Tri-Worlds Council Members to resign."

"Resign? Is that it?" Amos turned toward the door through which Tom Donough had passed a few moments before.

"Come on!" he said harshly to Cully over his shoulder.

Cully followed him as Amos opened the door. On the heels of Alia's father, Cully passed through into a larger room with a dais at its far end, on which was a circular table surrounded by seats in which five other men sat. The five had faces which Cully found familiar. They were the other Members of the Tri-Worlds Council; six of them, counting Amos, consisting of two men each from the Worlds of Earth, Venus and Mars. Standing to one side of the table was the figure of Tom Donough, the light from a window vision screen behind him aureoling his white hair.

Cully checked instantly, with the instinctive response of an animal stepping into a trap. But, just as he checked, he felt what he had already half-expected—his arms seized from behind and himself suddenly armlocked and helpless between two large World Policemen.

"Well," said Amos, going on up to the other five men at the table. "You heard?"

"Yes," said one of them, whom Cully recognized as Vlacek, the Senior Member from Mars. "We heard it all over your intercom. But," he hesitated, "you don't suppose there might be some point to what he says— that those Frontiersmen can handle the Moldaug without war?"

"Don't talk like someone who doesn't know anything more than he hears on the daily news!" Amos' voice had abruptly swelled. Suddenly it had all the vigor and strength that Cully remembered hearing in it years ago on Kalestin. Looking at Alia's father now, Cully saw that the older man seemed to have grown six inches. Dominatingly, he towered over the other, seated Members of the Council.

"That's not a fair accusation, Amos—" Vlacek was beginning, when Amos snapped him to silence.

"Not fair! Are we supposed to be concerned about what's fair? Or about saving the human race, here in the Solar System? A Frontiersman only has to say one word, and you begin to believe him. Don't any of you remember what we've established beyond a shadow of a doubt? Outer space destroys men—it destroys them, mind, body, and soul!"

"Now, Amos," said another of the men, one with his back to Cully, "this isn't a time for one of your campaign speeches—"

"Campaign speech? *Fact!*" Amos turned fiercely on him. "Maybe we don't know why, but we've got the evidence. The human race degenerates out beyond the Solar System. Look at these wild men of the Frontier. Look at what happened to those soldiers that were sent out to Fortown, on Kalestin, fourteen years ago! Those soldiers went insane, literally insane, out there. Are you telling me they didn't?"

Cully laughed, suddenly seeing the direction in which Amos was trending. Amos ignored the sound of that laughter.

"And I was there, let me remind you!" Amos' voice rose. He was all but raving now. But it was a strangely controlled raving, with a steady, chanting, almost hypnotic quality to it, which carried, even to Cully, a strong compulsion to be swept up into unthinking belief of what the aging man was saying. It was the compelling sound of a skilled persuader of men and women. "I'm not telling you what statistics say! I'm not telling you what's been reported. I'm telling you what's true, what I *know* is true . . ." A little spittle flew from the corners of Amos' mouth. "Space beyond the Solar System's not for normal humans. It takes aliens, creatures like the Moldaug, to exist out there. When men and women go out, it changes them! I know this! You *know* I know this, because I've been out there—as Governor on Kalestin—and felt what happens—and fought it off—so

that I could come back here to Earth—and warn you
about it!"

Amos leaned over and pounded rhythmically and
furiously with the flat of his hand upon the dark-brown
surface of the table before him as he spoke. His voice
lifted almost to a shout.

"*Are you going to deny the truth—when you hear it
from me—only to believe—lies when you hear them—
from someone like him?*"

His arm shot out, his finger pointing to Cully; while
his eyes, bulging, held the eyes of the other Council
Members. These stared back at him now like tranced
men, some rigid, some with fingers jerking against the
table top, some with mouths open and quivering.

"That's right, believe *me!*" Cully's voice slashed
sardonically across their trance, making them all jerk
around to look at him. "You'd better, because there's
something Amos has never told you. Actually, he ought
to disqualify himself—"

"Gag him!" shouted Amos, swinging about to the
guards.

A palm gag slapped across Cully's mouth and lower
face before he could finish his sentence.

"Now, take him away!" snapped Amos to the two
Policemen. "Lock him up! We'll keep him until Ruhn
gets back, and then we'll turn him over to the aliens—to
prove we've got nothing to do with the Frontier, that
it's all the Frontier's fault, this Moldaug war fleet moving in on us! Take him away—"

"Amos! Wait—" It was Vlacek again, on his feet now,
his eyes clear again. "Just a minute, Amos. He was
going to say something—"

"What if he was?" said Amos. "What if he even
believes what he was going to say? We know that
whatever it was, was a lie. It'd have to be, coming from
him. Take him away!"

"Wait—" said Vlacek, then almost cringed as the
darkly congested face of Amos swung once more upon
him. "He had something to say about you, Amos. If

there's something the Council needs to know about you—"

"Are you suspecting me of hiding something, Vlacek?" Suddenly, without warning, Amos relaxed. His voice became low-pitched, reasonable, calm and mild. "*Me*, Vlacek?" He spread his hands on the table. "How can you or anyone suspect me, of all people? Remember, I've got a mandate from the voters—not just the voters here on Earth, but the people on your Mars, too, Vlacek. The news polls show over eighty percent approved of me on all three Worlds—double the number approving their own Representatives, like yourself. Are you going to your voters—to your own voters on Mars, Vlacek—and tell them that you suspect *me* of something—just on the word of some Frontiersman?"

Amos stopped speaking. He stood where he was, leaning a little against the table with his belly, his eye fixed on Vlacek, the only other man around that table on his feet. Vlacek stood, silent.

"Sit down, Vlacek," Amos said softly. Vlacek sat down. "I don't blame you. I forgive you. We're all under a strain here. A terrible strain. But we'll come out all right. Yes, we'll come out all right when we hand this troublemaker over to Ruhn, and renounce the Pleiades and all those half-human settlers out there who've been stirring up the Moldaug."

He turned to Cully and the two World Policemen.

"Take the prisoner out," he said quietly to the Policemen. "Lock him up here, where we can keep an eye on him. But see he's comfortable. Give him anything he wants—in reason."

His eyes shifted to Cully.

"I'm sorry, boy," he said sadly, in a suddenly gentle voice. "I'm really sorry for you, Cully. I thought of you as a son once—and I still do. But we have to be ready to sacrifice anyone, even ourselves—even our own sons—if that's necessary to save the human race."

His eyes went back to the World Policemen. Slowly, he sank into his seat at the round table.

"Take him out, you two," he said.

The men turned Cully about and walked him back through Amos' office, down the corridor and out into the central lobby. The people there stared at the two uniformed men, still holding the arms of Cully's tall figure, as they went past. The Policemen took Cully down several elevators and various corridors until, at the end of one corridor, they unlocked a door and thrust him into a small room with a single, small vision screen on its otherwise bare walls.

They stripped and searched him, taking away his clothes down to his shoes. Instead, they gave him shower clogs, Police-issue underwear, gym slacks and sweatshirt. Only then did one of them pull the palm gag from Cully's mouth and jaw.

"That's better," said Cully, massaging his lips.

The Policemen did not answer. Cully felt his arms let free, and heard the sound of steps behind him, terminating in the slamming of the door by which they had entered.

Turning, Cully saw he was alone. A single light panel in the ceiling cast a dim illumination on a cot, a table, a chair and a small cabinet of drawers. A partition half-concealed a lavatory area.

Cully stepped over to the cot and sat down on it, rolling over to lie flat on his back. He stared at the ceiling. Undoubtedly there would be spy cells in the room, watching him.

There was nothing more to concern himself about for the present. Amos had done neither more nor less than Cully had expected him, to do. And in doing it, the older man had sown the seeds of his own downfall. Even now, Amos must be giving orders that Cully's appearance and current presence on Earth must be kept utterly secret; and already that secret would be leaking to an already terror-conditioned Old Worlds population, outside this building.

Cully closed his eyes, and in a little while he went to sleep.

22

The clash of the metal door to his room, opening and then closing again, roused Cully from his sleep. He propped himself up on one elbow to see that a tray with lunch on it had been delivered to the floor just inside the door. Cully rose, collected the tray and proceeded to eat.

Once he had finished the meal, Cully turned automatically to explore his cell unobtrusively with the eye of an experienced prisoner, in search of any weak points which might make possible an escape.

But it was a blank, metal-walled box of an enclosure. The vision screen gave him a view of New York Complex from some high point—which might or might not reflect his true location in the Tri-Worlds Council Building. The furniture consisted of the single bed-frame, with a combination foam spring and mattress unit and paper sheets. The single chair, also with hollow tubular legs, foam seat and back, and a tiny metal-legged writing table—these were the rest of the movable furniture. Nowhere was anything which might be used to pick a lock, or break a hole through a steel wall. Even the light in the cell came from an energized ceiling panel as metallic as the rest.

So much, Cully had learned of his place of imprisonment within the first thirty seconds of examination of the room. Two hours later, although he persevered, he had discovered nothing more. He lay on the narrow bed, staring at the unmarked ceiling with its single whiteglowing panel. There was, of course, the slim hope of somehow overpowering the guards when they came to feed him again.

But the next mealtime quenched that hope as well. Not one, but two guards held weapons on him, while a third carried in a new tray and set it down on the small writing table. Then they picked up the old tray and withdrew. Cully's attempt at conversation met a cold silence. Four hours after that—at nine o'clock by Cully's wrist watch—the illuminated panel in the ceiling faded to a dim glow that barely illuminated the room. It did not brighten again until seven o'clock the following morning.

Breakfast came at eight. Cully ate it more out of a sense of duty to himself than out of appetite. But then, lying in apparent apathy on his back on the bed once more, he began to calculate the time elements of his situation.

Amos had said that Ruhn was due back on Earth in eight days after conferring with his war-fleet commanders. Count one of those days as already gone. Count another off to make safe. Say that six days at the most, from now, Cully would need to be out of this room and in action.

Theoretically, he stood a good chance of being rescued by Leestrom before that time was up. Cully's imagination was both graphic and literal. Knowing his men, and the situations they would be facing back on the Frontier, allowed him to calculate just about how things must have gone since he parted from Leestrom at the Communications Point.

That parting had been—how long ago? It had taken

twelve days ducking and dodging to get to the Moldaug
Crown World, two days to kidnap the little Princes, ten
days to return here, one day since—twenty-three days
in all. Now, how would those twenty-three days have
gone for Leestrom, back on Kalestin?

It would have taken one day only for Leestrom to
return to Kalestin with his ships, and land them in the
uplands farm area. No more than half a day after that to
locate Emile Hasec and get him moving. But then—a
slow period. It would take Emile at least three days,
perhaps as much as five, to gather enough armed men
to move in on Royce's brush toughs holding Kalestin
City. Say, six of the twenty-three days gone so far.

Then one day for Emile and his men to move on
Kalestin City. No more than another day to take it—if
that. Those brush wolves Royce had hired were all right
in a street fight, but they lacked both the skill and
inclination for any kind of fixed battle. That was two
days at most for Emile to re-establish order in Kalestin
City. Two plus six—eight of the twenty-three days gone.

Then another slow period. Emile would have to send
ships to Dannen's World, to Casimir III, to all the
other Frontier Planets; and these in turn would have to
rouse themselves, organize, and send ships back to
Kalestin. Two weeks would be a miraculously short
time in which to get the Frontier and Leestrom supplied with spaceships. In particular, those ships with
which Cully had ordered him to move on the Solar
System and Moon Base. Eight days and fourteen more
made twenty-two. That meant yesterday was the earliest Leestrom could have left with his fleet from Kalestin.

Direct shift-time for that many ships moving together
from Kalestin to the Solar System, even with the advantage of known general distance between the two spatial
locations, would be four days. Leestrom, therefore,
could not reach the outskirts of the Solar System before
the day after tomorrow; and give him two days after
that—one for contacting Moon Base, one for reaching

New York Complex—to be any help as a rescuer of Cully.

Therefore, with six days to go before Cully had to be out of incarceration, four of those days would have to pass before any hope of rescue from Leestrom could be looked for.

It began to look very likely that Cully would have to count on getting out of this cell by himself.

Meanwhile, he must sit tight—and hope. Hope that he had not misread the present character of Amos, nor the character of the Old Worlds people as Amos had helped to form it. The Amos Cully had known on Kalestin, would not have failed to recognize the danger that he was not isolating the virus of Cully so much as incubating it, by putting Cully under lock and key while the inevitable rumor of Cully's appearance and arrest ran free.

But Amos was far gone from the man he had once been; and if it was true that polls showed eighty percent of the Old Worlds people approved of him, then most of the population of the three Solar System Worlds were far gone with him. The guards who brought his food, come to think of it, thought Cully—should provide an index to whatever changes were occurring in popular opinion outside his cell. Word would spread to the Three Worlds that Culihan O'Rourke When, having shown up to take over the Tri-Worlds Council and use the Frontier to protect the Old Worlds people against an approaching Moldaug war fleet, had been locked up, instead, on Amos' orders.

He who sows the wind, reaps the whirlwind—the old saw was still true enough, thought Cully a little grimly. Amos, sickening on his own mental poisons, had been whipping up terror on the Old Worlds for some years now, with two principal fears—fear of the aliens and fear of the Frontiersmen. The Madmen—and the monsters. Given their choice, squeezed finally between Moldaug invasion and Frontier takeover, which would the spacephobic peoples of the three Old Worlds choose?

The only tricky element to the whole situation, Cully reminded himself now, was that they must make that choice in time to save themselves. And with a Moldaug war fleet on the way and Ruhn due back in seven days now, time was at a premium for everyone but himself.

For him, personally, there were six days to kill, here in this cell. Cully lay back deliberately on the cot, forcing his mind away from the present problems, back into a past before those problems had even been conceived. Back to his younger days, after he had left the Governor's mansion on Kalestin, to go off trapping in the back-country brush by himself.

The memories flowed like water back into his mind now, how on those trapping expeditions, on the first few days away from even Frontier civilization, the consciousness of that civilization had still clung to him, like the smell of city smoke to the rough fabric of his brush clothes.

A sense of time, as being composed of discrete units, valuable fleeting hours and minutes demanding to be fully used, so that they should not be wasted—had hurried his strides as he left the city. A sense of limits and limitations had made him conscious of the weights of his pack and rifle. A burden of unaccomplished ambitions, like the memory of high walls and concrete streets, had filled his thoughts only with calculations of what his pelts would be worth, once he came back with them. For the first day or two, with all this in him, he had used to feel like an intruder among the brush, an alien among its earth and rock and trees, among its narrow, stony passages and white-touched mountain peaks, high against the day sky.

But, as with the scent of city smoke, these impediments of the mind had slowly begun to thin and fade with the first few days beyond town limits. With the first waking under open sky they had already begun to dwindle in importance; and with each new evening's

campfire, blazing redly against the dark, they faded still
further. By the end of the fourth day the great sea of
open country had swallowed him, his mind as well as
his body; and the thought of time as a convention,
composed of hours and minutes, gave way to the slow,
drifting thought of time as unhurried as the seasons of
the year.

In the end, always, he found himself feeling many
times expanded. His days were moments in a larger day
that dawned with the spring thaw and set with the
autumn frost. The distance from one mountain range to
another, hazy blue and white now in the distance against
the lighter blue of the sky, was only a single giant step
executed in peaceful slow motion through a number of
sunrises and sunsets and the steady, effortless, automatic movement of his legs.

Then at last, finally, the space between thought and
thought became a lazy giant step. Drifting through the
brush, so used now to the weights of the pack on his
back and the rifle in one hand that he was no longer
conscious of them, he had time for long, long thoughts—
thoughts that ran as far as from one mountain ridge-line
to another . . .

Wrapped up in his memories, Cully hardly noticed,
as the next five days passed, that the door to his cell
was no longer slammed, and that the meals he was
brought became steadily more varied and rich in quality. But the morning came when an inner clock chimed
its warning, and he returned from the past to realize
that it was the sixth day. Time had run out—and
Leestrom had not appeared to rescue him.

He sat up and ate the breakfast that had just been
brought him. The prospect of action now was as welcome as if it came on the heels of a long idleness.
Having finished the breakfast, he set about washing and
shaving with a new energy. Afterwards, he sat on the
bed, running his mind's eye back and forth over his
situation and his plans, checking his mental calculations

as a man might check the loading and action of a gun before using it.

Then, satisfied at last that he had overlooked no contingency, he got to his feet, strode over to the door of his cell and began pounding on it.

23

There was no immediate response to Cully's pounding.

"Guard!" shouted Cully. "Guard! Open up here! I want to talk to you!"

There was a hurried, muffled sound of voices on the other side, but the door did not open. Cully pounded again for a while, then went back to his bed, sat down and waited.

Some three minutes later, the door unlocked and was thrown open. Standing in the entrance was the usual quota of three guards—one of whom, wearing Sergeant's stripes, seemed to be breathing heavily, as if he had just run from some little distance to join the others. All three stared at Cully.

"What—" the Sergeant had to stop to catch his breath. "What's the matter, Mr. When?"

The polite form of address, the obsequious tone of voice were large changes from the hard silence these same men had shown when Cully had first been locked up in the cell. Rumor, Cully observed, must indeed have been at work on public opinion. He glared at them.

"Am I supposed to be left here just to stare at the

walls?" he asked. "Can't I have something to read—something to do?"

The Sergeant by this time had got his breathing pretty well under control.

"You can have anything you want, Mr. When," he said. "That's orders. Anything you want . . . within reason. Just tell me what you'd like . . ."

"Some book spools—and a viewer," snapped Cully. "And how about a pack of playing cards? I can play Frontier brush-bridge with myself, if nothing else!"

"Of course. Certainly," said the Sergeant. He fumbled in the inner breast pocket of his uniform jacket and came out with a black issue notebook and a stylus. "There's empty pages in the back," he said. "Just tear some out and write down what you want. Keep the stylus and some extra sheets if you think of something else. I'll have to get the list approved—but it'll just take a few minutes to do that."

Cully got up from the bed, took the stylus and tore out half a dozen sheets from the notebook. He sat down at the writing table and made out a list of several books of nonfiction and a pack of Kalestin-made playing cards. As an afterthought, he scribbled a request for the most recent news printings. He handed the sheet of paper and the notebook to the Sergeant without getting up.

"I made a note about it being a sixty-card pack of playing cards, the kind they make on the Frontier," said Cully. "There used to be an import shop here in New York Complex that sold them. If it isn't the Frontier set with the four different-colored jokers, you can't play single-handed brush-bridge. Make sure they don't give me one of your Earth packs."

"If it gets passed on downstairs, you'll get it, Mr. When—whatever it is," said the Sergeant. He stepped back, bringing his rifle up, and one of the other two Policemen pulled the door shut. Cully went back to his bed to sit down and wait.

About twenty minutes later, he heard the door being

opened again. The Sergeant stepped inside, alone, no longer flanked by his two armed companions.

"Here you are, Mr. When," he said. "I'm sorry— they said no news printings. If it'd been up to me . . ." He passed over four spools, a book viewer and a plastic-covered pack of playing cards.

"Thanks," said Cully. "Shut the door for a moment, will you? I'd like a word with you."

The Sergeant hesitated, then reached out behind him and swung the door closed until the click of its latch was heard.

"Thanks," said Cully quietly. "I just thought I'd take this chance to tell you I don't hold it against you, personally, for any of this." The Sergeant's face betrayed a flicker of gratitude. "For that matter, I don't hold it against Amos Braight. I suppose you know I was practically adopted by him on Kalestin when I was a boy? He was a great man then."

"He's still . . . a great man." There was the faintest of hesitations in the Sergeant's voice.

"You believe that, don't you?" Cully peered sharply up at him.

"Of course . . ." Again, the faint hesitation. "After all, he's the one man who knows both sides—I mean, here and the Frontier. For that matter"—the guard's voice strengthened—"he was the one man who could take the Frontier for a dozen years and come back—" He broke off, suddenly embarrassed.

"Still sane? Unchanged?" Cully suggested bluntly.

"Well . . . yes."

"That's interesting." Cully leaned back on the couch and smiled, faintly. "But what if he actually had been changed? What if he'd secretly gone to pieces out there, the way he says everyone else does?"

"But he didn't!" The Sergeant's voice was firm.

"Strange," said Cully, "him alone—out of all men and women—wasn't changed a bit by the Frontier. Out of all people, just *him*."

"That's what makes him a great man." The Sergeant

took a step backward and laid his hand on the door latch. "If you don't mind now, Mr. When, I have to be getting back to my—"

"But if the Frontier actually had got to him, only he'd hid the fact, and people begin to find out about it now, a lot of them might be starting to change their minds about him—don't you think?" asked Cully thoughtfully.

The Sergeant shot him a sudden, startled glance. For a moment the man stood without moving.

"You're saying . . ." he began, through stiffened lips, then stopped.

"What? Were you going to ask me something?" Cully raised his face innocently.

"No. Nothing." Sharply, the guard turned and went out.

Cully watched the door click shut, locked behind the uniformed figure; and shook his head sadly, well aware that the spy cells hidden around the room would be transmitting the picture of that gesture to the Sergeant, or others, outside that door right now. Then he turned and began, casually, to examine his new possessions, scattered on the blanket of his cot.

He put the book spools, one by one, into the viewer, glanced through each of them, then put them aside. Casually, he picked up the pack of playing cards they had brought him.

The plastic wrapping was smooth under his fingers and transparent. Through it, the words *First Frontier—60 Cards* stared at him from the label beneath. He nodded. This was the spacelifter's deck—the explosive tool he had described to Mike Bourjoi and the other crewmen aboard the *Nansh Rakh* as they hunted the Moldaug ship holding the human hostages.

Cully had gambled that the present owners of the import shop might still have some of the old spacelifter's sixty-card decks on hand, without knowing the true nature of such decks. Only a Frontiersman would be likely to order such cards unless they were on display. And the sixty-card decks had always been kept as back stock, their presence recorded in the memory bank of the store computer, but nowhere else. Now, Cully had both a weapon and a tool in his hands. He turned the pack over to examine the red wafer that was both a fuse and a timer.

But the wafer was gone.

Cully stared at the place on the plastic wrapping where it should have been. Abruptly then, he recognized what had happened. The pack had already been opened. His guards must have routinely opened it and spread the cards out—going through the motions of seeing that nothing useful to their prisoner or dangerous to them was concealed in the deck. Finding none, they had resealed the wrapping with a small piece of ordinary plastic tape.

The deck was still as potentially explosive as ever, but for Cully, without the fuse, it was just another deck of cards. Thoughtfully, Cully swept cards, spools and everything aside and lay down on the bed, closing his eyes.

For a little while he dozed . . . and then his mind came to, once more in working order. He got up and called the guard.

"Yes, Mr. When?" said the guard, opening the cell door.

"Listen—" said Cully, smiling engagingly. "How about something green around here to cheer up the place? Some potted plants or something . . ."

"I'll see!" The cell door closed with a clash. But less than an hour later it opened again, and the guard came in with a flowering salmon-pink geranium in a heavy ceramic bowl filled with earth.

"That's more like it," said Cully. "Put it on the writing table there." He went back to laying out four hands of cards on the bed, two up and two down, for Frontier bridge. The cell door closed again with a clash. Cully sniffed the spicy geranium odor filling the small room appreciatively.

He spent the rest of the day reading and playing

cards. Once the lighting panel in the ceiling dimmed for the night, however, he gave up and lay down.

The pack of cards was scattered over his bed. Uncaringly, almost petulantly, he swept them all off the covering blanket onto the floor near the head of his bed, so that they fell down the narrow crack between it and the writing table alongside. Then he stripped down to his shorts and undershirt and crawled in between the bedsheets, pulling the top sheet high up around his neck and turning his back to the lighted panel above the rest of the room. For perhaps half an hour after that, he stirred restlessly under the sheet; but eventually his breathing deepened, became steady, and he lay still.

For the rest of the nighttime period, as far as any invisible watchers were concerned, Cully slumbered on, hunched in his own deeper shadow with his face to the writing table, and his back to the dimly lighted panel in the ceiling. Several times during these darkened hours he stirred and got up from his bed to refill his bedside drinking glass with water from the lavatory area behind the partition. On each occasion, after he had drunk, he refilled the glass and carried it back with him to his bed. There he set it down on the floor in the narrow space between his bed and the writing table, and from time to time his stirrings under the sheet indicated that he roused himself enough to moisten his mouth and throat from the water it contained.

So much for what was to be observed. However, below the screen of the top of the writing table, in the shadow there, Cully was very busy. He had not begun to work until after nearly three hours of feigned sleep. But, at the end of that time, and with the least possible amount of betraying motion in the rest of his body, he had carefully set about the business of unscrewing the inmost of the two hollow, metal legs of the writing table next to the bed.

At first the leg had stuck and resisted his efforts to unscrew it. But gradually, with a fit of feigned tossing in his sleep, he had been able to bring enough leverage to bear to break it loose. After that, it was only a matter of turning it patiently, inch by inch, until the threads within its upper rim parted from the threads of the metal screw end in the table frame.

Once loose, he had carefully removed it, being equally careful to maintain the balance of the table upon the three legs still upholding it. Propping the removed leg upright, with its end held, but hidden in the crook of his left elbow, he went to work with his right arm and teeth on the Frontier-made playing cards that had been brought him.

Working slowly and carefully, one by one he shredded the cards with teeth and fingers, and soaked the shreds in the water of his drinking glass. When they were thoroughly wet to the consistency of workable papier-mâchié, he began stuffing them into the hollow interior of the metal leg, mixing them in with several handfuls of earth stolen from the potted geranium and enriched by scraps of half-masticated food from his dinner.

It was a long night's work, to fill the leg. When he was done, only five of the cards remained unshredded. Carefully, he began to screw the metal leg back onto the table, and persisted in tightening it until the pulped playing cards on top squeezed out in a thin dirt-darkened rim around the point of original contact between the top of the leg and its socket on the table. Then, wearily, he wadded up the original plastic covering of the pack, and stuck it in a shirt pocket, with the few remaining cards in front of it, just showing so that the shirt pocket bulged as if the whole pack was there—and fell honestly to sleep.

He roused when breakfast was delivered some three hours later. He made himself sit up and shovel a little of the bacon and eggs on his tray into his mouth, and drank the coffee that had come with it. Then he rubbed grainy eyes, got to his feet and went over to the washstand.

He washed his face, brushed his teeth and shaved.

Then, feeling more human, he sat down again—this time in the chair. He reached over to the writing table without getting up from the chair, and closed his hand on the book viewer and one of the spools. He brought his hand back, fitted the spool into the viewer mechanically, and began to stare into it. But it was the bomb image of the stuffed metal leg under the table on which his mind was concentrating and about which it was calculating.

For it was, indeed, a bomb. The nitrocellulose, mixed with the geranium's earth, rich in organic material, would fuse itself as the hours went by.

Cully was not enough of a chemist to figure accurately how long it would take for the guncotton explosion he had set up to reach the point of detonation. But he had played with this kind of nitrocellulose-organic mixture before, during his spacelifting days, and under the normal room temperature of his cell he felt fairly sure that it should reach the point of spontaneous combustion—and explosion—sometime between now and when the guards entered with the noon meal.

That left only two things to be done. Place the table leg into position as near to the latch-and-lock side of the door, and arrange as much protection for himself as possible.

For both things he had contrived a single excuse. Having stared through the book viewer long enough, he hoped, to bore any guard watching him through the spy cells, he began to houseclean his cell. First, using one of the sheets from his bed, he carefully dusted the floor, then put the now dirty sheet to soak in the washstand of the partitioned off lavatory area. Thoughtfully, he took a hand towel and wrapped it around his waist, under the sweatshirt. Then, as an apparent afterthought, he stripped the bed of all its other coverings—this required shoving the writing table over so that it partially blocked the closed cell door, with the loaded leg right up against the latch—and carried all the other bedding into the lavatory area, where he dumped it, ready to wash.

Finally, he even went to the extreme of removing the mattress from the bed and hauling that into the lavatory area also. Once there, he propped it up against the inside of the partition wall, so that there was now both a thickness of mattress and one of metal, between him and the table leg pressing against the side of the door where the door latch was. He began to wash his bedding.

He worked slowly but industriously at this, staying behind the partition, with one shoulder propped against the upstanding mattress. He was prepared with a number of loud and confusing arguments in case the guards watching through the spy cells should come in to question this rather eccentric behavior of his. But no one showed up, and he spun out his washing as the slow hours crept on toward noon.

He was washing away in this manner, half-hypnotized by the monotony of his actions, when a thunderous sound jerked him into action. The swift, conditioned reflexes of years sent him automatically diving to the floor, to cover his head with his arms and huddle against the base of the upright mattress.

But the impact of mattress and partition against his body never came. Abruptly, it dawned on him that it could not have been the table leg exploding that he had heard.

He leaped to his feet and stepped around the partition to see the room intact, undamaged. Then the thunder came again. It was repeated—a thunder of fists or gun butts against the metal door of his cell.

"Cully? Cully are you in there?" It was the voice of Leestrom. "Stand away from the door. We'll have you out of there in a moment."

Even as he heard the voice, Cully saw the area around the latch button of the door redden, and then a small black line appeared above the latch, that widened as the pale flame-tip of a cutting torch poked through. Beyond the door, suddenly, guns crackled, and a chorus of shouts and yells exploded, filling Cully's ears with tumult.

At the same time the thought of his own homemade bomb, liable to go off at any moment, sprang back into his mind.

He leaped for the door, seized the table, and, swinging it around, literally threw it back into the lavatory area, behind the mattress and the metal partition. Then he jumped into the corner furthest from the open end of the partitioned-off area and huddled there.

He looked toward the door, but the black line already made by the tip of the cutting torch was not extending itself; and, after a moment of staring at it, he realized that he could no longer see the pale tip of the flame. They had stopped cutting for some reason, out there, and the noise in the corridor gave no clue as to what the reason might be.

"Hurry up! Get me out of here!" shouted Cully at the door. "There's a bomb in here about to go off!"

The tumult in the corridor continued. The tip of the flame did not reappear.

He did not think they had heard him.

24

Cully continued to huddle in his corner. Still, the near-invisible flame-tip did not appear at either edge of the black line already cut through the door. But then, while the tumult outside still continued, a black dot appeared suddenly below the door latch, and grew slowly into another line displaying the cutter's flame-tip. It cut around and up on an arc, toward the other line already cut. Then it, too, stopped.

For a moment nothing happened. Then there was the slamming sound of a small explosion, it seemed right in the room with Cully, making him duck instinctively. When he looked up again, the door latch was torn off and bent inward, hanging only by the strip of metal where the two cutting lines had failed to come together.

The door swung open. People, headed by Leestrom's towering figure, burst into the cell. Cully exploded outward from his corner, shoving them back out the door.

"Out—" he cried. Appalled, he caught sight of Alia among them. "Out! There's a bomb in this room! It's due to go off any minute!"

They heard him this time, and scrambled away in front of him, out into the corridor and down along its length. Behind them, without warning, the cell erupted into flame-flare and whistling shards. Something like an enormous, flat sandbag seemed to slap against Cully from behind. He went down.

For a moment he was dazed, but even in his dazed condition his body was automatically scrambling to its feet like the body of a boxer not entirely out from a blow. As his head cleared, he found himself looking for Alia. But she had gone down under the bulk of Leestrom and she was already getting to her own feet. Now the others were rising also.

Alia's eyes, frantically staring around, located Cully, and sobbing, she flung herself into his arms, holding to him as if she would never let him go again.

Back on their feet, the rest looked about at each other. For a miracle, no one was hurt—no one was as much as scratched by the debris from the wrecked cell, which was now lying all about them. Suddenly someone began to laugh, the shaky laughter of relief. It was contagious. Another voice joined in—and then they were all doing it; all standing together in the corridor with the bits and pieces from the explosion around them, laughing like children at a party where some unexpected comical accident has taken place.

Even Alia drew away from Cully after a bit, wiping her eyes with shaky outward movements of the back of her forefingers, and began to laugh with the rest.

Cully was the first to sober. The sight of his no longer laughing face gradually quieted the others. They became solemn, looking at him. Cully looked about and saw not only Leestrom but Will, Doak, Pete Hyde, and the white-haired Tom Donough among the group surrounding him.

"How'd you'd find me?" he demanded.

Leestrom pointed toward Alia.

"She found out where they were keeping you," the

big man answered, "through this man here—" He jerked
his head at Tom.

"But what are you doing with Lee, anyway?" Cully
turned to Alia.

"I made him bring me," said Alia. "I thought if
something had happened to you, I could talk sense to
Dad . . ." Her voice dwindled off guiltily.

"Don't worry," said Cully quietly. "You won't have
to."

"That's right," said Leestrom. "But it's a good thing
she made me hurry, or we'd still be a full day's shifting-
distance out, on our way here from Kalestin."

And he proceeded to tell Cully what had happened.

Leestrom had followed orders and taken his ships
back to Kalestin, setting them down on a firm, dry-rock
plain less than ten miles from the wide farmlands of
that horny-handed, firebrand ex-spacelifter that was
Emile Hasec. Hardly were all the ships down before
Emile himself showed up with half a dozen neighboring
farmers. Leestrom told him the news about Kalestin
City and passed on Cully's orders.

A lesser man might have asked what right Cully had
to give him orders. But Emile was not a lesser man—
and proved it. Swearing in half a dozen languages at
once, he dumped the management of his plowed fields
and orchards into the hands of the beautiful young wife
from whom neither guns nor gain had been able to
separate him for the past year and a half; and, sweeping
the inland districts, he came sliding into Kalestin City
two days later at the head of an army of twelve thousand armed farmers like himself, in weapon-mounted,
upland brush-buggies.

The news of their coming ran ahead of them and
scattered the hired toughs of Royce's army. Emile dis-
solved what was left of the Assembly, throwing Royce
and as many others of its members in jail as he could
lay hands on, and set up a temporary new Assembly,
with himself as its Speaker.

His new Assembly sent courier vessels to all other

Frontier Worlds with word to crew and arm any space-ships they possessed, and send them to the Kalestin City Spaceport as quickly as this could be done. Meanwhile they were to set up home-defense units as quickly as possible.

By the time Leestrom's ships were crewed and ready at the Kalestin City Spaceport Terminal, three quarters of the available ships on the Frontier had arrived, fitted with weapons and men ready to fight. Any idea that such a space-going militia could stand up to even one full wing of the Moldaug war fleet in pitched battle was of course ridiculous. But on the alien large-scan screens a dozen such Frontier ships, flaring-in, in unison after a shift, masqueraded very convincingly as a section of warships on defensive patrol of a Frontier Planet.

Meanwhile, under Alia's frantic urging and with Emile Hasec's concurrence, Leestrom had headed for Earth with a motley assortment of some fifty spaceships of all types.

One shift away from the Solar System, this fleet was detected in the large-scan cube aboard the grounded *Nansh Rakh* by Pete Hyde, who, correctly judging it to be Leestrom rather than the Moldaug, lifted immediately from the Spaceport to intercept and join it. Which he did as the fleet halted at a safe distance from the sensory instruments of Moon Base.

At that point, Leestrom left the bulk of his makeshift fleet to play at resembling warships for the Moon Base instruments. He had sent the *Nansh Rakh* back Earth-ward with Alia to try and locate where Cully was being held. Meanwhile, he, with three of the Moldaug-built ships under his command, followed Cully's original orders about landing at Moon Base.

Privately, Leestrom's imagination had never been able to encompass the idea of a Moon Base being either tricked or cowed by the appearance of himself and his Moldaug ships. But he was stubborn about following orders and felt that the visit might work, at least as a bluff to back up Alia and the others on Earth. As far as his own three ships and crews were concerned, the big man felt relatively safe in landing. No responsible Old Worlds Spacefleet officer was likely to fire on a Moldaug ship until he was absolutely sure there were no Moldaug aboard her; and Leestrom was prepared to claim that in addition to his alien-supplied warships, out at the limit of sensor range, he carried Moldaug observers aboard all his ships. At worst, he should be able to get off again safely and rejoin his own ships. At best, he might be able to help bully the Tri-Worlds Council into releasing Cully.

But to Leestrom's considerable astonishment, Cully's arrival and arrest on Earth, plus the prospect of an approaching Moldaug war fleet had operated on the fears of the Old Worlds people as Cully had planned. It had already unnerved the Admirals commanding at Moon Base. Leestrom could not know that these officers, as well as everyone else on the base, had concluded at the first appearance of Leestrom's fleet on their sensors that the Moldaug, their patience finally exhausted, had come at last in force.

The Old Worlds' near-superstitious fear of the aliens, plus the reaction to Cully's arrest, had done the rest. The sickness of fear was here, too, among the officers and men of Moon Base, as well as among the general population of the three Old Worlds. Leestrom's own announcement, on landing, that the terrible aliens had made alliance with the savage Frontiersmen, finally washed away any last thought of resistance that remained on Moon Base. The Senior Admiral Commander, a man named Pilhard, knew that even if he should order his men to fight, most of them would not. With a sigh of only partial regret, for he was an aging man and had no personal stomach for an interstellar war tantamount to a human-Moldaug suicide pact, he chose swiftly to surrender now to the Frontiersmen—who were at least human—rather than take the chance of later having to deal with the inhuman Moldaug.

Nor did he check with his superiors at Tri-Worlds Council Headquarters on Earth, first. He was taking no chances of being countermanded.

In this manner, unexpectedly having achieved a bloodless conquest of nearly eighty percent of the effective fighting force of the human race, Leestrom was suddenly left at loose ends. Not ordinarily overimaginative, he recognized the necessity of moving quickly, now that he had set the conquest in motion. Leaving two of his ships to hold down Moon Base Headquarters, he headed for Earth and Long Island Sound Spaceport to join Alia, Will, and the others from the *Nansh Rakh* seeking Cully, who alone could coordinate the conquest.

By the time Leestrom landed on Earth, however, word had leaked over the laser-beam communications to Earth, ahead of him, and the voice of rumor had done the rest. Leestrom found Earth in disorganization, the Spaceport itself deserted, and the majority of Earth's population with no place to run to, quaking in their homes like rabbits at the ultimate end of their burrow, hearing the claws of the ferret scrabbling up the dark earth-tunnel toward them.

He landed almost beside the *Nansh Rakh* at Long Island Sound Spaceport, and made phone contact with Will, Doak and Alia, who were then with Tom Donough in Braight's private office outside the Council Building. Donough, shaken by events, and by the effect of them upon Amos, had located Cully for Alia by the time Leestrom, with Pete Hyde and a dozen armed men, had joined them. They had made their way to Cully's cell and, with only a last-minute resistance from the guard holding him, had set him free.

"Where's Amos, then?" demanded Cully as soon as the big man had finished.

"He's in the Council Meeting Room on the sixty-second floor," Leestrom answered. "Donough says you've been there, so you know what the place is like—"

"Let's go!" interrupted Cully, heading off down the corridor nearly at a run. "Which way?"

"This way," said Leestrom, catching up with him. "Head for the elevators."

They took the elevators. Riding up on one of the large, floating discs, Cully turned to Leestrom.

"You've got men in command at Moon Base now?" he demanded.

"That's right," answered the big man.

"Message them with your body-phone through the *Nansh Rakh* to put the whole Base on combat-ready alert. I don't think that Moldaug fleet's coming on in—but if they do, we have to be ready. Pete?"

He turned to the Navigator.

"How close is that Moldaug fleet, actually?"

"A good three shifts out," answered Pete. "But the last I heard from the duty Navigator I left on the *Nansh Rakh,* one of the ships from it was already shifting into the Solar System. That'll be Ruhn and his Brother Ambassadors aboard that ship."

"Then he'll be here soon," said Cully. "He may even have landed on Earth already. You've got the little Princes with you on the *Nansh?*"

"Right," said Pete.

"Get them. Bring them here—safely. If you have to use every man on the ship to guard them."

"Right," said Pete. He stepped off the disc at the next floor and turned to the *down* tube of floating discs.

"Will?" said Cully, turning to the older man.

"Yes, Cully?" Will's voice answered behind him.

"Send a man to the ground floor to find out how soon Ruhn is due here. Have him call up to you by direct body-phone as soon as he finds out."

Will turned to speak to a man beyond him.

"Cully . . ." It was Alia's voice. "What are you going to do?"

He looked at her.

"I'm going to try to talk to Amos, to talk him into letting me take over negotiations with Ruhn and his Brothers when they get here."

"What if Braight won't listen to you?" Leestrom asked.

Cully glanced around briefly at the big man, then turned back to find Alia staring steadily at him, her eyes a little dilated.

"Then . . . I'll have to take over anyway," he said.

"You mean you'll have to kill Dad, don't you?" said Alia in a dead voice. "The Moldaug won't believe you've taken over his authority unless he tells them so, or they see his dead body."

"Not necessarily," said Cully. "Anyway, I still think I can talk to him."

"You can't," said Alia. "No one can . . . now. But it doesn't matter any more. You do what you have to do for everybody's sake . . ."

"No, I really think I can talk—" Cully broke off, abruptly, glancing around. He looked past her. "Will, I want you and Doak—" He broke off. "Where's Doak?"

Will met the question with a strange look.

"He was the man I just sent down to find out when Ruhn was due here," Will answered.

"Get him back!" said Cully. "I need the two of you alongside me when I face Ruhn. He's got to see our whole personality unit, the personality unit of the Demon of Dark. Or am I wrong?"

"No," said Will slowly. "If you're going to pick up negotiations with a Moldaug Admiral in the place of the people he was negotiating with here on Earth, you'd better meet him as a full three-person individual."

"Well, then, get Doak back. Right away—" Cully broke off as Will turned slowly from him. "Wait a minute. Not you, Will. I'll need you with me. Harv—" he said, turning to one of the other men. "You go find Doak, and tell him to get back up here as fast as he can."

"Wait—" began Will. But the man Cully had spoken to had already turned, stepped off the disc and vanished on the floor now below them. Will checked whatever he was going to say, shrugged a little sadly, and turned back to Cully.

"Here we are," said Tom Donough. The disc halted.

They stepped off into the same upper lobby Cully remembered. It was deserted now. Tom Donough led them down the main corridor leading off from it, to where two heavy doors of carved mahogany stood ajar. Through their gap, Cully saw the open end of the room he remembered, past the door from Amos' office to the dais on which the round table stood.

Amos sat alone at the table, and the vision screen behind him showed the sky outside the Council Building with the sun lowering toward late afternoon. The room was as Cully had remembered it, except three of the chairs opposite Amos had been replaced by the hassock-like seats used by the Moldaug; and on the table, under Amos' right hand, rested a black object roughly the size and shape of a shoe box. Amos, his gaze on the table, did not see them as they tiptoed up to the partially open doors on the soft carpet of the corridor.

"All right," said Cully. "Alia, you come along beside me. You, too, Lee and Will. The rest of you follow— but not too close."

He turned, took hold of the handles of both door panels, and pulled. The massive panels, balanced so delicately that a child could open them, swung wide on either side at the touch of his hands. He led the way into the Reception Hall.

The clatter of their feet on the parquet floor echoed loudly in the silence of the Meeting Room. Amos looked up. His eyes fastened on them, watching them approach, and his hand closed about the box beneath it on the table.

"Stop there," he said in a strong harsh voice, when Cully was still a dozen feet from the dais. "Stop there, or I'll blow you and everything else up this minute. I swear it, Cully!"

Cully stopped.

"That's better," Amos said. "I think you know I never was afraid to do what I had to."

"No, Amos," said Cully. "I always knew you couldn't

be simply frightened out of something you'd decided to do. But what's this about blowing things up?"

Amos nursed the black box under his hand on the table.

"You see this?" he asked.

"I see it," Cully said.

"Well, I thought things might come to this some-day," Amos said, almost reflectively. "I tried to give the Old Worlds the will to prove to the Moldaug that here in the Solar System we're no threat to them out there, no matter what you Frontier people did. But I played safe—just in case, I fixed it so even if we didn't have the will to prove we wouldn't ever fight the Moldaug, we'd find we didn't have the means. This little console"— he patted and stroked the box again—"can blow up nearly every bit of offensive and defensive armament in the Solar System—and especially Moon Base. Tell them, Tom."

"It's true, Cully!" Tom's frightened voice broke in behind Cully. "The Council started booby-trapping every-thing without even telling the military, as much as five years ago, because Amos convinced them it was only a matter of time until you people from the Frontier tried to take over. He really can blow up—"

"Yes," interrupted Amos. "No need to labor the point, Tom. All Cully needs to know is that I *will* blow every-thing up if he comes a step closer. So just stand where you are, all of you. It won't be long. I got word less than five minutes ago. Ruhn and the other alien Ambas-sadors have already landed. They'll be here in less than five minutes; and when they get here, I'm turning you all over to them to do what they like with. Because you're all traitors to the human race."

His gaze went from Cully to Tom, to Alia, back over the others, and then returned to rest coldly on Alia.

"All of you," he said harshly. "All traitors."

25

There was silence in the Meeting Room.

"Five minutes?" asked Cully at last.

"Or less," answered Amos.

"That's too long," said Cully in a quiet voice that echoed strangely under the high ceiling of the room. "The Moldaug won't get here in time."

"In time?" Amos' deep-pouched eyes burned down at Cully.

"In time to save you," Cully said.

"Save me?" Amos laughed harshly. "From what?"

"Yourself," said Cully. "You're planning to use that trigger mechanism you're holding anyway, aren't you, Amos? When Ruhn and his Brother Ambassadors get here, you're planning to blow up Moon Base and all the other installations anyway. Just to show the Moldaug they've nothing to be afraid of from the Old Worlds, no matter what they do to the Frontier or anything else."

There was a sharp sound, like a click, from the throat of Will, standing just behind Cully.

"You'd do that?" Will burst out at Amos. "Don't you understand the Moldaug at all? Disarming yourself in front of them doesn't convince them you're not dangerous! Just the opposite! You don't understand how they think—"

"No, he doesn't," interrupted Cully, "but save your breath, Will. It wouldn't matter to Amos if he did. Because he's made up his mind to blow up those installations anyway. Haven't you, Amos?"

"Yes," said Amos coldly, looking down from the dais at him. "Just as soon as Ruhn gets here—as you say. And so you're thinking you might as well rush me now as five minutes from now, are you Cully? Don't try it. I can blow up everyone in this room as well, if I want to."

"That would include yourself?" Cully asked.

"That would include myself." Amos nodded. "Do you think including myself would stop me? I told you, I can't be frightened."

"Not by anything physical, no," said Cully.

Amos stared at him.

"Why? What're you talking about?" he said.

"Everybody's got some private fear," Cully said quietly. "A man who's not afraid of facing an armed mob can be afraid of a dark room."

"I'm not afraid of dark rooms," said Amos.

"Yes, you are," said Cully. "You're afraid of one particular dark room, Amos."

Beside Cully, Alia drew in a sudden sharp breath. Cully put his hand on her arm, checking her before she could speak.

"And, you've been out to busy that fear for years now," Cully went on. "Even if you had to bury the rest of the human race in a mass grave on top of it. You're spacephobic, Amos."

"Spacephobic? I've ridden in spaceships all my life," snarled Amos.

"I don't mean you've got a fear of space," said Cully, watching him closely. "You're afraid of what space contains. You ought to know about that fear, Amos. Most of the human race back here on the Old Worlds has it. That's why you were elected and kept on being re-elected, by such heavy majorities each time. That's why you could dictate terms to the rest of the Council. A society picks leaders in its own image. It's a cultural matter. You were the most powerful Representative on the Council because you most resembled the majority of the people who set up that Council to govern them."

"Cully," said Amos slowly, "you're not fool enough to think you can *talk* me out of what I'm going to do?"

"Maybe," said Cully. "But only if you listen to what I'm saying. If you don't listen, I can't save you."

Amos snorted.

"From what?"

"Your dark room," said Cully. "I told you you're spacephobic. I told you it was cultural. Deep down inside the animal part of you, Amos, and inside the people you represent here on the Old Worlds, there's an instinctive, animalistic picture of the territory that rightfully belongs to the human race—and inside all of you that territory ends at the outer limits of the Solar System."

"That's not animal," snarled Amos. "That's fact!"

"No," said Cully. "The picture of what human spatial territory needs to be has to be like the Moldaug picture of their territory—anything the race can use and hold. A truly interstellar culture thinks that way. That's why on the Frontier we aren't frightened at being outside the limits of the Solar System. That's why we don't make ourselves go to pieces, mentally and morally, to prove to ourselves that we shouldn't be out there—the way you and your fellow spacephobes do."

"*Make* ourselves go to pieces!" Amos laughed again, this time grimly.

"That's right," said Cully. "You fold up mentally and morally once you're beyond the Solar System, and then blame your fold-up on the fact that you're out where you shouldn't be."

Amos laughed again. He seemed to enjoy his laughter, for it grew until he threw back his head and roared at the ceiling. But when Cully took a step forward it cut off suddenly. Amos' eyes came down sharply, and his grip tightened on the black box.

"Stop there!" he snapped, all the humor gone out of his voice.

"I'm stopped," said Cully.

"All right." Amos relaxed. He chuckled again. "So we Old Worlds spacephobes make ourselves degenerate just to prove our point!" He chuckled again. "You're forgetting something, Cully."

"What?" asked Cully.

"Just," said Amos, leaning forward with a narrow smile, "that I went out and lived on Kalestin, and it didn't get *me* the way you say it should. If I hadn't seen what happened to poor devils like those soldiers in Fortown, I might be Governor of Kalestin yet. But after that, I saw I had to come back here and let the Old Worlds know what went on with humans exposed beyond the Solar System. But it didn't get to *me*."

He leaned forward again and lowered his voice harshly, staring directly into Cully's face.

"And you know *why* it didn't?" he demanded.

Cully said nothing.

"I'll tell you why not," said Amos. "Because I was too strong for it! And the people back here could tell I'd been too strong for it. *That's* why they elected me and trusted me to do what's right about it!"

Cully looked at him for a long moment without speaking. Then, slowly, he turned and looked instead toward the end of the room where the doors still stood ajar, giving a view of the approaching corridor and a part of the empty lobby beyond. He continued to stand there looking.

For nearly a minute longer, Amos went on staring at the back of Cully's head. Then, without moving he whispered harshly.

"What's the matter with you? What're you looking out there for?"

"Your dark room," said Cully without turning back to

him. "You wouldn't listen to me. Now it's coming for you. Any moment now."

Amos drew in a hissing breath and straightened up in his chair. He snorted a little and looked away from Cully, at the vision screen in which the sun was now only a little above the horizon.

"Cully—" began Will hesitantly.

"Quiet!" said Cully in a low voice, without turning his gaze from the corridor. "All of you. Don't talk!"

There was silence. The slow seconds passed . . .

"*Now*," said Cully—and his voice, low-pitched as it was, seemed to echo loudly in the silent, afternoon-lit room. "Now, Amos!"

"What?" Amos jerked his gaze away from the vision screen and turned to look out over the heads of Cully and the others, out through the partly open doors. Coming down the carpeted corridor toward the room was the small figure of Doak.

"What do you mean?" Amos leaned forward, shading his eyes against the direct, low-angled sunlight from the vision screen. "Who's that supposed to be?"

Doak was halfway down the corridor now, looking ahead somewhat puzzledly at the silent, watching group standing around Cully. His gaze slid on and over them, up to the figure of Braight seated at the table. He stared at Braight, his steps on the carpet slowly uncertain.

Still staring, he began to move forward more rapidly. His pace quickened.

"*Who's that—I say?*" Amos suddenly shouted.

At the sound of that shout, Doak broke into a run. Will shoved Cully aside and, turning, leaped up onto the dais beside the table, where Doak could see him clearly.

"Doak!" he shouted. "**Get** back! It wasn't him! I swear to you—"

But Doak was racing forward toward them, not seeing them, his eyes all on the frozen, peering figure of Amos, the mouth in Doak's pale, small face open and a wailing cry beginning to build from it—a single word drawn out until it was like the howl of a wolf . . .

"*Faaaaaaaaa . . .*"

Almost before they could move, he was among them, and there was a swirl of bodies around him like a swirl of water on a pond struck by a flung stone, and then a splashing outward, with big men falling away, falling down, as Doak burst from the midst of them, still coming on, with his prison-made knife now in his hand and glinting red.

"Stop him, Lee!" shouted Cully, throwing himself forward to block the way. But Leestrom, lunging forward, also stumbled back again, with blood running down his forearm; in the next moment Doak was coming at Cully—for a moment only, before, like a flickering wraith, he ducked under Cully's grasp and was two steps from the dais.

Behind Cully, even as he swung desperately about, knowing he was already too late, he heard the sudden double thunder of two shots from the old-fashioned revolver Will had carried all these months without ever using.

Full-turned then, Cully saw Will standing with the ancient weapon smoking in his fist, his face twisted in emotional pain under the white hair beside the stupefied figure of Amos; and the small figure of Doak tumbling floorwards, literally hammered to a standstill by the impact of the heavy lead slugs.

Will threw the gun aside and jumped from the platform to drop on his knees beside the small figure. From above him, Amos looked down, awkwardly holding the black box, his face stupid.

"What—" stammered Braight at the bowed head of Will, feverishly bent over Doak as the white-haired man ripped open Doak's shirt to investigate the damage of the slugs, "why did you save me?"

Will looked up at him briefly and savagely.

"He's your son," he said. "From Kalestin and Fortown."

Amos stood staring. For a long moment it seemed

that he had not understood Will. Then, slowly, the stillness began to leak out of him. Visibly, before the eyes of those still watching, he began to crumble.

"My son . . ." he muttered. "Then he wasn't killed with the rest. Oh, God . . . not my . . ."

The black box fell from his hand. He did not seem to feel or hear it go. He took one stumbling step to the edge of the dais, and another to the floor below. As he stepped down, his knees gave, and he dropped on his knees on the opposite side of the fallen Doak. His face lifted strickenly to Will.

"Yes," said Will grimly. "That's right. I tried to keep him away from you. I tried to keep him away from here—"

"Is he dead?" It was Alia's voice now. "Will—?"

"No," said Will harshly. His hands were flying swiftly, like independent creatures unconnected with his pale, suddenly old-man's face, under the white hair. "I'm getting the bleeding stopped, and if we can get him to proper medical care—"

He broke off, looking over at Amos even while his hands continued to work with Doak.

"He thought it was you who killed his mother because you always wore a uniform when you came," Will said to Amos. "I couldn't tell him it was one of the real soldiers who did it, without giving away the fact I'd known about her—and you."

"You?" Amos stared at him. "But how could you—?"

"I used to go to Fortown, to do what I could," said Will thinly, "after it started to go bad there. So I'd heard—about you, anyway. I found Doak's mother that night before you did, and she was already dead. One of the other women had already taken Doak away, but I didn't know about that until after. Doak never knew who you were. His mother always sent him away when you came so he'd never had a good look at you. All he had was a locket with a picture of you in it. So he thought you were one of the soldiers from the fort and you killed his mother because you were crazy-drunk that night. He's been hunting you all these years to kill you."

"He *should* have killed me—" Still on his knees, Amos began to weep like an old man. He sagged sideways, as if he would fall, and Alia caught him as a mother catches a child dissolving into tears He looked at her piteously.

"Alia . . ." he stammered. "I couldn't tell you—"

"Oh, do you think I didn't guess long ago!" she cried furiously, with her arms around him, half in tears herself. "Don't you think I knew all about it, even before we left Kalestin? But I knew if word got out, back here on Earth, of how you'd gone to pieces on Kalestin, you'd lose your Council seat—and I told myself that in spite of everything, you were a great man, the man they needed here! Until Cully—"

She broke off suddenly, looking up at Cully.

"But *you* knew!" she said to Cully. "How could you know?"

"He must have seen inside Doak's locket," said Will bitterly, not looking up from his bandaging. He had stripped off Doak's jacket and shirt, and the upper body of the unconscious man looked frail and helpless under the bandages.

"No." Cully shook his head, facing Alia. "Doak looks like you. Do you think I wouldn't notice something like that? Maybe somebody else might miss it, but I couldn't. And he walks like Amos. Once I made the connection, there were a hundred things about Doak that showed it."

He turned to Will.

"You know when I knew for certain?" Cully said. "When Doak turned and walked out on those sloping metal skids of the garbage area, when he was getting the Board of Governors to agree to letting you two be in on the escape. It was just the sort of thing Amos would do to make his point—and just the way Amos would have done it."

"All right," said Will to Leestrom, finishing up his

bandaging, "take him out of here and find a hospital. There'll be a directory on the ground floor—"

But as Leestrom bent to pick up the unconscious Doak, there was a swirl in the crowd between him and the door, and a man pushed through.

"The Moldaug—Ruhn!" panted the man. "He's on his way up from the ground floor right now—with two other Moldaug—"

"Quick!" snapped Cully to Leestrom. "Get some of the men up here into World Police uniforms—and take Doak out through that side door—it goes to Amos' private office. Amos, show him the way. Amos, pull yourself together—Doak can be cured, you ought to know that! The rest of you get out of here too. Not you, Alia. Or you, Will. I need you to help me face Ruhn!"

"What good can I do you without Doak?" asked Will.

He was on his feet now. Leestrom and Braight were leading the others out of the room through the door to Amos' office.

"You need a three-person unit to talk to Ruhn's tripartite individual-group," he said. "And do you think that Ruhn won't have seen full-description images of all three of us by this time? Who's going to sit in Doak's chair?"

"Alia," answered Cully economically. He snatched up Doak's discarded, bloodstained shirt, and threw it back into a corner behind a chair. He pulled the hand towel from around his waist under the sweatshirt, and shoved this into Alia's hands. "Here, cover your head with this."

Alia stared at him for a moment, then swiftly took the towel from him.

"What—?" Will gazed at them both.

"Didn't Cully just point it out?" Alia answered impatiently. "I look like Doak!" She began energetically to scrub the make-up from her face with a corner of the towel. "Will, pass me his jacket. Oh, I wish I had a mirror! There! Now, I'll fold this like a scarf to hide my hair with . . ."

She was already folding the hand towel into roughly triangular shape. Piling her hair up on her head with one hand, she wrapped the towel tightly around it and tied the ends behind her.

". . .There!" she said. "How do I look?"

She was just Doak's height, and his jacket fitted her. Except for a faintly piratical look that was a result of the bandana-like headcloth, she looked, indeed, like her half-brother.

"Fine," said Cully. "Let's get to our seats at the table now!"

The three of them had barely taken their chairs when several men wearing badly fitting World Police uniforms and sidearms appeared, and hastily took up stations at either side of the corridor entrance from the lobby. A moment later, three robed figures swung into view between the armed men, proceeding toward the Meeting Room and the table, where Cully, Will and Alia waited.

The Moldaug came forward, in their floor-length robes seeming to glide rather than walk, as if they were on casters. The middle one of the threesome was taller than the others—as tall as Cully himself. More than that, there was an erectness about him, almost a stiffness—and with a sudden twinge of emotion Cully realized that he was once more recognizing Ruhn. The unusual leanness and height, the erectness, were things he had noted back at Number One, that day of the escape, when he had seen Ruhn in the boat approaching from Amos' SA yacht.

The sight of them now brought back the momentary feeling of empathy that had touched Cully in that moment. Now that he had identified Ruhn, he began to see the little differences between Ruhn and his Brothers as well. The racial sameness of Moldaug features was breaking up to Cully's eyes, finally. He noticed now how Ruhn's cheeks were more hollowed than those of the others, and how the fine lines were more notice-able under the narrow eyes, and the skin over Ruhn's bony skull seemed to have a near-transparency that the others lacked.

In silence he watched the three Moldaug glide up to the edge of this dais and stop. He rose to his feet, feeling Alia and Will rise automatically on either side of him.

Ruhn's eyes met Cully's and the eyes of the tall Moldaug seemed to go back and back in his skull, like the eyes of the captured Moldaug spaceship Captain just before he had sprung at Cully, after believing that Cully had said that only the live captured Moldaug would be returned to their families.

Ruhn's tall figure was motionless for a moment and then his eyes moved down, down from Cully's face until they gazed at the blood from Doak's wounds, still darkly wet on the parqueted floor. For a long second his gaze rested on the blood, then moved back up to fasten on Cully's face once more.

Finally he spoke—slowly and deeply and carefully, in almost accentless English.

"We have come here," he said, "to speak to my Very Most Respectable Cousin Braight; and instead, we find ourselves met by the humans who have mocked us by pretending to be one of our mythical characters, and stolen our spaceships and hurt our people. Where is my Very Most Respectable Cousin Braight?"

"I am sorry—" began Cully unthinkingly in English. He switched to Moldaug.

"I am sorry," he said, "but the person to whom yourself refers no longer speaks for our race. Therefore, you must speak to myself, who am Culihan O'Rourke When, with my Brothers here—William Jaimeson and Doak Townsend. For there has taken place among us that which is equivalent to a Change in the Aspect of Respectability among ye of the Moldaug; and it is myself, the family, sept and clan of myself—being all those soft faces living on the Pleiades Worlds—who now lead our human race."

Ruhn stared at him for a long moment more, then spoke in Moldaug.

"Then it is yourself," he said with slow emphasis, "who now must answer to myself. For ye of the human race are under complaint of we of the Moldaug; and yourself must answer for ye all."

26

For a moment there was perfect silence in the room. Then Cully spoke.

"No," he replied evenly, "it is ye who are under complaint of we humans, and it is yourself who now must answer to myself."

Ruhn and his Brothers stood still. There was no change of expression visible on the alien faces. After a little pause, Ruhn spoke again.

"Yourself speak the tongue of the Moldaug very well," Ruhn said. "Yet it may be yourself believes yourself to be saying one thing, while actually saying yet another."

"No," said Cully. "There is no mistake. Let myself repeat what I say in my own tongue." He switched briefly to English. "I say, you and your Brothers and your people must now answer to me for grievances we justifiably have against you." He returned to Moldaug. "Will yourself sit with ourself and discuss this matter?"

Ruhn hesitated. Then he stepped up on the dais, his Brothers automatically following. They settled themselves upon the hassock-like seats facing Cully, Alia, and Will—seating themselves with their feet tucked up, not in the cross-legged position of a human from an

Eastern culture, but with toes tucked back in toward the crotch and their knees poking thier gowns straight forward.

"Perhaps yourself will begin," said Cully when they were seated, "by telling myself how it appears to ye of the Moldaug that ye have any complaint against we of the human?"

"Myself is surprised," said Ruhn coldly and remotely, "that yourself does not seem to recognize the complaint to which yourself refers. Yourself, or others like yourself, have stolen our ships, harmed our people, violated our territory, and finally stolen away the Heritors to our Throne. Does yourself deny these things?"

"Myself does not," said Cully. "Myself denies only that these actions should be any basis for complaint by ye of the Moldaug against us. Because it is these and other things which provide the basis for the complaint of we of the human against ye Moldaug."

Ruhn sat for a moment of ominous silence.

"Myself sees three possibilities here," he said. "First, that the words of yourself do not make sense because yourself does not possess sense, that ye are a race of madmen—in which case, there is no point to be gained in talking further to yourself. Second, that the sense of the words of yourself is deliberately twisted because yourself are attempting to outface us with bluff or lies—in which case, in Respectability the injury ye have done us is compounded beyond repair; and there is no point to be gained in further talking with yourself. Third, that yourself is both truthful and sensible; but that it is myself who does not understand. This last, third possibility alone is what keeps myself from ending this conversation now."

"The third possibility is correct," said Cully. "And in brief, that is our complaint against ye. Ye do not understand; and to the best view of myself, ye have not tried to understand the actions of we humans. Ye have instead misunderstood them, and tried to make them a basis for complaint against us."

"How can acts of violence against the Moldaug be otherwise than a basis for complaint?" asked Ruhn. His eyes had sunk into his skull.

"If an adult person strikes another adult person without cause," said Cully, "is there cause for complaint?"

"Certainly," replied Ruhn.

"If an adult person strikes another adult person to prevent the other person from committing an act which is not Respectable, is there cause for complaint?"

Ruhn's eyes seemed to come forward a little in their sockets.

"No," he said.

"Yet," said Cully, "in both cases a blow was struck—an act of violence committed. The question of whether cause for complaint exists depends upon the purpose behind the act of violence. Is this not so?"

"Myself will admit this," said Ruhn. "Yourself claims that there were purposes we did not know behind the acts yourself and others have committed against us? And that these purposes change the basis for complaint from we to ye?"

"That is what myself claims."

The sun was all but touching the horizon now, seen in the vision screen of the room. Its beams, flooding in, filled the room with a reddish, transparent light. In that light, the Moldaug looked darker; and Ruhn, in the middle between his two Brothers, seemed to loom under the darkened ceiling of the room.

"Then myself," said Ruhn, "wait to hear these purposes of ye; and on their validity will myself judge and act now for we of the Moldaug."

"Yourself shall hear them," said Cully. "They lie all in the palm of the hand of one fact—which is that we of the human have a different pattern and standard upon which we judge our actions than do ye of the Moldaug. Where ye think in terms of, 'Is this that I do Respectable or not?' we think, 'Is this that I do Right or not?' "

Ruhn's eyes receded a little, coldly.

"Myself am aware of this difference," he said. "We

had deduced it some years since. Yet ye are not unaware of the meaning of Respectability, since ye have a word for it in the language of ye humans. Therefore, ye are not ignorant of the responsibility to concern ye with Respectability where we of the Moldaug are concerned."

"Yourself," said Cully sharply, "continues to give grievance by misunderstanding. Ye, also, have the words for Right and not-Right in the language of ye. But would it comfort one among ye who had lost Respectability to know that himself was Right?"

"It would not," said Ruhn, "as I think yourself already knows."

"Recognize, then," said Cully, "that the opposite is true among we humans. That one of ourselves would find little comfort in the fact that himself was Respectable, if himself knew himself to be not-Right."

Ruhn went into one of his long pauses of silence. Slowly his eyes came forward.

"If this be true," he said, "it is an almost inconceivable thing, implying great misfortune, that the two races of ye and we should have the bad luck to be neighbors and yet so different."

"No, indeed," said Cully swiftly. "Yourself, instead, should praise the good fortune that makes us, as neighbors, so alike that there is only this difference between us."

"What says yourself?" Ruhn stared at him. "Does yourself pretend that this difference—which myself does not yet admit even exists, having only the word of yourself that it does—is small? Rather, it is wider than the distances between the stars of ye and we. For a race that has not Respectability is beyond comprehension. We had assumed that there were at least some shreds of the understanding of Respectability within ye."

"There are," said Cully bluntly. "But myself does not believe that an equal and opposite understanding of Right exists among ye. For yourself still speaks as if Respectability was the superior standard—whereas there are two equal standards, one for each race."

"Yourself cannot, indeed, show myself this," said Ruhn, with a variation in the tone of his voice that, by contrast to his normal, unvarying speech, was almost passionate.

"Myself can. Even as myself shows how ye have been failing in understanding of us, while all the while we have been understanding of ye."

Cully stopped speaking. He waited.

"Myself listens," said Ruhn after a second. "Speak."

"Excellent," said Cully. He softened his voice. "Myself will commence by showing yourself how we have understood the Respectability of ye from near the beginning of meetings between the people of ye and of we. Yourself shall tell me if myself am wrong in anything. Agreed?"

"Agreed," said Ruhn.

"Then, first—" Cully held up one finger. "In the beginning, when ye of the Moldaug first encountered some of us on the Worlds in the Pleiades region, ye did not consider us people."

"Correct," said Ruhn. "Those of ourselves who saw those of yourselves observed that ye had a technology that indicated cleverness, but there was nothing about your actions that was Moldaug-like. Therefore, we assumed that ye must be only intelligent animals, with whom, if we had no quarrel, neither had we any great or common interest."

"Second," Cully held up another finger, "ye became aware that the numbers of we humans were increasing in the Pleiades; also that we were building homes and exhibiting a social pattern—which, if completely un-Moldaug-like, was yet more than the pattern of mere animals. For the first time it occurred to ye that we might be un-Moldaug and yet a people. Therefore, ye closed the borders of ye to we, until the debate about our status as people should be resolved by common opinion among all ye of the Moldaug."

"True," said Ruhn, "Yourself have understood us in these things at least."

"Third," said Cully. He lifted a third finger. "Ye,

having discussed the matter of us among ye, and being Moldaug of open mind, took upon yourselves the hitherto unheard-of concept that we were indeed a people, though not Moldaug. That we were not animals, but people—with whom ye must therefore deal in Respectability."

"Yourself is correct," said Ruhn tonelessly.

"Therefore," said Cully, putting his hand down upon the table, "ye took the first step to deal in Respectability with we of the human. That step was to offer evidence of the Respectability of ye by making formal claim upon us for a portion of that interstellar space belonging to us. To show us that ye were a proud, courageous people, not so unsure of your Respectability that you dared not strike the first blow, ye laid claim to the Worlds we were occupying in the Pleiades."

"This is so," said Ruhn. "And to this claim ye did not Respectably reply with a counterclaim, that ye and we might in discussion establish the respective Respectability of our identities and the line of our common Frontier. Instead, ye replied with hints and implications through the one person, Braight, that ye might in fact yield the Pleiades to us."

"And this, ye knew," said Cully, "was a suggested action of such not-Respectability that it could only be a calculated insult to ye Moldaug. Ye conceived that we must be implying that ye of the Moldaug were not Respectable enough, in courage or in might, to lay claim to any area of ours, except ye knew in advance we would yield it to ye."

"This," said Ruhn, in a voice as close to grimness as a Moldaug voice might sound to human ears, "is very so. Inconceivable as it seemed, ye apparently were leaving us no option but to fulfill the letter of our claim—that was originally only a Respectable gesture—and make war upon ye. Still, we had seen ye and the armaments and spaceships which ye owned, and it was plain that they were no better than our own—therefore, war between ye and us could result only in mutual annihilation. Therefore, although the provocation was nearly unbearable, yet we forbore action and attempted to talk further with the person Braight."

"Who replied," said Cully with equal grimness, "even while he continued to offer the yielding that was not-Respectable to the point of insult, that ourselves on the Pleiades Worlds were the only humans who wished to war with ye. And this statement seemed to ye an intensification of the insult. For ye were aware that on the Pleiades Worlds, alone, there were of ourselves not enough to withstand ye for a single day."

"True," said Ruhn. "Yet still we forbore. And still was the insult increased. Yourself and others—whom the person Braight claimed came from the Pleiades Worlds only—entered our space, landed on one of our worlds, and committed grotesque and meaningless acts; among them, imitating the mythical Demon of Dark, as if to portend a Change in Aspect for our race. But yourself went even further, to violent action, attacking our ships and killing or capturing their crews. Finally, yourself went even beyond these affronts by stealing the Heritors to Barthi and his Brothers, who are leaders among the Moldaug—thus threatening a discontinuance of the family of Barthi, and an actual necessity for a Change in the Aspect of Respectability among us. With that, we reached the end of forbearance. Ye seem determined to force us to war, and in Respectability we can give way no further; so war it must be, unless yourself can convince me of some excuse for these acts—"

Ruhn pointed with one bony middle finger. It was a suddenly dramatic act, following as it did his motionlessness in his seat until now. His finger stabbed at the setting sun.

"—before that star sets, or war ye shall have with the Moldaug. War to the end!"

For a second Ruhn continued to point. Then his hand dropped back to the table.

"Answer. myself first," said Cully, after a moment's pause, "did not myself tell yourself just now, correctly, what was the meaning of the actions of ye Moldaug, up through the point where ye laid claim to our Worlds in the Pleiades?"

"Yourself did," said Ruhn. "But at this moment of crisis, what importance is there in the small fact that yourself understood these Respectable actions?"

"Because—!" snapped Cully, and the sudden violence of his tone made Alia and Will start. Cully in his turn pointed his finger at the Moldaug. He spoke in measured but emotion-charged tones. "I charge ye of the Moldaug, and yourself now present, with failing to understand the actions of us humans, even while myself and others were understanding the actions of ye. Therefore, ye have no complaint against us, but our complaint against ye is strong and real!"

Ruhn, who had not started when Cully's voice rose, did not move or speak now until Cully, in his turn, dropped his accusing finger once more to the table.

"Myself waits to hear," Ruhn said—and his eyes were back once more, deep within their sockets—"what misunderstanding yourself accuses us of making."

"Myself has told yourself," said Cully harshly, "that we of the human use the standard of Rightness, where ye of the Moldaug use the standard of Respectability. When myself needed to interpret the actions of my Respectable Cousins the Moldaug, as in the case of the claim ye made against our Worlds of the Pleiades, myself did not ask myself, 'What *Rightness* is at stake in this action of the Moldaug?'—even though myself judged the actions of my own self and my own people by the standard of Right or not-Right. No, myself asked myself, 'What *Respectability* is at stake in this action of the Moldaug?' Consequently, I saw the true reason for the action of ye."

Cully paused.

"But," he went on, "ye of the Moldaug—and yourself, who speak here for the Moldaug, did not do equally as myself. Yourself did not ask yourself, 'What *Rightness* is involved in the actions of Braight or they of the

human?' You asked yourself only what *Respectability*
was involved—and therefore neither yourself nor any of
ye saw the true reason for those actions. Therefore are
ye at complaint before us, and not we before ye!"

Cully leaned forward over the table toward Ruhn.

"Tell me!" he snapped. "*Among the Moldaug, who is
more Respectable? Himself who makes an effort to understand the actions of the neighbor to himself, or himself
who does not make that effort?*"

Ruhn stirred slightly in his chair. His voice was thinner when it answered, but he did not pause in answering.

"There is no question," he said. "Himself who makes
an effort is more Respectable than himself who does
not."

"I thank my Cousin Ruhn," said Cully coldly. "That
point is established, then."

"It is established," said Ruhn, still in the thin voice.
"But myself must then demand explanation from yourself, in terms of Rightness, of those actions which have
seemed intended to insult we of the Moldaug."

"Myself will answer," said Cully. "Let my Cousin
Ruhn listen. Ye of the Moldaug made a Respectable
demand upon us for response at a time when the equivalent of a Change in Aspect of Respectability was upon
us. Therefore, there was at that time no leader who
could speak for all we of the human in one voice."

"Myself will accept that as being the case," said Ruhn.
"But we of the Moldaug are concerned not with inabilities
to act, but with actions."

"Myself continues, therefore," said Cully. "Since there
was no leader to answer, there could be no answer—
immediately. We would answer, of course, as soon as
our Change in Aspect had been accomplished. But
meanwhile, we could not. We needed time—and neither Respectability nor Rightness required us to proclaim in plain words to the Moldaug that we were a
people divided and in a time of Change."

"I will accept that." Ruhn's voice was almost monotonous—but it was equally remote and void of any indication of his judgment upon the matter.

"Therefore, it was necessary that we try to gain time before answering; while, in Rightness, striving to convey to the Moldaug by sign or hint other than words that we were in a Time of Change and could not answer immediately," said Cully. "Does my cousin Ruhn know of any response from us other than an implication of our willingness to consider war with the Moldaug, that would have caused the Moldaug to hesitate this long in demanding a Respectable answer to their claim against the Pleiades?"

Ruhn sat for a long second.

"Myself knows of no other response," he said at last. "It is unprecedented we should wait this long—and only the grave prospect of such a war allowed us, in Respectability, to so wait. But yourself is saying that ye of the human deliberately misled us—which in itself implies an insult."

"Not," said Cully, "when we were attempting, by the actions of myself and others, to convey ye a sign of our true reason for delay. Cannot my Cousin Ruhn now see this for himself? Why should myself and my Brothers here, with others, enter Moldaug space and adopt the guise and actions of the Demon of Dark? It was a symbol of a change in Aspect myself knew ye must recognize. But why should ye think that a soft-faced Demon portended Change among the Moldaug? Surely, a soft-faced Demon must mean a Change among the soft faces?"

This time Ruhn sat motionless and speechless for a very long time indeed.

"Myself will admit," he said at last, and slowly, "that if all this be true, myself and we of the Moldaug have given ye some cause for complaint, rather than ye, we. But in stealing the Heritors of the family of Barthi, yourself committed an act too deep to be a sign or signal; for yourself, by removing them from their family, have actually periled the whole Aspect of Respectability among the Moldaug. This is an act which yourself can repair now only by returning their bodies together with an explanation which myself cannot conceive to exist—since nothing in Respectability excuses such an act."

"Quite right," said Cully. "Nothing in Respectability excuses the theft of the Heritors of the Moldaug leaders. Nor does anything in Rightness excuse it. But in the working together of both Rightness and Respectability there is an excuse—the *only* excuse. The Sons and Nephews of Barthi and his Brothers are alive."

"Alive?" Ruhn's eyes all but rolled back into their sockets. "How? You did not kill them? They did not suicide? The oldest is old enough to understand—"

"Ourselves did not permit them to suicide," interrupted Cully—aware that interruption in itself was an insult according to Moldaug standards, but betting that at the moment all standards were in question.

"Yourself did not permit . . ." Ruhn stared at him with deep-sunk eyes. "This runs close to seeming the uttermost insult of all! Then why steal them in the first place?"

"To show my Cousins of the Moldaug how Rightness could exist as the neighbor of Respectability," said Cully. "To demonstrate to ye of the Moldaug that our standard of Rightness permitted we humans to do easily what was unthinkable to ye—stealing the Heritors of the Moldaug leaders, particularly in a time when no true Change of Aspect among the Moldaug was taking place. But that our standard would not let us do what ye Moldaug would do easily. For Rightness forbids us to take the life of those who are young, even of our enemies' young, or to allow these young to take their own lives."

Cully paused. But he went on again before Ruhn could speak.

"In fact," he said, "Rightness, to we humans, implies a responsibility toward the young that is similar, if not the same, as the responsibility Respectability implies.

Yourself and myself may see fine differences in these two responsibilities; but to the young themselves—those of both our races who will be neighbors in the future—such fine distinctions do not show themselves. This, also, we hoped to demonstrate to ye Moldaug in the persons of your Heritors, while themselves were in the keeping of ourselves. And myself believes that it has been so shown—that the young of ye Moldaug, at least, can understand we humans, even as myself showed that myself could understand ye Moldaug."

Once more Cully paused. For a moment it seemed that Ruhn was not going to respond. But then he spoke distantly and coldly.

"Myself does not believe this," he said. "But, even if it were so, there has been shown no desirability for we of the Moldaug to understand ye humans and your strange standard of Rightness."

"Look around yourself, my Cousin Ruhn," said Cully strongly. "The universe has shown the desirability. Myself has from the beginning striven for this—to get across, to human and Moldaug alike, that two great races such as that of ye and we, powerful in armed might and of differing thoughts, cannot exist side by side in space without eventually either cooperating or destroying each other. And the key to cooperation is the responsibility upon both—we humans and ye Moldaug alike—to accept the other on the other's own terms, and judge them by their other standard—"

Cully paused. But Ruhn neither moved nor responded. Cully went on, leaning forward once more, urgently.

"True," he said, "there will be those things like Brotherhood or Sisterhood—the closeness-of-three among ye—that we can never feel. But likewise, ye will never know that powerful sense of self-dependence, of oneness-with-the-universe that comes to a single person of us who goes forth alone into wilderness. Truly, ye cannot know what 'I' means in our terms. But these fine, special understandings do not matter. For we need not embrace, only accept, each other—in order to survive

as friends and neighbors among the stars. And the
choice is simply that: between mutual acceptance of a
way not oneself's own; or blind misunderstanding and
misinterpretation, leading to mutual annihilation."

Cully stopped speaking. Ruhn sat, saying nothing.
Cully waited, but he still sat. The eyes of Ruhn's two
Brothers were on the taller Moldaug now, but even
they said nothing. Cully fumbled hastily at the surface
of the table before him until he found a phone stud. He
touched it.

The *connect* signal hummed in his ears, waiting for
the sound of his voice.

"Pete Hyde," he said, low-voiced, in English. "On a
body-phone, somewhere near my present location.
Pete—"

"Cully?" A small voice, directionally beamed from
the table top to reach his ear alone, sounded. "I'm out
in the lobby, Cully, just to the right of the corridor
entrance."

"Pete!" snapped Cully, still low-voiced, slurring his
words together to hide their meaning from Ruhn and
his Brothers, silent at the far end of the table; with
Ruhn staring stiffly ahead, and his Brothers watching
him as if in intense telepathic conference. "Where're
the three young Princes? Did you lose them?"

"Hell, no!" sang Pete's tiny voice up the directional
beam. "I've had them here with me for the last half
hour, seems like. I was waiting for you to tell me when
to bring them in."

Cully drew a slow, deep breath of hidden relief.

"Now, Pete!" he said. "Bring them in *now!*"

"All right—I was just waiting for you to tell me—"

"*Now,* Pete!"

"Right."

The line went dead. A moment later, Cully, staring
through the partly open doors, saw Pete and Leestrom
together bringing the little alien Princes down the corridor, holding them firmly by the hand. These two big
men and the little Moldaug came through the doorway

together—and then the Princes caught sight of Ruhn and his Brothers.

Immediately they tried to run forward, but Pete and Leestrom held them back.

"Uncle Ruhn!" shouted Hjrker, tugging to break away from the big left hand of Leestrom. "Uncle Ruhn, it is myself, Hjrker! And these soft faces will not let myself come to yourself!"

Ruhn's head snapped around; his Brothers' heads, also. Instantly, the three of them were on their feet, facing the doorway. Cully, Will and Alia rose likewise.

"Let them go!" Cully called in English to Leestrom and Pete. The two men let go of the small alien hands, and the three Princes ran forward together to the edge of the dais, where they stopped, lining up automatically with Hjrker in the middle.

Hjrker turned and pointed an accusing finger at Cully.

"Uncle Ruhn!" Hjrker said. "These soft faces yourself sees here stole ourselves from our Royal Family—and *that person* would not let ourselves accomplish an honorable action! So that ourselves are still alive!"

Ruhn stiffened. But before he could speak, the smallest of the three princely Brothers, Othga, piped up.

"And Uncle Ruhn!" he called, "will yourself go with myself back to the soft faces' spaceship, that myself may be allowed in to see the Control Room there? For it is not-Right even for a Very Most Respectable to be allowed into a soft-face Control Room without a Responsible Person of himself's family with himself!"

Ruhn turned to stare down at the small figure until Othga, abashed, bent his own gaze on the floor. Slowly Ruhn looked back at Hjrker, who was still pointing at Cully. Ruhn continued to look until Hjrker's arm finally wavered and slowly fell to his side.

"Very most Respectable Nephew," said Ruhn deeply, "himself whom you indicate is not to be addressed as 'that person.' For himself is your Very Most Respectable Cousin Cul'nan Orak Wh'n, who, together with his Brothers, is first among the family, sept and clan which now leads the soft-faced people—and himself with whom yourself will Respectably discuss many things pertaining to the two races, in years to come when yourself sits in the place of your Uncle Barthi and his Brothers. Therefore, as in high office there is high responsibility, yourself have been not entirely Respectable just now to your Cousin Wh'n, which, for the sake of the two peoples of ye, yourself should be."

The little Prince stared at Ruhn under the reproof, and finally swung his eyes unhappily to Cully.

"Myself am sorry," he said after a second. "Will my Very Most Respectable Cousin forgive myself in hopes that myself will do more Respectably from now on? For myself is very little," Hjrker added, in a sudden rush of confidence, "but myself do grow and learn very quickly."

GORDON R. DICKSON

Winner of every award science fiction and fantasy to offer, Gordon Dickson is one of the major authors of this century. He creates heroes and enemies, not just characters in books; his stories celebrate bravery and virtue and the best in all of us. Collect some of the very best of Gordon Dickson's writing by ordering the books below.

THE MANY WORLDS OF
MELISSA SCOTT

*Winner of the John W. Campbell Award
for Best New Writer, 1986*

THE KINDLY ONES: "An ambitious novel of the world Orestes. This large, inhabited moon is governed by five Kinships whose society operates on a code of honor so strict that transgressors are declared legally 'dead' and are prevented from having any contact with the 'living.' . . . Scott is a writer to watch."—*Publishers Weekly*. A Main Selection of the Science Fiction Book Club.

65351-2 • 384 pp. • $2.95

The "Silence Leigh" Trilogy
FIVE-TWELFTHS OF HEAVEN (Book I): "Melissa Scott postulates a universe where technology interferes with magic. . . . The whole plot is one of space ships, space wars, and alien planets—not a unicorn or a dragon to be seen anywhere. Scott's space drive and description of space piloting alone would mark her as an expert in the melding of the [SF and fantasy] genres; this is the stuff of which 'sense of wonder' is made."—*Locus*

55952-4 • 352 pp. • $2.95

SILENCE IN SOLITUDE (Book II): "[Scott is] a voice you should seek out and read at every opportunity." —*OtherRealms*.

65699-7 • 324 pp. • $2.95

THE EMPRESS OF EARTH (Book III):

65364-4 • 352 pp. • $3.50

WILL *YOU* SURVIVE?

In addition to Dean Ing's powerful science fiction novels—
Systemic Shock, Wild Country, Blood of Eagles and
others—he has written cogently and inventively about the
art of survival. **The Chernobyl Syndrome** is the result of
his research into life after a possible nuclear exchange . . .
because as our civilization gets bigger and better, we
become more and more dependent on its products. What
would *you* do if the machine stops—or blows up?

Some of the topics Dean Ing covers:
* How to *make* a getaway airplane
* Honing your "crisis skills"
* Fleeing the firestorm: escape tactics for city-dwellers
* How to build a homemade fallout meter
* Civil defense, American style
* "Microfarming"—survival in five acres
   And much, much more.

Also by Dean Ing, available through Baen Books:

ANASAZI
Why did the long-vanished Anasazi Indians retreat from
their homes and gardens on the green mesa top to
precarious cliffside cities? Were they afraid of someone—or
some*thing*? "There's no evidence of warfare in the ruins
of their earlier homes . . . but maybe the marauders they
feared didn't wage war in the usual way," says Dean Ing.
Anasazi postulates a race of alien beings who needed
human bodies in order to survive on Earth—a race of
aliens that *still* exists.

FIREFIGHT 2000
How do you integrate armies supplied with bayonets and
ballistic missiles; citizens enjoying Volkswagens and
Ferraris; cities drawing power from windmills and nuclear
powerplants? Ing takes a look at these dichotomies, and
more. This collection of fact and fiction serves as a
metaphor for tomorrow: covering terror and hope, right
guesses and wrong, high tech and thatched cottages.